Shutout

ST. CLOUD HOCKEY SERIES

MARI LOYAL

HEAT LEVEL AND CONTENT WARNINGS

Before reading this book, I encourage you to first read this section to determine whether it's the right fit for your personal circumstances.

This book is closed door, which means there is innuendo, kisses are descriptive (especially Chapter 32), and characters don't shy away from their attraction.

There is mild to moderate use of cuss words, particularly in emotional moments. However, there is no use of f-bombs, religious blasphemies, or known ableist terms.

The female lead is cheated on by her boyfriend early in the book. She also suffers from food allergies and there are mentions of her restrictive diet as result. The male lead experiences neglect from his parents. The characters are college juniors and are depicted drinking alcohol at a private party.

If any of these topics are troublesome for you, please protect yourself and read a book that better suits your situation.

Visit my website mariloyal.com for general content warnings that apply to all my books.

CHAPTER 1
BROOKLYN

leave my heart on the ice because I don't need it anywhere else. That's why it's extra shitty when my teammates don't even half-ass it. At this point they're just quarter-assing it.

"Tatum!"

I shift my eyes toward Bloom right in time to intercept a pass mid air as like I'm playing baseball instead of hockey. A Bulldog tries to barrel through me to steal the puck. Tries—and fails, because I'm not the biggest defenseman the St. Cloud Thunder Bolts have ever had for no reason. Dude tries to shoulder check me and hits my chest pads light as a feather. I just let him think he's won and right when he's sure he has the puck, I check him against the boards all proper. Enough to get a nice little *oof* out of him.

I carry the puck away from our zone and once again, I'm reminded that the only ones who seem to give a shit about this game are my defensive partner, Bloom, and I.

Yeah, I get it. We're down by five goals in a qualifier game. There's only a minute and a half left in the clock. But you'd think the seniors would be less eager to end their college hockey career so soon.

Worse, you'd think the juniors wouldn't want an embarrassing showdown like this one to weigh on them next year. But they're honestly the worst crop this team has ever seen in its history. I'm seriously dreading them taking over leadership next year. Does this mean I'll have to wait another stinking year after they graduate for my college hockey career to finally bloom?

Hah, my partner would've appreciated that pun. Especially because he's just as frustrated with the guys two years older than us.

"Do something, Blondie!" he shouts as I zoom by.

From the bench, I can hear Coach Green screaming his throat raw. "Pass! Pass the damn puck, Tatum!"

Nope, no sire. I don't trust any of these lazy suckers to do anything but burn the rest of the time off.

Fortunately—I think?—we've been so easy to jerk around that the Bulldogs don't try very hard to steal the puck from me. Or maybe they're running out of steam after spending the whole game skating circles around the Bolts. I take advantage of whatever the hell this lull is, my legs pumping all the power I have left into my muscles to eat the ice. One of our seniors literally gets out of my way. Two Bulldogs close in on me and I lean as low as I can to bowl through them. I'm not even close enough to the Bulldog's crease when I fire the puck like a cannon. My stick splinters in my hands but I ignore it.

Instead, I raise my fist in the air.

The puck sails through the air. The Bulldog goalie makes a swipe for it. It doesn't matter, that slapshot made my heart come back to life. Nothing in this world can stop it.

The alarm blares with the goal right as the net comes loose and slides back.

"Well, shit." My teammates are so far from me, it's actually one of the Bulldogs who speaks. "I'm glad the rest of your team isn't like you."

Wow, that's some classy heckling. Hurt them with the truth instead of yo momma jokes, huh?

That's legit the highlight of my last game as a sophomore, though. We lose five to one and even though it's not a shutout, it's an especially rankling loss when the only Bolts goal was scored by a defenseman. You'd think the Bulldogs just won the Frozen Four with how they're celebrating after the final buzzer, but that's probably to rub it on our faces. After all, they won on our home ice.

Inhaling deep from my lungs, I take one final look at the arena during the last official game of the season. The Bulldog heckler gives me a smirk as I skate away and I make a vow to myself.

I don't give a rat's ass about the to-be-seniors. They won't drag me down for another season.

"Good effort," Assistant Coach Thomas says as I walk into the locker and I bob my head in acknowledgment. We both know it wasn't good enough to merit a *good game* instead, but I'm not the kind of guy to shun a compliment.

Coach Green steps in last. His face is redder than a stop sign, which is also a sign in and of itself. I discreetly seek Dane Bloom's eyes. He and I make the team's top defensive pair, and after two wretched years of being under the yoke of self-entitled seniors and juniors, he can read my mind. Mine says *we are so damn screwed*, and his mind totally projects back saying, and *we deserve it*. I shift my weight and pin him with a *surely not us* gaze. He shrugs.

We both turn our attention back to the head coach as he stands in the middle of the locker room. I don't think I hallucinate the way he grows even redder when he catches sight of the seniors.

Especially because one of them is unaware as he says, "Hey, so what are we gonna do about all the booze and snacks we got at the Bolt House?"

"We'll put them to good use," the dipshit beside him responds. "Let's have a literal pity party. Get pity laid."

"You're a genius, bro."

I almost want to throw my skates at them if it'll get them to shut the hell up, before Coach picks them up like ragdolls and throws them at everyone else who also lives at the Bolt House. Like me.

But something worse happens. Coach Green takes a deep breath—which helps his complexion, he looks less like an over-fried shrimp now—shakes his head, and walks back out.

Like he's given up on this crop, just like they gave up on him and the team.

A trickle of ice crawls up my spine and I shiver to try to shake it off, but it still rises up to claw at my neck. Thanks to the therapist that the court mandated after my parents' divorce, I recognize what's happening. And I latch into what-ever is around me to not acknowledge my good ol' rejection sensitivity.

"Seriously?" I whirl around. "We just had the most embar-rassing game in Thunder Bolts history, and you want to party?"

"What's it matter with you, pretty boy?"

Sighing, I turn around to face the departing captain. Liam Roberts. He's wearing the same smirk that has ruined my life in more ways than one.

"Like, chill. You're already drafted. You'll bust your ass here for two more years before they send you to some farm team. No need to act like tonight was the end of your career."

It's like this dude never got the memo that nothing in life is guaranteed. Unfortunately, I got it via first class mail, by email, by text, from a messenger bird, and even damn fax just in case I forgot.

Liam Roberts and I are the same in some ways, but the opposite in most. He's also the son of a former NHL player. The genes and the clout have definitely favored him his entire life on and off the ice. He's used to winning in life, and maybe that's why this team doesn't matter to him. He thinks he's got it made. But I doubt that him dragging his feet around the ice is going to look good to the franchise that drafted him two years ago. His prophecy that a farm team comes next is coming true for himself from what I've heard.

Me? I'm also the son of a former NHL player. In addition, I'm also the son of a former Victoria's Secret model. My genes are the literal only thing I've won at in life. Everything else has been a pathetic Greek tragedy, and maybe that's why I'm hungry for a big W.

"Every game is the end all be all," I say in a low voice. Slowly, I force a smile onto my face. "But sure, let's have a party tonight to celebrate your mediocrity."

"What the hell did you just say?"

Dane breaks into an exaggerated holler. "Party at the Bolt House!"

"Yeah!" One of the juniors hollers back, not realizing that Dane was being sarcastic as shit.

Liam glares at me and I turn away from him to pull my jersey over my head. If I can have it my way, this will be the last time I exchange any words with this asswipe in my life. His coasting and douchebaggery will take him straight to an abyss, but I'll keep climbing out of my own.

"You okay?" Dane asks beside me.

Even though he doesn't know all my deepest, darkest secrets, Dane's the only person in this team who can read me like an open book. Liv used to say I should only play poker and with her after making millions of dollars in the pros, just so she could win every cent off me.

Thinking about her makes me even more sour, though.

"No," I admit.

He flops on the bench beside me and bends down to unlace his skates. "We'll be better next year."

Will we? But I don't voice my doubts aloud. He knows Liam corrupted the juniors too, and then there's the fact that Coach Green seems to have given up on us.

I shake my head hard to push that thought away from my head. There's only so much catastrophe my pea brain can take in one night.

So, after showering and changing into an Armani suit, I climb onto my Jeep Gladiator—both courtesy of my father's plastic—and head back to the Bolts House.

A few years ago, after the first generation of Thunder Bolts started putting the team on the North Eastern map, some St. Cloud alumni banded up to become our first boosters. Since our facilities were already top of the line, they instead bought this massive Victorian mansion near Main Street. It's more or less the team's frat house even though only ten people can live in it.

Once I reach my room on the ground floor, I toss my duffel bag under my desk and lock the door. Leaning my head back, I close my eyes against the prospect of an entire night dwelling on the loss and what that means for the program.

Should I just transfer to another college with a better team? Maybe this time I should pick one on the west coast. That way I could pretend the distance between me and the people I wish gave a shit about me is the reason why they don't.

"Sorry, guys." I mutter to the signed posters from Max Cassiano and Aran Rodriguez, both in their pro team jerseys. "I really wanted to follow in your footsteps, but it looks like I'm gonna have to veer off."

For now, I'm going to ditch this place for the night. I remove the suit jacket and toss it on my bed, followed by the tie. Before taking off my pants, I pull out the cellphone from the pocket and catch sight of a million notifications, none of which are missed calls or texts from my parents.

Whatever.

After changing into jeans and an Aelfric Eden graphic T-shirt, I pick my phone up again and fire up a text to Dane so he also ditches this joint. And because he's not quick enough to answer, I switch to check some of my notifications starting by Instagram.

The first post that pops up is from Liv and my entire attention zeroes in on it. It's just a picture of her hand, thumb down. All the rings she used to wear are missing and her nails are clear of polish. I recognize the sleeve of her sweatshirt as a St. Cloud branded one, which would've been too preppy for her until she started dating McDude.

The caption reads, *The last thing I want to do is go to a party at the Bolt House and yet—*

A text message from Dane pops up on the screen and I click on it by accident. When I return to Instagram, Liv's post is gone. I look up her profile, only to confirm she must've deleted it.

My ears are roaring. Liv said *and yet*, which means she's coming to this party—the same one I was just about to ditch.

My former best friend who hates my guts is coming to willingly share the same air I breathe.

I can feel my face stretching into a shit-eating grin and text Dane to announce a change of plans.

CHAPTER 2
OLIVIA

TRENT

Sorry, babe

We just really gotta finish this group assignment
tonight

ME

No, I totally get it

Guess I'll just study in my room

Brunch tomorrow tho?

ut my boyfriend leaves me on read, probably distracted by what his group mates are doing, and I flop back on my bed. With the motion, a strand of hair dips into my mouth and I splutter until it's out.

This is what my life has reduced to. A lonely Saturday night. I should follow in his example and pour my entire attention on all the material I have to cover for my midterms, which was the plan all along, but it'd have been nicer if Trent and I could've studied side by side at the library. Maybe get pizza from Romano's afterward. And just because the two of us are bookworms it doesn't mean we can't occasionally pause from studying to make out for a bit. Or at least that's how we used to be before. Lately, he's a lot more responsible than me.

Keys jiggle in the front door and it opens with a swoosh I can hear from my room. Right after, a voice calls, "Olivia not-the-singer Rodriguez, we're home!"

I roll my eyes, which I'm sure my roommates know I'm doing even though they can't see through the walls.

"Har har."

They burst through my door to catch me splayed on my bed with my limbs out in the shape of a star. Too slow I try to roll away but Dee Meyer's one-hundred-fifty pounds still crash over me.

"Oof!"

"We won!" She screeches in my ear. "You should've seen us. We were freaking electric out there tonight."

Grunting, I try to push her away from me. "No, thanks. I ha—"

"Hate hockey, yes," my other roommate says, sitting delicately on a corner of my bed. "But seriously, you should've un-hated it for tonight. If only to support your besties."

I lift my eyebrows at her. "Mina, you're not on the team. You don't even know how to skate."

She folds her arms. "But I'm their biggest fan."

"This is true." Dee finally rolls away from me and props her head up with her arm. "Her screams were the loudest from the stands. I'd have loved to hear you cheering too."

With a deadpanned voice, I say, "I don't scream." Not even for my siblings or for…

Nope. Not gonna think about him at all.

"Fine, but it'd have been nice to see your face supporting me from the stands."

"This face?" I motion at it, knowing it's set in a bored grimace.

It makes Dee laugh. "You're such a little shit."

"There are other ways you can show Dee how much you appreciate her accomplishments, though." When Mina Lee smirks, you know trouble's afoot. Dee and I exchange a glance that clearly means *uh oh*. "Like for example, crashing a party with her. And me."

"No, I have to study," I chime right away.

But Dee's confused. "Wait, what do you mean crash? We don't have to crash our own victory party, you know?"

Mina leans forward, holding her weight on her arms as her hands dig into the mattress. "That's because we're not going to O'Malley's like the team was saying. There's a better place that would boost the Strikes' morale even more, and as their alternate captain, you, Destiny Meyer, will help me steer them on the right path."

"Oh, yeah?" Dee chuckles. "And where's that?"

My eyebrows pinch but I'm not going to get into this. "Can you please take your mastermind self out of my room so I can get back to work?"

Mina's sharp eyes glint with a victory she hasn't yet attained, and she shares, "I just saw on Liam Roberts' Instagram that there's a party at the Bolt House tonight."

"Didn't they lose their game?" Dee asks, looking at me and I shrug like I didn't check the results a few minutes ago. It's not that I care about the team or the sport, but I haven't broken the old habit.

"They did, indeed. And you know who won? The Strikes. So what celebration would be sweeter than rubbing our victory in their miserable faces?" Mina finishes her speech off with a *gotcha* air that fools no one.

I blow a raspberry. "Admit it, you just wanna see if you can hook up with any of the Bolts."

"It's a scientific fact that people could do with a dopamine boost when they're sad. And you know what releases dopamine?" She folds her arms, her lips curving in that sneaky way of hers again. "The horizontal tango."

I level her with a look. "I thought this was all about celebrating the Strikes moving on to the final four?"

"Oh, please." Mina throws her hands in the air. "I was a good girl in coming to watch Dee's game instead of the Bolts. Besides, you're happily partnered up, don't I deserver a bone?"

"A bone or to bone?" Dee guffaws at her own joke.

"Both!"

At this even I laugh. Mistake, because Mina immediately focuses on me. "Does this mean you're in?"

"How in the hell does laughing at a raunchy joke mean I agree to this?"

"Well, do you have better plans?" she fires right back.

I stay silent for a brief moment that tells too much. Clearing my throat, I say, "Yes, I have a ton to study for my midterms."

"Really? On a Saturday night? Shouldn't you at least be boning your boyfriend?"

Heat explodes in my face. I'm not super comfortable with screaming into the four winds about what Trent and I do or don't do in private. "I, um—anyway, he already had plans."

The two of them do a double take at me. Then exchange a glance like I'm unable to discern that they're dissing Trent in their minds.

"It's not like that." I huff and push up to sit on the edge of my bed. "He's working on a group assignment."

"Right." Dee turns to Mina. "What was the excuse last time?"

Mina taps her chin. "Strep throat, I think."

I get up from my bed and slash a glance over my shoulder. "What? It's spreading like wildfire on campus."

"Sure, but when was the last time you two went on a date?"

Dee's eyebrows rise. "Or put plainly, why didn't you get strep throat from him?"

"We go on dates," I say, boredom dripping from my voice as I pick my hair up in a high ponytail. "We have lunch when we can, and we do coursework at the library together, and—"

Mina pins me with a wide-eyed stare. "But when was the last time you two had—"

"Anyway, shoo." I wave my hands toward the door. "Go to your party, whichever it'll be."

"No, I am duty-bound to not leave you alone and miserable, unlike that sorry excuse for a boyfriend of yours."

I fold my arms tight and glare at her. "Just because we're not glued to each other all the time, doesn't mean he's a bad boyfriend."

"You're absolutely right," Mina says with a contrite expression that I don't believe for a second because she never backs down. Sure enough, she adds, "You're totally happy with your boyfriend. So don't you want your bestie to find a boyfriend of her own to be totally happy with?"

Damn it, she's good. Even though I'm still miffed about her swipes at Trent, she has such a masterful use of sarcasm that I can't stop my lips from twitching. This is why we became friends in the first place.

Dee nudges Mina with her elbow. "I think she's starting to crack. Keep going."

But before Mina can utter another smartass word from her mouth, I groan. "Guys, please. You know how much I hate anything related to hockey, especially the Bolts. The literal last thing I want to do is be surrounded by them."

"You won't be doing it for them, but for me."

"And for me," Dee says with a grin. "Because I'm so texting the Strikes to rally the troops and go make a mess."

"Pretty *please*?" Mina elongates the word through a smile the shows off her perfect pearly whites.

"But…" I point at my textbooks strewn on my desk, but they're not even open already.

Maybe if I tell them the real reason why I don't want to go to this party, they'll let me off the hook. They know I had a best friend before them that was a guy, and that we had a big fallout after he acted like a grade-A jerk during our freshman year at St. Cloud.

What they don't know is that he's the star defenseman of the Thunder Bolts, one Brooklyn Tatum.

If I told them, I'm sure they'd let me off the hook. I could spend the rest of the night here in my room, chugging away at the materials that will take me closer to my dream masters in nutrition. Or I could even whip up another nice little recipe to post on my Instagram tonight. Something quick and easy for everyone else who is also studying for midterms.

But I know Dee and Mina would also make a huge deal out of it. They'd forgo celebrating the Strikes' win altogether to waging World War III on Brooklyn Tatum. And no matter how much he deserves it, I just don't want to deal with drama. It's why I've been avoiding him for a year.

So what do I do? Do I set my friends off on him so I can stay home tonight? Or do I put up with the possibility of seeing him tonight?

The latter will only ruin my night. The former will ruin my friends' night and I can't do that to them.

Defeated, I mutter. "Ugh, shit."

"Yes!" Mina jumps to her feet. "We should—"

"No." I cut her off. "I know exactly what you're going to say and no. I'm not changing into a barely-there dress. This is how you're dragging my ass to this awful party." I motion at my black leggings and the blue St. Cloud sweatshirt I swiped from Trent's closet.

"Fine, you're not the one who's looking for a man, anyway." Mina twirls around and finally heads to her room.

Dee's still in mine, her fingers furiously texting while her grin seems to grow bigger with every second. "And done. We have officially relocated the venue of tonight's victory party to one Bolt House. I'm gonna go get ready."

I scrunch up my face. "But I thought you're also not looking for anything at the Bolt House." Dee is allegedly in a committed relationship with hockey—allegedly because even though she doesn't waste much of her time trawling through bars or parties, she does occasionally find a hookup here or there.

Dee tosses her microbraids over her shoulder. "Yes, but I also enjoy looking like a damn snack. So if you'll excuse me."

I plop on my desk chair after she also leaves and put my face in my hands. Tonight isn't going according to any plan, huh? But it's fine—I'm fine. Even if I see *him*, I'll pretend like he's just a fly in the wall like I've been doing for a year.

And maybe I'll snap a couple of pictures for Trent. He's always complaining that I'm not social enough so this should prove him wrong. I make a quick Instagram post saying I'm going to this party so he can see it, but at the last second I decide to delete it and just surprise him later.

In the end, I get a bit of studying in while my friends doll up for the party. As we file into the back of an Uber together, I'm slightly less annoyed by this plan. In fact, I join in singing along to a song by Olivia Rodrigo, even though I hate it when people make fun of me because we have a similar name.

By the time we get to the Bolt House, I'm not even nervous. A year ago, a party at this place basically ruined my life. I won't let that memory get in the way of my chaotic friends' night out.

CHAPTER 3
BROOKLYN

The crowd parts with way more deference than necessary. I know I'm probably the biggest dude in the entire house, but it's not like I'm going to bowl them like they're pins. One girl by the kitchen sink stops talking with her friends and runs her eyes down my frame.

Meanwhile, I open the fridge and peer down at the war zone in there. Whatever food we had in here is already gone, and someone spilled salsa down the metal grill shelves. That's going to be a pain in the ass to clean later. However, there are still a few unopened beer bottles at the back so not all is lost. I grab one and shut the door, only to come face to face with the same girl who's been checking me out.

"You must be Brooklyn Tatum, huh?" She gives me one of those smiles that come along with a strategic lip bite.

I twist the cap open with my big paw, which doesn't go unnoticed by her. Leaning my shoulder against the fridge, I take a swig of the beer with my free hand. Her eyes lock on the tattoo lines on my forearm.

I tilt my head to inspect her. If she can eat me up with her eyes, so can I. She's hot. Blonde, wearing a Thunder Bolts jersey that she's modified to show a mile of cleavage, cinched around her waist with a belt. And I guess it's a dress now, because her legs are bare. Those heels look like they hurt, especially because she doesn't need them. She's fairly tall. Would make it easy to make out if she's interested.

Which I guess she is, because she takes a step closer, tucks her hair behind her ears, and—here's the clincher—rests her hand on my arm right where my bicep is curled as I hold the beer. Not even being subtle about the fact that she's groping me.

"The one and only," I answer at last, tucking my tongue against my cheek. "And who's asking?"

"I'm a fan." Her hand shifts to my chest, and she looks up with bright blue eyes that tell me she knows that I know what she's up to, and that at some point in this party she's going to be grabbing even more handfuls of me. "A big, big fan."

Puck bunnies are the best. If it wasn't for them my awkward ass would be discovered and I'd never get any action.

"Glad to see you're having fun now, Brooke." I shift my eyes over the blonde's head to Liam as he enters the kitchen. Very annoying to note how the crowd parts for him as well, and even worse that he decides to park his ass beside me and the blonde. He gives her a scan even as he says, "Especially since you didn't want to join the party in the first place, right?"

The girl shifts away from me to face him with a gasp. "Oh wow, Liam Roberts! Can you give me your autograph?"

"Sure thing, babe. Where do you want it? Your jersey?" He smirks. "Your skin?"

Instead of being creeped out, she giggles.

Puck bunnies are the worst. No loyalty and bad taste.

Should I be pissed that this isn't the first time Liam does something like this to me? Maybe. But hooking up with this girl would've been an added bonus for tonight, and not the real goal.

I pick myself up and part the crowds on my way out of the kitchen, leaving them behind to flirt or whatever. Once again, I scope out the faces all around the living room. There are two girls dancing on the couch to the bass that's making the walls vibrate. Right before them, a game of beer pong unfolds on the dining table. I recognize Dane's voice as he heckles whoever he's playing with, and I stifle a snort by taking another drink of my beer.

By the bay window at the front, Jamie Schwarz is performing an impressive keg stand. Especially because his T-shirt has fallen down his face, but he manages to keep his concentration even as some girl rubs his abs like she wants to make sure they're real. Jamie's cool, but I won't be cool with him if he and this girl end up going at it later tonight and I can hear everything from my room beside his.

One of the seniors behind him is chatting up three puck bunnies, and I'm even more glad that his room is in the west wing of the third floor, clear across the house and one level above my room. I definitely don't want to hear *that*. But a glance around confirms there's more than one Bolt House resident engaged in some form of flirtation. Which means there's not going to be any placid sleep tonight.

Is Olivia even coming for real? This is the entire opposite of her scene.

In fact, a scene exactly like this a year ago contributed to our friendship going to shit.

For the nth time, I pull out my phone and scroll through Instagram again. Her post is still gone. Why would she bring it back after deleting it? And yet, I wish I had some proof that I didn't hallucinate it. But an hour has passed since and there's no sighting of her, so maybe it was all in my head. Maybe I just miss my best friend so damn much that I'm trying to conjure her from thin air.

The front door opens and it's as if an invisible string pulls at my face. I turn, but it's not the universe finally listening to me. Instead, a group of Thunder Strikes walk in.

Their captain makes a grand entrance that includes saying, "Listen up, losers! The winners have arrived."

I bite my lips not to laugh as some of the puck bunnies start glaring at the newcomers. The Strikes and the Bolts hated each other when the program started, but throughout the years, it's turned more into good natured ribbing. I shouldn't be shocked that they're coming to rub their victory in our sorry faces. Except our faces aren't too sorry when they're busy sucking other faces.

I run a hand through my hair. Maybe I should give up on waiting for Liv or on getting any solid sleep, and follow in the example of my teammates to just hang out. That way I won't think too hard about how we blew the whole damn season.

I'm about to join the beer pong game when something catches my attention from the corner of my eye. But it's just some couple making out like no one's watching.

About to turn away, I do a double take and recognize one of the parties. I rub my eyes with the fingers of one hand and fix them on the couple again.

Indeed, it's Trent McFadden. However, he has his tongue down a redhead's throat and last I checked, Liv is still very much a brunette.

My whole body freezes. A flash of cold travels through my spine, followed by a lick of fire. No matter how hard I glare, the piece of shit doesn't stop. Only when the girl jumps to wrap her legs around him and their mouths disconnect for a quick moment, does he finally catch sight of me.

And his face blanches. Because he knows exactly who the hell I am.

I smack some random guy's chest with my beer until he gets the hint and takes the bottle. Trent says something to the girl that makes her un-Velcro herself from him. He's screwed, though. The living room is packed with people that block his exit.

"Brooklyn." His eyes travel down to my hands while I crack my knuckles. Meanwhile, what he cracks is his voice as he says, "Hi, fancy seeing you here."

I grab him by the collar of his shirt and yank him close. His eyes are wide, nostrils flaring as he breathes fast.

"Excuse me." I shift my glare to the girl. "You may want to step back for this."

"What?" She's still flushed as she glances between Trent and I. "What's happening?"

He releases a choked laugh. "Um, it's just a misunderstanding—"

I get in his grill, using the full force of my height. "Misunderstanding my ass. You're cheating on my best friend."

"What?" The girl hisses the question.

I frown at her. "You didn't know this slimeball has a girlfriend?"

"No!" Her expression morphs into total disgust.

He tries to push my arm away and I don't budge a single inch. "W-What the hell is it to you? You and Liv aren't even friends anymore."

Wrong thing to say, because now I'm even more pissed off. If I hadn't screwed things up with her, I could've kept this asshole far away from her.

He slobbered around her ever since they met at some chemistry class on the first semester of freshman year. The second I was no longer part of the picture, he pounced. I can't even believe Liv caved. Like maybe his decent looks prevented her from seeing what I saw all along—that he doesn't deserve a second of her time, let along a whole year together.

Through gritted teeth, I say, "This isn't about me, you steaming pile of horse dung. Does Liv know you're cheating on her?"

"Of course not." He frowns, a bead of sweat rolling down his face. "And it's going to stay that way, right? After all, you two don't even talk anymore."

"The hell it will, because you're going to tell her yourself or else I'm going to make you shit your own teeth."

He sucks in air through his damn teeth and opens his mouth to spew some garbage, except his words are drowned by a different voice.

"Trent?" A pause, and then… "Brooklyn?"

Slowly, I turn to face her.

And I mean, *her*.

The redhead for some reason hasn't scrammed and right beside her is Liv, along with two other girls that I vaguely recognize. All I care about is Liv, though, my former best friend. The feeling is obviously not mutual and her dark eyes shift away from mine, back to her boyfriend.

A boulder of guilt slams over me. I regret wishing she'd come to this party. It's like this house is cursed to give her nothing but pain.

"What's happening here?" Liv asks with that naturally raspy voice of hers. It doesn't matter that the music blares all around us, blending with a cacophony of other voices. I'd recognize hers in my sleep.

"Liv, babe. This Neanderthal is assaulting me. Tell him to back off."

"Shut the hell up. I haven't even hit you yet," I grumble under my breath.

"Yet! See—"

But Liv cuts him off. "And just why would he want to hit you?" After a blink, her eyes are on mine again even as she keeps her face turned to whatshisface.

The most curious thing happens. My body thrums back to life like it does when I deliver a particularly nice check against the boards, and I want to grin. The situation doesn't merit it, and I strain every muscle in my face to stay serious.

Her boyfriend takes advantage of my lapse to free himself from my hold, but he can't run any farther than before. "Well, um…" He clears his throat.

The redhead snaps. "Sis, is this your boyfriend?"

"Yeah?" Liv frowns.

"You may want to dump him, then. Because he let me believe he was single a second before he shoved his tongue down my throat."

"You were into it!" the dipshit says, pointing at the redhead. And that's when it clicks on him that maybe that wasn't the most important part of her speech. "I mean, I—"

Liv's lip starts trembling and she bites it. Her fists tighten at her sides.

"Ah, shit," I mutter. That's the same look I put on her face a year ago. I reach for her. "Liv, I—"

She steps away and all I do is grab air. "Let's go home," she says to her friends. "This party blows."

The two girls wrap their arms around her and steer her away, glaring at Trent over their shoulders. The redhead throws a double bird at him and pushes someone out of the way before blending with the crowd.

"Wait, let me explain." Trent starts toward the redhead or Liv, I don't know.

I can't give Olivia any comfort, unlike her girl friends. But there's another way I can help. I put my arm up and block his way. "You're going nowhere, dipshit. Not until we have a good conversation."

CHAPTER 4
OLIVIA

Canonically speaking, can people be turned into zombies even if they aren't bitten by one? Because that sure as hell is how I feel, except I don't remember any remarkable bites other than this morning, when I zoned out while having breakfast cereal and bit my own tongue instead.

I sigh as I follow the throngs out of the main building of St. Cloud's science faculty, where I just had my molecular and cell biology II final. And also the *final* final of the semester.

I survived. Somehow.

My steps are heavy until I stop outside in the middle of the grass. It's a shocking, luscious green. The exact same shade as Brooklyn Tatum's eyes. But the sky is the same true blue as my exe's eyes, and rather than reveling in nature, it pisses me off.

Yeah, I dumped his ass. And by text, too.

Of course, he didn't like that one bit. He spent weeks trying to corner me at the library or during class. It sucks sweaty cojones that he's also a bio major, but fortunately the more he deepens his marine bio concentration, the less we'll cross paths. I just have to hang tight in the meantime.

"Liv, wait!"

Shit, I should've kept walking. The flight reflex engages my amygdala. While my logical brain continues acting like a zombie ate it, my legs activate.

"Liv, please." A huff. "Why are you so damn fast?"

Because I have a gold medal in running from my problems, that's why.

Not that Trent McFadden is still my problem. I was very clear when I texted him saying we're through and promptly blocked him. Conversely, if that wasn't enough, I've become an expert at ignoring him every time he's tried to ambush me. And I've discovered some truly excellent hiding spots around campus like cleaning closets, storage rooms, remote bathrooms that smell surprisingly clean, and even under classroom desks. Turns out I'm quite flexible too.

"Would you just wait?"

Of course, life isn't like a K-Drama. If we were in one, he'd have grabbed my wrist and twirled me around smoothly. But in this crappy reality, he jerks me to a stop by grabbing onto my backpack. And my hair.

"Ugh!"

Trent lets me go. "If you'd just stayed still—I was just trying to catch you."

I pin the full force of my glare on him as I slowly turn, massaging my scalp. "Shouldn't you have taken the hint?"

He has the nerve to get annoyed. Huffing, he says, "I just want to talk."

"There's nothing to talk about. You cheated on me with some random girl at a party, which makes me think it's probably not the first time." Going by the way his face reddens and he swallows thickly, I'm right on the money. "How many times did you do it, Trent?"

"I—That's not the point."

I'm aware of other students getting front seats to some

drama, but I don't want this asshole to catch up with me if I try to run again. So, I finally square up to him.

"Then what is it?" I cock an eyebrow at him, and he grabs onto the strap of his backpack slung over his shoulder in a ridiculous way I can't believe I ever found cute. Like he's trying to imitate a five year old when he's 20.

"The point is that you can't just break up with me by text."

Vaguely I wonder if I'm losing my mind. Because even though I've been incapable of laughing for a month ever since that damn party, I now give out great guffaws that bend me over.

"You… you're shitting me, right?" I speak between wheezing. "What you want to talk with me about is how I dumped your stinking ass, and not about what you did?"

Trent's face pinches with anger, which turns him from a reasonably good looking guy into a brain-eating zombie. He points a finger at my face. "No, *I* dumped your sorry ass—"

"In what reality, buddy?"

"I *was* going to dump you." Trent pulls at his hair in frustration. "Ten minutes of making out with some random chick is always better than any sex with you, Olivia. If you weren't so damn frigid and boring I wouldn't have had to stray."

Frigid is the figurative bucket of water that washes over me.

My brain, ever so useful, runs through his words over and over until they're ingrained in my very being.

He'd been growing more and more distant in the final months of our relationship, never really telling me why, and rather than asking, I tried to keep acting as usual. But deep down I knew he wasn't reacting the same way to me as he did early on. Our kisses weren't so hot anymore. His hands weren't on me as much. He no longer wanted to play with me.

And this was why? Because all along he didn't find me attractive anymore, and didn't have the testicles to tell me?

His lips curl into a malicious smirk. "No comeback, huh? Even you recognize it's true. You're a—"

I snap out of the trance. My fists tighten and for once, I don't want to hold them back.

"Eat shit, asshole!"

I sock him right in the solar plexus.

Normally, I only condone violence in manga and superhero movie franchises. And I'm also too weak to open a flask with my own hands, so it's not like I can truly hurt someone. But it's so deeply satisfying when he folds over in pain, the breath rushing out of him with a satisfying *oof*. His backpack falls on the grass and that's when I notice the T-shirt he's wearing.

It's the vintage Free Willy T-shirt I got him for his birthday two months ago.

With a roar, I launch myself at him before he can recover. Clawing at him, not caring if I scratch him, I grab two big fistfuls of the fabric and tug.

"What the—" Trent's still disoriented enough that I can rip the T-shirt off of him. "Are you out of your damn mind?"

Someone snickers nearby. Some girls walking some twenty feet from us point at Trent's torso. I, too, found it funny that the only body hair he has is this little tuft in the middle of his chest. But I'm not in the business of making others feel bad about themselves the way he has clearly shown himself to be.

"No, I'm just not as boring as you thought," I say, instead of trying to bring him down like he did me. "And I'm going to be taking this back, since I bought it for you when I thought you weren't a piece of shit."

Erm, oops. Maybe I do want to bring him down a peg.

Still rubbing his stomach, he glares at me and says, "Fine. Then give me back my hoodie."

"You'll get it in the mail." Taking a page from the girl who outed him as a cheater, I give him the finger and march off.

The abrupt sound of applause makes me falter, but it's just the two girls who stayed for the whole show. One of them gives me a thumb up and the other one says, "Drag him, sis."

My lips twitch. Ugh, sisterhood is the best. The encouragement of these random girls helps me walk with my head held high across campus. And if it wasn't for Dee and Mina, I probably wouldn't have kept my priorities straight after the breakup and might've flunked my finals.

I pause to ball up the T-shirt that still smells like Trent's Axe Dark Temptation and toss it in a trashcan. My lungs work overtime to suck in fresh air and get rid of any trace of him, and the harder they work, the harder my tear glands respond.

Dabbing at my face only brings the freaking Axe smell back to my nose. I rush into the nearest building. I know it's part of the business faculty, and I pray that I don't run into Brooklyn. Running into a different kind of ex while I'm trying to wash off the stench of the newest ex is more tragedy than I can handle.

I make it into the women's restroom without any encounters. A girl stepping out of a stall gives me a weird look as I furiously rub soap all the way up to my elbows. I'm only satisfied when my skin turns red like a lobster.

As I stare at my reflection in the mirror, I let my arms hang limp at my sides, dripping water on the tiled floor. A clear tear streaks down my cheeks. My long hair, usually pin straight, looks like a bird's nest after that little tussle with he-whose-name-shall-be-excised-from-my-vocabulary. There are wet splotches on my white blouse, a little number I got because he liked it when we saw it at a store together even though I absolutely hate its lace sleeves.

In fact, I freaking hate these skinny jeans too. Maybe I should've noticed the red flag when he casually told me he liked skinny jeans on a girl. Because not only I used to wear baggy jeans all the time, but it also implied that he'd been checking other girls out.

I lift up my hands and inspect them. My nails are long, with a clear coat of nail polish, no rings or bracelets. All because he mentioned he liked natural, feminine girls. I picture the girl he'd apparently been making out with at the Bolt House party. Pretty. Lots of makeup. Hair a red that comes from a bottle.

"What a damn hypocrite," I say to the mirror, my whole body shaking as more little things start popping up in my head. In freshman year, I had my hair past my shoulder and kept meaning to trim it, but I'd been too busy to set time aside for it. And when I found out he liked long hair on girls, I decided to just grow it.

Except, how many of those decisions were actually mine?

When I think back to myself in high school, I realize I was a different person. I wore black, baggy clothes, styled myself however I damn well pleased. When did I lose myself?

How did I let him do this to myself?

"La madre que lo parió." I don't speak Spanish anywhere near as fluently as the rest of my family, but the feelings boiling in my gut can only be expressed in the tongue of my ancestors.

I run my wet hands through my hair, all the way down to the tips that fall to the middle of my back. I decide—me, myself, and I—to take myself back.

My asshole ex boyfriend might've made me lose sight of myself, but I never truly left. That boring version of me that allegedly made him cheat was the Olivia who tried to fit in his mold. But today I showed him who I really am. A take no shit badass. And that's who I'll be from now on.

With a deep breath, I walk out of the bathroom and keep my eyes forward. I make it out of the building without running into any undesirable boys, and haul my ass to the hair salon near campus.

Two hours later—mostly because I had to wait until they fit me in—I emerge out of the salon with a bob and already feel so much lighter. Not just because I lost like ten pounds of hair, but because this is one step closer to reclaiming my identity.

The apartment's empty when I arrive and that suits me well. I tear off the ridiculous blouse and throw it in the garbage can. I almost crash on my enormous ass while trying to peel off the skinny jeans, but finally succeed and also toss them. I'm all for sustainable fashion, but right now I need to get rid of every stitch that reminds me of him. Opening my closet, I start pulling out piece after piece, tops, bottoms, underwear, the pair of socks he gave me for Christmas. And finally, his damn hoodie.

That one falls at the top of the pile. I'm breathing hard as I glare at it. Before I know it, I grab a Sharpie from my desk and deface it with some colorful words, some of which he won't be able to understand because they're in Spanish.

I put my hand on my naked waist to survey the progress. "Good. Now, onto the next stage."

After bagging up all the clothes and dumping his sweatshirt in a box, I check what's left in my closet. It's all the stuff I brought from home that I used to wear until freshman year. I grab a rolled up pair of ripped boyfriend jeans from the back and put them on.

"Whew, they still fit."

After that victory, I grab a One OK Rock T-shirt and hesitate for a moment. This is Brooklyn's and my favorite J-Rock band. We went to see them in concert together the summer after graduating high school. But I'm the one who introduced him to them. He won't take this away from me.

I yank on the T-shirt, and head into the bathroom to get rid of the clear polish and trim my nails as short as possible. I find the angriest hard rock band in my Spotify playlist to keep me company as I paint my nails black.

"Boring? Frigid?" I mutter through gritted teeth. "I'll show you."

No more *pick me* energy from me. I'm going to do the picking from now on.

CHAPTER 5
BROOKLYN

Summer training camp with Coach Green is famous for being barrels of fun. And by fun I mean puke, which is what we all do at least once during the grueling week of punishment that he calls bootcamp. What's funny is that it's not the only week during the summer where sophomores and up train, but it's the welcome for the freshmen. And boy, it's filtered out a couple already.

"Congratulations on surviving the week," Coach voices from center ice, arms folded as he inspects each of us.

He does a double take when he finds me grinning from ear to ear.

Yeah, I'm soaked to the bone. My uniform probably weighs about fifty pounds more from sweat and slush. My calves throb like toothaches. My stomach is queasy, even though I've already given my offering to the barrel an hour ago. My head's still spinning around the ice as if we were in the middle of another skating drill, even though I stand in line with my teammates. Everything hurts and I'm positively dying.

But all this torture means one thing. He's not giving up on the team this year.

Neither am I.

Coach Green clears his throat and finishes taking stock of the team. He turns to whisper something to one of the other coaches, and they nod at each other before our head coach speaks again.

"The St. Cloud hockey program is still relatively new, but in its short existence it has made a name for itself in this tournament. Four Frozen Four championships in just eight years is nothing to sneeze at."

Two of those were won by Max Cassiano's first crop, and two by Aran Rodriguez's. And sure, I want to be the next Cale Makar just like any other defenseman, but Max and Aran are the ones whose legacy I want to surpass. It's impossible now that I'm starting my junior year, but maybe I can still tie them.

"But in the past two years..." Coach trails off to shake his head. "We have played worse than my kid at the mini mites."

A murmur rises from the line of players. I have to bite my lips to not scream because, honestly, comparing the Bolts of the last two years to mini mites is disrespectful.

To the mini mites.

"But now we have some fresh blood." He nods at the freshmen. "And we still have some veterans who want to fight." At this he nods at... me?

I turn to my left and there's Jamie. And to my right is Dane. Beside him, are some of the other juniors.

Wait, no acknowledgement for the seniors? Well, well, well.

Coach clasps his hands at his back. "So, we're going to do things differently this year. Normally, the captain and alternates are seniors." Except for Max's cohort, but I don't interrupt. "But this year, it's going to be a junior."

"What?" Kyle Warren shouts. He's a senior now, a buddy of Liam Roberts, and he was dead sure he'd be the next captain because apparently Liam recommended him for the job. Earlier in the lockers, Kyle was saying how, and I quote, having the C on his jersey would get him so much more tail. "But that's not right! I'm a senior." A second later he points at his other buddies. "We are seniors. Our time is finally up."

"You wasted your chance by playing worse than mini mites." Coach Green lifts up his hands like he can't freaking believe he has to repeat himself.

"Then I quit the damn team!" Kyle throws his gloves on the ice with all his might.

"That's fine. We have JV guys ready to take that spot."

I suck air through my teeth because that burn hurt even me. But for some reason this turns Kyle's ire at me.

"Or," I say in a sweet little tone now that I have his attention. "You could just man the hell up."

"You ass—"

"That's right. You either quit the team and forfeit your scholarship, or beg some other college to take you in as a late term transfer, or you do your job. Which is it gonna be?" Coach Green folds his arms and levels Kyle with A Look. The one that typically leads to a drill resulting in offerings to the puke barrel.

Kyle mumbles something I'm glad none of the coaches seem to hear, because it'd make us all do ten-minute planks. But the little shit stays in line, so I guess he's taking the not-outright-quitting route.

Nodding, Coach focuses back on the topic. "That said. The player who has shown the most grit on and off season will be the new captain."

I nudge my defensive partner. "It's you, Great Dane."

"Nope. It's you, Blondie." He smirks at me.

"And his job will be to keep up that intensity during this new season, while also infecting the rest of his teammates— and heaven knows this won't be an easy feat." He rolls his eyes skyward as if asking for patience. "Anyway, Tatum, you're it."

The grin wipes off my face.

Dane starts clapping even though he's still wearing his gloves. "Congratulations. Your life officially sucks now."

I don't appreciate how some of the guys in the coaching staff nod at that.

"I, er…" Kyle and the senior goons are giving me looks that say they'll try to shave my eyebrows while I sleep or something.

"Don't be too happy. Bloom, Schwartz, you're the alternates. Practice dismissed."

Dane stops celebrating. On my other side, Jamie cringes so hard he's close to turning into a black hole.

"Ah, shit."

"Is right," I murmur.

We start filing back out to the locker room. The younger guys take turns congratulating me, probably out of relief that Coach didn't go fully nuclear and make one of them lead this circus. My brain says this is going to be a shitshow, especially because the seniors have the maturity level of gnats and will try to sabotage this whole enterprise—if only by being lazier than ever.

And yet my heart hammers as hard as if I was in the middle of a game, nil-nil in overtime and during a penalty kill.

At my bench, I peel off my jersey and let it flop on the floor with a wet splat. I make quick work of removing my pads and twist around to fish around my bag until I produce my cell phone. I click on the text messaging app and…

Stop.

The thrumming in my veins dulls to nothingness when I realize I have no one to tell the big news to.

If I tell Dad that I just became only the second non-senior to be named captain, because technically Max is an outlier, he wouldn't care. He hasn't exercised a single molecule of enthusiasm for my hockey career, or me, ever since I announced that I wanted to play defense instead of being a forward like him. Which also coincided with the time he and Mom were divorcing.

Nah, he's much happier with his new wife and my half-brother, Lee, who's still young enough to look up to Dad as a hero.

And Mom? She hasn't contacted me in years. All my attempts to reach out to her have gone ignored and last I knew of her was through the tabloids. Apparently she's moved to Monaco to live with some guy from the royal family. Ridiculous.

Then there's Liv. She's never enjoyed hockey, but she used to make an effort because it was what made me happy. Except I made her hate my guts because I was trying to impress Liam Roberts back when I was a gullible little turd.

I slide the phone back into my bag and lean down to unlace my skates, sighing. It is what it is. Hockey's my only constant. Friends and family... not so much. It's why I got the weird tattoo I did. I've never told anyone what it represents because I know it's cheesy—they can just think it's some abstract stuff. But when I'm down in the dumps like right at this second, I look at the lines and remind myself I at least have one of the three things going for me.

After removing my undershirt, I run my finger across the lines that start at my inner wrists. A thick, fully black line for hockey. A fainter one in the middle that represents friends. And then a lighter one for family. The three lines run around my arms, over my elbows and triceps, to the back of my shoulders, and the meet in twin downward curves at the middle of my back. If I hold my hands at my back you can see that the lines make a giant heart.

Because these are the three things that are most important

to me. Two are incomplete, which means I pour my entire heart into only one. Hockey.

I smack my face hard to snap out of the sentimentalism. After undressing, I haul my ass to the showers. The icy spray of water helps me clear my head. I'll have to rearrange my semester schedule to make more room for hockey. It's not like practice will necessarily increase because I'm the captain now, but there are some admin duties associated to it that I'll have to accommodate. And maybe I should start paying more attention to plays, stats, how they all mesh with my teammates. That all is probably part of the *infecting* Coach wants me to do.

"O'Malley's to celebrate the fact that this year is going to suck but maybe not as bad as we thought?" Dane asks from the shower stall behind mine.

"Sure," I return with a snort. "But I'll catch you there. I need to do something first."

"And what's that? Squeal into your pillow?"

"No, squeal into your momma's pillow."

Somehow the lazy joke still gets me a round of chuckles, even though the mechanics are weird. Shouldn't I be making his momma squeal into her pillow? Whatever. I need to be more serious this semester, and being the biggest clown in the team isn't going to help my case.

First step, finish showering and get dressed. Step two, high tail it out to the admin building. I was going to take two electives this semester and I'm thinking it should now be zero.

*

Once I get to the admin office, I discover that the ticket machine is down. Like maybe it gave up after the place packed up with people like me, changing their minds at the last minute. Or complaining about something. The line moves pretty quickly, though, until I'm only three people away. That's when a little racket starts at the front.

Wait. I recognize one of the voices. I lean out of the line and a slow smile takes over my face.

It's Liv.

"I'm telling you it wasn't my fault. I'm a hundred percent sure I clicked on protein biochemistry and *not* on—" She pauses to read her schedule. "Reproductive biology I."

I stuff my fist against my mouth so I don't burst out laughing.

One of the two people ahead of me moves over to another booth. My blood starts pumping like I'm on the bench, waiting for the line change.

"Are you sure?" a softer voice retorts to Liv.

The person in front of me moves to the third booth that is now freeing up. I step forward and stand behind my former best friend as she throws her hands in the air.

"Can we please focus on what matters? The question is whether you can please, with a cherry on top, fix my schedule, and not on who made the error—which by the way, wasn't me."

Over her shoulder, I see the admin guy give her an eye roll. But then he catches me glaring at him. This gets Liv's attention because she turns around.

All the papers she had on the counter slide with her turn and crash down, but for a second neither of us moves. Other than she widens her eyes dramatically upon my sight, that is.

She cut her hair up to her jaw, shortest I've ever seen it. But the eyeliner's back and so is the obscure band T-shirt. I blink as I process what I'm seeing. She used to wear baggy band T-shirts and this one's cropped. Her chest casts a little shadow over the sliver of her stomach, right before the waistband of her jeans. I don't dare to meet her eyes again in case she thinks I was just checking her out.

And, uh, she'd be right. I didn't mean to. It just happened. But I don't know what that says about me.

So before she can react, I lean down and pick up her stuff. Right at the top is a printout of her schedule. My lips twitch at the reproductive biology I, which makes me wonder if there's a II, a III, or more. The puns I could make with this knowledge would be chef's kiss. And then my eyes snag on an elective.

Spanish I.

Her eyes meet mine as I hand her the papers. I hold them a second longer, buying myself some time to try to read her mind.

My brain plucks a memory from the box I try to keep shut. It's of Olivia and I during the first few weeks of the freshman fall semester. We were hanging out at the library, her studying for some bio class, while I did business school coursework.

"This sucks," I said with a whiny voice. "You want to open your own company so why couldn't you just major in business too?"

"Because," she said, her eyes still tracing a line on her textbook. "I need to know what I'll be selling at a molecular level first. I'll figure out the business side later. Or you can teach me."

I sighed. "Fine, but that means we'll never be together in class."

She hummed as her attention finally pulled toward me. I lay on the table, head resting on an extended arm as I looked up to her. Her hair cascaded around her face while she said, "Let's just take an elective together, then."

I smirked. "Now we're talking. But what?"

"I don't know… Spanish? You always said you wanted to learn more, and it's not like I'm great at it."

I stretched myself upright to sitting, suddenly excited at the prospect, and offered my hand out to her. "Deal?"

"Deal." She shook my hand, two hard pumps before letting go.

The Liv of the present looks at me like she wishes I'd self combust. She rips the papers from my grip and turns back to the admin guy, not noticing that she's given me a paper cut.

I lick my index finger while staring at the back of her head, a new plan forming in my mind.

CHAPTER 6
OLIVIA

'm a bit jittery driving to O'Malley's in my brother's old Toyota SUV, it still stinks like his disgusting hockey pads no matter how many times I clean or air it out.

That was the closest I've been to Brooklyn in forever and…

He's hotter than ever. Damn him.

It's not even just because we've turned into strangers. He's grown an inch or two since high school and filled out more in the past year and change—a lot more. The black Vans T-shirt he was wearing was tight around his shoulders and arms because he's become a fortress of pure muscle.

I bet his opponents get intimidated by the sheer size of him, even though he has a face that belongs in Hollywood, and is the goofiest boy in the planet.

The good news is that I'm as pissed at him as ever.

I grip the steering wheel tighter. This is why I've been avoiding him like the plague. Even a glimpse of his hair brings back a rush of unwelcome emotions.

In my mind I can still see the scene from that night crystal clear. We'd spent all day going back and forth between attending some Bolt House party or going to the movies instead. I didn't do parties much even then, but with some liquid courage and a killer outfit, I gathered my nerve to go to the Bolt House to finally confess my feelings for Brooklyn, even if that meant officially joining his world of stinky jocks.

That didn't happen, though. Instead, I found him in the kitchen talking with another hockey jock.

"Dude, that chick who clings to you all the time is the reason why you're not getting any," the dude bro said.

Brooklyn rubbed his hair and his back was turned to me. He had no idea said chick—me—had just entered the kitchen.

Dude bro did. He gave me a little smirk that chased a chill down my back. A sort of premonition to the catastrophe that was about to unfold.

"You think?" my asshole best friend asked, instead of telling his buddy to back off.

"Totally. Chicks ask me if you two are together all the time." At the ensuing silence, dude bro added, "But like you're in totally different leagues. She's a boring dweeb and you have everything it takes to rule this college. Plus, you said you want to get laid, right?"

"I—uh, right."

"So you're gonna ditch her and finally have some fun with the team?" He handed over a beer to Brooklyn as incentive.

And Brooklyn took it, saying, "Sure." Complete with a shrug and a swig, like he just didn't tacitly agree with the other guy who called me a boring dweeb.

Like he just didn't break my freaking heart.

Our friendship definitely started out of pity when we were five year olds at a classmate's birthday party, where I sat all by myself eating carrots with lactose-free cream cheese because I was allergic to basically all but one of the cake's ingredients. Everyone made fun of me, but not Brooklyn. He came and sat with me and we bonded over Dragon Ball.

Did he pity me for fourteen years?

And then if that wasn't all, Brooklyn also didn't refute the comment of me being well under his league. Which I've always known. Brooklyn's girlfriends in high school were the hottest of the hot. He always grew bored of them but kept me around. So I thought…

I really thought I stood a chance. Until that night.

My resolve about confessing was replaced by a different one. Before the dude bro steered Brooklyn away, I called attention to myself, looked dead into the deep green eyes of my about-to-be-former best friend, and said famous last words.

"Stay the hell away from me for the rest of our lives."

After that, I only endured a couple of days of Brooke's texts and phone calls until I blocked him and unfollowed him from social media.

No, not Brooke. Brooklyn. Or *that guy*, even. We're strangers now.

I pull into a public parking lot near O'Malley's and roll the windows back up. The preternatural stank will accumulate again but I don't trust the thick clouds on the sky. Before stepping out of the car, I rest my forehead against the steering wheel and close my eyes.

I know Brooklyn had no idea I had feelings for him back then. If it hadn't been for that little issue, I'd have just been pissed for a couple of weeks or something, until eventually giving him a chance to explain himself.

But it's now been a year and a half after that mess and I still don't have enough courage to face him. Even though he hurt me, I'm the one who destroyed our friendship. The longer time passes, the less I know how to fix it.

Finally, I can't take a second longer of the musty smell in the car and open the door. Thunder rumbles above me, which feels too cheeky for my taste. My keys and wallet are already in my pocket tied to my jeans with the kind of chain that was in fashion like twenty years ago. I grab my phone from the dashboard and stuff it in my other pocket with my emergency EpiPen, and off I go.

Mina and Dee are already at a table when I walk in. They must've arrived right before the crush of people, and it takes some elbowing and stepping on literal toes with my Dr. Marten's until I reach them.

"Hey, guys." I flop in the booth seat next to Mina. "Sorry I'm late. Big line at the admin office."

"Did you get it fixed, at least?" Mina asks me, genuinely curious after I spent the whole morning moaning about it.

"Yeah. It just shaved ten years off of my life." Of which nine and a half were because of Brooklyn freaking Tatum and his freaking shoulder muscles.

"Well, now you're here and that's what matters." Dee slides a chilled, unopened bottle of kombucha my way. "Here. To your singlehood."

Mina smacks a hand on the table. "No, I said we should toast to Liv's new sluttyhood."

"How about we just toast to whatever she wants to do?" Dee shrugs.

"Boom. Someone's got the right idea." I grab the bottle and smash its mouth against the edge of the table, at the perfect angle to pop the lid off. Never fails to delight people. "Cheers," I say, tucking my tongue out in a cheeky way.

As we clink various drink recipients, Dee asks, "Can you teach me that trick?"

"It's not that hard," I tell her. "All you have to do is—"

Mina leans closer to me and wags her eyebrows. "Are you ready then?"

"For what?" Dee asks, already forgetting the previous topic.

I turn the kombucha bottle in my hands. "I might have told Mina earlier that I'm ready." Dee leans forward from across the table like I'm about to give them the winning lottery numbers. "To fool around a bit."

"What? But I thought you hated men now?"

I chuckle. "I mean, kinda. But I can't make out with myself."

"It is a struggle." Mina shakes her head in the most defeated way. "But shall we hit the bar and see who we can flirt with?"

"Let's hit it." We slide off the booth, ready to go on the prowl.

Over the summer, I decided that the antidote to my boy issues is to treat them the same way they've treated me. Like I'm expendable. And since I have annoying hormones too, maybe this is the arrangement that will tide me over until I find my soulmate. Or don't.

I'm starting to think that romance books have been lying to me my whole life—which I can't ever tell Maddie, my brother's wife, since she writes my favorite ones. It's just that so far real life is far from what's on the pages, and I definitely prefer the latter.

It takes us some maneuvering until we make room for ourselves at the bar, our backs against it as we peruse the crowd. I hitch one of my boots against the bottom, elbow on the bar as I take a swig of kombucha like it's beer. A tryhard pose? Maybe. But I'm comfortable this way, which helps me curb my reflex of breaking eye contact with cute guys.

It takes a while. Dee's the first to get snatched up, proof of the Strikes' popularity in campus. I keep fanning my gaze across the place, until I make eye contact with a guy—and he doesn't look away. He's cute in that boy next door kinda vibe, and the second I offer a lopsided little smile, he starts heading over.

"Remember," Mina says beside me. "Whoever doesn't

manage to make out with anyone tonight is buying the groceries next time."

"I'll manage. You should worry about yourself."

"Oh, wow. I've created a monster." She laughs.

I smile at her. "No, you gave me confidence."

"You had it in you all along." She pats my arm right as cute guy reaches us.

"Hi there."

Not the most creative greeting, but hey. I'm not looking for a husband tonight.

"Hi yourself." I tuck my hair behind my ear. According to Mina, guys like that.

"Wow." He props his hand against the bar and leans closer. "You're like, really hot."

I can practically feel Mina vibrating with the need to laugh, and I know that's exactly what could happen if I even glance her way. So I don't. I focus on this decent-looking-but-not-show-stopping guy who thinks he has way more swag than he does.

Beggars can't be choosers and all that, especially when I have a bet to win.

"Wanna dance?" I ask him.

"Uh, sure?" He sounds uncertain now, like either he thought the riveting conversation was going to continue, or like maybe his dancing skills aren't great. Joke's on him—mine are probably worse. It's always fun though, and maybe if he drops the tryhard act we can work our way up to a kiss.

He offers his hand and I take it. His skin's a bit clammy, maybe he's more nervous than he lets on. *Me too, bud.*

"For the groceries!" Mina calls out behind me and I have to bite my lips not to laugh.

"What was that?" cute guy asks over his shoulder while navigating us to the only area that remains somewhat open. A few people are dancing to an ancient Flo Rida song.

"Nothing." My eyes fall on his shoulders. They're nice. Like they have no trouble carrying a backpack. I shouldn't compare them to a different pair I saw earlier. "So, what's your name?"

"Jayden. You?"

"Olivia."

Huh. Our initials would make a funny pair. OJ. Orange juice. Ex's and me made OT, overtime, which was an annoying hockey reference. Brooke and I made body odor, and I used to tease him about it.

I shake my head, forcing myself to stop thinking about him.

We start dancing and it's worse than I imagined. Not only are we extremely uncoordinated and he steps on my boots. But also Jayden grabs onto my sides, hands sliding under my crop top without asking for permission instead of easing me into this with some finesse.

Damn it, I knew this was going too well.

I grab his wrists and lower his hands to my hips over my jeans. Cute guy starts looking less cute when, instead of apologizing, he gives me a look like this is just a game and slides his hands back up.

"Okay, let's stop right here." I step all the way back.

"Wait, I'll play nice. I promise."

That all makes me think he'll do the exact opposite. I can't see myself possibly kissing him now.

"Pass. It was nice to meet you, Jayden." I turn to leave and the little shit grabs my side—again.

"It's just—you're so hot, I can't help myse—"

"She said no, asshole."

I don't have to turn to the third voice. Every cell in my body knows it belongs to Brooke.

No, *Brooklyn*.

Why the heck is he even here right now?

Jayden has enough cojones to glare at the star defenseman

of the Thunder Bolts and all 6 feet and 5 inches, two hundred twenty pounds of pure lean muscle. "She was mine first, dick. Find your own."

I blow a raspberry. "Dude, you wish."

"Let's go, Liv." Goosebumps break all over my skin as Brooke whispers in my ear. But I'm truly toast when he grabs my wrist and twirls me around.

CHAPTER 7
BROOKLYN

"Yo, Tatum! Where you going? We need one more."

I wave at Dane as Liv and I march by the pool tables. He shrugs and then works on recruiting one of the JV guys for the game.

"What the hell are you doing?" But even though her free hand grabs onto my wrist, she doesn't dig her heels in to stop me.

The place is packed tonight, which stands to reason on the last Friday of freedom before the new semester. I don't want interlopers for the talk Liv and I are about to have, so I navigate us through the bodies all the way to the back of the establishment, past the bathrooms and to the emergency exit. I know it doesn't trip any alarms, because this has become my escape route every time I'm out-peopled.

A drizzle greets us outside in the back alley. Liv finally twists out of my grasp and I expect her to beat it, but when I face her, she's still out here. Arms folded tight. Mean glare on her face. A strand of hair falls across her eyes and she puffs to try to move it. When that doesn't work, she releases a hand to push it back, which messes her hair in a way that suits her more. Just like the black nail polish and the chunky silver rings.

The Olivia I know is back, huh? Freaking finally.

Mimicking her, I fold my arms too and her eyes lower to my tattoos.

"What the hell are *you* doing?" I spit right back at her. "Like, I'm glad to see you're looking more like yourself, but shouldn't you have learned the lesson? Stay away from douchebags, Liv."

She scoffs in total disbelief. "And what gives you the right to say any of this shit?"

"I'm your friend," I say through gritted teeth, pissed out of my mind that I can't say *best* friend anymore.

"No, you're just a stranger now so butt out of my business." She starts for the door and I almost laugh when it doesn't open.

That's right, babe, one way only.

"And whose fault is that?" I mutter bitterly.

Slowly, she glances over her shoulder. "Yours, actually."

"Fine." I throw my hands out in that dramatic way she has. "I'm glad we're finally hashing this out. It's my fault, I was a total jerk. But that doesn't mean I've stopped looking out for you."

"Is that what you think you were doing?" Now she faces me again, incredulity pouring out of her very being. "Ever stopped to think I can take care of my damn self?"

"Sure. You could probably have kicked him in the balls. But what if he hurt you first?" I shake my head. "And what kind of person would I be if I saw what was going on and didn't intervene?"

"Uh." Liv taps her chin, pretending to think. "Someone who stays out of other people's business?"

"No, an asshole. That's what."

She blinks hard against the rain starting to prickle her eyes.

With an efficient swivel on her heels, she starts heading around the building back to the front. I follow because I'll make sure she gets back in safe.

As she fumes in silence, I ask, "Why are you even giving the time of the day to some random creep like that?"

"None of your business, Brooklyn."

I hate that she's calling me just like everyone else.

She used to have more nicknames for me than I can count. Brooke. Brookie—which is short for a brownie and cookie baked together, my favorite dessert. Body odor, because she said I always stank every time I gave her a headlock and made a mess of her hair. Blondie. Puppy, because I'm like a tireless golden retriever when I'm giving her crap.

And that's what I channel now, even though I'm annoyed as hell. This freaking rain isn't helping, either. "Are you looking for a rebound? Because if so I can hook you up with someone who isn't a slimeball."

She flinches, but I don't have enough time to inspect that when she suddenly gets in my grill. "Trust me, I don't need *your* help to find some stranger to make out with. No matter how below your league I may be."

Ouch. And not just from the words Liam Roberts said that time. Her index finger jabs at my chest once, twice. Hard enough to bruise.

Before the third jab, I curl my hand around her finger and seize it. Leaning closer to her, desperate to wipe Roberts' words from her mind any way that I can, I say, "Well, lucky for you I'm a stranger now, huh?"

Liv yanks her finger free and takes a step away. She rakes her fingers through her wet hair and pushes it back. It makes her crop top ride up and I get a glimpse of a black sports bra.

It makes heat burst in my gut and that's when my own words click.

I blink hard against the pouring rain and my own hair poking my eyes, but actually it's just so I process the moment.

Sometimes… often—okay, all the time—I talk without thinking and put my size sixteen foot in my mouth. It's why another one of her nicknames for me was blimbo. Blond himbo.

"Puh-lease." Liv snorts hard enough to drown a roll of thunder. "You wouldn't kiss me if your life depended on it."

"Is that a challenge? Because it sounds like one."

Shit, I guess I'm still in blimbo mode.

A condescending look falls on her face. "No, it's a fact—based on the whole me being under your league and all."

"Would you just freaking drop that? I'm not the one who said that crap."

"No, but you agreed."

"Aceituna," I say, using the nickname she hates the most in the world. "This is what I've been hoping to tell you for a damn year and a half. Yeah, I took the coward's way so I wouldn't have to stand up to someone I thought I had to impress. But I never really agreed, not for a single stinking second. You're not a nerd or a dud."

She huffs. "A boring dweeb and below your league were his precise words."

It's dark enough now that the street lights flicker on. Liv is bathed by an unnatural white halo that darkens her expression, and I don't know if that's why I can't read it. It's like she's angry, or pensive, or maybe both. She's capable of multitasking that way.

Then she lifts her chin. "Prove it, then."

"Prove what?" I push my hair away from my forehead, which lasts a whole second before the rain pounds it back down.

"That I'm not a dud." The corner of her lips curls into the mischievous smile that appeared every time she pranked me.

"You're a stranger now, right? So you should be able to kiss me with no problem."

My skin prickles. Red alarms blare in my mind.

This is dangerous territory. The kind I carefully maneuvered around all through high school. I vowed to myself to never, ever play with Liv like this. She's always been so much more important than any hookup.

Yet if I back down, she's going to walk off thinking that Roberts' words were true all along. And it chafes me raw that she even heard them in the first place because she's always been outrageously hot.

So, that leaves me with no choice but to kiss her.

Unfortunately, competition is in my damn DNA, and the surest path to victory is just rising to the challenge. I eat the distance between us in one long step. Her eyes flash with surprise as I grab the back of her neck and pull her against me.

I crash my lips on hers.

Apropos, thunder crashes above us and maybe a lightning bolt strikes me too. Except the sparks concentrate right where our lips touch. Liv gasps like she feels it too, and that's when my brain packs its shit right up and jumps off its socket.

Our mouths separate for a shared breath and I walk her back until she's up against the brick wall. The rain beats against my back and then her hands grab fistfuls of the back of my T-shirt. With my free hand, I push her hips against me and now we're close enough. Before she starts thinking I'm through with her, I swoop down again, coercing her mouth open with my lips.

A groan comes from my throat and I all but collapse against the wall. She tastes like rain and like Liv—something strong but sweet just like she is, just like she tries to hide. I need another taste and my tongue strokes hers, languid, deep, savoring the wet brush of our tongues, the gentle pull of my lips around her soft ones. She must have no doubt about what we're doing here.

Friends who don't find their friends hot don't kiss them like this.

I smile against her lips, opening my eyes for a second as I switch to the other side. Her eyes remain closed like she's given herself fully to every sensation.

I kiss the corner of her lips. Scrape my teeth against her bottom one. She grabs tighter onto my shirt like her legs are giving out.

That vaguely registers in my brain. *I'm making Liv's knees weak. Me.*

Then I tilt her head back even more so I can have more access. But while I plunge deeper in her mouth, one of her legs climbs higher against mine and the friction sets me on fire like a match. I shift my hand from her hip and down her thigh, at just the same excruciatingly slow way I'm kissing her. Finding the crook behind her knee, I hitch it higher until our hips are aligned. Until not even the rain can come between us.

Liv moans. If I was getting hot before, I'm pretty sure the rain's evaporating at the contact with my skin now.

My pea brain finally activates the flight reflex. If we keep going, I'm going to embarrass myself in front of her. Or worse, take her in some alleyway where anyone could see us.

This time our mouths make a loud, wet, sucking sound as I pull away. Her eyes fly open right away and the haze clears from them shockingly quick. Liv snaps her mouth shut, and I have to use all my willpower to not lock my eyes on her bruised lips. Just in case I'm tempted to keep bruising them.

We both breathe like trucks as I carefully lower her leg and step back. And back some more. Liv's dark eyes lower down to my lips, my chest and lower, before lifting quickly with an unreadable expression.

Since I'm nowhere near as good an actor as she is, I rub my face to try to wipe whatever is on it.

Namely, that I'm toast and I know it.

"Got enough proof, then?" I ask with a raspy, garbled voice that we both know what it means. That kiss turned me on so much that I could probably replace the Olympic torch.

"Yeah, I guess so."

I splay my fingers wide to peek at her. "You *guess* so?" Is she shitting me? That kiss was freaking epic. Lightning in a bottle. Or rather, a volcano in my veins.

Liv has the nerve to shrug. "At least it helped me win the bet."

I drop my hands. "What bet?"

"Make out with a stranger or buy the week's groceries." She tilts her head, eyes hooded as she inspects me again. Her voice is thick as she says, "So, thanks… stranger."

I stand still as a statue, watching her all the way until she rounds the corner and goes back into the bar.

I wish I could reactivate my legs but they've turned into lead. My eyes fall down to my Converse, St. Cloud blue, that are now soaked through. Which is a little bit like how I feel on the inside. Like I was okay a moment ago but now a storm has barreled through me.

"What in the actual hell just happened?" I ask they alleyway in a quiet whisper.

CHAPTER 8
OLIVIA

t's Monday morning of the new semester. I'm sitting in the classroom for my first lecture, the Spanish I elective. The front seat is for whoever loves to spend the entire lecture being asked questions, and ironically so is the very back. So I sit around the middle close to one of the doors, where it takes too much effort for lecturers to turn their heads to.

Here I won't get called out for not paying attention. Resting my elbows against the table, I rub my temples to try to subdue the headache courtesy of little sleep. Another consequence of not being able to stop thinking about that kiss.

The thing is that in all the years of having an unrequited crush on my best friend—*former* best friend, dang it—I never imagined that kissing him would be so… explosive. Spectacular. Fireworks are a puny comparison.

The whole thing lasted, I don't know, maybe ten minutes, and yet my body never flared to life anywhere near as much with my ex. Not even when we were getting frisky. Something was always missing.

I always knew Brooke would have it, whatever *it* is, if only on account of my gargantuan crush on him. And even now that I'm no longer pining for him, I wasn't prepared for the wave of sensations he'd crash over me. With his mouth alone. There was very little hand action going and it was almost enough to make me see stars.

Can't imagine what it'd be like if he kissed me with actual feelings. I'd self combust.

Yet, I know that whole episode was a glitch in the matrix. Something about that night was the perfect storm, and I don't mean just because of the rain. I was riding a high on kombucha and anger at boys that made me say, *screw it.*

And he—honestly, I don't know what his deal was. I think he's just become the player he wanted to be at college, and I've become just another girl in a crowd of mostly puck bunnies vying for his attention.

I can never face him again. Even if I wanted to.

On the plus side, I won the bet. Which means every ingredient of my gluten-free lunch sandwich was sponsored by my roommates. Small consolation.

Shaking my head, I unzip my backpack, take out my laptop and a few other essentials for notes. I may have chosen this elective in the hopes that it's an easy way to fulfill my semester credits, but I'm still going to work hard. And hopefully it'll distract me from only the most amazing kiss I've ever had in my life, out of all four of the guys I've ever made out with so far.

"Stop." I hiss to myself as I boot up my laptop.

A murmur rises among the students already in the classroom. I glance around, noting that most people have their attention fixed on the back of the room rather than up front, where we expect the lecturer to appear. I turn.

"No," I whisper, my eyes widening.

One Brooklyn Tatum walks down the steps in the middle of the classroom, those deep-set, bright eyes of his on me. There are flutters in my chest and chills rush through my skin. They're both warm and cold, which I know makes no sense.

But neither does he. Neither does *this*. He's never come to any of my classes. Why now?

My confusion skyrockets as he takes the seat right beside me. I'm reminded yet again of the sheer size of him, because the space should be enough for two people to sit comfortably without touching, but he needs to spread his legs open pretty wide to even fit on the seat. Which makes his thigh push against mine.

With the discretion of a bull in a china shop, I slide my things one spot away and move over.

"What the heck are you doing here?" I ask in a low voice, checking our surroundings for eavesdroppers. And yep, there are lots of them.

Brooke turns to me with a calm expression that I know very well. The twinkle in his eyes and the slight arch of his lips tell me he's holding back laughter. "I have class."

"What do you mean you—"

Someone clears their throat. Couldn't tell who, but they save me from making a fool of myself because when I face forward, the lecturer's here. And he's giving me a look like he's been here for a while.

Sliding lower on my seat, I give the true disruptor a flaming side eye. He's the picture of a diligent student, though, taking out his laptop and intently focusing forward like he's getting paid to do it.

I harrumph softly. Not even ten seconds into starting to pay attention, I get an email notification on the screen of my laptop. I know it's from the annoying blimbo without even looking. And then he pokes my side with his finger. I swat it away and give him another patented Olivia glare. He mimics a gesture he's seen in my family plenty of times and points at my laptop with his lips. The same lips that ate mine two days ago.

I click on my mousepad much harder than I should as I pull open his damn email.

> From: btatum@stcloud.edu
>> To: orodriguez@stcloud.edu
>> Subject: Hey bestie
>> Aceituna,
>> To answer your question, I'm taking this elective too.
>> Best,
>> Your bestie

I seriously have bad taste. What possessed me to ever fall for a little pest like this?

> From: orodriguez@stcloud.edu
>> To: btatum@stcloud.edu
>> Subject: RE: Hey Bestie
>> WHY???
>> P.S. You are NOT my bestie.
>> P.P.S. Stop calling me Aceituna. I am not food.

Brooklyn takes a hot second to read my short missive and slowly turns to cock an eyebrow at me. His eyes lower to my lips, and the traitors part with a gasp. His stretch into a little smirk, and then he's typing another response.

> From: btatum@stcloud.edu
>> To: orodriguez@stcloud.edu
>> Subject: RE: RE: Hey bestie
>> Oliva,
>> Because we made a promise in freshman year and I'm a man of my word. And I think you are too, otherwise you wouldn't have signed up either.
>> P.S. We'll see about that.

> *P.P.S. Kindly disagree, you are delicious.*

Heat explodes in my skin when I read his latest response and I cast my face down. At this second, I regret chopping my hair off so short because I'm not sure it hides the full extent of the blood rushing up my neck.

He chuckles through his nose softly. I wish nothing more than to sock him a good one.

> *From: orodriguez@stcloud.edu*
> *To: btatum@stcloud.edu*
> *Subject: RE: RE: RE: Hey Bestie*
> *Body odor,*
> *I am not a <u>man</u> of my word. I am a <u>woman</u> seeking an easy class to reduce my stress levels, which you are increasing right now.*
> *Bye.*

I'm not even going to deign his postscripts with a response. They're contradictory. In the first one, he's threatening with what, becoming my bestie again? In the second one, he's outright flirting.

Except Brooklyn never flirts with me, and if he wants to start doing that now because of that kiss, I'm gonna shut that shit down ASAP. Kissing him would've been a dream years ago —and on a physical level, it still is—yet it happened not because he wanted to, but because I appealed to his competitiveness.

That's basically the same as a pity kiss, which is why I never dared to pull that move on him when we were friends. Only that this time I settled for one because a body can only hold curiosity for so long, and we're strangers now.

So he's confused, that's all. The contradicting postscripts tell me as much. And being fresh off a breakup, I'm not interested in getting my heart toyed with again. Ever.

More emails from him pop up on my laptop, but if a trait defines me it is stubbornness. Right now, I exercise it by hyper-focusing on the lecture and taking the most comprehensive notes. Someone give me the model student award, please.

This time blondie pokes my thigh right through a hole in my ripped jeans.

I sweep a glare at him. If all the people who salivate over him had any idea how freaking annoying he is, they'd stop pining for him too.

Or they'd see him like the imperfect but cute little soul that he is, living in the body of a giant—and love him even more. Like I used to. But that's beside the point.

"What?" I mouth at him without making a sound. He motions at my laptop again.

Huffing, I check my inbox. There are four new emails and I click on the last one to view the thread.

From: btatum@stcloud.edu

To: orodriguez@stcloud.edu

Subject: RE: RE: RE: RE: RE: RE: RE: Hey bestie

Or I could make you laugh. I used to be really good at it. Bet I still am. Are your sides still ticklish?

> Can I help with that? I give a mean deep tissue massage.

>> Y U stressed fren?

>>> Pardon me, I didn't intend to be casually sexist. You are indeed a woman, obvi.

This just makes me want to cry. And scream.

From: orodriguez@stcloud.edu

To: btatum@stcloud.edu

Subject: RE: RE: RE: RE: RE: RE: RE: RE: Hey bestie
If you keep distracting me I'll bill you for the class credits.
BYE!!!!

From: btatum@stcloud.edu

   To: orodriguez@stcloud.edu

   Subject: RE: RE: RE: RE: RE: RE: RE: RE: RE: Hey bestie

   Do you take PayPal? Venmo? Zelle? CashApp? Good ol' cash?

   Listen, I'm just happy you're responding. Is all.

I bite my lip hard. My vision swims and I know if I move a single inch, I'm going to start bawling in the middle of this classroom right next to the last person I want to see me having a breakdown.

My fingers fly across the keyboard at lightning speed with another response, class be damned.

From: orodriguez@stcloud.edu

   To: btatum@stcloud.edu

   Subject: RE: RE: RE: RE: RE: RE: RE: RE: RE: RE: Hey
bestie

   Why are you acting like this is some great breakthrough? You could've emailed me any time.

Now he's the one typing up with enough intensity to draw attention from other students. I pretend like I'm concentrating on the lecture, but the hammering in my eardrums doesn't let me catch a single word the lecturer says.

From: btatum@stcloud.edu

   To: orodriguez@stcloud.edu

   Subject: RE: RE: RE: RE: RE: RE: RE: RE: RE: RE: RE: Hey
bestie

   You told me to disappear from your life forever. Blocked my number. Unfollowed me on social media. The only reason you didn't block my email was because the school system won't allow it. But I got the hint and I didn't want to make you even more pissed off at me. So can we please finally drop it?

When the email finally comes, I read and re-read it several times. This time, it's as if a block of ice descends to my stomach. Cold expanding all over my body until my fingers are so stiff, I can't even type again.

And then Brooke sends another email.

From: btatum@stcloud.edu

   To: orodriguez@stcloud.edu

   Subject: RE: RE: RE: RE: RE: RE: RE: RE: RE: RE: RE: RE: Hey bestie

   And by it *I mean the fight. Not this email thread. Unless you want to move on to text (unblock me plis).*

I lift my eyes from the laptop and turn.

Brooke's sitting closer to me, half leaning on the desk and propped up by his hand. There's no trace of humor in his expression. If anything, this is his game face. The one he has when he's dead serious about destroying the opposing team's morale with his plays. His eyes bore into mine like he's trying to dig up all my secrets.

And then he delivers the killer blow by whispering a single word.

"Please."

I wouldn't consider myself weak, but the little wrinkle between his eyebrows, the downturned curve of his lips, the strand of golden hair falling on his forehead, the almost imperceptible dip of the dimple in his chin… it's lethal. And I cave.

CHAPTER 9
BROOKLYN

The buzzer goes off. The arena is bathed in St. Cloud blue lights, the crowd roars in celebration of the biggest goal in my career.

Or at least that's how it feels like in my mind as I watch Liv reach for her phone on the desk, slowly tapping and scrolling until she unblocks me. And I know it's done by how she lifts her chin at me, with the same air of challenge from Friday night.

Stubborn little Olive.

Good thing I've always been persistent and I never gave up on her. I just had a feeling that after that incident, insistence would be the same as disrespecting her boundaries. Deep down, I always knew we'd eventually get over this and pick right up where we left off, though.

Ish. I couldn't have guessed that making out with her would be the ticket.

Pulling out my phone from my pocket, I fire a text over to her.

ME

Testing testing 1 2 3 1 2 3

OLIVE EMOJI

Seriously, let's talk later

Like half of the class is over already

Good enough. I'll hold her to that promise because she's never slipping away again.

I'm going to have to beg someone for notes after class. I've been paying even less attention than her and I actually don't want to flunk, even if I took the elective entirely for Liv.

Thank goodness that I accidentally saw her schedule. I was originally planning to remove the two electives I'd signed up for —and I did. Then I signed up for this one instead. Just this session alone has made spending extra time in future coursework worth it. Especially if Liv and I study together at the library like we used to.

See? Right where we left off. I can totally pretend like I didn't basically make love to her mouth.

I cover the lower half of my face with my hand and face forward. My lips tingle at the memory. Unfortunately, the rest of my body tingles too.

You're delicious. I nearly punched myself in the nose right after sending that email.

Liv was so cool after the kiss. In fact, the rest of the night she hung out with her friends at O'Malley's without even glancing my way once.

Me? I could barely tear my eyes off her. I especially fixated on the back of her neck, where my right hand parked itself the entire time we made out. It took all my self control to not tear through the place, pull her up against me, and kiss her neck like I had any right to.

It's like I've opened Pandora's box and I'm desperately trying to jam everything back in, meanwhile pretending like I haven't just unleashed the catastrophe all on my own.

Because I've always known this isn't a game I should play

with Liv. I would one hundred percent lose. There's no way a girl who calls her guy friend Body Odor has any interest in him. And if I make that play, she'd check my heart against the boards so hard I'd never recover.

I have to make sure she knows I'm only after the title of best friend, not the other type of BF. I can't risk losing her again.

Drumming my fingers on the table, I try to focus on the lecturer for once. But from the corner of my eye I can see Liv's fingers as she types on her laptop. The same fingers that clung to my T-shirt while we made out.

Back to the front my eyes go. And then the lecturer says something in English. "The assignments will be done in groups of four people so you can practice together and give feedback to each other." I look at Liv. She pretends like I'm not even here. The lecturer continues. "Go ahead and find your partners now. Just email me with the final groups after class."

"Liv, do you want to—"

"No." She glares at me.

"Well." I glance around. "Do you know anyone else in this classroom that you'd like to group with?"

The stubborn set of her lips falters and I get momentarily distracted by them. She opens them to say something when a different voice interrupts.

"Hi. You're Brooklyn Tatum, right? Captain of the Bolts?"

I catch as Olivia mouths *captain?* before turning to the speaker. Three girls sitting in the same row as us watch me. When the hell did they sit there?

"Um, yeah?"

The one nearest to me tucks her hair behind her ear. "We just need one more person in our group. Would you like to join us?"

I feel a shift on my left and turn to find Liv standing, looking around like a meerkat trying to find other meerkats. I curl my hand around her arm and pull her down to sit flush against me. Circling my arm around her shoulders and ignoring her outrage, I turn back to the other girls and say, "Sorry, but we just need two more people. Thanks, though."

Rather than being daunted, the girl in the middle says, "Rock, paper, scissors?"

And as if this was par for the course, they do three rounds until it turns out the one in the middle loses. There's some shuffling until she, and the girl farthest from us, trade seats so she can find a different group.

"Are you sure you wanna do this, blondie? You might lose some fans this way."

Liv's husky voice so close to my ear is torture.

I turn to face her and have to use my considerable willpower to not stare at her mouth. Blinking slowly buys me some time until my brain manages to scramble words that make a coherent sentence together.

"What do you mean?"

Liv pushes against my side and since I don't budge, she ends up sliding away back to her previous seat instead. "Don't give people the wrong idea," she responds before shifting her attention to the other girls. "Hi, I'm Olivia Rodriguez and—"

"Oh my gosh, like the singer?"

"No." Liv's brow plummets and I almost laugh. The murderous look on her face keeps me serious. "Anyway, what are your names?"

"I'm Emily Garcia and this is my friend Alyssa Tuft," says the one nearest to me, while the other girl leans forward to twirl her fingers in a little greeting. "And we're such big fans. Could we have your autograph, by the way?"

I tuck my tongue against my cheek and shift to give Liv a look. She rolls her eyes and pulls up the email tab, probably to follow through on the lecturer's request. During class. How edgy of her.

"Sure," I return to the other girls.

It's always bizarre when this happens because it's not like I'm some professional superstar. I wasn't even the first round's first pick in the draft. I was second, which for casual fans—or my father—means shit. If people requesting my autograph knew half of what Liv knows about me, they'd think I'm the biggest loser in the world.

No wonder she calls me Body Odor.

"Thank you," farthest girl says. Elisa?

"Also," her friend—Amelia—adds, "I guess we should all exchange phone numbers. To plan the meetups and such."

"Right." I grab my phone and click around to punch in the first name, before giving the nearest girl my phone to add her number.

Her smile falters. "It's Emily. Not Elisa."

"Oh, sorry." I lean forward to look at the other girl. "What was yours again?"

"Erm, Alyssa."

"Emily. Alyssa—What?" I turn. Liv's expression is impassive, but I'm pretty sure I heard a muffled chuckle.

"Nothing."

Nothing my ass. She was laughing at me. It's the most glorious sound I've heard in a long time. This is why Liam Roberts used to give me so much shit about her, because I always turn into a clown in front of her to make her laugh. Or smile. Her happiness has always made me happy.

Phone numbers exchanged, correct names stored, and when the class finishes up the new girls try to strike a conversation. The problem is that Olivia is faster than a mouse, and I basically have to trip on myself to catch her before she vanishes.

I grab her by the elbow. "Hey, you said we'd talk later."

Her lips pinch in annoyance but she doesn't shrug off my

hold right away. And now that I've caught up, she slows her pace down.

"Later could mean tonight. Or tomorrow. Or in ten years."

"As if." I snort. "Especially not after you've unblocked my number."

"I can just as easily block it again." She gives me a sweet smile that lasts all of one second. "You should've stayed behind to do some more fan service instead."

"Jealous?"

Liv scoffs. "In your dreams."

Yeah. Definitely in my dreams as of this weekend.

Changing gears, I shrug on my backpack. Her eyes set on the strap by my shoulder for some reason. "So, you didn't know I'm the team captain now?"

"No, I'm not your groupie."

"But friends should know what their friends are up to."

She stops. "For the last time, we're not—"

"Nope, we're past this." I raise a hand, palm facing her. "We're back to being friends. And we're never going back to not being friends. You hear me?"

She blinks those big, brown eyes up at me. "Friendship isn't a switch you can just turn on and off."

"It was never off for me," I whisper. And that makes her look down at the floor, a casual admission that it had been off for her. I grab her arm again, making her meet my eyes. "I've missed you, Liv."

Air filters through her lips. "No. Not the puppy eyes."

"Are they working?" I smile a little.

"Kinda." She mumbles, shaking her arm free of my hand.

"So, friends again. But this time forever, am I right?" I nudge her side with my elbow and yep, she's still ticklish going by how she all but jumps away.

Liv cuts a quick side eye to me. "Yeah, friends *forever*, I guess."

CHAPTER 10
OLIVIA

Friends forever, *my ass*.

An unrequited crush on a best friend is a sweet little way to package what essentially is ulterior motives.

I had the hots for the guy who was my best friend for years. It turned me into a chicken shit who needed years to gather her nerve to confess, at the risk of losing his friendship if things got too awkward. Then it became a self-fulfilling prophecy. Last week, I gathered a lifetime's worth of nerve to challenge him to kiss me—and he did.

And all that still changed nothing. Friendzoned again.

I accept my fate now. Fully. And yes, it's taken me perhaps too many wine coolers, one of which I'm sipping right now. And maybe I've also soaked my pillow through from crying a few nights this week.

But I get it. There's no way B-heart-O is happening, ever. That dream is finito. It'll take some time for my heart to catch up to what my head now understands—especially because I have to see his pretty face all semester—but it'll get there. Even if I have to gaslight myself into not feeling like this is a second breakup in a row.

If not, I'll always have my ten thousand Instagram followers.

I sniff and suck wine through a straw at the same time, which is not the sole extent of my multitasking. I'm sitting in the living room couch, editing a video on my phone that I'll upload tomorrow. I'm doing a series where I whip up a quick and healthy recipe, including allergen modifications in the captions, to the tune of some heavy metal. It's funnier because I keep a deadpanned, almost arrogant expression on my face as I record. You'd think Beethoven is playing in the background.

My account has been active ever since I started college, but it's really taken off after chopping my hair off and playing the music I actually like. I've gained half of my followers in the past two months alone.

And one of them is Brooklyn. Now that he's unblocked from my life, he's spent the past five days liking every damn video and giving me commentary on the side. His favorite so far has been the strawberry and date smoothie, and I don't know if it's because he has a sweet tooth or because the background song is one of our faves from Memphis May Fire.

The straw makes that gurgling sound that means I've reached the end of my wine cooler, and even though it's only five thirty in the afternoon, I consider getting another one. Or maybe switching to something that won't get me plastered on an empty stomach.

I have my head buried in the fridge when my roommates arrive together.

"Um, hi, Liv. How are you feeling, sweetie?" Dee's tone is so careful, it weirds me out enough that I abandon the quest.

Closing the fridge, I mutter, "Fine? What's going on?"

She and Mina exchange a glance and Mina sighs in relief. "Okay, at least she sounds more human now."

"*What?*" I scrunch up my face.

Dee toes off her sneakers and drops her messenger bag by the door before joining me in the kitchen. She goes straight for the cereal. Dry. Like a monster. "Well, you've been kinda weird this week. Unresponsive."

"Catatonic, more like." Mina's eyes zero in on the wine cooler still clutched in my hand. "And also you single-handedly went through our entire wine stash."

"Oh." I toss the empty container in the trash and push my hair away from my face. "The start of the semester was rough. That's all."

"Wanna talk about it?" Dee asks between crunchy mouthfuls.

Maybe I should. Fessing up might relieve some of the burden. But I know I'm the one acting like a brat, so I don't know. I don't want to get set straight quite yet. I want to wallow for a bit longer. Maybe ten more years.

"Actually, I just don't want to think about it."

"Fair." She goes back to crunching.

"Hmm." Mina narrows her eyes at me, obviously dying of curiosity. But she surprises me by saying, "What you need is a change in your routine to really distract you from whatever this is that you're gonna tell us all about later."

I snort. "What do you have in mind?"

She folds her arms. "Get dressed to find out."

"I am dressed." I motion at my sweats.

"In something that is more chic than hobo, please."

I turn to Dee. "Do you know what she's planning?"

"No, but whatever it is, I'm in."

I frown. "I'm not sure I like this."

"Just trust me."

Those are famous last words for a reason. And an hour later—because that's how long it takes for Mina to approve of my outfit—I try to cling to the car door while Mina uses her entire weight to pull me toward the St. Cloud hockey arena.

"Nope! Not gonna happen."

"It'll be fun, I promise."

"I hate hockey and you all know it."

"And yet you know almost more about it than Dee."

The alluded stands placidly off the side and says, "Well, she's the sister of two hockey legends, so…"

"Mina, I don't—oof."

My words are drowned by the blow. I land partially on her, one of her knees digging into my butt cheek, my elbow knocking the wind out of her.

This is my chance to escape her evil crutches. I roll to the side and push up on all fours. But I'm not even able to get on my feet before Dee stands in front of me, crouched down ready to check me against the car. She plays defense and is clearly on Mina's side, so she definitely would.

Slowly, I stand up and raise my hands. As if they were marching me into prison and not to the hockey arena, Dee grabs me by one arm and Mina by the other. If Dee isn't playing, it obviously means that tonight is some Bolts game. We're two weeks from the opening of the season, which must mean this is a pre-season game.

We walk into the premises and the smell of popcorn assaults my senses, making my stomach grumble like a lion. I mutter, "If you're gonna kidnap me, at least have the decency to feed me."

"Fine." Mina shrugs. "Dee, convey our guest of honor to our seats while I get us some snacks."

"Yes, ma'am." Dee promptly obeys by pushing me toward one of the doors down to the stands.

And down we awkwardly shuffle through the steps. And down some more. The ice is getting dangerously close. "Hmm, don't tell me we have front row seats."

"Sure do!" Dee beams up at me from a rung below. "It took pulling some strings, but we got them."

I make another attempt to escape, but there's no way I could possibly out-maneuver an elite hockey athlete. She may look cute and sweet on the outside, but Dee's made of solid muscle. Like someone else I know. Someone I'm dreading to see.

Yet, the second my behind is parked on what apparently is my seat, my eyes immediately dart around looking for blue jerseys with grey and white details. But the ice is devoid of any players yet.

Funny how relief and disappointment can mix so well in someone's gut, huh?

This is why I don't like hockey. It can bring you up and down faster than a rollercoaster. Like when you're six years old, watching your older sister skate up the ice like she's a super-hero, and then she gets checked so hard that her spine breaks and she doesn't get up. Or like when your older brother and your best friend are still obsessed with the game after that, even though they saw the accident too. Like that.

My knee starts bouncing. Every time I watch a game, I spend the whole time praying that no one gets hurt too badly, which sucks any fun out of it. For the year and change when I shut Brooke out of my life, I still checked the news after games to make sure he was fine. I do the same for my brother and my brother-in-law in the pros. Thankfully I don't have to keep tabs on Luz anymore now that she's officially retired from playing. But somehow I can't escape this damn game.

"Okay, I got salted popcorn for the hostage, salted caramel for the athlete, and buttered for me. And my purse is full of soda and water bottles. Grab what you want," Mina announces as the shuffling of the line begins and I end up sandwiched between them. Mina sits on my left and starts passing goodies along.

Corn is thankfully a safe food for me, and my roommates know very well that I can't do dairy. Even if tonight sucks, I at least get a free popcorn and Coke out of it.

"Okay, can someone please tell me what we're doing here now?"

Dee motions at Mina. "Please, do the honors."

"Very well." My other roommate turns her hair behind her ears, dyed platinum blonde and styled in waves. "Back at the party that eventually led to the breakup, Dee and I noticed how Brooklyn Tatum stood up for you."

It takes me a moment to realize she's talking about the breakup with my ex *boyfriend*, not the one with my ex *best friend*.

Mina continues, "You never told us why and well, we know how hard all of this has been for you, so we didn't want to press. Until now."

I clutch at my popcorn tighter. My heart rate goes from normal to full steam. "Why now?"

"Here's where Dee comes in."

We turn to her. "Jenny, who is Maggie's roommate, said she saw you and Brooklyn all chummy chummy in class. And Maggie told me at practice two days ago."

"Who the heck is Maggie?" I ask, doing my best to not screech with the horror I feel on the inside.

Dee gives me a look. "Um, our goalie."

"Don't give me that look, I'm not your groupie."

"The point is," Mina says, drawing my attention back to her. "It looks like you have found the perfect target for your rebound. And since he's the new captain of the Thunder Bolts, what better chance to get his attention than cheering for him tonight?"

I stare at the board across from me for a moment, without really registering anything.

Closing my eyes, I mumble, "I know you guys are trying to help, but this is entirely the opposite of that."

"What do you mean?"

The floodgates open—and by that, I mean players from both teams emerge onto the ice. I raise my popcorn bucket to hide behind it, but it's not like I'm the only person sitting in the stands. The arena has been filling up with people steadily, and I'd say at least seventy percent of them are girls. No way Brooke will spot me. I should be safe.

"It's not like that between Brooke and I," I say, ignoring how Mina repeats *Brooke* in a little squeal. Squirming, I decide the time to fess up is now. "Remember the guy I told you about in freshman year?"

Dee's brow furrows. "The childhood best friend you were going to confess to, who turned out to be a total jerkface?"

"Yep." I suck in a deep breath. "That guy's Brooklyn Tatum."

Mina mutters. "Oh, shit."

We sit in silence for a good moment, even as the audience cheers at the Bolts circling the ice and warming up. I grab a handful of popcorn and eat it like a squirrel, trying to store my weight's worth of food in my cheeks.

And of course, that's when a Bolts player abruptly brakes right in front of us, raining sludge against the glass boards.

Slowly the sludge slides down and my eyes fall on the C stitched on the chest of his jersey. I lift my eyes up.

Brooke rests an arm against the glass to lean forward. He's wearing that grin I've always found annoying, and even more now that I know what his lips feel like against mine.

And his eyes twinkle like damn fairy lights.

"Well, well, well," Brooke says, loud enough that we can hear him through the glass and over the noise. "If it isn't my best friend. Did you come to watch me?"

I recover enough to spit out, "*Former* best friend. And no, I was dragged under duress."

"Sure." The word drips with sarcasm and his smirk deepens. "But it's okay, I'll make it worth your while." He winks before skating away.

Winks.

At. Me.

Pretty sure my friends know they could fry an egg on my face right now.

"I feel like I'm missing more details," Mina says on the verge of laughter.

Sliding lower onto my seat, I launch on the epic tale of my old unrequited crush.

CHAPTER 11
BROOKLYN

'm the busiest player on the ice. A lot of people think my
job as a defenseman is to block the opposing players from
executing their plays, and dassit. But that would be if I was
a run of the mill defenseman.

On top of that, I'm in charge of protecting my forwards so
they can carry the puck to the opposite net. And also of insti-
gating key opposing players—especially the short fused ones—
so they focus on me and not my forwards, which means
drawing penalties.

And when we get them? I'm on the special team to kill
them too. Not to mention, I'm the last line of defense before
our goalie. Who by the way, I have to protect with my life if
that's what it takes, plus do whatever I can so he can keep a
shutout for the team stats. And if there's a slight chance? I'm
going to slap the puck so hard that I blow a sixth hole through
the opposing goalie and bag us a goal.

It's why I average over thirty minutes of play every game,
while some of the other guys hit half of that. It's also why I
have so many chances to show off.

The first one comes in the first period. A Brighton guy

breaks away, salivating at the chance of a goal. But I've mastered the art of positioning myself, and even though I have a late start, I dive right when he swings hard and tap the puck with the tip of my stick. It veers off into the air and Schwarz, our goalie, makes an easy save.

"Show off," he tells me while the play's stopped.

We both know that play could've gone wildly different and end up in a Brighton goal anyway, but it didn't. "You're welcome."

Chewing on my mouthguard, I slightly turn to the seats across center ice and spot Liv right away. She's talking with her friends, more animated than I've ever seen her. Hand gestures, shifting from one side to the other.

And totally ignoring the game.

I narrow my eyes. Challenge accepted, Olivia Rodriguez. I'll make you watch me.

By the second period, no one's on the board yet. I figure I can instigate some shit and the chance couldn't be more perfect. I spot Brighton's top defender tailing one of my first line forwards as he carries the puck from the sides. I take off like a freight train and crash into the Brighton guy just like one, all legal like, but he still goes down like a boulder.

I lift my head up and make eye contact with Liv right through the glass. There's a cringe on her face, like she knows just how much the other guy must be hurting. But the play's still going. Fallen guy tries to hook me with his stick and gets a penalty.

He glares at me as he gets sent to the sin bin, and I stick my tongue out and wave my gloved hand like a damn brat. Gets them every time.

"Wow, I'm really glad you're on our side." Bloom chuckles as we skate off to the bench for the PP. "You are absolutely insufferable."

"Talk dirty to me," I say with a fake roar.

"Let's order pizza from Romano's for the after game party."

We climb over the board and plop our asses on the bench. I say, "Are you asking me out, Bloom? I'm single right now and I may get ideas."

He shakes his head. "Sorry, Blondie. You're not my type."

"Well, neither are you. My type is…" I trail off, my eyes sliding across center ice again.

Liv's watching me now.

I tilt my head.

She's not my type. I gravitate to sporty girls. In fact, Liv knows my first ever crush was her sister—no doubt one of the items in the long list of embarrassing reasons why Liv thinks I'm the cringiest.

Anyway, my girlfriends in high school were two cheer-leaders—separate occasions, of course, I'm not a douchebag —and a tennis player. I briefly dated a figure skater at the start of freshman year. I haven't dated anyone steady since, but most of my hookups have been jocks of some sort. They understand the lifestyle. They know the game goes first. School second. Them third, maybe tied with friends or even in fourth place.

Liv is the kind of girl who should be in first place. I know that—I've always known that. This is what has never made her my type. So why am I looking at her right now?

She's not my type, I repeat to myself.

My brow furrows as I focus on the ref dropping the puck for the faceoff. Brighton is a good team, a Frozen Four contender. I don't know if it's because they're severely underes-timating us after years of us sucking sweaty armpit, but plays are developing as if this was a choreographed practice drill. I squirt water on my face as the PP special team scores our first goal of the night.

Liv doesn't jump to her feet like the rest of the arena, if

anything she looks bored. My lips twitch. I've missed seeing that.

She used to come to every one of my games even though she abhorred every second. She was the only familiar face in the crowd for me. Is tonight an outlier, or is she going to become my person again?

I should ask her. I'll find her after the game. But first, we have to win it. The least I could do to acknowledge her efforts is to not lose like a clown.

When the lines change again, I hit the ice like a boulder. The Brighton guy who fouled me is out now, and he immediately gets in my grill. "Hey, asshole. You think you're so tough?" He pushes my chest hard.

I tuck my tongue against my cheek but can't keep the grin off my face. "If I wasn't, what would that make you? The worst defender in the conference, I guess."

I dodge the swipe, laughing my head off when it gets him a misconduct because the refs aren't messing around tonight. I skate across the Brighton bench, biting my tongue in an *oopsie* expression that gets them all shouting lovely epithets at me. Boo freaking hoo.

Right before play resumes, I catch Liv shaking her head at me. It's like she might've forgotten my style. A lot of defenders use their physicality to intimidate their opponents. I could, too, yet I just amplify my blimbo personality until I become truly insufferable. That, paired with my top notch stamina and conditioning, is what makes me an effective D-man.

Aka I'm a pest who doesn't quit. Which is also the approach I'm going to use with Liv now that she's let me back in her life.

The game ends with the Thunder Bolts winning by shutout, the most satisfying game of my life so far. I follow my teammates through the tunnel and pick up a pair of skate guards, my ears roaring with their chatter but even more with the rapid drum of my heart. Without telling anyone, I split right where I should've gone left for the locker room. I pause to shoe on the guards before leaving the players area.

"Brooklyn!" Some girl exclaims. "That was such a great game. Would you—"

"Yes, thank you." I glance over her head, scanning the faces until I spot the one I want. The girl keeps talking and I give some non committal sound as I side step her. It takes several *sorry* and *excuse me* to wade through the throngs. Fortunately, it raises enough attention that Liv notices me quickly.

And she tries to run.

I shout, "Aceituna." It stops her dead in her tracks, if only so she can glare over her shoulder. My lips twitch. "Stay still, woman."

She turns her face to one of her friends who's saying something as I approach. When I finally reach her, the full force of her brown eyes is on me.

Damn, she could be a hockey player with that glare.

I prop my hands on the butt end of the stick. "So, what'd you think?"

"Barbaric, as usual." She folds her arms, face pinching in even more annoyance.

"I know you liked it," I say, nodding, which makes sweat drip down my nose. "You were proud of me for drawing a penalty without fighting."

"I—what?"

"It was all over your face."

"You were watching Liv's face during the game?" one of her friend's asks. She's one of the girls who was with Liv on the night I caught Trent cheating.

I startle. "Oh, hey. I'm Brooklyn. Who are you?"

"Mina Lee." She presses her lips tight as if trying not to smile. "Not to be confused by chopped liver."

I blink slowly.

"Good game out there, Tatum." I turn to the other voice and find Dee Meyer standing next to Liv. Her I recognize because she's a Strike.

"Huh. What's up with the sudden sportsmanship?" I ask her.

Meyer waves a hand. "Credit where it's due. If y'all keep playing like tonight, you'll crush the season."

Oh, this is an opening.

"It depends." I slowly face Liv again. "Will you come watch my games again?"

"How does that even relate?"

I grin. "I play better when you're rooting for me."

Her long eyelashes swoop up and down with rapid blinks. "Um. You'll have to pay me, Brooke."

A rush travels up my spine. Brooke. Not Brooklyn. This is an improvement.

"Name your currency." One of the other girls clears her throat and once again I'm reminded that we're not alone. Time to shift gears. "Anyway, are you all coming to the after game party?"

"No—" Liv starts to say and is cut off by the non Strike.

"Yes! Where?"

"Bolt House," I respond.

"No." Liv frowns. "Definitely not. That place is the source of all my traumas. What if something terrible happens again tonight?"

"Or…" I drag the word in a way I know irritates her. Sure enough, her expression darkens even more. "You could go, have a good time with your friends—" Here I motion at the other girls and myself. "And conquer your fears like the badass we all know you are."

The non Strike nods sagely. "Your former best friend has a good point." She gives me a sly look. "I'm her bestie now, bud. Sorry."

Meyer rolls her eyes. "No, *I* am Liv's best friend."

I smile. "I'm extremely competitive, in case you didn't notice."

Liv rubs the bridge of her nose. "Can't I just go home and wallow in my misery?"

Misery? Is she still pining after her asshole ex?

I grit my teeth. Rather than showing how annoyed that makes me, I hook my arm around Liv's neck and pull her to me. She knows what's coming.

In a lethal voice, she says, "Don't you freaking dare, Body Odor."

I sure must be reeking right now, which will make this more effective. Dropping my free glove on the floor, I dig my fingers in her hair and mess it up, making sure she's trapped between my arm and my side. The angry squeaks make me laugh. My veins thrum back to life, as if I was starting a new game shift.

"Say you'll come and I'll stop."

"No! Stop!"

Her hair is so soft I may not stop anyway.

"I'll tickle you next."

"Fine, we're coming." Her voice comes out distorted and I finally let her go. Liv takes large gulps of air, her face as red as a tomato. "Oh. My. Word. You stink so freaking bad, I almost died." And for effect, she dry heaves.

Same as usual.

I bend down to pick up my glove. "See you there." I glance at the other girls. "You too, of course." And with that, I basically skip back to the locker, where Coach Green will blow my eardrums up for disappearing for a few minutes.

CHAPTER 12
OLIVIA

"He's definitely into you."

I give Mina a look. "Wow, so this is what two butt cheeks flapping to produce words sounds like."

Her lips twitch but she manages to keep herself serious. "Listen to me, you stubborn human being. He basically didn't even acknowledge our existence throughout that whole interaction."

"Yep, we were definitely chopped liver." Dee waggles her eyebrows.

Sighing, I nurse the half empty Solo cup in my hands. We found ourselves a corner of the Bolt House living room, just off the side of the fireplace. We have to basically scream at each other over the myriad of voices and loud rap bass already blaring in the house—and this is before the team even arrives. I imagine it'll get much rowdier after.

"It's not like that. Brooke is a one-track mind kind of guy. He had a mission, which was to make me come to this horrible place, and he wasn't going to entertain distractions until he succeeded."

"He touched your hair," Mina says, patting her own head.

I cringe. "To give me a stinky headlock."

"No, it was to touch your hair. Guys who are into girls do whatever it takes to touch their hair—and other places, obviously," she says, as if flexing her psych major muscles.

Except she's dead wrong. "No, he's always given me headlocks like I'm his younger sister. Even though I'm older." By two months, but it mattered a lot when we were kids.

"His eyes were on you like ninety five percent of the time," Dee says. The traitor. "That's another sign. It's like body language one-oh-one."

Mina leans forward and puts her hand on my shoulder. "He ditched the after-game team huddle and made his way through the crowd to find you. That boy is whipped."

I throw one hand in the air. "You guys don't get it because you don't know him. He's *always* like that. He's like a freaking puppy with a bone. This is nothing compared to how he is with his girlfriends. He treats them like princesses, not like sisters. There is no one more disgustingly sappy than him."

"Fine, ignore all these facts that your real best friends are laying on you." Mina waves her hands in the air, as if wiping the slate clean. "The actual point here is, what are you going to do from now on?"

"What do you mean?"

"You had a massive crush on him, it went badly, you've reconnected. Now what?" She blinks up at me. "Friends forever or friends to lovers?"

I throw my head back and beg the heavens—through a ceiling spotted with gross stains—to grant me patience. "I already told you that he's the one who cooked that *friends forever* special. There's nothing else on the table."

Mina gets in my grill. "But is that what you want?"

I blink down at her. Even though she's almost a head shorter than me, she's scaring me. Her eyes look feral. Like she wants to maim me right now.

"What I want," I say slowly and her eyes widen in anticipation. "Is peace. Which is the opposite of drama. Which is exactly what would happen if I develop another hidden agenda."

She whines. "Having a crush on a friend isn't the federal crime you're painting it to be."

"Actually," Dee cuts in. "I agree with Olivia."

"See?"

Mina whirls around to her. "The hell do you mean?"

"He already made his intentions clear when he said friends forever." Dee tosses her microbraids over her shoulder and shrugs. "And I get it. He's definitely sending mixed signals. But maybe he just doesn't know what *he* wants right now, and the worst thing Liv can do is to get herself hung up on him if he's going to be all wishy-washy, especially after the whole debacle with Trench Coat."

We've decided avoiding his name is too hard, and I came up with this silly nickname that isn't the kind of insult I'd have to go to confession for, but still makes it very clear that we don't appreciate him. In the least.

"Thank you." I motion at Dee with one hand. "You're officially bestowed with the title of Olivia's best friend."

Mina gasps. "Outrageous!"

I bite my lip, debating whether to share what's really circling in my head right now. But these are my friends. They're not people who would dismiss what I think or make fun of me for it. Maybe they'll even help me make sense of myself.

"What if…" I trail off, looking down at the beer growing flat in my cup. "What if I can't help myself and I catch feelings again?"

"Again, she says." Mina snorts and elbows Dee next to her. "As if her feelings had gone away at all."

I glare.

Dee shrugs. "No think. Only do you."

"Do *him*." Mina drags the word until some other girls nearby glance our way.

"Stop! Oh my word." I cover my face with my free hand.

Something like a yell sounds from the outside and then the front door opens, followed by a squeal.

The St. Cloud Thunder Bolts must be making their appearance, huh.

Sure enough, one guy in a navy suit struts in. What appears to be a random girl from the crowd launches herself at him and next thing, they're sucking faces right in front of everyone.

Is this going to be what happens every time one of them walks in? And when Brooklyn comes in too?

I watch with the same kind of curiosity as someone about to witness a car crash as the next guy makes it to the threshold. Two girls pull him by the arms, although no PDA yet. Maybe the first guy was an exception. The third guy instead high-fives some of the other people, and the fourth heads straight to the kitchen without bothering to be social.

I sit back against the windowsill, so relived that I don't even care if Mina can read me like a book.

See? This is the problem. I become this unhinged, jealous, insecure person when Brooklyn is concerned. Deep down, no matter how much it hurts, I know he has the right of it by sticking to just being friends. If we were more it would be too… too all consuming, never ending, too *everything*. It's scary.

That's when *he* walks in, wearing a deep emerald suit that probably costs as much as this house. His blond hair is longish at the top, and he's combed it aside in a way that makes the natural wave look intentional. If some guys are a snack, Brooklyn Tatum is a whole damn four-course Michelin-starred meal, including dessert. I couldn't look away even if someone paid me a billion bucks.

How did I even manage to keep my cool all those years back?

Brooke's talking with one of his teammates when, suddenly, he swings around and locks eyes with me. I startle. Sheer willpower alone keeps me from hiding.

Slowly, his lips curve in a lopsided smile. I read them say, *"You came."*

No, I didn't. The ghost of me did for I am dead now.

Mina singsongs. "Chopped liver."

I fix my attention on her. "If you ever accidentally or on purpose say anything that gives away my feelings for him to anybody outside of this triangle of trust, I will turn you into chopped Mina."

"Bit morbid but you can count on my discretion." Then why is she smirking? "So, you admit you have feelings."

"Ugh. I think I prefer you when you're chasing after boys. Go find someone to spend all that energy with."

She picks up her Solo cup from the fireplace mantle. "Fine. Then let's go play beer pong with some jocks to see if I can play with any of their pongs later."

I burst into laughter and meanwhile our other roomie cringes. "Yuck, I never wanted to think about Bolts' pongs." Dee sticks her tongue out. It's funny that she acts like Bolts are gross, when I know for a fact that she's had some intra-team fun in the past.

But anyway, as I follow them to the center of the living room, I take a discrete look around and I don't spot Brooklyn anymore. Did he already find someone to bring to his room or something?

I shake my head hard. It's none of my business. He can do whatever and whoever he wants.

Unlike Dee, Mina and I are as uncoordinated as newborn foals. Unlike Mina, though, I don't enjoy any kind of physical activity outside of reading on my couch or lightly head banging to a jam. So when we try to be fair and I end up pairing with Dee, while Mina ends up with a random girl on the other team, all I do is drag Dee down. It works out great, because gradually I stop even trying. Dee's competitive spirit alone carries the team.

Some movement catches my attention from through the crowd around us. Brooke's heading down the stairs, now wearing one of those graphic T-shirts that would look awful on anyone else, and a pair of ripped jeans that show a hint of powerful hockey thighs. He's not even on solid ground when a super hot girl in tiny shorts and a crop top intercepts him.

I swallow hard and try to focus on the game. Okay, so he went upstairs not for a hookup but for a change of clothes. Turns out the hookup found him, though.

How do I make myself not care? Did it really take finding a boyfriend—any boyfriend, as it was—to fool myself into thinking I was over him?

And yet, I take a look around and spot a few good looking guys I'd have tried to make out with a week ago. But even that plan has been foiled after knowing what being properly, thoroughly kissed is like. And by *him*, no less.

The girls are so into the game, I don't have the heart to pull them away from their fun. Slipping into the crowd, I slowly make my way through the living room in search of a bathroom I can have a lil cry in. Hopefully that's all I need to remind me that going down the path of crushing on Brooke leads nowhere good.

CHAPTER 13
BROOKLYN

"____ith me?"

"Hmm?" My brain scrambles the speech this girl's giving me, which is rude, though probably not as much as if I vaulted over the stairs to really bypass her.

"I said," her annoyance penetrates through my thick skull and I finally look at her. Her mouth is downturned into a pout, one hand delicately resting over her chest. Her well-displayed chest. "Do you want to go somewhere more quiet with me?"

My eyes trail over her head, over the multitude of people talking, dancing, drinking, or playing games in the living room —and they land right on my best friend. She's watching a beer pong game from the edge of the crowd circling the dining table. Maybe she's warm, because she pushes the sleeves of her hoodie up her arms. Now she's laughing at something one of the competitors says, and I don't know why but my gut twists. I haven't heard her laughter in so long—don't even know if I could get a chuckle out of her now.

"Well?"

"Sorry," I say on autopilot. "I'm looking for someone."

"A girl?" the stairs troll asks.

I tuck my tongue against my cheek and nod. "Yeah, a girl."

"Well, I'm a girl too." She licks her lips in a way I'm supposed to react to, and she even goes as far as running her hand down my stomach.

I pluck it well before she reaches the waistband of my jeans and offer a tight smile. "A specific girl, that is. Can I please get going?" Huffing, she finally lets me through, not without muttering some colorful language. Funny that it comes from someone who a moment ago wanted to undress me.

Right before I reach the landing, though, I take another peek at the beer pong game and—

Where's Liv?

I focus harder on the players. Maybe she's joined the game. But there are only the two Strikes and the other girl Liv was with earlier, and Liv is still MIA. I crane my neck this way and that, pop into the kitchen and nada.

Did she go off on her own? Or did she go off with someone? Is it someone she can trust? What if she gets in trouble? We try to run a pretty tight ship in this house but the guests can sometimes be an issue.

And then I hear a very sharp, "Excuse me." I whirl around and find some people parting down the hallway with grunts and curses. But that was her voice.

They move out of my way more easily. And there she is, by herself, trying to open the first door on the right.

"What are you doing?"

Liv jumps in her skin. "Brooke? What are you doing here?"

"This is where I live." I stuff my hands in the pockets of my jeans.

"I mean, here *here*. Weren't you flirting with some girl earlier?"

My eyebrows rise.

So she noticed that?

Her expression is starting to darken so I don't dare to tease her. Instead, I say, "I just wanted to make sure you're okay. You shouldn't ditch your friends when it's this crowded."

"I just need to use the bathroom." She blows a raspberry that lifts a strand of her hair, only for it to fall back on her face.

My fingers tingle, and I know that the only way to cure the itch is to tuck her hair back. Or to comb it, the pads of my fingers softly caressing her scalp.

What the—where did that come from?

I clear my throat. "Well, that's not a bathroom. That's—"

Abruptly, the door opens and someone stumbles out, crashing into Liv from behind. I react in time to catch her before she face-plants on the floor. Instead, she smacks hard against my chest.

"Ow!"

I wince. "You okay?" But then the drunkards get their own feet tangled and almost take us out.

"Sorry, captain." One of the freshmen in the team grins at me, an equally tipsy girl behind him. Her makeup is all smudged and her skirt is on backwards. And he's missing a shirt altogether.

"You better behave, Michaels," I warn with a frown. Dude salutes and turns around, giggling girl in tow grabbing *his* ass. Strong hint that whatever that was, at least was consensual.

I remember the girl in my arms and glance down. Liv rubs her nose with her hand, face scrunched up in pain. All I can do is bite my lips when she pins me with the full force of her glare.

"Is your freaking chest made of steel?"

"Titanium," I chime, sounding serious. "And as you can see, that wasn't a bathroom."

Liv harrumphs and she puts her hands on me, one against my chest, the other against my stomach. I freeze, muscles contracting at the shockwave the touch sends. Sensation travels all the way down to my toes and I have to steel myself against a shiver.

But then Liv pushes me away, and I have no choice but to let my arms fall.

"So anyway, where's the bathroom?" she asks with impatience.

I comb my hair away from my forehead, biting my lip so I don't whine like a wounded animal. That's how I feel now with the distance between us.

"You don't want to use the ones downstairs, trust me." I lean forward and grab her hand. "Let's go upstairs."

"Fine." She sighs like it's no big deal that this is the most contact we've had since we made out in an alley a week ago.

I shift my hand to lace our fingers together, holding tight as I navigate us back upstairs. There's a couple about to round at least base two at the top of the stairs, and a wild mental picture forms in my mind. It's of Liv and I just like that, her legs around my waist as I prop her up against a wall and devour her mouth.

Shit. I'm messed up. We're supposed to just be friends— barely. I haven't even earned her trust back. I shouldn't be thinking about things like that.

"Where are we going?" Liv asks while we climb up the second set of stairs, this one tucked against the east end of the second floor.

"My room." My voice comes out weirdly deep and raspy, and I keep talking so I can pretend I didn't get turned on all on my own. "Now that I've been made captain of the team, I've moved up to the third floor that is normally for seniors."

Our steps echo through the quiet. We keep partygoers off this floor, unless one of its residents intentionally brings company upstairs.

Uh, I guess like Liv and I now.

"Congrats, by the way. I know how important all that is to you," she murmurs.

I pause at the top of the stairs to glance back at her. Liv meets my eyes slowly. A tightness in my shoulders ebbs away, one I hadn't even noticed until now. It's like I'd been waiting for this moment and it dawns on me how much I wanted someone I care about to confirm if this was an accomplishment at all.

Swallowing hard, I face forward again and resume the walk. "Thanks, Liv."

Some voices echo around the hallway as we make it upstairs. We pass by a door that barely muffles some pretty clear sounds as to what's happening behind it. Behind me, Liv expels the kind of breath that makes her sound exhausted.

We reach the end of the hallway and I dig my keys out of my pocket to unlock my room. I open the door with my free hand and mumble, "I cleaned my bathroom this morning. Holler if you need anything."

Liv uncurls her fingers and slides her hand from mine, not looking up as she steps into my bedroom. "Thanks."

"No worries. I'll wait out here, okay?"

She glances over her shoulder. "Uh, sure." Then she closes the door with a soft click.

I turn to rest my back against the door, twirling my keys around my finger. Liv is in my bathroom. Why does this feel so weird? We used to visit each other's houses all the time in high school, would do our homework side by side on my bed, or she'd sit on her bedroom windowsill while I sat on the floor below her. It was no big deal.

This feels like a big deal.

Did we really turn into strangers? Is that why? Because this is like getting to know each other again, getting familiar with our spaces again.

No. It's because for a second I had the wild notion we

should be doing something else in my bedroom. Or in the bathroom. Wherever she wants.

"She doesn't, asshole," I mutter to myself, running a hand down my face.

My pants vibrate, but it's not because of the blood rushing down my body. I take my cellphone out of my pocket and the name that pops up on the screen is more effective than an ice bath.

MALE PROGENITOR

Why didn't you show up for Lee's birthday party today?

I stare at the text from my dad, my eyebrows scrunching up with the effort it takes me to decipher it. But it's not some secret intelligence code. I swipe open the text app to look at the thread between us, in case I missed the invite. But the last text was from me saying I'd just made team captain, and I'm pretty sure he hadn't read it until now.

Just in case, I also check my emails, and there's nothing there either.

ME

I didn't know about it

Isn't his birthday tomorrow?

My texts show as read immediately. I wait for the three dots but they don't appear. Clicking out of the app, I stuff my phone back in my pocket right as a bedroom door opens down the hall.

I narrow my eyes like I need that to sharpen my already perfect vision. But they're not deceiving me: that is indeed Trent McFadden walking out of a room with a girl. And like what they were doing is not obvious enough, he stumbles while trying to walk and zip up his pants at the same time.

Something like a hot hand grabs me by the throat, or it could just be from how hard it feels to hold back from cussing the shit out of him. I lock my muscles tight so I don't rush down the hallway and pound him to the floor. He should be feeling absolutely wrecked after losing someone as amazing as Liv.

And then one neuron in my pea brain produces a spark of important thought.

Liv can't see this—see *him*.

Before her shitface ex spots me, I slip into my bedroom and lock the door. The water stops running in the bathroom and a moment later, the door opens.

CHAPTER 14
OLIVIA

'm in Brooklyn's bathroom.

It's funny, because he still buys the same brand of soap. Pretty sure it was the housekeeper who used to buy it back when he was a kid, but he must still like this brand now that he has a choice to buy whatever he wants for himself. It makes me feel like maybe some parts of him are still the same.

But there's been changes. For example, when I came in, the toilet paper roll was almost out. I had to—out of necessity, not out of stalking—look into his cabinets until I found a stack of rolls on a shelf right below a giant box of condoms, like a regular size one wasn't enough. Brooke's never had a shortage of girlfriends and hookups ever since he bloomed in high school, but he used to be shier about it.

Leaning down, I splash water on my face for as long as it takes to cool it. I turn off the faucet and grab a handful of his towel to dry my face.

His towel. That maybe he dries himself with.

I drop it like it's on fire but I'm the one who's burning up.

"*Friends forever*, he said," I mutter to myself through gritted teeth. "Which is the entire opposite of what you're thinking about, you freaking perv."

Taking a deep breath, with water dripping down my chin and on the skin of my chest, I open the bathroom door and step back into his room. I calculate I have maybe five seconds to scan it before leaving—

Zero seconds. Because Brooke's in his room, his back against the closed door. He lifts his eyes from his phone screen for a second and does a double take. For a long moment there's only silence.

"Uh, need a towel? I thought I had one—"

"Yeah, you do. I just… didn't know if…"

"Oh." He snorts. "Yeah, it's fresh. You can use it without catching any cooties."

"Right." I swivel around and march into the bathroom to pat my face dry with a corner of the towel. On my way out, I stick my tongue out to my own reflection because she's an embarrassment. "Thanks," I murmur in sarcasm.

Brooke sticks his hand up when I'm back out. "Actually, let's not go outside yet."

My lips form several silent words but the one that eventually comes out is, "Why?" At the same time, I pray that I'm not blushing too hard. His room's only illuminated by the streetlights streaming in through his window, and from the screen of his cellphone. Hopefully this means he can't see how red my face probably is.

"There's, um, some people behaving indecently outside. I don't think you want to see that."

I wrinkle my nose. If it's anything like what I've seen in past occasions at this house, then I definitely don't.

"Okay. Can we at least turn on the lights?"

"Sure." He twists around and flips a switch.

Soft yellow light bathes the room. It's one third of his home bedroom size, but nicer somehow. Back at his father's place, everything was stark white, stainless steel, black tinted wood—orderly and clean to the point of obsession.

Here, everything is navy blue and white, and messier in a way that shows it's lived in. His desk has one pile of school textbooks and material, and one pile of hockey magazines. I pick up the first one, a *SPORTY* issue, and he's on the cover wearing the jersey from the pro team that drafted him two years ago.

I cock an eyebrow at him. "Bit narcissistic."

Brooklyn folds his arms and they momentarily distract me. Forearms flexing, with thick ropes of veins traveling under smooth skin and tattoo lines, and a dusting of blond hairs. They should be illegal because they're an attack on public moral.

"Okay, sue me. I was proud of myself for getting that cover."

I check the magazine's issue date. It's from a year ago when I was in the thick of my anger, unable to even stomach the thought of him. Of course I missed all the important moments he had throughout that time.

Now that I realize that, my eyes prick and I try to keep them from spilling by rifling through the stack of magazines. But there's only one thing that can relieve the stab of pain in my chest, and that is apologizing.

"I'm sorry, Brookie." My voice is soft. Biting my lip, I brace myself to meet his eyes and add, "For being such a bad friend."

And I mean this, in more ways than one. It's not just that I wasn't there for him, but the *why* of it too.

He blinks hard, forehead scrunching as more seconds tick. "What do you even—" His phone pings and he checks it by reflex. Grunting, he says, "One second."

"Okay." I stack all the magazines again, making sure they're perfectly aligned while he furiously types on his phone.

"Sorry about that." Brooke slips the phone back in his

pocket and lifts a hand to run his fingers through his hair. "Anyway, back to the topic. What in the hell are you talking about?"

I poke at the magazine at the top. "I missed this. I've missed all your accomplishments in the past year and a half because I was too selfish."

"You weren't." Brooke looks down, shuffling one foot against the blue carpet. "You were angry, and you had a right to be. I'm the one who… Basically, I drove you away." His voice trails off into a whisper.

Oh, he has no idea, huh?

"No." I take a step closer but pause. What am I going to accomplish by touching him? Instead, I dig my hands into the sleeves of my hoodie. "I was unreasonable. I—I'm the one who abandoned you. You shouldn't even want to be my friend anymore."

I press my lips tighter, but that doesn't keep a tear from falling. I divert my eyes because I'm not trying to manipulate him or anything, and I really wish I wasn't crying in the first place.

Sighing, he takes a step forward. But instead of hugging me like I figured, he reaches down at my waist level. It takes some seconds for my mind to process that he's grabbing the two ends of my crop hoodie, his enormous fingers delicately fitting the tabs so he can zip it up. And up. All the way to my neck. Like maybe he had enough of looking at my black sports bra.

I will my face not to heat up but I don't think it's working.

Meanwhile, Brooke's expression is pensive. "I told you that's all in the past."

"Is it?"

His eyes soften. "You're here now, aren't you?"

Yeah, and I never want to leave. I never did in the first place. I just thought it was what I had to do for my own sake.

"I am," is all I say.

"Good. Now, let's take a seat while we wait." With two

giant steps, Brooke bumps against the edge of his bed and lets himself plop on it. He pats the bedding, in case it's not clear where I should sit.

I'd have got the hint even if it wasn't so heavy handed. After all, his desk chair is loaded with what seems like clean laundry. At least going by the smell. And there's literally no other surface than the floor where I could sit.

I even consider it for a moment. I'm not worried about cleanliness because out of the two, the messiest one has always been me. But I worry about what it would say if I choose to sit on the floor rather than next to him.

I join him but still keep a decent distance. "How long do you think it's gonna take?"

"Hopefully, it'll be over quickly." He lifts his shirt to fish for his phone again, accidentally showing a sliver of taut skin. "Hmm, not yet."

"Is someone giving you updates on what the so-called indecent scene is?"

"Yeah, my man Dane is on it."

I tuck my hands under my thighs. "Who's Dane? Your new best friend?"

"He's my defensive partner." His eyes immediately catch on what my hands are doing. He knows it's a nervous tick. "But he can't replace you, of course."

"Please, he and your parade of girls have." I face forward, trying to avoid his knowing gaze, and freeze.

Two giant posters, one of my brother-in-law, and one of my flesh and blood brother, cover the wall by the bathroom. How did I not see them earlier?

"Well, they haven't." There's laughter in his voice now. "And if it makes you feel even better, none of my parade of girls have kissed the crap out of me like you did last weekend."

I suck in air. Slowly, I turn to him but only so I can deliver a punch to his shoulder. It definitely hurts me more. "You are hereby banned from talking about it."

"Can I think about it?" A corner of his lips lifts.

"No! That's not what friends do."

Brooke bobs his head. "But friends do get curious about what their friends are up to so, is that why you decided to come tonight? To see if you could find someone new to make out with?"

"I plead the fifth."

"But I bet you talk about things like this with Meyer and the others all the time."

I give him a look. "Yeah, but they're girls."

Brooke tilts his head back a bit, as if needing a different vantage to observe me. "Right, and I'm not."

"Obvio microbio," I say in Spanish like my mom does when she's feeling sassy.

He hums from his throat and turns around to face the posters. Max and Aran are in their NHL team uniforms but helmets off. It's funny because Max was captured in the middle of a nice smile, the kind that makes women cry that he's happily married. But Aran is with his usual serious expression, the one that makes me wonder what his wife even sees in him.

In their wedding vows, both of these men said some crap about how they each married their best friends. I remember weeping each time, hoping one day that would be me as well.

Alas, who knows who Brooke will end up marrying—if he even does. I'm not sure he's a fan of the sacrament or institution, considering his family history.

"Isn't it creepy to have them looking down at you when you're, um… you know." I casually point a thumb back at the mattress.

"Sleeping?" Brooklyn asks in an overly sweet voice.

I give him some serious side eye. "You know what I mean."

A full smile blooms on his face. It transforms him from

staggeringly handsome to heart attack inducing. Chuckling, he says, "Actually, I'd never thought about it but I'm definitely going to be creeped out now. I'll take them down."

"Yeah, maybe you should," I mumble, remembering the surprise sitting in his bathroom shelf.

Brooke gets up and starts peeling off the tape from the corner of Max's poster. His T-shirt stays a little bunched up, showing a patch of skin between the hem and the waistband of his jeans. The wild part is that despite the narrow sliver, there's an impressive muscle display.

He used to be way skinnier the last time we hung out. What the heck happened?

There's another ping and he pauses the work to check his phone, leaving half of Max's poster sagging forward. "All right. Coast is clear now," Brook announces. "We can go back to civilization."

"Was my company some kind of savage jungle?" Sarcasm drips heavy from my words.

His eyes flash as he opens the door and flicks off the light. "Oh yeah, I now know you bite."

"What?"

He taps his bottom lip with his finger. "I had bite marks after we kissed."

I gasp, trying to draw in enough oxygen to restart my brain after his abrupt topic switch. After spluttering for a second, I point at his face. "Liar! *You* are the one who bit me."

"Oh, so you were paying attention." He grins as we walk down the deserted hallway.

"Didn't we just agree to never talk about this?"

"Nope, I never actually agreed." Brooke whistles some old school, jolly tune as we start walking down the stairs. Extra annoying that he's right behind me.

"Well, stop. It's embarrassing."

"Why?" he has the nerve to ask.

I pause and grab onto the railing so I can turn over my shoulder. "Because we are *friends forever*, am I right?"

Brooke seems bigger than usual from this vantage. I have to crane my head back to meet his eyes, otherwise I'd be staring at his waist. His face is uncharacteristically blank, but I don't have the luxury of discerning what it could mean when he starts talking again.

"In other news, as your friend who is concerned for you, how are you enjoying the party? I know you don't like this house."

I resume the trek downstairs and when we're both safely at the landing, I say, "Well, other than you clearly trying to embarrass me, nothing catastrophic has happened just yet. So I guess it's okay."

"Good, let's keep it that way."

Later, well after Brooke conveys me to my friends again and goes off to find a beer, I discover exactly what he meant by that.

Turns out, while we were waiting upstairs during what I feared was people having excessive public displays of affection, Brooklyn was orchestrating an operation for his hockey bros to remove a certain ex of mine from the premises.

That is the exact moment where I discover something. What I felt for him in high school was a crush. A first awareness that he was a boy, I was a girl, and that he smelled good and made me laugh. That maybe it'd have felt even nicer if he kissed me.

But this thing burning me up from the inside now… this is something else. Bigger. And it can turn into the kind of thing that destroys our friendship for real if I don't rein it in.

CHAPTER 15
BROOKLYN

know I'm in trouble when I screw up during a warmup blue line shuffle drill. Last year, I posted the best record in the team's history, but today it's almost like I'm trying to hit the puck with the butt of my stick. The fact that Coach Green is dragging me by my practice jersey over to center ice, far enough from everyone else, is confirmation enough.

He folds his arms as he faces me. "Tatum, we're just days away from the season opener and you're performing worse than ever. Why are you making me regret assigning you as captain?"

I wince. "I'm sorry, Coach. I, uh… my head's a bit of a mess right now."

A bit is an understatement.

"With what?" he hisses the words. "Girls?"

Yes.

Actually, no. Just one. One I foolishly told that we'd be friends for freaking ever, even though I've been having nightly dreams about her—of the spicy variety. Of course, every time I wake up after the dreams with the desperate need for a cold shower, I can't fall back asleep again. The lack of proper sleep is actually what has me moving slower than a sloth today.

Of course, I say nothing.

Coach Green continues talking by himself. "Family?"

My face pinches. That's also a yes.

I went home the Saturday of Lee's birthday, two weeks ago. I bought some fancy pads for him because I know he's as obsessed with hockey as any other Tatum man. Dad has probably given him every piece of equipment imaginable, but I literally wouldn't know what else I could gift to the favorite son of a millionaire.

Except, I stood outside ringing the doorbell for long enough that I figured they weren't home. I finally let myself in and texted Dad. After an hour, he replied that he was sorry, but they'd decided to take an impromptu trip to the big city to take Lee to an NHL game.

I'd have liked to go too. The Division I season hadn't even started yet, so I was free. Which Dad should've known.

So anyway, I'm constantly horny and mildly depressed. At the same time, I have mountains of coursework that I can't chip away as fast as I wish, because I spend most of my time either at practice, or at the gym, or studying our playbook, or watching game film, or texting Liv without giving away that she's driving me feral with need.

And yet, these are all first world problems I have no right to complain about. I'm on a full ride, I'm already drafted, my father is loaded, I don't have any injuries…

So many guys in the team have it so much tougher. Like Dane. He's probably the hardest working guy on the team. All the way from here, I can see him crushing the drills. And it's all because he feels solely responsible for breaking his family out of the poverty cycle. Frankly, I was even happier when he got drafted this summer than when I did.

It makes me pissed at myself. I have everything and yet I feel like it's not enough. I don't even have a right to want more.

Shit, Coach's speaking again.

"—And apparently, I shouldn't meddle in players' personal lives." His expression is deadpanned, sarcastic. "But if you don't fix whatever the hell this is, I'm going to meddle, all right. I can give that C to Warren instead because at least he really wants it."

Sure, Kyle Warren has been moaning in the lockers about how he should've been the C because he's a senior. But he cares more about himself than the team, which makes Coach's threat terrifying.

"I'm sorry, Coach. Won't happen again."

"Yeah. Go make sure of that."

"Yes, sir."

After that, no matter how exhausted I feel, I give it my all during practice. It only amounts to two thirds of my normal performance, but if Coach isn't staring daggers at me or pulling me aside again, it must be progress.

Freshly showered after class and in a comfy St. Cloud hoodie and joggers, I make my way through campus toward the library. I'm early for the study session with the Spanish I group, so I'm just going to catch some Zs at a nice little corner while I wait for them.

We said we'd meet on the second floor, since it's the one the librarians don't care to keep people quiet. I climb up the stairs slowly, although three steps at a time. Upstairs, I sweep my eyes around, trying to locate the best spot for a nap, preferably shady. But then my eyes are immediately drawn to someone.

Of course Liv would be here early.

She's sitting at the end of a long table by a window, her full attention on the open textbook before her. Her pen is wedged between her nose and upper lip like a mustache.

"What a dork," I say in a mumble, although I don't stop

the smile forming on my face. It doesn't matter that she's right under a sunbeam, I just found my spot.

I take a step forward toward her and movement from the corner of my eye gets my attention. Some guy is headed straight for her and I hesitate. Maybe they know each other. It's early enough that Liv could've scheduled another appointment. But she'd be looking out for him, right? Maybe she wouldn't be quite as absorbed by her textbook.

I don't know if I'm doing the right thing, but I eat up the floor with long steps and reach her table well before the other guy. Liv looks up in surprise as I drop on the seat at her right side.

"You're here early," I mumble to her like it's not obvious.

From the corner of my eye, I catch the guy frowning at me but he does a U-turn. If he'd had any actual business with Liv, he wouldn't have minded my presence, which confirms he was just coming to bother her.

"So are you." She quirks an eyebrow at me unbeknownst to what just transpired.

I take the bottle with my after-practice protein shake out of my backpack, and set the backpack down on the table. I try fluffing it as if it was a pillow, but it doesn't help that inside it's full of hard notebooks, texts and a laptop. Whatever.

"Yeah." I lean all the way down and grunt as something in the front pocket stabs at my face. After rearranging it, I say, "Just need a little cat nap."

She turns her attention back on her textbook and I stare at her for a moment longer. It's just me, so she gets back to balancing that pen on her lip without a care as to what I might think about it. But I think about it, all right. It sucks my attention to her puckered up lips—lips that I'm now familiar with. If I could, I'd be running my tongue across them right this second. But I stay still, just taking her in.

A section of her hair is tucked behind her ear, and I hadn't noticed until now but she has a lot of ear piercings. One, two… five total. Those are new, at least from sometime after the fallout. Like my tattoos. Is her other ear the same?

"I hadn't noticed these." I reach up, gently pinching her earlobe between my fingers. Air rushes out of her mouth, which makes her pen drop on the textbook, and I let go. "Sorry, are they new? Did I hurt you?"

"No. Just startled." Liv clears her throat. "And they're not new. I've had them for a while but I'm using them again now that I don't have a boyfriend who wants to control my appearance anymore."

I slide my free hand under the table so she doesn't see how tight I'm squeezing my fist.

Not wanting to get into the topic of her asshole ex, I ask, "Do you also have five on the other ear?"

"Yes." Liv nods seriously. "I'm all about symmetry."

My lips twitch. I try to hold myself back but the words still spill out. "Where else do you have piercings?"

Slowly, Liv turns a mighty glare at me. "Nowhere else, you freaking perv."

"You should've just said it was none of my business and left it to my imagination."

Her eyes open as wide as saucers. "I don't want you to imagine anything."

Too late.

I started imagining things right after we made out.

"Well, would you get more piercings somewhere else?" I wiggle my eyebrows in a way that's always annoyed her, so she clearly knows I'm not serious.

"More in my ears, maybe. Anywhere else is too impractical." Liv's raspy voice turns excessively sweet. "Would you get pierced somewhere not your ears?"

I scrunch up my nose. "Hell no. I'm too sensitive."

"And yet you got tattoos." I still as she reaches over to my extended arm, the one I'm using as a pillow over my backpack, and lightly pulls at the sleeve of my sweatshirt until the black lines are visible. "How far do these go?"

"Should I show you?"

She pulls back. "Didn't you say you were going to take a nap?"

"Maybe you shouldn't have distracted me."

"Me?" Liv places a hand on her chest delicately. "I'm not the one who started touching my ears." I tear my eyes off the anime T-shirt that fits maybe a bit too snug across her chest, to the frown on her face.

"Fine, the bling bling distracted me. I'm going to sleep now." I bring my other arm back up and tuck my hand under my cheek before closing my eyes.

A few quiet minutes go by. The only noises are the low buzz of activity around the library and the occasional scrape of her pen on paper. Her chair creaks and I open my eyes in time to see her rearrange herself. Now, one of her legs is over the seat, her knee bumping into my thigh.

Her eyes find mine. "Sorry."

"It's okay," I drawl.

But it's not okay. I wish we were so much closer. I need to touch her again. After just one kiss, I'm already addicted to her and it's resetting all the ways I used to act around her.

Her hair's fallen from its hold behind her ear and I reach over again. This time, I drag the pads of my fingers deliberately slow across her temple, gathering her hair until I can tuck it back against the shell of her ear. Then, I run my fingers against it, caressing her ear over and around the piercings, some glinting and some solid metal, until I drop my hand.

"Brooklyn." My name comes out through gritted teeth. "Do that one more time and I'm going to pull at your ear."

"Oh yeah? Should I do this instead?"

Wariness takes over her expression as I sit back up with dramatic flare. Before she can react, I grab her on a headlock and pull her against my chest. A little shriek gets muffled against my sweatshirt as I brush the palm of my hand over her hair.

"You—you—" Liv can't finish her threat under the attack, and I almost think she's given up on retaliation until I feel her trying to grab at my stomach.

I slow down the motions and ask out of curiosity, "What are you doing?"

"I'm trying to pinch you," she responds gravely. I stretch my neck to see, and even though she's using her fingers as pincers, all she can grab onto is my sweatshirt. "Why isn't it working?"

The second I release her, she sits back at a distance. But whatever epithet she's about to throw my way, it dies in her throat as I grab the hem of my sweatshirt and lift it.

Her eyes pop wide open at the display. I keep my body fat at maximum ten percent, and every muscle of my body is cut. I don't have to glance down to know that even though I'm sitting, my abs are more defined than if someone had Photoshopped them on my picture

"This is why you couldn't pinch me, Aceituna. There's just no fat."

After tearing her attention from the numbers tattooed down my left side, she says, "Watch me." Faster than a lightning strike, she digs her fingers around a ridge of my abs and pinches. Hard.

"Ouch!"

Harrumphing, she lets me go and starts trying to comb her hair. I rub my skin, biting down a grin because her face is red as a beet. It could be because of the headlock situation, or because she liked what she saw.

I'm playing with fire but this is the most alive I've felt in weeks—months, even. And yeah, maybe I'm the damn author of the infamous *friends forever* words, but what if we *should* be more than friends? What if I could gradually show her that we could be so much more?

CHAPTER 16
OLIVIA

He's killing me and he has no freaking idea.

Brooke and I have always been handsy but not like this. Back in the day, we used to smack and pinch each other like nobody's business. He'd grab me in his infamous stinky headlock and I'd punch him and kick him until he let go. It was wild to me that it made some of his girlfriends jealous when they got to kiss him and touch him in ways that didn't cause pain.

But this? This is weird. It's like a mix of the two. I've never been gladder to be on the receiving end of a headlock, because after those casual touches to my ear I was ready to pull him into a corner. Who knew ears were so sensitive.

Surely not him, or he wouldn't have touched mine on purpose.

By the time Emily and Alyssa finally join us, I almost want to kiss them. I can't take anymore of sitting next to Brooklyn, watching him snooze on his backpack. Why does he need eyelashes so long? Or lips so luscious? But also, he should shave because that little stubble is offensive to my sensibilities. Sensibilities that are a bit too tingly right now.

"Sorry to keep you waiting," Emily says as she takes the seat across from Brooke. "There was too much traffic this morning coming from my boyfriend's."

I try not to perk up at that. She has a boyfriend? And here I thought she was angling for a chance at Brooke. Still, I keep my head down in case my thoughts are visible on my face.

Alyssa chuckles. "And I just didn't want to get out of bed."

That's not gonna help her become a hockey girlfriend, if that's what she wants. Brooke gets up at five in the morning everyday for a run before practice. It's been like that since high school. But this is none of my business.

"Nah, you guys were right in time. We were early." He rubs his eyes with a big yawn and I don't know why I hadn't noticed before, but he has massive dark circles around his eyes like he has barely got any sleep for days. I wonder what's wrong.

"Uh…" I drag my eyes away from him and try to focus on the girls. "Shall we get started?"

"Yes." Alyssa clasps her hands, a bit more excited than she should be for what is essentially a pretty basic assignment. "I came up with a few scenarios we could create some interesting dialogues from."

In the end, we end up choosing the career option because it'll make it easy to talk about ourselves. The next half hour transpires in easy silence as we individually come up with bullet points about our career paths that we can translate, and then turn into a conversation. It's like the kind of stuff Brooklyn and I did in high school Spanish, except a lot more expensive, but it sure is going to fulfill my goal of easy credits.

The scraping of his chair on the floor pulls me from the monologue I've been typing up. "Sorry," he says in a whisper. "I'm gonna take a bio break. Anyone want anything from the vending machine?"

"A Sprite for me, please," Emily says with a smile I now guess is sweet, rather than flirty.

"Red bull. I still need to wake up." Alyssa's eyes still carry the glint of interest, though.

Brooke stands to his full height and looks down at me. "I know what you want, Liv." He has the nerve to pull at my earlobe softly before he leaves.

I'm going to murder him when we're alone.

"What was all that about?" Emily leans forward. "He knows what you want? Whew, that sounded charged."

"It's nothing," I mumble.

"Hmm, *nothing* doesn't look like a blush like that." Alyssa folds her arms and leans over the table to speak closer. "What's the deal between you and Brooklyn?"

And, here it is. What eventually happens every single time other girls are around us. *The inquisition.*

Sighing, I say in a deadpan voice, "Nothing. Brooke and I are just childhood friends."

"Brooke?" Emily leans her chin on her hand in a tell-me-more move.

"*Just*?" Alyssa instead latches onto this word. "Do you wish you were more?"

"No." I'm so practiced in this lie, it sounds natural. "You're free to put your hat in the ring."

Alyssa lifts both hands up. "Whoa, don't get me wrong. I have the super hots for him, but I'm not going to step on another girl's toes to get me there."

"That's right." Emily nods. "That wouldn't be cool. And even though you say there's nothing between you guys, I beg to disagree. The tension between you is making *me* sweat, and I already have a boyfriend." She giggles.

Under the table, I rub my own sweaty palms up and down my jeans. "I assure you, there's nothing going on."

"Okay, so if there's nothing going on, can you give me some advice?" Alyssa's smirk could mean one of two things. The first, she doesn't believe me and is just testing me to make me admit I also have the super hots for Brooke—not gonna happen. Or two, she legit wants me to help her get his attention.

That's the other type of conversation I've had to endure for years. If the inquisition goes well because the other girls are decent, they inevitably ask for help.

"I don't know," I say, truthfully. "He seems to gravitate to hot girls, so you're good."

"Why, thanks for the compliment." Her mirth intensifies. "But ever stopped to think that you're hot yourself?"

I cringe so hard, it narrows my eyes into slits. "No, trust me. I'm not his type. Can we please drop this conversation?"

"Okay, fine," Alyssa says a bit too innocently.

I push my chair back and mumble that I'm also going to the restroom. Hopefully, if I wash my face there will be no visible trace left that inside I feel like I'm dying.

But right as I round the bookshelf behind the table, a hand sneaks out and grabs my arm. I look up at the owner. Brooke has a finger against his lips while he drags me across the corridor, until we're several shelves away from our group mates.

"What are you doing?" I whisper.

He stops before me, folding his arms. "What was that?"

I notice that he's not carrying any of the requested beverages, which means he didn't go far in the first place.

I swallow hard but it does nothing to slow down the rapid pace of my heartbeat. But I didn't say anything weird, so what gives? Lifting my chin, I ask, "What was what?"

Brooke jerks his head in the general direction of our table. "I was just about to leave when I heard that little conversation."

I stuff my freezing hands in the pockets of my jeans. "Why are you saying it like it was my fault?"

"That's not what I mean." His eyebrows pinch a little.

"Why didn't you just shut them down? You usually don't take any shit."

"Because—" I sigh so hard that I end up blowing a raspberry. "Even if I tried to cut them off, they eventually find me in some corner and interrogate me. It's what always happens when there are girls around you and I'm in the way."

"What?"

"You didn't know?" I lift my eyebrows.

He blinks hard. "*Always?*"

"It was much worse in high school, trust me." I shrug, but I don't plan on telling him the worst of it. Or that the worst of all was one of his ex girlfriends.

"I—I'll tell them something to leave you alone."

"No." I put my hand on his chest to stop him before he walks over to our group mates. "That would make it worse."

"What? How?" Brook frowns.

"This is why I've never told you about this. Most girls would think I ran to you and pit you against them." Slowly, I drop my hand back down. "I don't think that'd be the case with these girls, anyway. I don't get mean girl vibes."

"I did." If anything his expression's darker. "They could've come straight to me and asked if I was single. Instead they tried to drill you. That's not cool."

I tilt my head. "Or they're just nervous."

"Why are you defending them?"

Because I know what it feels like to have a hopeless crush on him. I saw myself in every single girl who approached me asking for some in with Brooklyn, because who wouldn't possibly fall for him?

"Just pretend like you didn't hear anything. Let me handle it as usual."

"As usual." Brooke mutters in a dark way, staring at me with his intense game face. "How many times has this happened?" I bite my lips so I don't laugh at his sweet, naive ass. "How bad did it ever get? Did someone ever bully you because of me?"

"Weren't you going to the restroom?"

"Olivia, don't change the topic."

I tilt my head back, closing my eyes as I sigh in defeat. "Anywhere from a mild chat like this one to hair pulling."

"*What?*" he hisses in horror. Next thing, he digs his fingers into my hair and massages my scalp as if the hair pulling had just happened. "Who the hell hurt you?"

"I'm not hurt now, you dork." I grab his wrists and push his hands away before he can give me even more tingles. "That was like four years ago."

He does the math quickly. "When I was dating Jenna?"

Oops, getting too close to the truth. I turn around to head to the restrooms.

"So, it was Jenna," he mumbles behind me and I stay quiet.

Down the stairs, I veer left for the women's restroom and he follows. I give him a look. "Drop it, before you walk into the wrong restroom."

"Fine, we'll talk about this another time. But promise me something." He takes a step closer to speak lower as a girl walks out of the restroom and gives us a funny look.

"What?"

"If someone else gives you any shit because of me, you'll give me the chance to intervene."

"Why?" I wrinkle my nose. "I've been able to take care of myself just fine."

"And it's killing me to find out I put you in that position more than once." He tugs at a strand of my hair, which makes the back of his fingers brush against my cheek accidentally. "Promise me."

Before I shudder, I say, "Fine." I rush into the restroom before he can see how much he's affecting me.

CHAPTER 17
BROOKLYN

We lose the first game of the season, 6-5, against the Falcons. They were last year's champ and some of the seniors are happy that it wasn't a total embarrassment.

"I beg to disagree," I say from my bench, a towel on my head as I work on loosening my skate laces. "This feels a lot like *so close, yet so far* to me, and that's not worth celebrating." I grit my teeth. We have a decent chance with this roster but only if they stop screwing around.

And then Kyle Warren opens his stinky mouth. "Oh wow, what a demoralizing thing to say from the guy who is supposed to be our captain. We should all be out celebrating that we held our own against the reigning champions, right?"

His buddies agree with him like drones and start rallying the rest of the team for a night at O'Malley's. I leave it alone because at least they didn't half-ass it tonight at the game, even if Kyle's error is what led to the Falcon's sixth goal.

I'm so annoyed, I scrub my skin in the shower like I'm trying to peel it off. Be the Captain, they said. It'll be fun, they said.

"What do you wanna do?" Dane asks me afterward, when we're putting on our freaking suits and ties. "Hit O'Malley's too, or go to a rage room?" He chuckles but the idea has merit.

I shake my head. "No, I think I need quiet. See you at home later."

"Okay, honey. Don't be too late or I'll worry."

I flip him off on my way out of the lockers, hauling my sports bag on my shoulder as I head to the parking lot. Maybe I should've blow dried my hair because the chill bites me as I walk into the night. I didn't tell Dane that there's a third option, one that centers me better than a crowded place or smashing things ever could. One that's on speaking terms with me again. But if I told him, he'd have gotten jealous.

I toss my bag in the backseat of my Gladiator. After climbing in the driver's seat, I pull out my phone from the pocket of my slacks, wishing I could surprise Liv and show up unannounced at her place. Except I don't have her current address, so I have no choice but to ruin the plan on my own.

ME

What u up to

I turn on the vehicle and crank up the heat so it starts working fast. With one hand, I tap on the steering wheel as I wait for a response. With the other, I doom scroll through social media to pretend like I'm not being impatient at all.

But then Liv's face pops up on my screen. I pause to watch a video of her showing how to make a quick allergen-free salad to the tune of Motionless in White. I snort a laugh at the contrast. She moves through her kitchen as though it's a totally domestic scene without the strident background music and she looks at the camera like she's bored. It's hilarious.

Or it would be if she wasn't so damn hot.

I rub my chin with my hand while I watch her. Does this make me a shitty person? I'm her friend. Her best friend wannabe. I'd break my own face before making her uncomfortable.

But I like what she's wearing. It's some kind of black top, so tight it shows off her curves. The neckline swoops down, not drastically, but enough to show some skin. When she turns around for a second to retrieve something, I can see a lot of her back. If I had her permission, I'd kiss her neck slowly, savoring her skin the way I would her lips, and I'd make my way down her spine until I map every inch of her.

That's when my phone pings with a response.

OLIVE EMOJI
Studying, why?

ME
Would you like some free pizza with that?

OLIVE EMOJI
Uhh I am confusion

ME
Text me your address to unconfuse yourself

I squirm on my seat while her three dots reappear, trying to convince myself that the thought of kissing her back hasn't affected me.

OLIVE EMOJI
Free you said? Why yes, thank you

"Yes." I pump a fist as her new address pops onto my screen. I add it to her contact info, put on my seatbelt, and drive off to Romano's. Not only is it the best Italian place in town, they're owned by the family of Olivia's brother-in-law. They know the Liv special by heart now, which is the only pizza guaranteed to not trigger any of her allergies.

As always, the place is an overwhelming explosion of sound

as I walk in. Weaving through the tables, I head directly for the counter where the matriarch of the Cassiano clan is checking a couple out.

"Bambino, you are too skinny!" she exclaims when it's my turn.

I know for a fact that I am not skinny. I could eat the whole kitchen if they let me. "How are you, Mrs. Cassiano?"

"Busy." She puts her hands on her hips. "Trying to convince that son of mine to come visit his elderly mother for the holidays. Apparently he has 'a game' before Thanksgiving."

Ah, she's talking about Max. The fact that she made quote marks with her fingers before 'a game' is funny. She doesn't care at all that her youngest son is the hottest forward in the league.

Grinning, I say, "Give me two years and I'll make his life on ice so miserable, he'll want to escape home for the holidays."

"I'll hold you to that." But by the way she's smiling, I can tell she doesn't believe anyone can take her son down. Would that I could have a mother like her. "What can I get you, bambino?"

"Extra large pepperoni pizza with extra cheese," I say, pausing for her to key it into the computer. "And also one Olivia special."

Her eyes lift from the screen. "Well. It's been a while."

"I know." I stuff my hands in my pockets, trying to appear nonchalant. Even though everyone in this town knows that Liv and I weren't speaking. In fact, I'm surprised her brother hasn't already called me to warn me off. I don't think Aran ever liked me much.

He'll find out after tonight, though. Because Mrs. Cassiano will tell Max, who will tell his wife, Luz, who will tell her younger brother without a doubt. I'm sure Aran will rant about the little shit who's back in his sister's life to his wife, Maddie.

She might mention it in passing to her mom, and Mrs. Berkley, being Lee's teacher, might end up passing the message along to my father through my half-brother.

I wonder if this is enough to get him to talk with me. After all, he's never liked Liv either. But he's a man of incredibly bad taste, otherwise he wouldn't have married my mother.

I'm ridiculously jolly as I pay for two ginormous boxes of piping hot pizza and drive off to Liv's address. It's in an apartment complex smack between campus and Romano's, which I don't think is a coincidence. I balance the pizzas expertly as I climb up the stairs until I find her door.

After ringing the doorbell, I shout, "Extremely hot delivery!"

It gets Liv opening the door in record time. "Oh my gosh, you dork! You're going to bother people."

"Please, grandma. It's only nine."

Liv moves aside and opens the door wider. "Shoes off, please. Or Mina will kill you."

"Is she around?" I ask as I walk in, trying not to visibly react at the vanilla scent that clings to Liv's skin.

"Yeah, she's taking a shower right now."

I will not show disappointment that we're not alone, no sire.

As she takes the two boxes so I can remove my shoes, I mutter, "Crap, I hope she likes the two options I got."

"It's okay. I've seen her eat pig's intestines. This is very pedestrian in comparison." Her voice twinkles with a chuckle and…

I immediately feel better. Like magic.

Kyle who? Falcons whomst?

I wipe the clown's grin off my face the second Liv turns, before she can see it. As she lowers the boxes on the coffee table, I force myself to take some more steps out of the entrance and into the actual apartment. The first area my attention goes to is the kitchen.

"So this is where the magic happens, huh?" Is that pile of dirty dishes in the sink all the stuff she used for the latest video?

But she's not wearing that nice little top anymore. She's in a grey St. Cloud sweatshirt that would fit two of me, and leggings. I'm severely overdressed, but I can somewhat fix that.

"What magic?" she asks, looking up at me now that she's sitting on the carpet, while I undo my tie.

"Your videos," I say, my eyes fixed on hers. "I've been a fan from the beginning, but I'm really enjoying the rocker domestic queen collection."

"It's not a collection." She blinks slowly. "I think this is it for me."

Yeah, I agree. Although I'm not sure we'd be talking about the same thing.

"Motionless in White, though? We loved that in high school." I stuff the rolled up tie into the pocket of my blazer and then remove it, settling it down on the couch.

"I know. I'm thinking Mudvayne's next," she says, watching me take a seat on the floor right beside her. She scoots a bit farther, except that almost puts her at the end of the table. "Um, is this comfortable for you? We could use the kitchen island instead."

I watch her as I unbutton the left sleeve of my shirt and start to roll it up. Her attention's drawn to my tattoo right away, and she keeps staring at it even when I say, "No, this is fine." It's perfect. She's perfect.

"You never told me you wanted a tattoo." She motions at it with her lips in a way I used to find funny, but now gets a chill traveling through my spine.

Clearing my throat, I say, "That's because I didn't know I wanted one until I did."

"Okay, fair."

I look away from her to work on the opposite sleeve now. "Do you want to know what it means?"

"Can I?" Liv reaches forward to pop open the first pizza box. When it turns out to be her special, she swings it open all the way and grabs a big slice of gluten free, no cheese, marinara, black olives—ironic—capers, and artichokes. No meat, because deli meats have an additive her stomach can't tolerate.

I bite down a smile as I watch her tuck in with gusto. She trusts very few people in her life to keep her food safe, and I happen to be one of them. Always made me feel special.

Now I want more. I want to keep her safe, not just her food. I want to be her special person. I want *her*.

But I don't want to freak her out. I have to take it easy.

I place my hand on top of my pizza box, palm facing up so the start of my tattoo is visible. "It's kind of silly," I continue, my voice a bit deeper than I intend. "But these three lines represent the most important aspects of my life."

"Doesn't sound silly," she says with a mouth full of food.

There's a smudge of marinara on her cheek and before I can process, I reach forward and wipe it with my thumb. I lick the sauce off my finger but keep my eyes fixed on my tattoo because I'm afraid she'll read my mind if I let her look into my eyes. Yet I can't stop myself from touching her. From craving her skin.

So much for taking it easy.

"This one," I say, touching the fully black line on the outer edge. "It represents hockey, which is going pretty well for me, even though we lost tonight."

"I saw the score." Her voice is soft, airy. "Must've been tough. Wanna talk about it?"

I look up. "You want to talk about hockey with me?"

"Notice how I asked if you wanted to, instead of saying I wanted to?"

Grinning, I touch the line in the middle, which is faded

compared to the hockey one. "And this one is for friends, like you, who put up with my shit even though I annoy them."

"Ah, yes. That makes sense," Liv says in a dark tone. "Why is it lighter than the first one, though?"

"Because…" I busy myself with getting a pepperoni pizza slice and force myself to respond. "Because I once drove away my best friend in the whole wide world." I take a big bite and start chewing.

As the silence stretches, I glance at her and freeze.

Liv looks like she's about to cry.

"Uh…" I set my slice down. "Sorry, I didn't mean to—"

She takes a deep breath. "And the last line? The one that's even more faded."

I swallow down the pizza, which is suddenly not tasting so great. My stomach churns with a cocktail of emotions that don't work well together. Severe attraction for my best friend, who still has sauce on her face. Annoyance after the game. Hurt, so much damn hurt, that a restaurant owner cares more about me than my own parents.

"That one's for my family," I say with a thread of voice. I don't need to explain why it's the faintest line. Liv knows. She's seen the worst of the Tatums from the front row.

She slides her fingers between mine and holds my hand tight. "I'm sorry, Brooke."

For some reason, what I manage to say is, "You're getting gluten on your hand now."

"I know, I'll go wash it later." Sighing, she lifts her eyes to mine and her lips part.

But a different voice comes out. "Well, what do we have here?"

Oh, shit. I forgot there was someone else home.

CHAPTER 18
OLIVIA

I pull my hand from Brooke's right before Mina gets in position to see it. I almost grab my slice again until I remember I might've picked up flour crumbles from his hand.

"Brooklyn's here, and he brought pizza," I announce as I stand up and walk around her to the sink.

"Wow, you won't catch me complaining," Mina says. "A hot guy in a button shirt and free pizza in my living room is truly a one of a kind experience."

No me digas, I almost say. Brooke nearly gave me a heart attack when I opened the door and saw him outside.

But then, every interaction since has been just as dangerous. If Mina hadn't come out of her room at that moment, I might've leaned forward and... completely ruined this new delicate balance by kissing him. Also, potentially sending myself to the hospital from the taste of normal pepperoni pizza on his mouth. Small details.

"Do you have any dietary restrictions?" There's concern in his voice, which makes me shake my head. I'd have thought that telling him she can eat any part of an animal would give him a hint.

"Nope. I could even eat you up if you were interested."

I choke.

So does Brooklyn.

Meanwhile, Mina casually comments, "Oh, sounds like you guys need some water. Be right back."

I'm still coughing while I dry my hands up with the kitchen towel. Mina pulls open the fridge to get a pitcher of cold water, and uses it to hide her face as she gives me an exaggerated wink.

What is this devious woman playing at?

It's not like she's legit hitting on him. I know what her flirty tone of voice is, and that wasn't it. And also, after a few parties at the Bolt House, she's started to develop a little thing for Brooke's friend, Dane Bloom. He's a ginormous brunette who'd look very nice wrapped up around her little finger—her words, not mine.

She also knows I unfortunately still have a thing for my childhood friend. So it's almost like she wanted to make me give myself away with that comment. I wouldn't put past her.

I walk back to the living room like it's a mined field and not a regular floor with linoleum tiles. Mina's setting down a tower of clean cups along with the water pitcher when I join them.

"There's enough pizza for an army," she says as she surveys the two massive boxes.

Brooke motions at it as he chews, one cheek full to bursting. "Speaking of armies, where is your other friend?"

Mina gives him a side eye. "She has the away game tonight, you know."

"Right." He sounds more distracted than usual. I wonder if the loss really hit him that hard? But now I don't know if he'll want to talk about it with Mina here. He's always extra sensitive after a loss, so he tends to hide all by himself rather than socializing his feelings.

Speaking of, Mina's eyes are narrowed, head tilted in a thoughtful expression. "Brooklyn Tatum, are you self-absorbed or clueless?"

"Clueless," Brooke and I say at the same time. We look at each other.

"Ah." Mina presses her lips tight.

While his curl into a goofy grin, I pick up my abandoned slice and lament that it's grown cold. To distract myself from that sad fact, I add, "This is why I have a special nickname for him."

"What's that?"

"Blimbo," we say at the same time again, which makes Mina's eyes widen.

"Blond," I start.

"Bimbo," he finishes. "Sadly, I'm a walking stereotype."

"I wouldn't say it's sad," I volley while chewing, because there's no point in pretending to have manners in front of two people who have seen me at my worst in different occasions. "It's quite funny, actually. I once watched him walk into a closed crystal door."

Mina cocks an eyebrow at me and I can read her mind. She's wondering how I could still fall for a guy like that. But it's because she doesn't know him yet.

"So not funny." He frowns, even though his eyes twinkle. "It gives me a headache just to remember."

"What were you even thinking about that had you so distracted?" I ask, pouring myself a glass of water.

"Back then?" Brooke's forehead scrunches up as he harkens back to that time when he almost shattered the glass door to the high school library. "I think college admissions? It was around the time I didn't know where I was going yet."

Ah, yes. Back when we were both freaking out at the possibility that we'd have to go our separate ways. We ended up going to the same college and growing apart anyway. Life's funny like that.

Maybe he's thinking the same thing, because he's suddenly grown quiet.

"So, Brooklyn." Something in Mina's voice gives me pause. "I'm a little aware of the history between you and my best friend Liv, who I have never put through any suffering in my entire life—"

Uh oh. Should I stop this?

Yes, I think so.

"Oh, that's right. I made a bunch of salad that would go nicely with the pizza. Anyone want some?"

Brooke looks at me, eagerly. "Yes, please. I'm intrigued by the flava beans."

"Fava beans, you dork."

"Those."

Mina takes a deep breath and asks, "So, what are your intentions with her? Are you planning on hurting her again?"

My jaw drops and I freeze, locked between sitting and standing. Which makes me collapse on the couch.

Brooke's eyebrows pop off. He slowly turns to Mina. "Uh, what?"

"You heard me." She folds her arms and glares at him with all her might. It's strong enough to make him swallow hard. "Because in my opinion, a little party here and a little pizza there aren't enough to make amends."

Brooke blinks hard—at me. "I thought I'd only get this kind of speech from your brother."

"Might as well practice now," I mumble, picking myself back up to head over to the fridge.

"My intentions?" he muses aloud while I grab the salad container along with some serving cups and utensils. When I return, he's got one arm across his chest, hand hooked on his other arm that is raised as he rubs his chin. The raspy sound hits me as I sit back down next to him. "My intentions," he repeats, facing Mina head on, "are to reclaim my rightful position as Aceituna's best friend."

Mina looks positively murderous. "Those are fighting words, blimbo. Especially from someone who hurt her so much."

"Salad?" I ask, popping open the container.

Brooke grabs a serving plate. "Yes, please."

As I pass him the container and serving spoon, I give Mina what I hope is a discreet glare.

So this was the angle? Not some awkward attempt at matchmaking, but a declaration of war? I don't know if I should be relieved or annoyed, because this must mean she doesn't approve of Brooke and I as a couple. Or maybe she just thinks I stand no chance with him.

"Salad?" He offers her the container, and she reluctantly takes it from him. As he leans back against the couch, Brooke places a forearm on his raised knee and says, "And for what it's worth, I'll spend the rest of my life apologizing for being a jerk to Liv if that's what it takes."

Mina pauses to reassess him. That's the thing with Brooklyn. He always has his head in the clouds but occasionally he'll deliver a biting zinger that cuts through people's defenses. And this is one such case, because with that he rendered Mina's argument moot, and her speechless.

This is why I didn't want to talk with him after the incident. I knew he'd make me come around and I wanted to hold onto my anger longer. Except I hurt him too—bad enough that he got a tattoo about it.

My eyes focus on the ink as he picks up a second slice of his gluten bomb of a pizza. My eyes fall to his side, encased in a perfectly tailored button shirt. The other time at the library, when he flashed his abs and nearly made me die of a nosebleed, I caught glimpse of another tattoo against his ribs. It was a bunch of numbers. I wonder if he'd been about to tell me about it before Mina interrupted us.

"Anyway," Mina continues, "I'll be pleasant for tonight since you're feeding me. But from tomorrow you should start watching your back."

"You're on," he says as if this was a normal conversation that he feels the need to keep entertaining.

I shake my head. "You guys are weird."

"Speaking of," Mina says, brushing flour off her hands. "I have to go work a late shift at the school library now, where I'm sure to see weird things like the guy who always sits alone in the history hallway to pick his nose for an hour, or the couple who are technically banned because we keep finding them getting it on in random corners."

Slowly, Brooklyn turns his head to me and I think he's going to remark on how particular my friend is, except that he says, "Tell me you're not hanging out at the library on your own where any of these weirdoes could do something to you, right?"

I snort. "Of course not, big brother."

"Ew, I'm not your brother," he says in a deadpanned voice. "I'm also far more handsome than him. And talented. And popular. And frankly, my communication skills are so much better than all his grunts and glowers."

Next to him, Mina gives me a look that is supposed to convey a lot of meaning, except I don't get it. Finally, she mouths, "We'll talk."

Well, that doesn't sound good.

Aloud, she says something even worse. "Anyway, I'll leave you two alone until Dee arrives."

"Enjoy your exhibitionists," Brooke returns offhand as he chews.

Mina makes a rude gesture that only makes him grin. One

day they're going to be the best of friends and that day I'll start living in fear of the terror they'll inflict upon me. Terror that I'm already feeling the first tendrils of as I watch Mina wash her hands and collect her purse. She twirls her fingers in farewell before leaving.

The sound of the front door closing echoes around the quiet.

I am not going to look at Brooklyn now.

"I'm full," I say too loudly, hoping he takes that as a hint to start packing up. "Thanks for the pizza." I start closing the box with three fourths of the pizza still in it.

"I can help you pick up."

"No, take your time eating. You're probably still hungry."

I could kick myself. Brooke himself gave me the perfect out and I didn't take it. Almost like I don't actually want him to leave.

Who am I trying to fool? I wish he could stay all night, not necessarily for nefarious purposes, but just to chat. We used to stay up super late talking about any and everything before I went and gave him a reason for a tattoo. Not that I'm the sole person responsible for it. I'm only a fraction of its meaning.

My head's a mess already and it's only been five minutes since Mina left. I need an outlet for all this nervous energy that won't make me screw things up.

"I, um, I'm gonna get started on the dishes." I can feel him watching me while I stand up.

"Okay."

I can breathe easier in the kitchen, with a whole island and barstools in between. After rolling the sleeves of my sweatshirt, I squirt a big dollop of soap on the sponge and get to work.

"So, you wanted to talk about the game?" I ask, picking up on a thread of conversation from before Hurricane Mina.

"I did."

I jump in my skin, because Brooke's right behind me.

Glancing over my shoulder, I find him on this side of the kitchen island. How did he even get all the way here without me noticing?

Right, he's not wearing shoes either.

He's just leaning there, torso slightly curved to make himself a smidge shorter to rest his hands back on the island's surface. One of his legs is folded over the other one, like he's going nowhere. His chin's tilted back as he watches me.

I whirl around right in time to nick my finger with the knife I was trying to wash.

"Ow!" A drop of blood forms on my fingertip.

And then Brooklyn's arms are around me.

CHAPTER 19
BROOKLYN

Her breath hitches when I grab her hand to inspect the cut. It's maybe a quarter of an inch but bleeds pretty profusely. What probably makes it sting even worse is that her hand is all sudsy.

I reach forward to run the tap again. It brings me flush against her, and I don't move away even as I rinse her hand under the water spray. Instead, I pluck the soggy sponge from her other hand and toss it away, before bring her hand under the tap too.

"I can wash my own hands." Liv tries to tug free and I don't let her.

Tucking my chin on the top of her head, I say, "You should also be able to do the dishes without hurting yourself, yet here we are."

"Touché," she grouches.

The sane, logical part of my brain is screaming at me to stop. Friends don't do what I'm about to. But I still let my pea brain take over.

I circle my left hand around both of her wrists, locking

them in place. With my right hand, I pick up the hand soap container and squirt a little on her hands. I start rubbing the soap on her damp skin, slowly sliding my fingers between hers, up and down—just making sure her skin is thoroughly cleaned off food debris and the more abrasive dish soap. I'm extra careful with her left hand, running the pad of my thumb just under the cut to wipe a way a trickle of blood.

"You know," I can't even pretend like my voice isn't NSFW right now. "You gave me a paper cut recently."

"Hmm?" That almost sounds like a moan, or it could be my wishful thinking.

I clear my throat slightly. "At the admin office, when I gave you back your schedule."

"Oh, really? I was in a hurry and didn't even notice."

Her voice has always been husky and right now it's doing things to me. It's nothing short of a miracle that I can still form coherent sentences.

"In a hurry to not see my face?"

"That's right." She chuckles softly. "Feels like a lifetime ago but it was what, a month ago? Two? And now you're everywhere."

Not everywhere. I haven't been in her bed yet.

Shaking my head hard, I step away from her so she can grab the kitchen towel. She passes it over to me and picks up the kitchen roll for herself.

"Go put on a Band-Aid."

"Yeah, okay." She keeps her head down as she walks by me, but even her hair can't hide the blush on her face.

Once I'm alone in the kitchen, I run my lemon scented hands down my face. "What are you doing, asshole? This is the opposite of taking it slow." Now I can't get the picture out of my head of her in the shower and my hands soaping her up.

I slap my cheeks hard enough to sting possibly as much as

her injury. Tugging my sleeves past my elbows, I set out to work on the dishes now that she won't be able to.

"Hey, that's my job," Liv complains as she returns, her voice dancing behind me as she circles around the island, bringing her vanilla scent closer.

"You're on drying duty now," I say, motioning at the growing pile of dishes I've placed on the rack. She unhooks a different kitchen rag from a cabinet handle above me, and starts working. "So, the game."

"Right."

I offer a grim smile to the cabinet because I've never heard her sound so excited to talk about a sport she despises.

"It's not like I'm complaining that we lost our first game. Our opponents are the reigning champions and they're just tough, you know? But…" I trail off because this saucepan has some gunk I just can't get out. "What the hell did you cook on here?"

"That one wasn't me. It was Mina, grilling pig intestines on it." I gag and she starts laughing. "I'm kidding, it was regular sausages for breakfast."

I dry heave again anyway. Suddenly the smells are a little less tolerable.

"Surely you've seen worse at a house packed of gross jocks?" She's still laughing, and I guess I'm glad it's helped dispel the weird mood I incited. Pretty sure Mina would be extra pissed at me if she found out I tried to make a pass at Liv.

"Well, yeah. But I won't give you any details because then you'll be the one puking your dinner."

"Gah. Back to hockey."

"Right." I shake my head, grinning even though getting back on the topic should make me miffed. "What was I saying?"

"You're allegedly not complaining."

"I'm not. But I just wish the rest of the team cared half as much. Especially the seniors." I lean my head back and close my eyes, sighing. The good mood's vanished. "Yet, they're pissed that I was made captain even though they just don't care enough to even deserve a jersey."

"So, let me get this straight. They're lazy but self-entitled?"

"Pretty much, yeah." Just like their buddy Liam Roberts. But that's not a name I'll ever bring up in her presence.

"They sound like the opposite of you. No wonder you're annoyed."

I gasp. "Was that a compliment just there?"

"Yes." She gives me a look like I'm possibly having my biggest blimbo moment. "Brooke, you do know you're at the level of your heroes, right? I'm surprised the pros are even letting you finish college."

I blink hard. "I, uh…."

Liv's eyes leave mine to focus on the pot lid she's drying. "I've watched your games."

"But you weren't there tonight."

She glances up at me again and I don't care to correct my slip up.

Yeah, I noticed. I've been looking for her in the stands my whole life, even when I knew she wouldn't be there.

"I mean…" She glances back down. I try to focus on the remaining dirty dishes as she speaks. "Back during the Dark Age—that's what I'm dubbing the last year and a half—I still watched your games sometimes. Not in person, but on the computer."

"Huh. Why?"

Liv shrugs. "I just wanted to make sure you didn't get hurt."

Shit.

Why is my whole body tingling?

Especially behind my eyes?

My voice is garbled as I say, "So let me get this straight. Even though you hated me, you still kept tabs on me?"

"I never hated you."

My pulse spikes the way it does when I'm about to deliver a heavy check against the boards.

"And you think I'm a good player."

"Yes, purely from an objective standpoint. If you keep it up, you're going to have one of the most amazing careers in the pros. And that… that's terrifying."

The cup I'm washing slips from my hands. I fumble but it still falls. At least it's plastic and doesn't break.

Slowly, I turn to her. "Why?"

"Because you could get hurt," Olivia says with a soft voice. Sighing, she says, "I've never told you why I hate hockey, right?" She sets the drying rag down and looks up at me, biting her lip.

"No." I swallow hard. We've skirted around this topic all our lives, because I think I've always known why.

"I can't…" She cuts herself off to shake her head. "I can't see what happened to Luz again. And every important guy in my life seems bent on getting hurt playing the most reckless sport in the world." Her chin trembles.

I shut the water tap and stand there for all of one second. That's as much as I can resist.

In the blink of an eye, I breach the distance and wrap my arms around her. Liv stiffens and takes a deep breath, her nose buried in my chest. And then she shifts to settle her cheek on my chest, and I follow suit by resting mine on top of her head. Closing my eyes, I inhale the scent of her hair, holding her a little tighter.

Slowly, she lifts her arms until they circle my waist. I thought everything was perfect earlier, while we sat together eating pizza. But I was wrong. *This* is perfection.

"Liv." I sigh her name and then, to mask the longing in it, I try for levity. "I'm going to be okay. You know I'm the lovechild between Wolverine and Deadpool."

Her voice is muffled as she mutters, "Your bones aren't made of adamantium and you can't infinitely heal yourself."

"I'm strong as an ox."

"But you're not an ox."

"My point is, I'm going to be fine. So are Aran and Max. What happened to Luz…" I squeeze her tighter. "That was a freak accident. A one in a million thing."

"That's already too many chances." Her hands squeeze at the back of my shirt with more force. "Every time one of you is playing, all my head does is spin one horrible *what if* after the other."

I pull away just enough for her to look up at me. My heart pangs as she sets her chin against my chest, and I rub a hand up and down her back to distract myself from the fact that I'm yearning for her even though she's in my arms, as close as our clothes allow.

"And yet you, yourself, said I'm a really good player, right? So you should know that I'm trained on how to protect myself, on how technique can keep me safe and healthy, and that there's a whole staff that will look out for me even if I get a paper cut."

"But you wouldn't get a paper cut during a game." She gulps hard. "You could get seriously hurt instead. Did you see what happened to—"

I brush the hair off her face, leaving my fingers in her hair. "Liv, this is literally the only thing I know how to do. The only thing that makes me feel alive." Besides her, that is.

"And what if it kills you?"

"It won't." I smile at her frown.

"But what if—"

"It won't," I repeat more firmly. "We're going to manifest

good things and not tragedies, okay? Besides, what would kill me would be to not play."

More subdued, she starts pulling away from my embrace and I have no choice but to let her go. Unless I want to steer the conversation to even more dangerous waters.

"But you're going to retire eventually, what then?"

"That's hopefully twenty years down the line, after I've given it my all and squeezed as much hockey out of life as I can." I switch the water tap back on to finish the last dishes. "Besides, I could coach a little league after that. Or maybe join a team's staff."

"You could become an anchorman."

"Would you like that better?" She gives me a weird look that makes me worry I let on too much about how I want her in my life twenty years from now—and beyond. So I rephrase, "As in, would that feel safer to you?"

"Yes, a lot. I'm sure your future wife would appreciate it too."

I choke. She definitely picked up on my train of thought. "W-What?"

"Or maybe she'd be just as reckless, going by Luz and Maddie. I don't think anyone sensible would marry a hockey player." Liv makes a face. "Couldn't be me."

I hum from deep in my throat, my mind churning.

This sounds a lot like a preemptive rejection, but the fact that she's bringing up such a wild topic all on her own means she's thought about it—about being with me. Maybe marrying me.

My body vibrates with energy. Couldn't be her, she says, while revealing that she's terrified about my wellbeing. Because that's how much she cares about me.

"Come watch my games," I spew all of a sudden. "Exposure therapy, right? It's what makes people pull through their phobias."

"No, thanks. I'm really happy with my hockey phobia."

"Seriously." I huff. "The more games you watch, the more at ease you'll feel. And whenever I get hurt, you'll know exactly under what circumstances. Taking the uncertainty off it should reduce the impact, right?"

"*When*? Shouldn't it be *if*?" Her face scrunches up.

I nod. "When. It's inevitable. Max sprained his ankle pretty bad during last year's playoffs. And your brother pulled his groin two games ago. Did you freak out then?"

Liv cringes. "I literally don't need to think about my brother's groin ever."

"It's a very common injury for goalies." I roll my eyes. "And you haven't answered the question."

"Well, no."

"So what's different with me?"

She startles, her eyes widening as she looks up at me. "Um, nothing, I guess," she says with a high pitched voice.

Which means entirely the opposite.

I use all my willpower not to grin in victory. Maybe she says she doesn't want to marry me right now—and fine, we're only twenty. But she worries about me more than about her brother or brother-in-law. She may not realize what this means. That she could get to love me.

And I viscerally remember how she kissed me—like she'd been waiting her whole life for someone to make her mewl like she did. At least on a physical level, she already knows we work.

Liv's the one. She's always been the one. I was just too much of a shithead to understand that. All those athletes I dated were like me, more focused on their sports than on anyone else. And that was safe. That was the opposite of Liv, who couldn't care less about hockey or anything else that features in the Olympics. It's the one thing we've never had in common, the excuse I used all the way since high school as to why we'd never work.

When all along she's been the only person to make my heart beat as fast as hockey. And now that I get it, there's no way in hell I'm letting her slip away a second time.

Calmly, I turn back to the dishes and say, "I'll get you season tickets."

CHAPTER 20
OLIVIA

After a couple of weeks, half of my body weight is now made out of popcorn and Coke. I'm sitting in the middle of the stands of our home arena, watching the latest iteration of the Thunder Bolts vs. Bulldogs classic. This means the whole place is packed to the brim with a blue ocean, not even leaving a single row for any brave Bulldogs fans to come heckle our guys.

Yeah, *our*. By virtue of getting puppy-eyed into coming to these games by a certain captain, I'm now part of the blue ocean. Very annoying.

I jam my hand in the massive tub of popcorn and grab a handful that I can eat like a chipmunk. Mina's laughing beside me.

"Whodda thunk that the biggest hockey hater would become a puck bunny."

"I am not a puck bunny," I snap while crunching on my snack. "I'm not chasing anyone's jersey here."

"Are you sure?" She wiggles her eyebrows. "Like, if Brooklyn all of a sudden asks you out, you wouldn't?"

I cough. Balancing the tub between my knees, I pick up my

cup of soda between the heels of my hands to take a big sip. If I try to grab it with greasy fingers, it'll slip and cause a catastrophe. Like it happened last week.

"I'm here for myself, not for him," I retort, lifting my chin. "If I don't come to his home games, he'll bombard me with texts begging me to come. And I really value my peace of mind."

"I'm going to spare you the racy pun I could make there and just say this." I brace, because now that she's said it I can see how this conversation could get so much worse. "First, if you weren't hoping for something, this man wouldn't bother you at all no matter how persistent he is."

True. Then again, Brooke is my weakness. He's always been.

"Second," she continues, "Don't you find it funny how he can spot you in an arena packed with some three thousand fans?"

That lands like a record scratch. "Uh, it is weird. But I mean, since tonight was gonna be a full house, he did ask for which section we'd be sitting at. But maybe also the ticket counter passes along the info?"

"That all makes sense, which means he cares enough to check." Folding her arms, she regards me with raised eyebrows. "And otherwise, if the guy can spot you among thousands of people... what do you think it means?"

I speak with a choked voice after stuffing my face with more popcorn. "He has eyes sharper than a hawk's."

Mina snorts. "Not at all, because he wouldn't be able to pick me in the crowd. In fact, he doesn't even notice me if I'm standing next to you. What I'm saying is that the guy likes you and eventually you'll end up in his jersey."

"He doesn't." I shake my head. "Listen, Brooke isn't a shy guy. If he was into me he'd have said so."

"Didn't you say he hugged you from behind once like you

were reenacting some K-Drama? Because girl, that would so do me in."

Nearly did me in, too. I don't know how I managed to stay upright as he washed my damn hands, which is not something I ever contemplated would get my engine revving.

"The thing is," I say loudly so she can hear through the noise in the crowd. "He's always been a touchy-feely, affectionate guy. He's the male human version of a golden retriever. Always seeking attention and very fluffy."

She tips her chin down to give me an incredulous look. "You mean to tell me that guy who has an ass of steel is fluffy?"

"His hair is." Heat creeps up my neck when I remember that nothing else of his seems fluffy, at least going by his abs that look carved in marble. I'm still not over those, either.

"I'm telling you. Before the season even ends, you two are going to be swapping bodily fluids of some kind."

I punch her in the arm and she cries out in pain because she isn't made of steel.

But now my whole body's tingling and heating up, which is cooking me under my coat. I try to focus back on the game and ignoring her, but Mina keeps making random kissy sounds for the rest of the intermission.

Only when the game resumes does she let up. She's got so into the game and the culture the past two years and change, that she knows the rules probably better than me. And she's very invested in both the Bolts and the Strikes winning when she's in attendance. Especially on a certain alternate captain she has her eye on.

The relative quiet from her teasing, welcome as it is, also means I have no other means of distraction but to keep munching on bottomless popcorn, or watching the freaking game. My heart hammers harder as Brooke's line jumps back on the ice.

The way I view it, there are three types of hockey fans.

Casual ones can barely follow the puck with their eyes, that's how unused to the pace they are. Average fans can follow plays without issue, but the numbers on player's jerseys are still a bit of a blur and they rely on the screens quite a bit. Super fans could narrate the whole thing not just down to who's who in the middle of play, but their stats too.

I'm a Brooklyn Tatum super fan. He's averaging thirty one point eight minutes per game. He's only two goals away from tying with the top forward in the team. He has middle of the pack penalty minutes, which is a feat considering his line has been dubbed the top penalty killers in Division I men's hockey this year. And I could spot him in the middle of a brawl.

Which… is this the beginning of one?

I sit closer to the edge of my seat. Two Bulldogs are chirping at Brooke. I'm sure he's dishing it right back, especially the more aggressive they get. One of the Bulldogs grabs Brooke's jersey but the refs don't care because none of them have the puck right now.

"Hey, shouldn't that be a penalty?" Mina asks.

I'm about to explain when the play heats up. The crowd starts booing as a Bulldog basically carries the puck coast to coast, and it becomes pretty clear to me that what they were doing was trying to distract the Bolts' best defender. But Brooklyn's big and powerful. He breaks off their hold to intercept the opposing forward and—

"No!" I shout, jumping to my feet. I watch through a rain of popcorn how Brooke crashes on the ice. Hard.

"Those assholes!" Mina's on her feet too. "That was high sticking, refs!" She shrieks with all her lungs.

But then I see my worst nightmare coming true.

There's blood on the ice. And Brooke's not getting back on his feet.

My knees knock on the seat in front of me. I catch myself right before I buckle down. Mina's arms are suddenly around me and she's saying something. I can't hear her over the roaring in my ears. My harsh breathing. A weird whistling that doesn't stop.

"It's good, he's sitting up. Look."

Signs of life from him penetrate the fog even more than her words. Brooke pushes onto all fours. The arena's gone completely quiet as he sits back on his haunches and sheds his gloves. All I can see is the giant 3 number at his back, so I don't know how bad he's hurt. Or where.

"Please." I shake my head. "I need to see—I need to…" I don't know what. I just need to know he's not bleeding out of an eye. Or his neck.

"Okay," my friend says softly. "Let's find a better spot."

She grabs me by the hand and navigates us down the row. Some people throw insults at us and I don't care. They can say whatever. I just need to get closer, I need to…

We climb down the stairs toward the boards, and Mina makes room for us among other snooping fans. From this vantage, I can see him more from the side. But someone from the Thunder Bolts staff is in the way now. The guy is crouched before Brooke, inspecting the injury.

Biting my lip, I send my fiercest glare at the Bulldog who high sticked Brook on purpose. And while he didn't even have the puck. This should be a misconduct that gets him kicked out of the game. Or a suspension. Because it was one hundred percent targeted at the guy carrying the entire freaking team.

Someone starts clapping and I return my attention to Brooke. He's standing up now, pressing a towel to his face or neck. I can't tell. But the staff members grab him by the arms as he skates off the rink.

"I'm going."

"Where?" Mina asks me.

"To the locker room. I need to make sure he's okay."

"Um, is that even allowed?"

"No, but good luck to whoever tries to stop me," I say in a voice even I recognize sounds absolutely unhinged.

"Oh-kay. I don't shy from an adventure. Let's go."

Together, we climb back up the arena and I motion at her to follow me. Her eyes go as wide as saucers as I strut us in through the staff area. Back when my siblings went to this school, Brooke and I used to sneak in to the training area all the time. If we go through this hallway and take the first door on the right, we land in a janitorial room that connects to the hallway where the training gym is.

"How the hell do you know the way?" she asks in a low whisper, as if we were filming a spy movie.

"Luz gave us the layout so Aran, Brooke and I could sneak in to see her and Max."

"Shouldn't the staff know that their security's kinda meh?"

My face pinches. "Okay, that's a good point. We'll tell them after this."

"Yes, after."

I point left after we're through the janitorial room. Men's voices echo faintly down the hallway.

"I'll wait here," Mina says all of a sudden. I turn to her and she waves me with her hands. "Go, do your grand gesture for the man you love. I'm gonna stay back so hopefully they don't catch me and ban me from the arena."

"So you're a coward now?"

"No, I would just prefer to keep coming to games." Her expression softens. "Honestly, I wanted to make sure you don't collapse. And you look better now."

Sighing, I grab one of her hands and squeeze it. "Thanks, Mina. I know I got a bit, um, intense back there."

Her lips stretch in a concerned smile. "I get you, boo. Now go."

Taking a deep breath, I swivel around and walk over to the men's locker. My hand hesitates at the door, but what's the worst that can happen? They kick me out, but at least I'll get a glimpse of the situation.

I barge in.

Three men turn around. As they move, one of them clears the view between Brooke and I.

"Oh!"

My vision swims.

"Liv!" Brooke shoots up to his feet. "It looks much worse than it is, I promise."

"Thomas, get this woman out of here," a man barks.

"No, I—I—" But I can't get an argument out. Not when I take in the bleeding gash on Brooke's cheek, or the blood smear on his neck and on his jersey.

"Coach, she's family," Brooke says.

Barky man glares at him. "She looks a bit too young to be your mother, Tatum."

Brooklyn shakes his head, which sends crimson drops through the air. "She's the only real family I have."

"Can you at least wait outside while I stitch him up?" an older man asks me, not unkindly but impatient. And that's when I realize he's wearing surgical gloves and has a needle and thread in his hands.

With a weak voice, I say, "Shouldn't that be done in the hospital? Um, in a cleaner environment?"

"It's okay, Liv. He's the team doctor."

The man I assume is Thomas motions for me to step out. "It'll only take a moment."

Nodding, I retreat until the door shuts back in my face.

The first sniffle comes out. And then it's a full on torrential rain on my face.

"Liv?" Mina asks from behind me, and her hand starts rubbing circles on my back. "Is it really bad? Should we call nine-one-one?"

"No." I'm not a sobber, but I've always been a sniffer. I rub my forearms against my nose, smearing the sleeves of my coat with tears and who knows what else. "He's okay. They're taking good care of him. But his face… his pretty face…"

Mina's expression is set in a grimace. "Well, scars are attractive too."

I shake my head. One day she'll make a great WAG. Unlike me. I can't fathom becoming a member of the wives-and-girlfriends club when it means making light of injuries. Who wants to see their loved ones getting hurt? Not this girl.

The door opens and the two coaches walk out. The nice one says, "He's waiting for you now."

"But don't you ever barge into this area again, little miss," the head coach says, pointing at my face. "I'll get you banned, even if my best player claims you're family. You hear me?"

"Yes, sir."

He seems to like that, because all he does is glare for a second longer before walking over to the tunnel.

"I'll wait for fifteen minutes," Mina tells me. "And if you're not out by then, I'll assume you're doing naughty things and leave."

"I'm not going to—fine. Whatever." I push the door again and at the last second, I retreat and grab her in a tight hug. "Thank you."

She pats my back. "Now go get your man."

"Ugh."

When I finally walk into the locker, the doctor is almost done packing up as he speaks. "—Ibuprofen if it hurts too bad and try not to get water on it until I see you tomorrow, okay?"

"Yes, sir." Brooke speaks through a mostly closed mouth as his eyes find me. He's no longer wearing the bloody jersey. "Hey, you okay? You look like you're gonna faint."

I shake my head hard. "You're asking if I'm okay? I'm not the one who lost half his blood!"

"You sure? Because you're looking mighty pale there."

"Besides," the doctor says as he zips up his bag. "If he'd lost half his blood, he'd definitely be dead."

"Not helping," I mumble.

"Also…" The older man motions at Brooke and at me several times. "Don't you do things that could rip out his stitches."

"Thanks, Doc," Brooke says far too loud. "I really appreciate you."

He and I wince as the old man chuckles the whole way out the door.

Brooke, in his full uniform sans bucket, gloves, or jersey, leans back against the closed locker. His hair is damp and matted against his head. He looks a bit tired, probably from an adrenaline crash. It's a look I'm very familiar with myself. The doctor taped up a strip of gauze that takes up Brooke's right cheek from just under his cheekbone to his jaw.

My chin starts trembling and Brooke lifts his hand like he wants me to hold it. I cross the locker room and when I grab his hand, he pulls me to sit on his left side, where I can't see the gauze.

His head rolls over so he can look at me. "It's really not that bad. Just five little stitches. Doc just didn't have a smaller gauze."

I sag a little. "But it looked so bad."

"I'm a bleeder. Remember when I scraped my knee in the fifth grade?"

I frown, observing how his massive hand seems to swallow mine up. Lacing our fingers together hurts a bit because his are so much wider, but I wouldn't let him go for the world.

"That was your fault," I murmur absentmindedly. He'd been chasing me with a frog, which I absolutely hate. He got what was otherwise coming to him via my fist.

His thumb runs across the back of my hand. "And it didn't even leave a scar. So I'm sure this will be the same."

My strength gives out and I lean on him, my head resting on his stinky shoulder pad. "I'm sorry. I should be the one comforting you, not the other way around."

"You are." His voice is feather soft. "You braved Coach Green to make sure I was okay. That's… wow."

I bite my lip. "That—That's what friends do, right?"

For a long moment, the only sound comes from the whirring of the ventilation system. And then he sighs.

"Anyway, I'm out for the rest of the night and I was gonna watch the game from the bench, but I'm actually not feeling so hot now."

Gasping, I pull away to observe him more clearly. He doesn't look particularly pale. His eyes are bright. But you never know.

"Are you on concussion protocol? Should I find the Doc? Or—"

"Shhh. Take a deep breath for me, Olivia." I do, and he mimics me for three more breaths until he nods and continues. "No, I'm just in a lot of freaking pain right now and I want to ice my face. Can you drive me home?"

"Yes. Of course." I jump to my feet and freeze when a car doesn't magically appear before me. And now he's fighting hard against a smile. "Don't laugh, you could rip out the stitches."

"Right." Brooke braces his hands against his knees and stands up. He's normally a head and a half taller than me, but he's truly a giant while on his skates. He doesn't notice how weak in the knees I am because he turns to yank his locker open. After rummaging, he comes back with a car key. "Can you warm it up while I shower? Unless…" He lifts his eyebrows. "You wanna see me get naked?"

I whirl around. "I'll wait for you in the parking lot. And don't get your face wet."

"Sure."

I duck my head even though he can't see my blush from the back. On my way out I mutter, "Pervert."

And only when I'm sitting in his ginormous pickup that smells like his expensive cologne does my mood change. Once I deliver him to his place, I'm going to kill him for scaring me like this.

CHAPTER 21
BROOKLYN

Olivia gives me one last withering glare over her shoulder, and slams my bedroom door with so much force that it rattles the wall.

I think… she's mad at me.

A tense silence took over the entire drive from the St. Cloud home arena to the Bolt House. I could tell by the way her expression gradually hardened, how her knuckles grew whiter as she gripped the steering wheel, and by how she refused to meet my eyes, that she moved well past the worry stage and into anger.

I kept my mouth firmly shut, first, because it hurt less than opening it, and second, because anything that could spill out of it would only make her angrier. I can't help but feeling like I won the lottery seeing her react so strongly. The pain's worth it to know she cares this much.

The best I can do for now is give her some time to cool off, and then start a subtle plan of attack. But how do I get her to start seeing me as a guy and not as her friend who puked green slushie in the seventh grade?

Obviously, my brain hates me, and once I recall that

memory I wince—which makes my face really freaking hurt. I sit down on my bed and toe off my sneakers, removing my bomber jacket at the same time. It's probably going to take nothing short of a miracle for Liv to look past all my embarrassing moments.

"Yeah, I'm doomed," I utter in the quiet of my room.

Slowly, I pull the hem of my long-sleeve shirt up and take it off in a civilized way, rather than grabbing a random handful of it and pulling it off. I'm going to have to be a bit careful when doing anything for a while, now that I have three-inch slice on my cheek.

I can't believe I convinced Liv to come watch my games and got injured basically right away. It's pretty insignificant and if it hadn't been because she was so distraught, I'd have stayed to watch the rest of the game and driven myself home.

She's never going to forgive me for this, though. And that's going to make it that much harder to make her fall for me, no matter how much she cares about me.

"Stop. You're not made for thinking, Brooklyn," I tell myself as I remove my socks and ball them up with the rest of my clothes. I toss them clear across the room and they land in a haphazard heap on my desk chair. "See? You're a man of action. You'll act when the time's right."

Nodding, I recalibrate myself. Give Liv time and space to cool off. Act like nothing's amiss. Push the agenda that scars are sexy. And for now, maybe take a nap. That's as far as my pea brain can think of. The big stuff will have to happen on the fly.

Getting back up, I hook my thumbs around the waistband of my joggers and pull them down before—

The door opens.

My eyes fly up. Liv stands on the threshold holding up a bag of frozen peas. Her eyes lower. I check myself just in case I forgot to put on any underwear after showering. But no, there's the black boxer briefs. Yet, there she is, soaking every inch of my bare skin up with her eyes. She seems particularly into my thighs.

Interesting. Maybe this won't be as difficult as I feared.

"Are you gonna keep staring?" I bite my lip so I don't smile. "Or should I just take it all off?"

Her brown eyes snap back up to mine, her glare intensifying. "Why the hell are you undressing?"

"I thought you were on your way home."

"No, I was trying to get fresh ice for your face but your fridge is disgusting." A crease forms between her eyebrows the more she talks. "Well, aren't you going to dress back up?"

If all she needs is a modest amount of nudity to get affected, I'm not going to fold so easily. All I do is pull my joggers back up. Surely she can deal with a naked torso and bare feet, right?

I lower myself back to sit on my bed and paraphrase her question. "Well, aren't you coming in?" As I lean back with my hands on the mattress, her eyes seem to fixate on my shoulders.

How funny, most girls would lose their marbles at my abs. I wonder if they lost their impact because she already saw them at the library.

Maybe she's finally realized that I'm teasing her because her eyes narrow. Liv pushes the door shut with her elbow and activates her feet. My heart pounds faster with every step she takes, even though I know she's not going to suddenly sit on my lap and eat my face. She wouldn't even do that if I wasn't injured. To her, I'm still her annoying guy friend.

Her hand rises abruptly and I flinch at the cold against my face. "Here, hold this so I can call an Uber."

Instead of doing as told, I keep her hand firmly in place. I tilt my head back to look up at her, into her eyes. "Stay a bit longer."

Liv's quiet as she observes me, her eyes roaming around my

face as if searching for something. But just when I expect her to argue back that she has to go or something, she instead runs the fingers of her free hand through my damp hair. "Damn puppy eyes of yours. You could rob a bank with those."

Would she get upset if she found out I'm trying to rob her heart?

Well, is it really robbery if I give her mine in return?

Clearing my throat, I pull her hand away from the thawing bag of peas and maneuver back until I lay down on my bed, my head on the pillow closest to the wall. Then I pat the empty expanse beside me and crank up the sad, watery puppy eyes that disarm her.

"Ugh." She huffs, but she unzips her leather jacket and retraces a few steps to hang it on the backrest of my busy desk chair. I swallow hard as her knee sinks into the mattress, then the other. My bed is a king size for tall people, which means she has to crawl on all fours for a brief stretch to get to the other pillow.

All throughout, my ever helpful brain supplies a fantasy of Liv doing precisely that, but with a lot less clothes.

I smack the pea bag on my face hard enough to hurt. At least it snaps me out of it before I can start openly salivating at her.

We lay on our backs, staring at the ceiling for a long moment. It's not what I wish we were doing, but at least she's still here. Her warmth seeps through my arm and I know if I stretch my hand just a bit, maybe even my pinky, I'd touch her hand.

I'm debating it when she says, "Does it hurt a lot?"

If I say yes, would she use it as an excuse to fight or would it make her stay longer?

"It hurts a lot less with you here."

There's rustling as she shifts on her side to face me. I'm happy to do the same and turn to my left, folding my left arm under my head. I balance the pea bag on my face as I watch her. She has both hands tucked under her head in a kind of praying position. A few strands of her hair have fallen over her face and they must be tickling her. With my right hand, I brush them away and she stays very still through the motion.

Whatever I thought she might say after that, isn't what actually comes out of her mouth. "I really think you should put on a shirt."

"Is this bothering you?" I ask in a droll.

"No," she says in a calm and level-headed way that annoys me.

"So what, is it my body odor?"

"No, you smell fine." Fine? *Fine?* I smell damn amazing after a shower. Is this woman made of steel? I guess that must be it, because she shrugs. "You're going to get cold."

"Trust me, I run hot. I normally sleep naked."

Liv blinks hard and avoids my eyes. "Um, but I mean, you have the frozen bag on your face and your hair is still wet so…"

I take a deep breath, trying to calm down before she can hear the wild thumping in my chest. The problem is that it brings the warm vanilla scent that clings to her and inundates my lungs. I blame the lack of oxygen on what I do next.

Lifting myself up for a moment, I slide my left arm under her head until I replace her pillow with my shoulder. The bag of peas slides off my face and back, where it's going to stay forgotten now. With my right hand, I pull her against me by her waist. Her hands form a barrier against my chest and they feel like ice on my skin, either from the frozen peas or because she's the one who was cold.

"See? I'm plenty warm."

"Ah, yeah. I see."

I smile into her hair, not even caring that it feels like a knife is stabbing my face. My arm under her neck curls up to hug her shoulders and with my other hand, I rub lazy circles on her back. A shudder racks her body and I hum from deep in my throat. "Looks like you're the one who was cold." Or something else.

"It's an uncharacteristically cold October," she says with a serious voice. "Lucky for me you're a furnace, huh?"

"Very lucky," I say into her hair, my voice surprisingly drowsy.

"You must be tired," she says, her breath fanning against my neck, soft as a feather.

"Hmm." I'm not tired, I'm content. I close my eyes anyway, just trying to savor this moment. Liv doesn't speak again, and after a moment I feel her body relax against mine. That's the true bliss, knowing she's comfortable with me.

Our breathing evens with every passing second, and next thing I'm really asleep.

*

I try to shift to my other side, but a weight prevents it. And the weight is warm, too. And it smells delicious, like a dessert I want to run my tongue over.

My eyes pop open. It takes a moment for them to adjust to the dim light of my bedside table. I must've left it on overnight. Then I lift my head from the pillow, but all I can see is a head of dark hair. Laying my head back down, I blink up at the ceiling.

It's Liv. She's sprawled over me like she owns me.

The most shocking part is how she's not waking up, even though she can probably feel the furious beating of my pulse against her face, which is buried against my neck. I can feel softness of her chest pressed up against mine. Worse, her thighs straddle my left one. And if that wasn't all, my right hand found its way under her sweater and yep, her skin is so much softer. The softest. So warm. My fingers twitch and the minuscule friction sets me on fire.

I'm breathing fast. Heat travels down my body, focusing on every contact surface. Especially my freaking thigh, all snug against her as if it had any right. I need to—she can't wake up to this. I have to make this right.

Gritting my teeth like I'm bench pressing twice my body weight, I lift my hand away from her bare back. Liv gives out a little moan and I squeeze my eyes tight. Slowly, I continue removing my right arm from around her.

"No." The word comes out from her throat like a whine, and I freeze. "Don't leave me."

It takes me a moment to realize she's talking in her sleep. And another moment to figure out it's probably not me she's talking about. After all, I've never left her. She's the one who left me.

So, is she dreaming about her ex, whatshisface?

A pained groan lodges in my throat. I'm such an asshole. Who cares if I want her now, when she's still dealing with her feelings for her ex?

Sighing, I grab her shoulder to shake her awake—and my phone starts going off at the same time.

Liv jolts. She pushes slightly against my chest, but instead of jumping the hell away like I thought she would, her nose brushes against my jaw as she looks up.

We blink at each other. My phone still rings on the nightstand. Realization about what kind of position we're in falls on her slowly, her lips parting to form a small circle.

My voice is raspy as I mumble, "Aren't you getting off me?"

But it's like her brain's short-circuiting because all she can manage to say is, "I—I—"

And I guess mine does too, because all I can think about is: she's not running away. She knows exactly what all is pressed against her and she's not jumping away like I'm burning her.

Licking my lips, I hold the back of her head with one hand, and her back with the other. Her breath hitches as I roll us over. It's not my fault her thighs ended up spread apart, or that it's so easy to kneel between them and stretch over her to grab my phone. Or that it puts us right where I want us to be, our hips against each other, her thighs around my hips, and when I look down at her I could kiss her so easily.

But Liv doesn't seem to be breathing. Either I'm too heavy or she's in shock. So this is enough teasing for today.

I push up onto my hands and lean back on my haunches. While I glance at my phone screen, I feel the mattress shift with Liv sitting back up. I will murder Dane later but for now I cancel his call. It's two in the morning and I could've enjoyed sleeping with Liv for three more hours if it hadn't been for him.

"Sorry about that." I murmur, watching her fold her leg so she can scoot over to the edge of the mattress. "It's just Dane, but we can—" My phone starts going off again.

Liv clears her throat, her back to me as she lowers the sweater that had ridden up. "It's okay. Maybe pick up the call."

She sounds normal. Too normal.

I narrow my eyes as I watch her head over to my desk chair, but pick up Dane's call. "What?"

"Dude, you finally give signs of life. We were worried."

"I'm okay, just taking a nap." Liv's eyes flash to me for a second as she shrugs her jacket on. "Let's talk later," I say, hanging up before he can get another word in. Jumping from my bed, I grab Liv's arm before she makes it to the door. "Hey, let me get dressed and I'll take you home."

"It's okay, I can just grab an Uber—"

"Liv, please." I sigh heavily. "It's the least I could do, okay? Let me."

"Okay," she whispers, folding her arms but keeping her eyes downcast to the side. Like she's embarrassed.

Shit. I pushed her too hard.

I make record time of putting my socks and sneakers back on, and shrug on my shirt fast enough that it catches on the bandage stuck to my cheek and makes me wince. I grab the jacket, my phone and keys, and we walk out of my room in silence. This one's worse than during the drive.

Should I apologize? But she's the one who was all over me. I should apologize anyway. I could've just crawled over her to get my phone.

"Liv, I'm—"

"Sorry," she says before I finish. "I didn't meant to, like, grope you in your sleep."

I rub the back of my head. "If anyone should be apologizing, it should be me," I say as we walk down the stairs with her leading the way. "I'm the one who made you stay and fell asleep all over you and I'm sure you could, uh, feel stuff." I don't even have to say what stuff.

The fact is that I went to sleep with her in my arms, and she was in that same spot in my dreams. The other fact is that I'm a healthy, red blooded male. Things happen. Things that are going wild because of her.

She keeps her attention forward, back to me, and I can't take the awkwardness anymore. "Listen—" But before I fess up about *things*, we pass the kitchen and two people there freeze me in my steps.

"Well, well," Dane says, his mouth curling into a smirk as he eyes Liv and I. "Looks like we had nothing to worry about. Right, Jamie?"

The other stooge looks equally smug. "Yep, seems like someone kissed the poor, injured guy better."

"You two," I say, my voice changing drastically. "One more word out of your yaps, and I'll feed you your own teeth."

Jamie covers his mouth but his eyes are all shiny like he wants to laugh.

Meanwhile, Liv gives me a deadpan look over her shoulder. "Wow, they're just like you."

"Excuse me, I'm their captain and therefore so much more mature."

"He's lying to you. It takes the whole team to gather a single braincell." Dane pushes off from the counter while blowing a raspberry. He offers his hand to Liv, saying, "I'm Dane Bloom, alternate captain."

"Olivia Rodriguez. If you say one single joke about my name I will make you eat your own teeth." She smiles as she shakes Dane's hand. My chest squeezes with something I have no right feeling. Liv's free to smile at whomever.

"Oh." Dane turns raised eyebrows to me. "So this is the infamous childhood best friend?"

"You talked about me?" She lifts an eyebrow at me.

I stuff my hands in my joggers' pockets and produce my car key. "We should go. It's pretty late."

"Wait, I'm Jamie Schwarz, the other alternate." He also shakes Liv's hand. "Glad to know you're real. I thought blondie was making you up every time he talked about you."

Liv snorts.

I grab his wrist hard and yank his hold on her loose. With one last glare, I steer Liv away by her shoulder. There are snickers behind us as we walk out of the Bolt House and I'm surprised Liv's not giving me heaps of shit for that little interaction.

The temperature outside has dipped a lot since earlier. Liv shivers on our way to where she parked my Gladiator, and I put my jacket on her shoulders. She snuggles into it the whole way over to her apartment.

Either because it's late, or because she's tired, we don't talk much until I leave her at her front door.

"Thanks." She yawns as she slides my jacket off and returns it.

"Buenas noches," I say with my heavy gringo accent, but it garners a small smile from her. "See you in Spanish on Monday?"

Liv nods. "Yep. Drive safe."

I wait until she opens her apartment door and slips inside to put on my jacket. It smells a little like her now. Which means my pillow must also carry her scent.

There's no way I can sleep now. My body's still burning with all sorts of things, but I'll focus on the safest of the red hot ones for now.

When I barge back into the house, I find my two alternates still lounging in the kitchen while they tuck into heaping sandwich plates. My stomach gurgles, but before that I have a different mission.

"Hey, assholes," I say as a greeting. "Let's be a hundred percent clear about something."

"Wha?" Dane asks with his mouth full.

I point at the door as if Liv was there. "That I have no idea what I'm doing but I'm really, desperately into my best friend, and your teasing doesn't help me at all." My anger deflates at admitting the truth, and I sit on a barstool to prop my elbows on the massive kitchen island, putting my forehead on my hands.

"Wait, do you have a crush on me?" Dane gasps in an exaggerated manner. He gets his karma when he starts choking on his food.

"What should I do?" I ask with a groan.

"Here, bro." Jamie passes Dane a glass of milk. To me, he asks, "What do you mean?"

"I can't just spring up feelings on her."

"Feelings?" Dane lowers the borrowed glass of milk. "So like, not lust. *Feelings*."

"*Feelings*," I repeat in a dark tone of voice. "And everything else too."

"As in, you want to change her status from friend to girlfriend?"

"From *best* friend to girlfriend, to be more accurate," I say just to be a little shit. "Which normally might be hard, but she just started giving me the time of day again."

"I don't know, man." Jamie pauses to bite into his sandwich. "The whole tale about how she bypassed Coach Green to see you after the penalty already spread like fire through the team. We all thought it was either a very enthusiastic puck bunny, or your girlfriend."

"Don't panic," Dane says. "That conversation was like ten minutes long tops. Everyone's still at O'Malley's either trying to get plastered, or laid, or both."

"Good to know the team's worried about me."

"Please, we know you're built like a damn ox. We thought the puck bunny would give you all the comfort you needed."

"And that's why you said that flaming piece of garbage to Liv when you saw us, I see." I lift a hand toward him, opening it and closing it.

Dane looks at it warily. "What does that mean?"

My response is, "You either come here so I can punch you in the throat, or you give me the rest of your food. Choose."

He pushes his plate over to me. Wise man. "The point is," Dane continues saying as he watches me eat his other sandwich. "I don't think you need to work very hard to get with her. Just don't treat her like you used to, or like she's any of us, and you're golden."

Jamie nods. "Yeah, man. Open a few doors for her. Carry her stuff. Be nice or something. Girls like that."

I snort and talk while chewing. "I don't treat her like I treat you. I…" But my voice trails off.

A massive cringe shrinks me to half my size. I've been known to put Liv in headlocks, which isn't something I've ever done to a girlfriend. And Jamie's right, the physical contact with a girlfriend is so different. Softer. Lingering. Hotter. Much more intentional.

"That's right." Dane smirks as he watches the realization slam me like a puck to the face. "Treat her like a girlfriend and she'll want to become one."

See? I really am a man of action—and there are plenty of actions I can take with this knowledge. Starting Monday in Spanish.

CHAPTER 22
OLIVIA

"I think if we say it like that, it sounds too colloquial. Right, Liv?" Brooke explains from so close, it almost feels like he's speaking over my shoulder. I swallow hard, keeping my eyes on the screen of my laptop on the table.

Ugh. Why is he turning the attention on me?

I try to scoot to the edge of my seat but it doesn't matter, he still has his left arm on the back of my chair. His thigh's still glued to mine. And none of this is going unnoticed to Alyssa and Emily, who have been giving me funny eyes ever since we sat down at this table at Thundercloud, the school's cafe.

I deeply regret choosing this venue over the library. We'd have had so much more space there. More importantly, I wouldn't be struggling so hard to contain how much he's affecting me. Why does he have to smell so good? I know he wears some fancy cologne and aftershave, but the end result of them on his clean skin is too much for anyone whose orientation is hot hockey players. It almost makes me miss the stink of his pads because at least that keeps me level headed—if not horrified. And like, I'm legit angry every time the smell of coffee or freshly baked muffins compete for my nose's attention.

But my biggest complaint is that he's so damn warm. I wish I could just lean into his side and snuggle like we did on his bed. Especially now that I know how, even though he's hard like granite all over, he can still mold himself around me in a way that feels so soft. Safe. Comfortable. If only for the little issue where he makes my hormones rage like magma in an active volcano.

Alyssa lifts her eyebrows in an indiscreet way. "Olivia?"

I clear my throat so loud that the people in the next table look at me. Face warming up, I redirect my attention back to the assignment. "I think we can continue using tú instead of usted. It's supposed to be a conversation among friends, you know?"

"Right, *friends*." Alyssa nods like a bobble head, slowly turning to her friend who is barely containing laughter.

"Anyway, let's make a pause here." I shut down my laptop and push my chair back with more force than necessary. It forces Brooke to drop his arm. "I don't know about you all, but I'm starving."

"Oh, me too," Brooke agrees, and the two perverts across the table are now on a serious struggle to hold back their laughter.

I shake my fist at them while Brooklyn rises from his chair, his back slightly turned to us.

"I'll get in line," he says to us. "Take your time, ladies."

"Sure, thanks." Alyssa smiles sweetly at him, but when he's out of earshot she whispers, "Okay now you have to admit that something's definitely going on between you guys."

"Nothing is going on, and if you keep making faces at me I will do you bodily harm."

Emily pats her friend's shoulder. "Easy, girl. I think these two are just delusional."

"What?" I scrunch up my face.

"Yeah, you guys are so in love with each other, it almost hurts to watch." Alyssa lifts her hands, palms up. "So, either I tease you a little or I start seeing green. You'll just have to put up with it, I'm afraid."

"I can't wait for this presentation to be over," I murmur, acid dripping from my voice. Their chuckles follow as I weave around the packed tables in the cafe. Brooklyn's by far the tallest person in line to order, and as he scans the menu overhead, he seems largely unaware of all the looks he's getting.

Some are nice, like the guys over by the window who are probably debating whether to ask for Brooke's autograph. He's, after all, the next highest draft this campus has produced after my brother-in-law.

Other forms of attention aren't quite as nice—to me, at least. Like the girls two tables over from the line who are undressing him with their eyes. There's one in particular who sits at an angle Brooke would be able to see, since he's still pretty far back in the line. She's biting her lip in that way I know drives guys wild. And if that wasn't enough, she's unzipping her hoodie slowly and I don't think she's wearing a shirt underneath.

But Brooke nods to himself like he's just decided what to order, and he turns from the menu to me. His eyes find mine, them a south pole magnet and mine a north one. Dude's completely oblivious to the disappointed girl behind him.

"He literally has eyes only for you," one of our Spanish group mates says behind me.

I huff. "Oh, stuff it."

There's a lot less bite in my words than before. This is the kind of situation that for years lifted up my hopes until they soared like a balloon in the sky, but something would always deflate it and I'd come crashing back down to earth. After so many violent crashes, I just can't genuinely tell if this is a me-thing or if Emily and Alyssa are right—if Brooke is starting to look at me like something other than his former bestie.

"No, *you* stuff it." Alyssa laughs. "And you know exactly what and where—ow! Did you just pinch me?"

I retrieve my pincer hand. "Yes, and I only regret not doing it earlier."

"What was that about?" Brooke asks as we join him in line. A random dude tries to complain, thinking we're cutting line before him, but when he sees who he'd have to take his complaint against—a bigass hockey player—the guy clams up and falls back behind us.

Meanwhile, blimbo here doesn't notice anything. How he manages to have almost perfect view of the ice when he's playing is a mystery. I shake my head.

"Nothing," I respond. "What are you getting?"

"The egg sandwich." As the three of us blink up at him, he grins. "Sandwiches. I know it's tiny so I usually order six."

Alyssa gives me a look. "Suddenly, I have a different type of jealousy."

"Yeah, I also wish I could eat that much," Emily says.

This is when Brooke decides to be sharp, because he tilts his head and asks, "A different type?"

"What are you guys getting?" I ask the other two girls, loudly.

Emily knows exactly what I'm doing but she's the nicer one of the bunch. "I think I'll go for the breakfast bagel."

"Avocado toast for me." Alyssa tosses her brown hair over her shoulder.

Brooke nudges my side with his elbow. "You, Liv?"

"I'll get the garden salad," I mumble.

"But it has walnuts."

I lift my eyes to his. Of course he knows I'm allergic to walnuts and like half of the other edible foods on this planet.

But did he scan the whole menu and memorized the items that have any of my allergens, or what?

Please, someone tell his boy that he doesn't need to do anything further to make me love him. I'm already too far gone.

"I—yes. I always ask them not to put them in."

Brooke nods and rejoins the conversation with our study partners. The two girls mustn't have noticed the significance of his question, or otherwise they'd be teasing me again.

I hang back a little as they chat about the presentation we're assembling, occasionally giving my input when they ask for it. None of us is a native speaker, but Brooke always defaults to me because he knows I grew up in a Spanish speaking household and can understand it, even though he took more Spanish lessons in high school than I did. That's been our dynamic since we were kids; Brooke's always been happy to let me lead whatever topic I'm passionate about, even if he has comparable or more knowledge about it.

He's such damn good person. How could I have ever painted him as the villain a year and a half ago? Was I really that in my feels that I felt justified in treating him like crap?

My shoulders droop with a deep, sad sigh. I don't deserve this second chance at his friendship, and I have zero right to crave more.

Suddenly, Brooke angles a bit and gently pushes me forward with a hand at the small of my back. A shiver raises goosebumps all across my skin, and I pretend like I'm just cold by burrowing deeper into my enormous Linkin Park hoodie.

The gentle push brings me up to the counter, and an annoyed girl stares at me from behind it. "What are you ordering?"

Yikes. If they had a chill pill in their menu, I'd order it to give it back to her.

"The garden salad, please. No nuts."

She punches the order in the iPad, and then turns a much nicer expression to the guy behind me. "And you, captain?"

Oh. She knows who he is. And if she hates me on sight, she must think Brooke and I have something going on because of how close he's standing. I take a long step aside that brings me up against Alyssa and Emily. Brooke gives me a weird look before placing his order.

When I turn, I find the two girls wiggling their eyebrows. "Not a word."

One of them zips up her lips. The good thing is that the Thundercloud is pretty fast, and we don't have to wait long for our food. It stems off the worry that these two will spill something incriminatory in front of Brooke. Soon, we're back at our table and I'm pleased, because not only I'll finally get some food, but everyone's mouths will be too busy to speak.

Grunting, I give a second try of popping open my salad. The lid's stuck with industrial grade strength because even though I strain my muscles, I can't get it to budge.

"Gimme," Brooke says, his cheeks swollen with food. He takes the container from my hands and anyone would think his gigantic paws would be clumsy. But no, he tucks his fingers under the lid easy enough and pulls. It opens with a loud pop of air releasing. Nothing spills and he looks too proud of himself. "Here," he says, giving me a wide smile. The kind that stops traffic and makes people secretly take pics of him—yep, like zipper girl is doing from her table right now.

"Um, thanks." I slide lower in my seat.

I need to find a way for him to stop beaming at me that way, or he's going to fulminate me. And everyone around us, if I can go by the way Alyssa looks at him like he's a dream.

At least I manage to rip the balsamic vinaigrette packet open on my own. But just as I'm about to sink my fork into the salad, Brooklyn grabs my wrist and stops me.

"Wha—"

The question dies on my lips. His face has transformed into an expression he only shows during games against Bulldogs. Pure anger.

I watch, frozen in my seat, as he snatches my salad and jumps back to his feet. Our group mates look just as confused. Pushing my chair back, I follow as Brooke cuts the line and squares up against the cashier who has the hots for him.

"No nuts, she said." Brooke's voice is deep and growly. My entire body tenses.

When I reach them, the girl is blinking fast and has grown pale. "Um, what?"

The vicinity quiets down. Whole tables and a line of people cease their activity to listen in on what's got the Thunder Bolts' captain's panties in a twist, including me.

Brooke points at me and then the salad. "She said no nuts, but there are nuts here. Ever stopped to think why someone might request no nuts?" He leans closer to her. "Because they could be deathly allergic. You could've killed her."

My entire face prickles at the attention, especially my eyes. I hook my arm around Brooke's and pull with all my might. "Brookie, it's okay. Nothing happened."

"But it could have!" He turns over his shoulder, agony in the way his forehead wrinkles. "You could've ended up at the hospital—again! And I... I..." He shakes his head and swallows hard.

"I could make a new salad?" the girl offers with a small voice.

"No! You should apolo—"

"Brooke, come with me." My voice is hard enough that it snaps him out of the haze. I drag him outside of the Thundercloud amid stares and whispers. We're only a few steps away when I realize I'm pulling him by the hand, our fingers interlocked as if they had any right to be. But changing my hold would waste precious time where I need to just lead him away.

Finally, I stop under the shade of a tree with leaves the color of fire. They almost twinkle against the cold breeze, a happy little sound at odds with the expression on his face. Brooklyn looks like someone died. His eyes are glazed over, and I just know he's imagining a horrible worst case scenario that hasn't happened, since I'm still obviously breathing.

I let go of his hand. When that's not enough to awaken him, I step closer until I crash against his chest and squeeze my arms tight around his waist.

Finally, he sighs against my hair and curls himself forward. His arms wrap around me with urgency, like I'm a slippery balloon trying to escape between them. "Sorry I lost my shit back there."

"Thank you for looking out for me," I mumble against his chest.

"Always." If anything, he holds me tighter.

We stay like that, just listening to the leaves dance in the wind, wrapped in a cocoon of each other's heat, feeling each other's heartbeat. I was embarrassed before, but now I'm thankful that the scare brought us this moment.

And it's only a moment, because it ends too soon when another voice rings beside us.

"What do we have here?"

I stiffen. Unfortunately, that makes Brooke pull away fast.

My ex stands a few paces away, still on the pedestrian path that curves around Thundercloud's building. He's smirking, arms folded like he has permission to show his face in front of me.

"Are you two together now?" he asks, looking at Brooke and I. "I mean, I always knew there was something weird going on between you. You only started paying attention to me when he disappeared from your life, you know?"

I suck in air. That's not a truth I wanted revealed, *ever*.

Through gritted teeth, Brooke mutters, "Get lost before I rearrange your face, you little shit."

Trent puts an offended hand on his chest. "Aren't you a student athlete? You'll lose your scholarship if you act violently."

"Wanna test that *if?*" Brooke cracks his knuckles.

"Whatever, good riddance." Trent makes a sardonic expression. "Just remember, Liv. Rebounds don't work. I'm on my third already, so I speak from experience."

I know he's saying all this to see if it affects me. Yet I couldn't care less about how many people he dates or sleeps with.

What I can't let him know is that the thought of Brooke being a rebound is disconcerting. Or rather, that trying something more with him and having it fail is a possibility… That's what freaks me out about Trench Coat's implications.

I take a step forward. And another. I raise my hand sharply and my ex flinches. Now that I know his body remembers, I give him a feral grin. "Go before *I* punch you. Again."

"Again?" Brooke asks behind me, amusement in his voice.

Trent spits on the ground—a habit I always hated—and he turns away. "Oh, and I hope you liked the package," I say to his retreating back. It makes him accelerate the pace.

Brooke's eyes gleam when I face him again. "What package?"

"I may have returned a defaced hoodie to him via post."

His grin stretches so wide, I know he's forgotten the bad feelings lingering from the earlier incident. "That's my girl."

If only.

I clear my throat. "Can we go back to the cafe and you won't behave like a Neanderthal anymore?"

Brooke sticks out his hand. When I do nothing but stare at it, he opens and closes his fingers around air. Slowly, I slide my hand to his and he tugs it into the pocket of his hoodie. With a bright voice, he says, "Nope. I'm never going to stop being a caveman about you."

I have to keep my head down on the way back so he doesn't see how hard I'm grinning.

CHAPTER 23
BROOKLYN

Thank goodness I have an uncanny talent for switching my brain off when I'm not playing hockey. Otherwise, I'd go full caveman in front of the entire classroom.

The thing is, Olivia looks steaming freaking hot today. She's in a white, long-sleeved blouse that doesn't even have a big cleavage and isn't particularly clingy, and the world's most boring, wide-legged black trousers. But the whole thing emphasizes her unreal hourglass shape, and more than one guy is noticing. I know exactly what the asshole in the front row is thinking by the areas where his eyes seem to focus.

Somehow, I manage to parrot my lines convincingly enough. "Espero comenzar mi carrera en la NHL dentro de dos años," I say, forcing my eyes to stay on one of our group partners.

She nods as if all of this was brand new information. "Suena muy interesante. ¿Cuál es la parte que más te emociona de convertirte en un jugador profesional?" She trips on the last few words, just like I want to trip that dipshit over there who's salivating over Liv's ass.

Yeah, she has a superb ass. But it's not his to look at.

Brain off, autopilot on, I tell myself.

Releasing a deep breath, I say, "Lo que más me emociona es formar parte del mismo equipo con mi amiga, Olivia."

Very rehearsed, the other group mate asks, "¿Cómo es eso posible?"

"Es que mi sueño es ser la nutricionista de su equipo," says Liv. Her voice transforms when she speaks the language of her parents. It seems a little deeper, smoother. I wonder what it sounds like when she uses it to say dirty things, and not lies about how she dreams about being my team's nutritionist just so we could have a conversation pinging back and forth among the four of us.

Damn it, if I catch one more horny animal looking at her like she's meat, I'm going to flip a switch back on.

It was so much easier back in high school. None of the guys dared to even look her way because they knew I was her best friend. If they tried anything funny, I had the body mass and disposition to turn their faces into pulp. But here? I have no stake on her. I'm just a classmate. And Trent's little comment was kind of true. I have to stay in perfect behavior so I don't jeopardize my path to the pros. Being drafted doesn't mean I'm set.

"Thank you, group three," the lecturer says once we've finally finished the whole spiel. "Up next—"

I stop listening after that. I blame my turned off brain for putting my hand on the small of Liv's back as we make our way back up to our seats. She gives me a puzzled look over her shoulder, but I don't drop my hand until we sit back down. The biggest offender, all the way down at the front, makes sure to give me a glare loaded with screw-you energy before turning back out front.

"It's over." Liv sighs and sags on her seat.

I nudge her shoulder with mine. "You were amazing, Miss Spanish-is-actually-not-my-mother-tongue."

She snorts and whispers back. "Thanks, Mr. I-studied-more-Spanish-than-the-one-who-is-supposed-to-be-a-native-speaker."

"Wow, I have such a long name."

The upwards curl of her lips wedges itself right in between my ribs, until it finds the fleshy part of my heart that I normally only exercise on the ice.

I finally understand how I've been lying to myself all along. My heart was only dormant because I just didn't understand who it belonged to.

Now, how do I tell her this in a way that won't send her packing?

I drum my fingers on the table as I watch her profile. Unlike me, she's trying to pay attention to the next group. They could be talking about how their dream is turning lead into gold and leaves into money, but I couldn't care less. I'm trying to determine if Liv's lips are a few shades darker because she bit them or because of lipstick.

"Did you put on makeup today?" I ask her with my lowest voice. She's right beside me, our legs flush together, so she hears me clearly.

She turns to me. "Yeah. Why?"

"Lipstick too?"

"Yes?"

Ah, so that means I can't kiss her right this second. Even though that's too bad, because her lips look so thick and soft.

"Hmm, looks good. But you always look good anyway."

My attention shifts down as her throat works with a heavy swallow. Liv turns back to the front. "Thanks, I think so too," she returns all sassy.

I bite my lip. Brain's still off, though, because I twist myself enough to release my arm and put it on the back of her seat. Now even closer, I whisper into her ear, "I'm curious about something. Are you the kind of girl who puts on her makeup before or after her clothes?"

Her breath hitches. The skin of her neck breaks into goosebumps right where my breath hits it.

Slowly, Liv turns to me. Our noses brush and now I'm the one catching my breath as she lifts her eyes to mine. "Before," is all she says. Then she leans all the way away, resting her elbows on the table to prop herself forward like she's riveted by the presentation.

My jaw hangs.

It's been almost three weeks since the accident at the Bulldog's game, which means I have a scab that now allows me to have facial expressions again. Whole lot of good it's doing to me, when now I can picture Liv in her underwear as she leans closer to a mirror to put on her makeup. Or naked. What if that's how she does it?

My knee bumps hard under the table. Heads turn my way and I hide half of my face behind my hand. And it's a good thing, because with how hot my cheeks are, I know I'm red like a stoplight. It's the curse of being such a blondie.

That's when I catch our two other group mates on Liv's other side, watching me like they're this close to cackling like hyenas. Even if they didn't hear the exchange clearly, there's no doubt they know my mind is firmly in the gutter.

That's where it stays the rest of the class until at the end, the lecturer drops a bomb. "Now, for the second half of the semester we're going to work on a similar exercise. For that, you're going to form new groups."

Liv and I exchange a glance. I'm glad she's as distraught as I am.

"Pairs, actually," the lecturer continues saying, "so that this time the conversations are deeper."

Someone at the front raises a hand. "Question. Can it be with someone from the previous group?"

The lecturer sighs, either tired or bored out of his mind. "Sure. But I have the scripts from today's presentations, so if you talk about the same topics, I'll flunk you."

Some guy two rows under ours turns to Liv. Before he can open his pie hole, I slide my arm around her shoulders. "Tag, you're it."

Liv's eyebrows arch in a haughty way. "Fine, at least I know you're not a slacker."

"So you guys will pair up?" Emily asks us, blinking in a weird way. Is she okay?

"Um, yeah. I guess." Liv's voice darkens.

"Good luck, then." Alyssa winks at Liv, and this makes her grow stiff as a plank.

"What's that about?" I ask.

Liv swivels a murderous look at me. "Nothing. Can you get your tree trunk of an arm off my chair?"

"But it's more comfortable this way."

Pursing her lips, she reaches over behind her and lifts my arm up. I let her, but then leave my arm all over her space on purpose. When class ends, she jumps to her feet in an attempt to leave faster. Except our now former group mates take their sweet ass time, and I have no motivation to get out of Liv's way.

I chuckle behind her after we've left the classroom and she's still stomping her feet. "What's got you hot and bothered, Aceituna?"

She grinds to a halt. "I am not hot. In case your eyes are failing you, I'm wrapped up from head to toe and I'm breathing little clouds." This is true, basically only the top of her head pokes over a thick black scarf.

I jam my hands in the pockets of the Tom Ford coat I paired with my suit for today's presentation. "Fine, why are you so annoyed, then?"

"Because—" She stops herself by gritting her teeth. "Nothing."

"Would you look at that? I can feel my curiosity growing by the second."

Liv resumes walking. The strap of her bag slides down her shoulder, but she's wearing so many thick layers that she can't pull it up on her own. I push her struggling hand away and lift the strap back to her shoulder. I catch myself right before leaning down to kiss the wrinkle off her forehead.

"Thanks... giving," I blurt out instead, grasping at straws.

"What about it?"

"Bye guys!" The girls who were our group mates walk around us with their third friend. I wave at them and as they turn away, I let that same hand travel through my hair.

Liv's attention is pulled by a lock of hair that's now fallen on my forehead, and I leave it there. "So, I was wondering what you're doing this Thanksgiving." I was wondering no such thing, but now I'm thankful for my brain coming up with that random topic change because I legitimately want to know.

"Well, the usual. The prodigal daughter and son are coming home with their spouses, so it's going to be the same big mess of every year." She looks down at the opening between my coat. "And you?"

"The usual too. A miserable dinner at my father's."

Liv bites that lower lip I desperately wish to be biting for her instead. "Would you... like to come over? I mean, since we're on speaking terms now, and all."

My eyebrows rise. "You mean, since we have resumed our best-friendship?"

"Sure."

My cheek twitches. Is this a good thing? Being her best friend again? Or is this a deeper level in the friendzone?

But she wouldn't have admitted to putting on her makeup

while semi- or fully-naked before, so I'm confused. Like, any allusion to nudity was strictly off bounds before the Dark Age.

The only thing I know for sure, is that I can't be apart from her for a second longer. The rest I'll have to take as it comes. Thus, I say, "Yes, I'd love to come over again."

Her expression softens. "For old time's sake, right?"

No, for new time's sake. Hopefully, by next year's Thanksgiving I won't be her best friend, but her boyfriend.

CHAPTER 24
OLIVIA

"Brookie, just how much coffee have you had today?" I ask as we walk up the steps to my childhood home. We stop by the front door and because no one in my family is the snoop I am, it's okay to have a little chat here.

My former best friend turned friend that I wish would turn into my boyfriend rolls his shoulders—not against the cold, but like he's about to throw down against an opponent's enforcer. He even shakes his hands wildly.

"It's not caffeine, it's nerves."

My eyebrows would shoot to the sky if they could. "Um, why?"

He lifts those brilliant green eyes of his, which today match his beanie. "You're kidding, right?"

Our breaths blow puffs that almost look like clear cotton candy. We're technically still in the fall, but we had the first snow of the year just last night. There are patches of white still hanging on the steps and the porch rails, and the grass is mostly frozen. It looks a little like Brooke's eyes right now, green and glittering.

When it's clear I'm still confused, he says, "I didn't come last year."

"And?" There's an uncomfortable note in my voice and I jam my gloved hands in the pockets of my coat.

Brooke chews on his bottom lip. "I don't think they'll be too happy to see me if they know why I didn't come last year. What if they kick me to the curb?"

Ah, so this is what my uncomfortable feeling was. Remorse.

I dig my face deeper into my scarf, looking up at him from under the black wool wrapped around my neck. His cheeks and nose are flushed with the cold, and there's a crease between his eyebrows as he worries his lip. If he continues, he's going to bruise it.

Sighing further fogs up the air. Fearing that he could vanish like my breath, I free a hand and grab onto the sleeve of his jacket. "That's not gonna happen at all. They kept asking me about you last year. It annoyed Trent to death."

His shoulders drop a smidge and a wide smile forms on his face. "Oh yeah?"

"Yep. So chill, okay?" I ring the doorbell.

"I'm chill. Why are you ringing the doorbell to your own house?"

"Because I said I was bringing a surprise." I grin up at him and bump his shoulder with my fist. "Tag, you're it."

The door bursts open and my mother's expression is a kaleidoscope of emotion. The first one is annoyance that anyone would dare ring the doorbell on Thanksgiving. After all, the actual people she expects to see all have keys to the house. The second one is confusion because she sees me first, and then a super tall guy next to me. And then joy breaks out of her pores. I wish I was recording the way she spreads her arms wide, eyes and mouth just as big as she squeals.

"*Brooklyn!*"

"Mama Estela." He opens his arms, one of them flying over my head and thankfully not knocking me over.

I leave them behind to hug it out and step into the warmth of the house. It smells like pabellón criollo and maybe I've turned into a cartoon, but the scent carries me over to the kitchen. I find Dad right in the middle of stealing a forkful of the carne mechada, his face blushing at getting caught.

"Mija!" He quickly dumps the meat back in the pot and puts the lid back on it. After tossing the fork in the sink, he engulfs me in his arms. "How's my baby girl doing?"

I squeeze him just as tight. "You mean your favorite and least problematic child?"

"Er…" Dad clears his throat as he pulls away. "Did you bring your EpiPen just in case?"

"Yes, Dad." I shake my head. "It's not like there's any gluten or nuts in an extremely Venezuelan Thanksgiving meal."

"That's why we do it." He chucks my chin.

I blink hard, processing.

Here I always thought it was because they wanted to celebrate their homeland just a bit, to remember its flavors, to not think of it with the sadness or the hurt of so many other immigrants. But it was because of me all along. Because the turkey stuffing has gluten. And so do pies. And some pies have nuts. And some other typical American staples of a Thanksgiving meal could also kill me on the spot because of the food coloring.

I'd take back the whole least-problematic-child if I could, except now Brooke's in the kitchen and Dad's greeting him like Brooke is the prodigal son who has finally returned.

While they're all busy with that, I grab a new fork from the drawer and sneak in a little taste of the meat. The flavors hit me with so much force, my mouth turns into a beach. Or maybe this is the first time I'm truly appreciating it.

Sudden banging makes me freeze, but when my parents keep fussing around Brooklyn without a hitch, I figure it's no big deal. I sidestep them and head out of the kitchen, looking for the source. Then I spot two sets of legs rushing down the stairs, until my sister Luz, and her husband Max, appear before me.

"Did I just hear Brooklyn's voice?" she asks me without stopping to say hi. Behind me, she screeches. "Look at you! You've turned into a freaking mountain. Max, come see!"

"Hey, Liv." My brother-in-law gives me a quick one-armed hug before following after his wife.

Brooklyn gasps like a fanboy. "Max Cassiano? The leading forward in the NHL?"

Max plays along. "Brooklyn Tatum? The highest drafted defenseman last year?" After that, I hear the unmistakable slaps of a dude-handshake, followed by weird back thumps.

I hang my grey beanie from the coat hanger by the door, and as I unwind my scarf I count how many coats it already boasts. It tells me Aran and Maddie must be on their way. I take up my favorite spot, which is peeking through the curtains until I catch them walking up to the house.

That's how Brooke finds me. He takes up the same spot but by the window on the other side of the door. "That wasn't so bad," he says in a mumble. "But the real test is coming."

I press my lips tight. Aran's gonna be the challenge. I didn't have to tell him earlier, but I know that Brooklyn knows that Aran was the only one who didn't miss him last year.

"Why do you think he hates me so much?" Brooke asks as if he could read my mind.

"I don't know." That's a lie. I'm sure Aran's always known I've had a huge unrequited crush on Brooke since forever.

"Who's up for a game of catch?" Dad asks from the living room.

"Well, the catcher hasn't arrived yet," my sister says.

But that's when I spot movement from the corner of my eye, and sure enough, that's my brother and his wife walking up to the house. Maddie's in a green coat that brings out the almost imperceptible red in her hair. My brother's in all black. Boring. Or like a grim reaper. Depending on his mood.

I glance at Brooke. "Ready?"

He swallows hard and is doing the shoulder rolling thing again. "I got this. I'm taller than him now. Boxing is one of my dryland trainings. I could plow through him now. We can do this."

"Okay…" Without warning, I swing the door open. Aran and Maddie pause, and where her face breaks into a huge smile, his is the picture of wariness. "Greetings, you must pay a toll to pass through this door," I say, extending my hand out for payment.

To my surprise, Maddie digs into her coat and pulls out a book. "Here's my payment. An ARC of my next release."

Now I'm the one shrieking like a banshee. "Oh my word, oh my word! Is this finally Kent and Ophelia's story?"

"That's right. Friends to lovers at last."

I snatch up the book and hug it tight to my chest. This is the book I've been waiting for ever since she started her self-published hockey romance series years ago. And of course, it's so I can live vicariously through it.

"I love you so much," I whisper fiercely as I hug her in a vise. "You're my favorite sister-in-law."

"She's your only sister-in-law, you twerp," my brother says in a deadpan.

Pulling away from Maddie, I glare at him. "Pay up, jerk."

He has the nerve to pinch his chewing gum between his teeth, before plucking it between his fingers. I move my hand away before he can dump it there.

"Wow, I hate you."

A corner of his mouth twitches. "Missed you too, Aceituna."

I wrinkle my nose as I watch them step into the house. Luz or my mom, I can't tell from outside, exclaim upon their arrival. And then my oaf of a brother freezes at the door. I know why, but I still push him with all my might until he grunts and I can finally shut the door behind me.

I stand there, watching the faceoff between my brother to my left, and Brooklyn to my right. Brooke's hands are in the pockets of his jeans, shoulders curled inwards as if making himself smaller. So much for him being taller than Aran.

"Oh my." Maddie puts a hand on her cheek as she looks up at Brooke. "I can't believe you got even cuter, kid. How is this possible?"

Aran grunts. "He's no TDH."

"Huh?" I ask.

Maddie leans closer to me. "Tall, dark, and handsome."

"Oh. Yeah, no. Brooke's tall, light, and…" I trail off when three pairs of eyes turn to me, equal amounts of amusement between them. Folding my arms, I say, "Super ugly. Like it hurts to look at him."

"Excuse me, I am not ugly." Brooke turns his nose up and points at the faint scar on his cheek. "I'm ruggedly handsome."

"Hey, Dad," I call out, ignoring Brooke. "The catcher's here."

"Finally." Dad smacks the armrests of his armchair and gets up. "Catcher, pitcher, batter, and centerfield, let's go," he says, pointing at Aran, himself, Max, and at Brooklyn.

Aran's the first out the door, since he's the only one who didn't even get to take off his winter wear. I try to make my way through the mass of dudes now blocking my way but it's like they're doing it on purpose.

But then two pairs of hands cinch around my waist and

next thing, I'm flying. When I land away from the melee, I turn over my shoulder and Brooke winks at me.

Did he just lift me up like I'm some fairy princess or something?

"Mierda." I whisper when I notice that Luz, Maddie, and Mom all saw that little exchange.

I stand still as the men walk out the door. Our backyard is ridiculously tiny, but there's a nice park a block away where Dad takes the hockey bros in our family and forces them to play baseball with him. Normally, the women stay back in the warmth of the house, sipping hot, spiced wine and watching trashy reality shows. Except I have a feeling I'm the reality show now.

"Well, well." My sister singsongs.

"That was so cute." Maddie pulls up her cellphone. "I'm so gonna write that into a book."

"What?" I swallow hard.

My sister-in-law looks up with wide eyes. "He just Patrick Swayzeyed you."

"He did not."

"So, is this finally happening?" Mom wiggles her eyebrows.

I scrunch up not just my face, but my entire being. "What are you talking about?"

"Are you two finally getting together?"

"No!" I scream and hold tighter onto Maddie's book against my chest.

"Why not?" Luz twists her face in confusion. "It's about damn time."

"Yes, but no—I mean..." I sigh, exasperated out of my mind. "You don't understand."

"Then explain it to us." Maddie pats the open seat on the couch next to her.

And because it's Maddie, who is sweeter than sugar itself, and not because it's one of my evil relatives commanding it, I drag my feet over to sit next to her and I give them the gist of it. No one's shocked when I admit to my feelings for him. There's a bigger reaction when I finally fess up to why he didn't come for Thanksgiving last year. And complete outrage when I tell them my feelings are one-sided.

"One-sided my ass!" Luz throws her head back and laugh. "Aran and I have a running bet since you were in middle school about whether the two of you had hooked up or not."

Mom gives her a warning glance. "And what exactly does hooking up mean?"

My face flames up. Luckily, Mom's attention is on my sister. "Erm, kissing. Getting together as a couple." We all leave the possibility of sex out of this conversation. Not that it's even relevant.

"So, uh. What are the bet's terms?"

"Aran bet that you're never hooking up." She grins at the way I grow visibly grouchy. "And I bet that you're definitely hooking up at some point. Who's winning?"

All three of them lean forward.

I place the book on my lap, running my fingers across the title. That's when I notice that the hero's illustration is a tall blond. And the heroine is a brunette with mid-brown skin tone. Even though her hair's long, she looks a lot like me.

I give Maddie a side eye. "Wait, Kent… like a place. And Ophelia, which is a similar name to Olivia?"

Maddie nudges me with her shoulder. "Ophelia will get her happily ever after. How about you?"

"We kissed once," I blurt out, and before they can even react, I also add, "But that's it. He hasn't even tried to kiss me again."

Mom's hands are on her chest, but she's not even mad that her little girl's up to no bueno. Meanwhile, my sister slaps her thighs. "But what about you? Have *you* tried to kiss him again?"

"Of course not." I sink back into the couch. "We're just hanging out again. The kiss was a fluke."

"I don't think so. The boy doesn't tear his eyes from you." Maddie shrugs.

"He's *never* torn his eyes from you." Luz's widen, as if she was trying to pass along a telepathic message.

In turn, I roll mine. "What are you talking about? He had a crush on you and then on a million girls but me after that."

"Whatever." Luz waves her hand. "That all was before he knew himself. I'm telling you he's looking at you like he wants to eat you up now."

"No sex," Mom says right then. "Not before marriage."

Maddie and Luz stay uncharacteristically quiet. Then again, so am I. Even if the sky turned green and the grass blue, and Brooke and I hooked up in the not-safe-for-work definition of the word, he wouldn't be my first. That honor was wasted on my gross ex—ugh, I best not think about that.

"Anyway, I think you really have a chance now." Maddie reaches over and squeezes my hand. "Don't be a fool like your brother who almost wasted ours."

My mom and sister nod. The three of them are dead set on the same opinion, which is a feat from three headstrong women.

I'm a headstrong girl too, but maybe right now I'm being stubborn in a bad way. A ray of warmth pierces through my chest, and I don't dare to breathe in case it expands everywhere. I know it's hope, and hope is scary for someone who isn't used to allowing it in her life.

After biting my lip, I ask, "Okay, so what should I do?"

CHAPTER 25
BROOKLYN

The Rodriguez family Thanksgiving feels like a distant dream, with its flavorful food, pregnancy announcements—there's a mini Aran coming into the world; thankfully he or she will share half of Maddie—and a generally chaotic, but cozy feeling I starkly missed last year.

Now, Olivia and I stand in front of the front door to my dad's house, and nervous energy's coursing through my body again. I've rolled my shoulders enough that they still shouldn't feel so tight, and I've shaken my hands enough that now they tingle.

But then Liv snatches the one closest to her and clasps it so tight, I couldn't possibly move it again. "It's going to be fine. You're not alone."

Soon, I'm going to tell her how much I love her for it. I'm still in the planning phase as to how, but it's happening.

For now, I just need to survive Thanksgiving dinner at the Tatum household. "Thank you," I tell her. "For being here."

"And I'm really sorry I wasn't, last year."

I shake my head. "Let's forget last year even existed."

"Great idea." Liv nods. "Shall we?" She waits until I shrug to ring the doorbell.

This time it takes a moment for the door to open. When it does, all I can see is the hallway packed in fall decor. Until I look down. Way down. And find my half-brother's grinning face.

"Mom! Dad! Brooklyn's here!" After the shockingly loud screams, Lee turns his attention to Olivia. Back to me. Back to Olivia. Down to our joined hands. He sucks in air and screams over his shoulder again, "And he brought a new old girlfriend!"

Liv drops my hand like it's suddenly burning her.

Trying not to be annoyed by that, I ask Lee, "New old?"

He shrugs. "Well, you were always together so…"

From the corner of my eye, I try to inspect Liv's expression for any clues as to how this makes her feel. Except she could really win a poker tournament if she set her mind to it.

I clear my throat. "So, can we come in or not?"

"Oh, right." Lee steps aside. While Liv and I work on removing our winter layers, Lee disappears down the hallway into the opening that leads to the living room.

There's a strong smell of cranberry sauce in the house. Lauren, Dad's wife, loves the stuff. I wouldn't be surprised if I get served a vat of it.

"You hungry?" I ask Liv as I take her coat and hang it by the door.

"Not really, so you don't need to worry too much about me."

"Mkay." I'm sure at least the mashed potatoes will be fine. Unless Lauren smothered them with gravy already.

"You?" Liv asks as she balances herself against the door to toe off her boots, since Lauren likes to keep a shoeless household.

"I'll eat your share." I try to offer a smile that comes out more watery than I wish.

Liv pushes her hair away from her forehead. Her face is still flushed from the cold outside, and the combination of that and the sadness in her expression is doing something to me. I rub my chest before I know what I'm doing.

"It's going to be okay, blondie."

"I hope so." I bite my lip for a moment. "Last year was hard."

Liv plucks the hand I have against my chest to squeeze it between hers again. "Didn't we say last year didn't exist anymore?"

I straighten up and force a wide smile on my face. "Last year who? We don't know her." Liv opens her mouth but instead of her voice coming out, a different one rings in the quiet.

"Brooklyn."

But both Liv and I freeze at the sound of my dad's voice. I squeeze my eyes tight, wishing for a second that Liv and I could be transported literally anywhere else right now. Even a hot desert with no water in sight would be better.

Slowly, I take a deep breath and turn to face my father.

He looks older. I don't know why, but that's the first thing I notice. The lines around his mouth are deeper, and there's a new permanent one between his eyebrows. Must be from frowning upon me so much. I didn't get his dirty blond hair or his blue eyes the way Lee did. I also didn't get Dad's smaller build, and I'm now realizing just how much bigger I have become. I know I had a bit of a growth spur in the past year but it's only now that I'm realizing how significant it was.

Dad's eyes roam up and down my frame, before settling on my hand clasping Liv's. She tries to free herself and I don't let her. Instead, I lace my fingers between hers.

Dad folds his arms. "Son."

"Dad."

"Olivia," he says, icy eyes shifting to her.

"Mr. Tatum."

This is a drastically different welcoming compared to Liv's family. I can't help but snorting.

But before Dad remarks on the gesture, Lauren glides out of the kitchen in a knit dress that I'm sure is something out of a catalogue. She holds onto Dad's arm while offering a polite smile. "So happy to see you guys together again."

"Hi, Lauren," I say back, amiably enough. "Food smells good. Thank you for having us."

Liv squeezes my hand. She knows I'm never this flat with anyone, but it's no wonder family's the most faded line in my tattoo. My connection to the Tatum's is just as thin.

"You're so welcome. Would you like something to drink while we wait for the turkey?"

"Give him the same as Lee," Dad tells her. "He's still not an adult yet."

"Milk it is." Lauren gives us another perfect housewife smile. "And you, Olivia? Milk too?"

"I'm lactose intolerant," my best friend responds with the most deadpanned tone of voice that almost makes me laugh. With how many times Liv has been over, Lauren and my dad should remember about her allergies and intolerances very clearly.

Brimming with sarcasm, I add, "Wow, Dad. I'm surprised you remember my age."

His scowl grows deeper. "What is that supposed to mean?"

"Nothing." To my step-mother, I mumble, "Aside from water, do you have anything Liv could drink?"

"Well, I didn't know she was coming so…" Lauren blinks as she thinks. "How about chamomile tea?"

"Perfect, thank you." Liv's back to cold blooded politeness.

"You got it." The older woman turns back into the kitchen, but Dad's still blocking the hallway.

I motion at his tight stance. "Does that mean we're not welcome to sit, or…?"

"No, of course. I—" He cuts himself off and waves us into the kitchen.

Liv and I take adjacent barstools and Lauren sets a glass of milk in front of me. If there were any cookies around, it wouldn't annoy me so much. She busies herself with boiling some water in a kettle while Dad starts or resumes sharpening his carving knife. I don't know if that's what he was doing when we arrived, or if this is for show.

What I do know is that my sanity's best preserved in this house by volunteering as little words as possible. It's not like I'm a complete stranger, even though they treat me like one. Lauren's one of those country club women whose worlds have to be perfect, and that's the entire opposite of what happens when Dad and I talk. So we just don't talk for her sake. And that's also probably why Dad forgets to invite me to things.

Then he gets mad when I don't show up because that's the real issue. Whatever I do, he's not going to be happy with it. It's why growing up, the only one I could be my full goofy ass self with was Liv. Here, I had to act like a cardboard cutout of myself.

Luckily for me, Liv hasn't let go of my hand for a second.

Unluckily, Lauren notices this as she sets a steaming mug of chamomile tea in front of Liv. "So, you guys finally became an item?"

Dad stops moving to turn his stare on me, disapproval dialing up by the second. "I thought you were focusing on hockey."

What would he know about what I do with my life?

Instead, I say, "I am."

"Congratulations, you guys," Lauren chimes, her back turned to us as she stirs something in a pot on the stove.

"Uh."

Liv and I turn to each other. Her expression's asking me if we should tell them we're not really a couple. Mine's telling her that they don't actually care, and the less we engage the faster we can beat it out of here and head back to campus. Liv shrugs, and we remain silent.

"How's hockey?" Dad asks offhand, grunting as the knife catches on the sharpener.

"Hockey's great."

"Is that why you have a scar on your face?"

I'm surprised he even noticed.

"Yep, it's a badge of honor."

I know I've said too much, because it sends Dad down the tried and true path of looking down on me. "You wouldn't get hurt so much if you'd become a forward like me."

"Actually." Liv surprises us all by speaking. All three of us turn to her. "This is Brooke's first injury in his entire college hockey career, which you'd know if you watched his games."

You could hear a pin drop.

I'm doing everything I can not to pull Olivia into a kiss that would scandalize Lauren. Especially when Liv turns twinkly brown eyes at me, like she knows she did some mischief that can backfire on us but is still proud about it. I at least allow myself to run my thumb up and down the skin at the back of her hand.

"Well." Lauren puts her hands on her hips. "The turkey still needs at least an hour in the oven. Why don't you two go watch a show in the meantime?"

"Or you could play with your brother," Dad says.

I ignore that because Dad complains about me the most in occasions where he considers I could be a bad influence on Lee. "C'mon, Liv. Let's go see if my room's been converted into a storage closet yet."

She bites her lip not to laugh at what a little shit I am. I'm much more pleased that she lets me keep her hand in mine as we slide off the stools, though.

"Fine, but keep the door open," Dad says in a dark tone of voice.

I don't retort jack squat to that. He's been giving us the same shit since Liv and I hit puberty, even though back then Liv could've kicked my ass to kingdom come if I got too close. She'd still do the same now if I tried anything.

Upstairs, it turns out that my room is intact. I don't know why it surprises me, because it's not like they're actually lacking storage space in a house with six rooms and half as many occupants. I don't know if it's that they're too lazy to do anything with the space, or that the possibility of me coming over on occasion isn't as remote in their mind as it is in mine.

I stand by the door as Liv walks in. Our arms stretch but she keeps going, until our hands eventually break apart. She sets her tea mug down on the bedside table and grabs the remote before crawling on my bed like we're back in high school, face down with her feet toward my pillows. Although not on them, because she's too short for the massive bed.

Tension finally drains from my body. This is okay. Familiar. Much nicer than downstairs. I take my usual spot on the carpet at the foot of the bed, facing the massive TV.

"What are we watching?"

"I don't know," she says from above me. "Let's see if we find a classic from our time."

I snort. "Don't make us sound so old."

"You're right, we're not even old enough to graduate from milk."

Dad would be pissed if he knew the kind of crap that goes down at the Bolt House, then.

Or not. He wouldn't bother to ask.

Liv flips a few channels until she finds some Naruto rerun and stays there. I lean my head back against the edge of the mattress and grunt. "That wasn't so terrible. I don't know why I was freaking out."

"The possibility of a big fight is still there." Her sigh fans against my hair. "Sorry if I turn out to be the spark that lights that fire. I just got so annoyed earlier."

"He has that effect on people."

I freeze when her fingers start playing with my hair.

This is also familiar. Sometimes, when we were kids, I'd lay my head on her lap while we were reading comics or studying, and she'd absentmindedly play with my hair. But it's been so long. And it doesn't feel the same anymore. She rakes her fingers on my scalp just the same, but it's no longer relaxing. If anything it makes my blood boil even more.

"Did you fight last year?" she asks.

I groan, not necessarily because of the question. "I thought we weren't talking about last year."

"Last time, I promise."

I lean my head back all the way and open my eyes. Her face is right above mine, and the last thing I want to do is talk about my father when her lips are right there. When I could be stroking her tongue upside down and exploring her mouth even deeper, Spider-Man style.

"No, last year was worse," I respond in a quiet voice at last, my eyes glued to her lips and the tiny gap between them. "He didn't even ask me a single question about myself. It was like I wasn't there at all. A whole day of that."

But Liv surprises me by resting her forehead against mine. "I'm sorry, Brooke."

I blink hard. "What the hell for?"

"I…" She lets out a forceful breath. "If I hadn't been so selfish, you wouldn't have been alone last year."

My chest twists. The pain is so strong, I almost think someone's stabbing me with a sharpened hockey stick again.

"Liv, no." I raise my hands to cradle her face, and she lets me lift it so I can look into her eyes again. "It's not your fault that my father doesn't give a rat's ass about me."

"But it's not fair." She whispers. One of her hands falls on my shoulder and I feel the touch like a brand through my clothes. "I just don't understand why he's like this. And worse even, your mom."

I drop my arms slowly, bringing my face forward in time for the Sasuke and Itachi fight to start. Drumming my fingers against my thighs, I say, "I know why."

"Why?" she asks sharply.

"Because I'm not lovable." I shrug. "I know what love looks like. Your parents worry about you and your siblings to death. That's love. Even the way Aran gives you shit all the time is love." I point at the TV. "Just like those two clowns over there, fighting each other because they have no other way to express how much they care. But none of my parents feel any of that for me, and I'm the common denominator. So that's why."

For a moment, everything's quiet except for the action on the screen.

But then my bed shakes, and suddenly Liv's legs are beside me. And even more suddenly, she kicks me. *Hard.*

"Ow! What the hell?" I rub my ribs where she dug her toes.

"Who fed you that spoonful of horseshit?" Liv looks down at me, hands into claws as if she wanted to choke me. "What about your girlfriends? Or your fans?"

"What? What about them?" I frown, confused as hell.

"Don't they love you?"

"No." I run a hand through my hair, wishing it was her fingers doing it instead. "They don't even know me—the real me."

"Yeah, because you keep all your relationships shallow on purpose. That's why even though you have—what were their names—James and Daniel?"

"Jamie and Dane." I'm going to keep to myself how pleased I am that she didn't remember their names.

"Them." Her face pinches with grumpiness. "That's why even though you have them, I bet they have no idea about what your relationship with your parents is. Or that you're a huge nerd under that hockey uniform. Or that you have a huge man-crush on Max and Aran. Or that you're legit so sweet it gives me cavities. I mean—" She throws her hands in the air. "If any of the girls you've dated even knew this, they'd have never let you go."

I blink up at her. "A man-crush?"

"That's not the most important take from my speech."

I press my lips to hold back the sudden bubble of a laugh. "Then what is it?"

"You're damn lovable, Brooklyn Tatum." Liv folds her arms tight. "Anyone would be a fool not to see that."

My throat works with a hard swallow. Especially because I really want to know what *she* thinks, personally. Like if she could come to love me the way I love her.

And even though it feels too soon for that conversation, I'm also not a coward so I ask, "Are you a fool, then?"

Liv's eyes widen. Her lips part, just as her cheeks start to redden. Clearing her throat, she answers, "Of—Of course not. I'm a smart girl. I know a golden retriever when I see one." She leans down and rubs her hand on my hair like I'm a real puppy.

What?

Does that mean she loves me or not?

Or does she love me like a dog?

I can't believe I'm jealous of a hypothetical dog.

Or was that a clever sidestep? It's true that she's smart and I'm not exactly the sharpest tool in the shed.

But I haven't even figured out what to say back when Lauren announces that the damn turkey's ready ahead of time, so we end up sitting at dinner without being able to talk about this at all.

And later, as I drive us back to campus, Liv keeps her nose in the book Maddie gave her. Like she doesn't want to talk.

Or like she said too much. Like maybe she does feel something for me. And this time, it might be more complex than just friendship if she can't say it loud and clear.

Or maybe I'm too desperate to be loved for real.

CHAPTER 26
OLIVIA

Back at the apartment, the Saturday after Thanksgiving, Mina and I watch as Dee primps herself up for a date with a mystery guy. She's in the bathroom, applying mascara to her eyelashes while we oversee her efforts, Mina from the hallway, and I perched on the edge of the bathtub.

"Make sure to apply a second layer," Mina says in a grouchy tone.

"Yes, ma'am." Dee happily applies another layer, but I don't think it matters. Dee's a knockout even wearing her baggy, sweaty hockey uniform.

"Ugh, how come you have a date lined up after Thanksgiving but not me?" After asking, Mina jams her hand in a bag of trail mix and all but stuffs the whole mouthful into her mouth, crunching in such an aggressive way that I fear for her enamel.

At least I'm trying to be productive by painting my nails with glittery black polish. But don't get me wrong, I am jealous as can be, too.

"Maybe it helps that I found this guy at an empty O'Malley's during Thanksgiving, and we had a few drinks together?"

"Okay, I detect the sarcasm and I respect it." Mina laughs, her mouth open and showing a lovely view of mashed trail mix.

After applying the last coat of top polish to my toes, I lower my foot and really look at Dee. She's the one who taught me the art of applying my makeup before putting on my clothes, after the one time I got eye shadow all over a nice blouse. But damn, if that guy gets an eyeful of Dee's undies he'll get a heart attack.

My eyebrows shoot up. "So, I take it this is not the kind of date we need to wait up for you?"

"Who knows." Dee smacks her lips as she applies gloss. "I might or not get lucky, we'll see."

"We are so not lucky." Mina's face scrunches up like a kid about to throw a tantrum. "We are so not getting lucky tonight, just to clarify."

Dee pauses from her ministrations. "Or… you could, like, hit up a bar or something."

Mina's eyes brighten immediately and set on me. "Can we?"

"I'm not interested in looking for guys." I shrug. There's literally only one I'd love to be getting ready for a date for.

"But think of your poor, cold and lonely friend." Mina directs her pout at the screen of her cellphone instead of at me. "Instagram, here we go. Let's see where the hockey players are."

"No, please. No more Bolts." I put the palm of my hand on my face. The last thing I want is to send a weird signal to Brooke, which is exactly what would happen if I start hanging out around his guys while I'm trying to figure out how to seduce *him*.

"Oh!" She exclaims. "Dane Bloom and Brooklyn Tatum are at O'Malley's. Let's go."

Okay, if Brooke is there that's a different story.

My spine straightens as the two of them turn to me. I bite my lip but there's no holding back the heat taking over my face. "Um, okay."

"Oh, shit. Is this finally happening?" Dee drops the tub of gloss on the sink from the shock. Meanwhile, Mina's eyes widen dramatically.

"Well." I clear my throat and rock a little on my seat. "I may have had an epiphany or two over the holiday."

"And?"

"I might or not have decided that I want to get out of the friendzone?" I finish the comment with a weak little cringe. "I just don't know how." Luz, Maddie, and Mom weren't exactly helpful. They were all of the consensus that I should tell Brooke I've had a crush on him for the longest time, and ask if he'd consider dating me. But that's the very last thing I want to do.

The thing I learned from my ex is that if men don't want something—me, I'm talking about me—there is no way you can make them. I tried to mold myself into the version of Trent's ideal woman according to his little comments here and there, and he still cheated on me. Because he never wanted me. And that was solely on him, but it's just the damning case that proves this hypothesis.

Brooklyn has to want me first, and no amount of me telling him that I want him is going to convince him of that.

After explaining all of this to them, I add, "We held hands basically the whole day and he did nothing. Nada. Not even give me a spicy little look. Forget about eating my mouth."

Mina gives me a glacial stare. "Ever stopped to think that maybe it's because you're not coming onto him?"

"But like I just said—"

She raises her palm. "Hold. Coming onto him isn't necessarily about spilling your feelings. Just like, dress sexy around him and see how he reacts."

"Oh yeah, that's an easy one." Dee leans her hip on the sink and motions to herself. "That's what tonight is all about."

I frown. For Thanksgiving, I wore a normal black sweater tucked into boyfriend jeans. Comfortable. Me. But not exactly screaming throw-me-against-the-wall-and-devour-my-mouth.

"Okay, good point."

Mina points at her phone. "How about tonight? We have the perfect occasion."

"Let's do it."

The way the two of them squeal makes me cover my ears with my hands. Then I freeze. "Crap, wait. My nails are drying."

"That's fine, baby girl. It buys us plenty of time to pick an outfit."

Dee gives Mina a look. "We won't find anything useful in her closet, though."

"Actually…" The two of them turn to me, expectant. "There might be something."

"Oh?"

"I originally intended to wear it for Trent—"

"Girl, no."

"Ew."

I'm healed enough from that episode that I can chuckle. "I know. Big mistake to wear something for a guy, and yet here I am."

"It's different. This is to make you confident enough to finally bag the love of your life." Mina folds her arms. "Don't you two give me that look. It's true. I'm pretty sure Brooklyn and Olivia are soulmates."

"We are so not passing the Bechdel test," Dee mutters.

"I want to wear it for myself, though." I lift my chin. "And that's actually why I bought it. Because I wanted to feel sexy in it."

"What is this *it* you speak of?" Mina asks.

After a brief expedition to my room and with her help to dig into my closet so I don't damage my nails, she plucks out the *it* from the bottom of a drawer. The two of them ooh and aah at it.

Dee tilts her head and says, "Wait, but he won't see this unless things have already progressed quite far, you know?"

"Not unless Liv wears it as a statement piece."

To Mina's surprise, I nod. "Yep, that's what I was thinking about."

"Wow, Thanksgiving has changed you," she says, her expression sparkling with admiration.

I grin. "I'm very thankful I have another chance."

"Let's do this!"

My heart kicks hard, almost to the point of giving me vertigo. "Wait." They pause in the middle of walking out of my bedroom. "I, uh, could use with a little booster."

A moment later, we bust out the wine coolers that Dee is officially old enough to buy on her own. She's reasonable and only has a glass, and since she had a big head start, she finishes getting dressed and hiding all her va va boom-ness under a massive down coat before she's out the door for her date.

Mina and I stay behind to get properly ready. This implies more drinking, which makes the makeup application more challenging, but the whole process less barf-inducing than it'd be if I was in my senses.

"Am I doing the right thing?" I ask her while she's doing my makeup.

"Totally. You're going after what you want."

"And what if he doesn't want me? What if this really destroys our friendship?"

Mina snorts. "I'm pretty sure he already wants you."

"I want to believe you. I'm just so used to getting deflated at the end."

"Once you get married, you have to make me the maid of honor and not Dee, though."

I give a noncommittal hum from my throat, not just because I know Dee would dispute that. But also because I'm not trying to get Brooke to propose to me here. I just want him to notice me first. To really see that I'm not just his friend he can talk about anything with—including his girlfriends. But in fact, his next girlfriend.

I'll focus on being his *last* girlfriend after that.

After we're dressed up sans coat layers, we look at each other on the full-body mirror in Mina's room. Unfortunately, the sweet wine swooshing in my belly doesn't imbue me with confidence anymore.

"What was I thinking? This sucks."

Mina smacks my butt. Hard. "Stop that shit. You look really freaking hot. In fact, you're making me look frumpy."

"Shut up, you look amazing."

"So do you, silly goose."

I run my eyes down my reflection. The most comfortable part of the outfit is my black combat boots. But I must've forgotten to throw out this pair of black skinny jeans, and I deeply regret it now. "Can I at least change into a different pair of jeans?"

"Why?"

I shrink into a little raisin. "You know I'm self conscious about my hips and my butt."

I've always hated that my bottom is one, sometimes two sizes larger than my top. My ex was an ass-guy—in more ways than one, I suppose—and he's the reason I took to wearing skinny jeans. But at least I used to balance it out with looser tops that disguised how disproportionate my body is. And wearing a tight corset top made of black lace and wires might be a bit too much highlighting the problem. I close the blue jean jacket tighter.

"Listen to me, you fool." Mina grabs me by the shoulders and either she sways, or I do. Maybe both. "There is no guy at O'Malley's who will be able to keep his eyes off you. So you better focus on Brooklyn because Dane is mine, okay?"

"I thought you were going to give me a pep talk, not that."

"That was the pep talk." Her eyes pop. "You're so hot, you could snag any guy you wanted tonight and whenever. Remember that. Now, do I look like I want someone to keep me warm?" She's in a blue bodycon dress that doesn't hide any of her curves, and see-through tights that will literally make her freeze.

"Yes, I think you're in real danger of hypothermia."

"Excellent. Then we're ready."

CHAPTER 27
BROOKLYN

Something Liv said two days ago stuck with me and unfortunately, a lonely Friday where all I did was work out and do homework, really made me marinate it.

I don't really talk with people.

Sure, I'm a goof. I've definitely been down for a good time since Liv's hiatus from me. And I can spend a whole week talking about hockey with anyone who cares to listen for that long. But I don't really open up to anyone other than Olivia.

I thought the friends line of my tattoo was dimmer because I'd lost her, but honestly, I don't try very hard with anyone else. And I'm not saying that I should've replaced her because that's impossible, but she's right. Literally the first time I talked about something personal with my teammates was when I admitted I'm head over heels for my childhood best friend.

That's why I'm sitting with my defense partner at O'Malley's bar. Maybe that was strategically a bad call, because we're facing the TV screens showing a game from the team that drafted me. And all I can say are things like, "Their second line is lacking depth right now. It's like they're a Frankenstein that wasn't sewn together properly."

He nods while popping a French fry in his mouth. "Yeah, that's what happens when you lose so many players to injuries this early."

Another silence falls between us. Dane's a chill dude who only gets amped up when we're on the ice, so it's not like this is uncomfortable for us. It might be a bit easier with Jamie, who is as much of a dork as I am. But at the same time, Jamie might've been freaked if I attempted a serious conversation with him.

Except, Dane would probably freak out too if I suddenly spring how much Thanksgiving at my dad's sucked because he basically hates me. And it's not like Dad's abusive, but neglect feels very shitty too.

"So…" I tap my fingers on the chill surface of my ice tea glass. "How was your Thanksgiving?"

His eyes still follow the on-screen action as he speaks. "It was okay. My Aunt Sheila got so sloshed she almost killed herself walking down the stairs. And my mom complained that the turkey was too dry the whole night even though she's the one who cooked it."

I snort. "That sounds fun. Did you get drunk too?"

"Oh yeah, off my freaking face. Mom almost smashed her broomstick on my head when she noticed."

"She sounds great."

That tears his attention away from the game, if only to give me a very confused look. "What part of my mom almost murdered your defensive partner sounds great? Do you secretly hate me?"

"No." I tuck my tongue against my cheek, eyes focused on my empty plate. "I mean, the fact that she cares so much. And is there for you." Wow, shit. This is actually worse than the Dad-talk I intended. The burger and fries in my stomach are trying to claw up my esophagus.

"Why do you sound like a wounded puppy?"

My lips twist in a sneer. "Because I am, I guess."

"Hey, Barry," Dane calls out to the bartender. "We'll need a couple of whiskey shots down here."

The bartender, a grumpy-ass guy who's been here since time immemorial, gives us the driest look a living human can muster. "Two more iced teas coming. Unsweet."

Dane and I slouch. There's no fooling this guy.

"Anyway." Dane turns back to me. "Lay it all on Uncle Dane. It'll help."

I sigh. "There's not much to it. Mom's been out of the picture since my parents got divorced like twelve years ago or something. But Dad…"

He perks up even more and that reaction reminds me of something. Bryce Tatum was a star forward until just fifteen years ago. He had a long career despite the injury that firmly put a lid on it. So many kids, including myself, grew up idolizing him, trying to emulate his dirtiest dekes in practice, or even the celly that made him a popular fixture of sports magazines—something like the Rhodes thinker but on ice.

Whenever I tried to talk about Dad with someone who knew him, they inevitably fell into starstruck mode. Except for Liv. She also saw more of his father self than his professional athlete self, and doesn't give a rat's ass about Dad's fame.

Clearing my throat, I ask, "Are you gonna get weird if I talk about him in a way that doesn't make him sound like a perfect public figure?"

"Hmm." He presses his lips tight. "I'm sensing the right answer is no."

"It's definitely no."

"Okay, then totally no. Cuss the shit out of him."

That makes me grin. "I wouldn't quite give him a curse word middle name but we're not exactly on the best terms."

"Yikes. Is he like a helicopter Dad? Doesn't even let you breathe without his permission?"

I shake my head. "On the contrary. I could die in a ditch and he wouldn't notice."

"Whoa, that sounds worse than if you called him foul names."

"You asked." I shrug, as if my heart wasn't trying to race my dinner out of my throat. "Dad only cares for his second family."

"That certainly makes for an awkward Thanksgiving." He puts a paw on my shoulder and gives it one squeeze. "Sorry, bro."

I raise my eyebrows. "Thanks, bro."

"I'm here if you want to talk actual shit about them, but I admit I'm not the best with tears."

I punch him on the shoulder. "Do I look like I'm about to start weeping?"

"There's some shiny stuff on that corner of your eye." He vaguely points at my face.

"Whatever, asshole."

"Hey, should we get more fries?"

"Definitely." I signal Barry and put another order.

From the corner of my eye, I observe my closest buddy in the team. His focus is back on the screen, even though we're in intermission now. But there are no traces of pity on his face, or of disbelief that my hall-of-fame candidate father is anything but perfect. There's still a ton of adrenaline coursing through my veins, but I didn't die from opening up just a notch.

Liv will be so proud when I tell her.

I fish in my pocket for my cellphone. Her contact sits at the top of my list and I have to bite my lips so I don't grin like a freaking clown from seeing it there. Just a few months ago, I didn't think she'd speak to me ever again. And now we basically text every moment of the day and night when we're not hanging out. I wanted to see her so badly yesterday, but I'm trying to not crowd her. This is fine for now, though, I can just update her by text.

But just as I'm about to hit send on the simple question of *guess what I just did*, I hear her voice right behind me.

"Hey, Brooklyn."

I almost fall off my barstool with how fast I spin around. But there she is, along with one of her friends. Just in case, I rub my eyes to make sure it's really her and not my mind playing tricks.

"Liv?"

She snorts. "Who else?"

I sweep a glance around O'Malley's. It's almost empty, with most people in campus still at home for the holidays.

"Let me just make sure you're not a mirage," I say, reaching out to pinch her cheek. It's warm. Really warm. And red. But then she does the same, her fingers closing around my cheek hard.

"You guys have a really weird handshake," Dane jokes beside me.

"Hi there," Liv's friend says to him. Still prisoner of Liv's hold, I turn a bit to watch the action. Dane discreetly checks Mina out, and smiles widely.

"Hi Mina."

Oh, they already know each other?

Wait, based on the way they're looking at each other, I think they're going to get to know each other *deeply* very soon.

Back to Liv, I say, "Unhand me, woman."

"You first."

"On the count of one… two…"

"One order of fries and two more ice teas," the bartender says behind me. "You two, what's it gonna be?"

Mina ventures to say, "Two gin and tonics."

I don't even have to look at Barry to know he's scanning

the two girls and making mental math. Finally, he says, "Two more ice teas."

I chuckle, and the stretch makes Liv's fingers release my face. My skin tingles, not because she squeezed it too hard, but because it misses her warmth. It's a shame that Dane and Mina are around, because their scrutiny will make it so much harder to slip Liv's hand in mine like I did two days ago.

Unless I send them away.

"Should we play a round of pools? Darts?" I ask and very discreetly elbow Dane's side.

He yelps. The sucker. "Ouch. What? Oh. Yeah! Let's go, Mina."

I want to die. Or kill him. He couldn't be less tactful if he tried.

"I like pool," she says, sliding her arm around his once he's got both feet firmly on the floor.

"But are you any good? Because I'm not going to let you win just because you're really pretty."

"Oh, you're on, boy."

Liv's caressing her cheek as she watches their retreating figures intently. Almost like she didn't want them to go, either because she didn't want to be alone with me or…

Nah. She can't possibly be into Dane, can she? I mean, her friend wouldn't steal the guy Liv likes from under her nose. Unless Liv's never told a soul, which I can also see happening. If I'm private about some aspects of my life, Liv can be a downright vault. For example, it's only recently I found out some of my past girlfriends used to bully her in high school behind my back.

I gnaw the inside of my cheek as she hops on the barstool that Dane vacated and looks sadly at the fries. They're cooked in peanut oil and while delicious, they would send her straight to the hospital. Hooking my finger around the basket, I slide it over until it's basically behind me.

Sighing, she unbuttons her jean jacket and—

I start choking.

"Uh…" She stretches over to pat my back, which makes everything so much worse.

"What the hell are you wearing?" I manage to spew out between coughs.

Liv looks down at herself, her bottom lip still jutting out too damn cutely. But that's a massive contrast compared to whatever this outfit is. It's like lingerie, because there's no way that's a blouse or something. It's too tight. It frames her chest in a way that has me in a crisis, and I don't just mean the coughing fit. And if that wasn't all, it's too damn transparent —at least around her torso. Like, I can't see any of the saucier bits, but never has my brain had more input than this to imagine them.

"Clothes?" she asks, sarcasm dripping from the word.

After taking two punishing gulps of ice tea, I mumble, "Those are not clothes. That's underwear." My voice comes out thick and raspy. Hopefully, she thinks it's because of the coughing and not because I'm more turned on than a torch.

Maybe I should just look at the game, or she's going to start noticing that her bestie is a total horndog for her. Talk about easing her into the idea of dating me, huh?

"Is it too much?" She grabs the flaps of her jacket and opens it further while inspecting herself.

I have to drink more tea or I'll choke again.

"I just wanted to wear something different. See if…" She trails off to bite her lip. "See if it got me some attention."

I'm so aggressively happy we're facing the bar, and that the only one on duty right now is the grouchy owner who couldn't care less about the college kids that contaminate his establishment. If we were sitting at a table, or playing pool right now, the like, three other guys around the place would be salivating about her. Like I am.

I run a hand through my hair. My voice comes out a bit breathless as I ask, "What kind of attention?"

"A guy's." She closes her lips around her tea's straw and sucks.

I look away. I can't believe I'm jealous of a damn straw.

"Dane?"

"What?" She snaps.

"I saw you looking at him funny."

"No—I'm just happy for Mina. She's the one with a thing for him." Liv raises her index finger in warning. "Don't you dare tell him. She'd kill me."

"My lips are sealed." Would that I could seal my eyes too, before they bulge out. The problem is that with her jacket open so wide, I can see a peek of her side under her arm, and there's a little curve of her skin there that is absolutely killing me. I want to taste it so bad.

I sip more tea, too.

"So, it's not a particular guy, then?" I ask.

Liv swirls the drink in her glass with the straw. Almost too softly to hear, she responds with, "My next boyfriend, hopefully."

My heart trips against itself.

She came here looking for a guy. A guy to get together with. My fingers tap against the surface of the bar. I didn't tell her I was here with Dane, so it's not like she purposely came for either of us. But this *has* to mean she's over whatshisface. So maybe I finally have a chance.

"You don't need to dress like this to get a guy's attention, though." Especially not mine. I love her even in ratty old T-shirts ten times her size.

Liv's face scrunches up. "Do you know what my ex said when we officially broke up?"

"No." My entire body clenches with the desire to check

him against the boards with all my strength. Alas, Trent McFadden isn't a hockey player.

Propping her elbow against the bar, and the side of her face on her hand, she looks as me as she says, "That I was too boring and frigid."

"*What?*"

Even Barry turns toward me.

Liv nods like we're talking about the weather. "The boring part is his fault. He wanted to dictate how I dressed and what we did, so that's what he got. But frigid? That was a he-problem, right?"

Abso-freaking-lutely. She boils me up even when she just smiles my way. Forget about the vision she is right now.

Liv pauses to motion at herself. "Like Mina says, I'm freaking hot. And I'll make sure the next guy really, really wants me."

"Liv, listen." Before she kills me from excessive blood flow, I grab the flaps of her jacket and pull them close. She sits quietly while I work on the first button, the one at the bottom, and steadily make my way up to close her jacket. When I'm done with the top one, I look into her eyes and say, "The right guy will come and he'll want you with every fiber of his being, regardless of what you're wearing, okay?"

Her expression softens a bit and she expels a breath. "I hope so."

She can be sure of it because that next guy is me, and my brain churns ideas on how to tell her soon.

CHAPTER 28
OLIVIA

I am confusion. Confusion's definition in the dictionary is me.

I recall an occasion or two when Brooke openly checked out a hot girl. So I know how the damn-I'd-tap-that expression looks like on his face. The subtle narrowing of his eyes. The little lip bite. The head tilt to get a better look. That's not at all how he looked like at O'Malley's when he saw my outfit. Instead, he acted all brotherly and shit trying to protect my modesty.

Yet here we are six days later at the library, and he won't stop touching me.

We commandeered a quiet corner behind the history shelves, against the window. The heating's actually nicer here than it is over at the long, open area with the tables, which is why we'd rather sit on the prehistoric carpet than on chairs. Brooke took off his winter coat and set it on the floor for me to sit on, and ever since, he's been parked flush against me. Our shoulders and arms brush every time we move, and he even dumped his ginormous, rock solid leg over mine when I tried to move away. A bit later, when I stretched out my arms and shoulders, he sneaked his arm around me and hasn't let me get away since.

Brooklyn has always been like a puppy, constantly seeking touch and affection. And even then, this is weird. It's like… boyfriend-y stuff. Which doesn't track with how he didn't openly salivate over me.

Worse, even though I've been trying to act mature about it, it hurt me that he didn't.

This is messing me up even more. Especially because I'm drowning in the masculine scent that clings to him, and the curve of the back of my neck fits against his shoulder like a lock and key.

"How's that?" His side rumbles against mine with the deep timbre of his voice. I'm super glad to be wearing thermal leggings and a tent-like St. Cloud hoodie, so he can't see the goosebumps it raises all over my skin.

I swallow hard and have to squeeze my eyes hard to focus them on the screen of his laptop. He has it half rested on his thigh, half on mine. Obviously, this tilts it heavily against me because his thigh is so much bigger. I desperately wish I could chuck the device away and just map the muscles of his powerful hockey thighs with my hands.

"It's a good start, but I think we should make the dialogue more personal." My voice comes out weird but I refuse to clear my throat out of principle.

"Hmm." Brooke scrolls down, his two middle fingers brushing the trackpad softly. "Okay, I see your point. It almost sounds like a TV ad."

"I really think the lecturer is going to evaluate us on this. I mean, he did say he wanted the pairs to go deeper."

"Deeper, huh?" he muses aloud, casually making me want to scream.

His phone goes off right then, the screeching almost acting as my proxy. Finally, Brooklyn unwraps himself from around me and stretches away to pull his phone out of his backpack.

"Aww, man."

"What?" I ask, my eyes fixed on the short true-blond hairs at the back of his head.

"I have to get going. Can't be late for the game prep."

I press my lips into a tight line, right in time to keep a groan inside. When I can trust myself again, I say, "That's okay, we can finish the rest by text."

Brooke pauses from packing his things up to turn to me. His lips are twisted in a thoughtful expression. "Hey, Liv. What are you doing after the game?"

"Not working on the Spanish assignment, if that's what you mean." I roll out of the way so I don't step on his coat and get to my feet, before bending down to pick it up. I shake the garment and pat the contact areas to clean it up a bit.

"Cool, I don't wanna do that either but there's something I want to ask you." I freeze, watching as he gets up, strap of his backpack on one hand, and a blue bundle on the other. When he faces me, he says even more bizarre things. "So, I'll find you after the game and then we can go get some dinner. But in the meantime, take this."

"What?" I stare at the thing. It's fabric, and at first I don't make sense of the mix of colors. Some blue, grey, white, a dash of yellow. Then Brooke splays it open and I get it. It's a Thunder Bolts jersey, complete with the C at front. I lift my eyes to his. "Why are you giving me a hockey jersey?"

"Not just any good ol' jersey. It's mine." He turns it around, showing the TATUM 3 at the back. "It's game worn, but I promise I washed it."

It's interesting how a person can choke with their mouth firmly closed, yet here I am. I have to cough a couple of times and swallow hard before I can speak again. "Why are you giving me your jersey?"

"Because I know you don't have one, and it'd be cool if you could support the team?" His lips widen into a cheeky grin. "And by team I mean me. There is totally an I in Captain."

"Um, are you sure? It's like…" I wave my hand, not knowing how to explain what could potentially backfire. This is a hockey girlfriend thing, which I'm not. Yet, I want to be. Except he didn't jump my bones last week. I'm not strong enough to open this can of worms right now.

"Look," he says, dropping his backpack on the floor and working the jersey in his hand. I don't move a muscle as he puts the neck opening over my head. Brooke takes his coat from my hands and with one of his, lowers the jersey down my body until I'm trapped. And even more confused. It must be showing in my expression, because if anything he's even more amused now. "Liv, you're my favorite member in the audience and literally the only person who's there because she genuinely cares about me. That's why I want you to wear it."

"Okay," I say automatically. It's not a declaration of love. He's obviously not asking me to be his girlfriend. But I'll take it. I'll take whatever crumb he gives me right now until I can eat the whole pie. And I will, no matter how long it takes me to make him look at me the way I want. I slide my arms into the sleeves of the jersey, and then spread them wide. "How do I look?"

He rubs his chin while he inspects me, head to toe. "Shorter, somehow."

"Go." I point toward the exit.

Chuckling, he grabs his stuff. "See you after the game."

"Yeah, whatever."

I watch him go, my heart racing faster even as he disappears down the stairs.

Then I look down at myself. It's not a mighty big deal. Plenty of girls on campus wear his jersey, and it's not like people would know at a glance that this one is an actual player's jersey. There's no stake being claimed here. But is it bad if I feel like it is anyway?

I wish I could ask Siri what this means. Boy doesn't go awooga at the sight of me wearing something racy, but he gives me his jersey. And now he wants to ask me something after the game.

"Fool," I whisper to myself. If I hadn't gotten so distracted by the jersey, I could've asked him what his question was, instead of now having to agonize over it during an entire game.

I try to do a bit more work for a different class, but I can't focus. The library feels drastically colder now that I don't have the human torch right beside me. What if he was all over me just because he knew I was cold, not because he can't get enough of me?

Ugh. I need to do something definitive. I can't keep living like this.

Maybe tonight, after the game, he's going to ask me if I have a thing for him or what. Heaven knows I've been acting unlike me around him for weeks. And if so, screw it, I'll confess. I can be chill about this. I'm a grown ass twenty year old woman.

*

Two hours later, I am absolutely not chill while I sit alone in the stands. Mina wanted to come since this one's a home game and the Strikes have the away one tonight. But she has a library shift that prevents her from cheering for her potential man. Unlike Brooke and I, Mina and Dane seem to have hit it off pretty well after last weekend and already went on a date. Why can't I be that bold? Why do I have to overthink every damn thing?

My eyes latch onto Brooke the second he jumps the bench

to start a shift. I jam my hand into the popcorn carton, all the way down until I reach the empty bottom.

Dinner. That's what he said. We're gonna have dinner after the game, which means he's going to be in one piece after the buzzer—and he better, or else. But it also means I should stop stress-eating. I can always stress drink, but my soda is also out.

My knee bounces as Brooke zooms down the ice like there's no one there. If his opponents were any smart, they'd stop him no matter what even when he doesn't carry the puck like right now. But they're too busy trying to score a goal on us and they give Brooke too much leeway.

He checks an opposing forward so hard, the sound echoes all around the arena before the audience breaks into cheers. Brooke doesn't stop. He's a blue whirlwind as he steals the puck and passes it over to Dane with such accuracy, you wouldn't think this is a live game.

Too late an opposing player tries to come at Brooke. I jump to my feet. But he doesn't take the hit. He bends down low even as he glides down the ice, and the other guy goes flying over him. It's a party trick that makes the whole place roar. In contrast, I melt back on my chair.

Good, he's still safe. No new scars. Whew.

The buzzer goes off to end the second period. Nervous energy courses through my veins, making my limbs springy. I let them carry me back to the concessions area, which suddenly strikes me as a great idea. Not my fault if I miss a portion of the third period if the line is too long, right?

My chest pangs. What if Brooklyn tries to find me in the crowd and can't see me, though? That'd disappoint him. Worse case, it would unfocus him and that could be dangerous.

Swiveling around, I head back the way I came when something in the corner of my eye catches my attention. Two tall men stand between the moving crowd, and I'm at an angle to recognize one face. It's Coach Green. I keep going, because it's none of my business.

Except, I'm close enough that I can now see the second guy. And while I have no idea who he is, I sure recognize the pin on the lapel of his suit jacket.

It's the logo of the team that drafted Brooklyn.

"Sorry," I mumble to some girls as I change path and get in their way. "Sorry, sorry." I twist and turn to navigate through the crowd until I reach them. I position myself just off Coach Green's back, where he won't see me and where it doesn't matter if the other guy does.

Lucky for me, I catch the conversation still at its inception because Coach Green's saying, "—Owe this visit today?"

"I wanted to check in on Tatum," the second guy says.

My stomach drops.

Of course. I mean, I know for a fact that no other Bolts have been drafted by this professional team. This is why I *had* to eavesdrop. But why am I still surprised?

"I see you made him captain."

"Yes. It was an easy choice." Coach Green's shoulders lift. "He's the best player in the team by far, and the rest of them look up to him."

"That's good, leadership skills are important. But his on-ice skills are what I'm here for."

I wish I could ask him, well? What does that mean? Is there a *but* at the end of his sentence? Because if so I will fight him. Brooklyn is the most hardworking guy I know, and that's even excluding his abundant talent.

I find myself pushing my sleeves up before Coach speaks again. "The kid is wasted on this team."

Oh.

I mean, yeah. He is. He wasn't the highest drafted defenseman by accident. The only reason he wasn't number one is because he's not a forward, and those are always the ones with the highest demand.

"I agree," the pro guy says with a nod. "That's why I'm here to take him."

I freeze.

"I—sorry, what?" Coach asks.

"We've had a lot of injuries this season and we need horsepower. I know it's going to screw up your season, but this is a great opportunity for the kid."

"Of course." Coach Green rubs the top of his head. "When do you need him?"

"As soon as you can spare him."

"Okay." No! Not okay! But the Bolt's coach obviously can't hear my mental screaming. "He should finish off the semester first."

"And when's that?"

"There are two weeks left."

I smack my hands against my mouth, otherwise I'll start screaming. My eyes fix on the spotted granite floors until it blurs. I blink hard, but there's no stopping the torrent of tears.

"That works," the other man says. "It gives us plenty of time to do the paperwork."

"Very well. I'll talk with him and get it started," Coach says with a sigh. I hear the smacking of hands shaking. "I'm angry that you're taking my best guy, but thank you for putting our program in the map."

"My pleasure. I'll make sure the organization compensates you for your loss."

Coach mumbles something I can't hear but makes the stranger laugh. A second later, their voices disappear and I'm alone in the crowd.

My heart shatters into a million pieces and that's how it's going to remain, because there's no way I'll ask Brooklyn to stay for me. To give us a chance. Not when he's about to achieve everything he's been busting his ass for.

CHAPTER 29
BROOKLYN

"That's what I'm talking about, baby!" I crash into Jamie, our goalie, and we wrap our arms awkwardly around each other. His stick bumps my helmet, but it doesn't matter. We just won by freaking shutout.

Dane's voice approaches from behind. "Aw yeah!"

I turn and we jump to bump our chests hard enough that I feel it under the pads. But a zamboni could drive over me and I wouldn't feel it. My whole body is a cocktail of dopamine and serotonin, the best mix right before my date with Liv.

Okay so she doesn't know it's a date yet. I said we're going to dinner, but then I'll ask her on an official date over the best pasta in town.

My eyes scan the crowd, looking for a girl with light brown skin, short brown hair, and my jersey. She does me the favor of always buying tickets around the same area, right behind our bench, which helps me spot her quickly. Her back is to me and she's climbing the stairs, following the trickle of people slowly starting to make their way out. I'm sure there's going to be a massive party right after this but I won't go. All I want is some alone time with Liv.

"Let's go," I tell the guys, still celebrating in huddles on the ice. I skate over to the tunnel at full speed and all but skip toward the locker room. I toss my gloves on the bench and open my locker, tearing through my bag until I find my phone.

ME

Can you sneak in to the players area?

I stare harder at the screen, probably making veins bulge in my face, until my text is shown as read and her three dots appear.

OLIVE EMOJI

I don't think your coach would approve

ME

Okay fine, I'll find you at the main entrance

I'll be super quick

OLIVE EMOJI

Ew no, make sure to wash properly

I tilt my head, about to ask her just what she wants me so clean for, but I settle for a generic *fine*. I can't come on too strong or she'll balk. She's the kind of person who naturally goes against the grain, which is why I have to give her a very soft introduction to dating me.

First, I'll ask her to be my date to the team benefit gala. If she wants to assume that it's an invitation as friends, that's okay. But at the gala, I'll show her what a date with me looks like. Then I'll ask her on another one over Christmas break, and on that one we'll kiss—I'll make sure to find some mistletoe or carry it in my pocket.

And if our first kiss was wild, unexpected, a little angry and a lot wet, this second one will seal the deal. Of that I'm as sure as the fact that my parents named me Brooklyn because they conceived me at a hotel in the New York borough.

Okay, weird factoid. Maybe my mind's going in the gutter way too fast.

I make lightning speed work of stripping out of my uniform, chucking my skates and helmet wherever they fall. I grab a clean towel from the rack and dash buck naked across the locker room.

Coach Green and Coach Thomas walk right in the middle of that. "Tatum—"

"Sorry, Coach! In a hurry."

The bathroom tiles are cold under my feet and help me acclimate to a freezing cold shower. Just in case. I soap myself thoroughly, also just in case, my eyes stinging as shampoo drips down my face.

"Uh, dude. What's got into you?" Jamie asks from beside me.

Behind us, Dane says, "He has a date that is not really a date because the girl he's going out with doesn't know it's a real date."

"Shut up," I grouch.

"Is this with the girl we met at the Bolt House the other night?"

"Yep." Dane confirms. "The ex best friend who has our boy more whipped than cream."

"Shut up," I repeat as I stand under the punishing spray of high pressure, ice-cold water.

Jamie chuckles. "Good luck. Although I don't think you need it."

I turn off the faucet and run a hand down my face. "Why not? Do you think she's into me?"

"I have no idea. I just mean because you're a chick magnet."

I shake my head with a sigh. "Yeah, that doesn't work on Olivia."

"*Sure.*" Dane's still soaping up his pits as he stretches the word.

I basically whip myself with how quick I try to towel dry myself, and skip back out to get dressed.

"Are you in a hurry, Tatum?"

I suck in air and turn while in the middle of zipping up my jeans. "Coach. Hi. Yes. Sorry. I am. I have plans. What's up?"

His eyes are narrowed, mouth pinched as if he was trying to put a complex puzzle together. "Fine, we can talk tomorrow after the game. But no bailing from that conversation."

"I—uh. Everything okay?"

"Yes. More than okay." Except his smile is more a grimace than a demonstration of happiness. "This can wait twenty four hours."

"All right." This is weird enough that, normally, I'd drop everything like a hot potato to figure it out. But Liv's waiting for me, and I can't think of anything in this world that would be more important than this crossroads in my life. One just doesn't walk out of the friendzone with no effort. "Thanks, Coach."

He nods a bit more than necessary and retreats, giving me full permission to resume. I put on my long-sleeve shirt so fast that it bunches up around my torso. But I have to let it be so I can quickly put on my socks and jam my feet in my boots. After making sure every layer is in place and that I'm not flashing anyone, I dump all my things in my sports bag and run.

My boots skid against the floor as I change direction. After badging through a door and walking through a second one, I'm finally in the public area. There are still people milling about but they're all blurs in the periphery. I spot my girl right away, though. Her coat hangs from her arms and the TATUM 3 faces me again.

"Liv."

She turns. "Oh. Hey, Brookie."

I drop my bag. Before she can react, I'm picking her up in my arms and spinning her around. Liv lets out a squeal and has no choice but to wrap her arms around my neck for support. My face is smooshed against her chest and stomach, and I'm momentarily upset that she's wearing so many layers. I have no complaints about her butt basically sitting on my arms, though.

"Oh my word, put me down. Everyone's watching!"

They can watch a bit longer. Like a damn creep, I inhale her rich vanilla scent until it filters through my lungs and into my bloodstream. Slowly, painstakingly, I lower her down to her feet, making sure her body slides down my entire frame. The jersey and the sweatshirt she wears underneath catch against me, and I'm not even apologetic that my hands land on her hips right on top of her leggings. Liv's eyes are wide as she looks up at me.

The corner of my lips rises a notch. "Did you see that?"

"Um." She blinks fast. "You barreling down to pick me up like a toddler in front of basically the whole school?"

"No." I snort. "We won by shutout."

"Oh, that. Yes, I saw it." She shifts until she frees her arms from my grip and places her hands against my chest, where she can probably feel my heart racing faster than I did to find her. Her eyes lower to a spot on my throat. "You played really well. Like, professional-level well. Which I guess is more than really well. You were amazing."

I grin so hard that my face hurts. "Why, thank you. Shall we celebrate with pasta?"

"Sure." Liv shrugs out of my hold to pick up her fallen coat and put it on.

I have a feeling like she won't let me grab her hand on the way out, but I don't let her walk too far. When she tries to get in her car, I grab her by the back of her coat and steer her all the way to the passenger seat of my Jeep Gladiator.

"Did you like the game?" I ask her during the short drive between the arena and Romano's downtown.

"Like is a stretch." She's looking outside the window as she speaks. "But thanks for not giving me a heart attack this time."

I bite down a grin. "You're most welcome. I totally didn't get slashed, hooked, checked, or punched because I knew you were watching."

Liv turns to give me a fierce little glare. I fantasize with grabbing her chin and pulling her in for a quick kiss, and she's only spared because the light's still green.

Even though parking downtown on a Friday night is a pain in the ass, we strut right in to Romano's where a table is already waiting for us. It was the lesser reason why I was in a hurry, to not lose the reservation.

The main reason is across from me. She hangs her coat on the back of the chair and squeezes between it and the table to sit. Then, knowing full well that I'm the size of a mountain, she pulls the table toward her from under the mantle. It gives me enough room to sit down. My knee bumps against her legs before I spread my thighs wider so hers can be comfortable between mine.

Not the first time we do this dance, but the first I realize how perfect we fit.

"Ciao, bambino," Max's mom says next to our table, or more like screams. She turns to Liv. "Your usual pizza or the pasta?"

"Pasta this time, thanks. How's the family doing?" For the first time, Liv smiles a little.

Huh. Why am I only noticing just now?

"Messy as usual." The older woman looks at me. "And you?"

"The lasagna, please."

"Double?"

I grin. "Of course."

The woman turns over her shoulder and yells. "One order of the gluten free garlic knots!"

Liv and I cringe at the extreme volume of Mrs. Cassiano's voice, and as the matriarch moves onto the next table, my-date-who-doesn't-know-she's-my-date and I have a chuckle.

But then Liv's expression falls again, and I don't know if it's the dimmer lighting in the restaurant, but her eyes seem puffy.

My eyebrows bunch in the middle. "Hey, is there something wrong?"

Her brown eyes snap up to mine. "What? No. Everything's perfect. What did you want to talk about, by the way?"

I know she's deflecting, but I can definitely pivot to this other topic and come back to get the reason she's feeling off out of her later, right when she thinks I forgot about it.

Folding my arms, I lean on the table so I'm closer to her and have to scream less in the noise. "So, you know how every year the team puts out this event to get money out of the boosters and sponsors, right?"

"Right. This was one of Luz and Max's projects together after they announced they were a couple and got their teams to stop acting like turds."

"Correcto," I say, emphasizing the final o in a way that makes her scrunch up her pretty face. "And because they're geniuses, they scheduled it right before Christmas because it's the season of giving."

"Uh huh." A crease appears between her eyebrows. "If you're about to ask me to donate to the cause, you're shit out of luck, pal. There's only dust and dead moths in my wallet."

I shake my head, amused that she's so clueless. "Of course

not, you brat. I'm going to ask you to be my date for the event."

"I—" She cuts whatever she was going to say off, eyes bulging. "What?"

"Olivia, will you be my date to the St. Cloud Thunder benefit gala?"

"D-Date?"

She doesn't seem to be processing and I'm ever so helpful. "Yes, date. As in, we dress up nice, I pick you up, we go to the thing together and stick to each other's sides the whole night, and then I convey you home in one piece. Nothing major."

Totally major. Even though I deliver the speech with a smooth voice and a hefty dollop of sarcasm, my heart pounds harder with every second she doesn't respond.

Abruptly, she pushes to her feet. The space is so narrow that her hips bump against the table. I have to grab it before it topples over. "Liv—"

"Restroom," is all she says.

I twist to watch her disappear down the hallway. Then a shadow appears before me, and it's one of Max's way older brothers putting a basket of gluten free garlic knots on the table.

Well, this is going kind of weird.

I pluck one of the knots from the basket and stuff it in my mouth, folding my arms as I chew. I don't know how to work with this situation. If she'd laughed or straight up said no, I was ready to play the be-my-date-as-friends card like the clown I am. But I have no flipping clue what's going on with her right now. Guess it's time to return to asking her what's wrong.

But then she comes back. I try to stand, but Liv's already swinging a leggings-clad leg over her chair to slide down vertically. She's panting when she finally faces me, and her face is dripping water.

"Yes."

"What?" I ask.

"Yes, I'll be your date."

I blink hard. "Why do you look like you just agreed to get dental surgery?"

The determined mask in her face cracks a little. "Do I?"

"You do, but no takebacksies." I push the basket toward her. "Now, are you going to tell me what's got you all high strung?"

"There's nothing." Liv grabs one of the knots and tears it open. Steam rises from the dough. "Back to the gala. I've heard it's pretty fancy, is that true?"

"Oh, yeah. Black tie kinda shit."

She wrinkles her nose as she chews. "Dang, I have nothing to wear."

Curse my traitorous mind for picturing her wearing nothing, and my even more traitorous body for reacting to it.

I tap my fingers on the table just as a great idea occurs to me. "Let's go shopping, then. Tomorrow before the game."

Her eyes are still focused on the bread basket as she says, "Okay."

Nice, scoring myself another incognito date. I pump my fist under the table.

Back to the other topic. "So you're seriously all right? Got any bad news or something?"

Liv rests her chin on her fist and looks me dead in the eye. Instead of spilling whatever's bothering her, she says, "So is the gala cocktail formal, or like prom dress formal?"

My eye twitches. We both know I only win battles of will on the ice and never against her. For now, I settle for talking about the event and making plans. There's plenty of time to interrogate her later.

CHAPTER 30
OLIVIA

On Saturday, nothing and nobody can get me out of bed. Dee and Mina try to coerce me with the promise of a nice little brunch somewhere, but I tell them I'm not feeling well and don't want to pass this along to them. They enlist their services to do pharmacy runs if necessary, but I don't have the heart to admit that what ails me isn't physical. Although, I sure feel it in my gut.

Brooklyn's leaving.

My time with him is coming to an end. I should be jumping out of my room and racing straight into his arms, kind of like he did yesterday after the game, but I have no energy.

Last night, I thought I could push through the grief twisting my gut and agreed to go to the gala with him. But today, I don't think I have what it takes to pretend like I'm happy in front of him.

Pawing under my comforter, I bump against my cellphone half tucked under my pillow. His contact sits at the top and I bite my lip. There's still two hours before we agreed to meet at the mall, but there's no way that's happening. Not while I burst into tears every ten minutes.

ME

Hey

Can we postpone the dress shopping?

COOKIE EMOJI

Sure but what's wrong

He's been asking non-stop since yesterday, but he's the very last person in the planet I want to talk with about this. And especially not before he tells me the news himself.

ME

Just under the weather

COOKIE EMOJI

Should I bring you soup?

Ice cream?

Period pads?

Alcohol?

Pizza?

My arms?

"Ugh." I bury my face in my pillow and kick my mattress.

I'd love for him to bring all of the above, except for the pads because I'm not really on my period. But mostly, I wish he was here. Spooning me. His face buried in my hair. My back pressed up against him. His arms around me.

But then we'd have to talk. And I really would break this time—ugly crying, snot and everything.

ME

Just need a nap

Have a good game and don't get hurt

I toss my phone on the night table away from me, and twist until I'm facing the ceiling. The sheets are all wrapped awkwardly around me, immobilizing me when I hear the device buzz with more incoming texts. I close my eyes and tears roll down into my hair.

"Wow, you're being *the* melodrama," I say to the quiet.

The funny thing is, I didn't even feel this shitty when Trent cheated on me or when he basically admitted he felt no attraction for me.

Slowly, I pull myself up by my elbows until I sit. I rub my face hard. Maybe I should study. I'm in the middle of finals and this drama is setting me back. I busy myself washing my face and fixing up my bed. But after cracking a textbook open and trying to lose myself in the world of organic biology, my mind keeps drifting back to him.

It's four in the afternoon now. This is when, in a different universe, we'd have met at the mall to start looking for a fancy dress.

I could try to film a new video. There's a recipe for cookies I've been tweaking with. I'm trying to make a gluten- and lactose-free brookie that doesn't taste like newspaper. And Brooklyn would definitely love to eat it after a game. I'd love to feed it to him. Slowly. With my fingers. And then, I'd really enjoy kissing the crumbs from his lips.

There's no point. He's leaving during the Christmas break.

I need to get out of my head, and there's only one place in town where I can do that. I pack an overnight bag, including my textbooks and my laptop, and hop on the stinky SUV my brother passed down to me when he graduated college and was hired on as the most expensive free agent in a professional team on the other side of the border.

See? That's what the hockey guys do. They work very hard to leave everything behind. It's my turn to be left behind again.

Some half hour later, I'm on the opposite side of town parking by the curb of my parents' home. I skid on black ice as I get out of the car, and for a second I think how shitty it'd be if I die cracking my head on the pavement right now. But I manage to stabilize myself and step more carefully to the other side to retrieve my bag. My heart's pit-pattering hard as I stand on the porch and realize I forgot to grab my keys to the house.

I feel more pathetic than ever by ringing the doorbell. But Mom opens the door, takes one look at me, and pulls me into a hug. "¿Quieres unas arepitas, mija?"

This is why I came. Mom and Dad's way of showing affection is feeding us. Unless we want to talk, they don't probe.

From the living room, Dad asks in excellent Spanglish, "¿Qué? ¿Tienes que hacer un laundry?"

I snort into Mom's shoulder. Correction, food and laundry. I blame my siblings, because that's all they ever did when they visited home after leaving for college.

"Food," I say.

While Mom goes off to fix some arepas, I crash on the living room couch next to Dad. Unfortunately, with so many hockey goons around him, he's come around and now follows the sport closely. He's watching a rerun of an old game of Aran's where my brother's pulling saves that should get him this year's Vezina. One of those saves has Aran doing the splits like some Olympic gymnast, and now I get why Brooke said that pulling their groin is a common injury for goalies.

That sure helps me focus on my textbook until Dad asks, "You okay, Aceitunita?"

I sigh, perennially annoyed at the nickname that likens me to an olive. "I'm okay."

He hums from his throat but keeps watching the game. I push through my reading for at least fifteen minutes until Mom calls me from the kitchen. The house smells like freshly grilled arepas, and I let my nose trace the scent to the plate waiting for me on the kitchen counter.

"You're too skinny, Olivia," she says, obviously not realizing I've loaded on the pounds from stress-eating vats of popcorn with Coke at Brooklyn's games. "Are you eating okay? Or is it something else?"

I chew on my arepa with avocado and pico de gallo and say nothing.

"Something else, then." Mom nods to herself and turns back around to the kitchen. "I'll be here whenever you need to talk, okay?"

A memory hits me smack in the face. That's exactly what Mom said the night I came home crying, after Brooklyn agreed with those terrible things a hockey bro said at the Bolt House party almost two years ago.

I set the arepa down and swallow hard. That's why I came home. Not because my parents are less snoopy than my friends or my siblings, but because they're my parents. And whenever I feel sad, hurt, or I'm sick, I look for them. Or for Brooklyn, which right now and back then I couldn't do.

"Mom." My voice shakes and it makes her drop the bowl she's washing. The entire kitchen blurs as tears pool in my eyes. "Mom?"

"Mija, what's wrong? Are you sick? Arturo!" She calls to Dad. "Get the EpiPen!"

"No!" I shake my head. "I'm not sick. It's not… not that."

"No EpiPen?" Dad screams from the living room.

"No." Mom confirms, before appearing back at my side. "¿Qué pasa, Olivia?"

I draw in a shaky breath. "It's Brooklyn."

"But I thought things were finally going the way you wanted?"

"I did too." I squeeze my eyes shut and lean against her. "But he's leaving."

"What do you mean leaving?"

I tell her everything I know, which isn't much but is definitive enough. "Ma, he's getting the opportunity of his life. I can't just get in the way."

"But why would you be getting in the way?" She strokes my hair with one hand, the other holding me tight against her.

"Because I dallied. I didn't tell him what I feel in time and if I do that now it might make him hesitate." I shake my head against her shoulder. "I can't do that to him. Hockey's all he has."

"He has you too. He wouldn't choose one or the other."

I frown. "What?"

"People can have several loves without favoring one over the rest. Just look at your father and I. We love you three just the same."

"That's not true." I scoff. "Luz is the favorite child. I'm the middle of the pack. Aran's the third fave."

"What?" Mom screeches and pulls away. There's abject horror on her face. "Is that what you kids think?"

"Uh…" How did I just make this all worse?

"Olivia Maria…"

"Well." I scratch my head. "It's in the level of attention."

"What you just mentioned is the level of neediness." Mom smacks my arm pretty hard, making me wince. "Your sister's injury screwed us all up, and then there are your allergies. We just didn't have to worry very much about Aran." Her eyes glaze over as she gasps. "Oh, no. Does he think we don't love him? Arturo!"

"EpiPen?" Dad calls out from the living room, his voice still coming from the same place on the couch where he's attentively watching his son's game.

"Apparently the kids don't think we love them enough!"

I shake my head. "Sorry, Mom. I didn't—"

Dad takes a moment to say anything. "Should we buy them more gifts for Christmas?"

"Yes!" The word spills out of my chest automatically. "For your youngest! After all, your two eldest have very well-paying jobs already."

Mom starts laughing and for the first time in twenty-four hours, I do the same. I lean back into her and squeeze my arms tight around her, taking in her familiar scent. It's enough to calm me down.

"So what you're saying is that I don't have to make Brooke choose between me and hockey?"

"Yes." Mom kisses the top of my head.

"And what do I do if he leaves for the pros anyway?"

"Maybe give him the chance to help you come up with a plan."

I mumble. "Well, that's if he likes me too."

"Oh, he does, Olivia. You've always been that boy's world."

CHAPTER 31
BROOKLYN

We must've crushed the other team's spirits so badly last night, that tonight is an easy win. Almost embarrassing, even. A whopping seven goals to one they managed to score during a power play. Yet, it tastes funky. Liv wasn't at the game and something's clearly off with her. The last thing I want to do right now is celebrate.

"Tatum," Coach calls me from the door of the locker room.

This time, I drop everything and follow him out into the hallway. I'm in my socks and sans jersey, the pads still cinched tight around my elbows, chest, and shoulders. A mix of sweat and water drips down my face and I try to wipe it with my hand. "What's up, Coach?"

"I'm going to have to replace you as team captain."

"What?" I shout, my body stiffening like a plank. "What did I do wrong? The team's been playing well. Even the seniors have stopped talking smack."

"Nothing's wrong. Actually, I just have major news for you." He makes a dramatic pause I don't appreciate, and while my expression darkens, his slowly splits into a smile. "You're being called up to the pros, son."

The words *the pros* seem to echo around us. They keep bouncing against the walls and hitting my head with violence, and even then I don't process them. I can't reason at all.

What does react is my body. My stomach takes off like a cart being pulled at several times the force of gravity around rollercoaster loops.

In contrast, my heart plummets to the floor. And it keeps going until it disappears all the way down the center of the earth. The pro team is in a different state—shit, it's clear across the country on the west coast. That's as far as it can possibly get from Olivia without having to use a passport.

I stagger. Coach takes it as normal shock. He pats my shoulder—actually, my pads. "I know. It's a big deal. It's not everyday that college kids get called straight up to the pros without going through the farm team. Especially when it isn't even the playoffs."

My eyes close. I sat with Dane at O'Malley's just last week, watching the team that drafted me struggle. "They've had a lot of injuries this year," I say with a faraway voice.

"That's right." He expels a long breath. "It's going to suck for our team to lose you. Hell, it may cost us the season. But it's your chance, Tatum."

"Right." I swallow hard and shake my head. "Um, do I have a choice in this?"

Coach Green does a double take. "A what? What other alternative do you have?"

"Staying?"

He gives me a look like I'm shitting him. "Sure, you can choose to stay in your Division I team and maybe carry it to Frozen Four for two years in a row. Then you could either get dropped by your pro team, or go to the farm team. And then there, you certainly have the choice of working your ass off, or slacking off and getting dropped like Liam Richards."

"Whoa, what?" My head's reeling from the barrage of words coming out of Coach's pie hole, but especially that last part.

"So, sure. You have the choice of squandering away the opportunities that come to you. Be my guest."

I lift a shaky hand and run it through my wet hair. "I still want to think about it."

"Fine, but I do have to tell your father because you're still a minor."

"Okay." Before he leaves, I add. "And Coach? Can we please not tell the team yet? I don't want to cut their momentum."

He jams his hands in the pocket of his official sweats. "Fine by me. But you can only hide it as long as it takes for your pro team to make the announcement." He says this, one hundred percent sure that I'm moving up to the NHL, no ifs or buts.

I watch his retreating back for a moment, my lungs working even harder than if I was in the middle of a shift.

I don't know how I manage to take myself back to the locker room to keep getting undressed. Most of the guys have already hit the showers, except for a couple of seniors who give me nasty looks. They probably heard. Now the whole team's going to find out.

I lean back. How should I tell Liv?

Actually, the more important question is, how can I tell Liv I'm in love with her and also ask her to get into a long distance relationship with me?

A few minutes later, I use the cover of the shower spray to hide the fact I'm crying like a freaking baby. The guys would give me so much shit if they knew, but no one's paying attention to me. They're chatting about the goals we scored, the saves Jamie made, the sick deke Dane made in the third, the party they're going to crash from the engineering kids. I have to brace myself against the wall so I don't crumble.

Who knew that getting everything I've been working for could feel so crushing?

Unlike yesterday, I take so long to shower that Dane's already toweling off when he asks, "You okay, blondie?"

"Yep." I say in a snappy way. "I'm all good. You can go ahead of me."

"Okay…"

I basically turn into a prune. That's as long as it takes me to wait for everybody to leave. I plop on the bench, still wearing only a towel. My elbows fall to my knees and I lean forward to rub my face, my hair, and my face again. My heart must've returned from wherever the hell it went when Coach dropped the news, and now it thumps painfully in my chest.

After getting dressed, I drag my ass out of the locker room, my head still spinning around. I need to talk with someone, think about this aloud. Maybe I should hash this out with Dane and Jamie. That's what friends are for, right? But they're working up to the same goal of going pro, and I think that wouldn't make them objective enough.

"—Review the tape?" A familiar voice drifts closer, and I lift my head to find Coach Young and Assistant Coach McDonald walking into the facilities. I must've taken so long getting showered and dressed that the Strikes have already returned from their away game. We make eye contact and the two women tip their heads in acknowledgment before returning to their conversation.

I clear my throat and on impulse, I ask, "Coach Young, can I speak with you?"

The two women freeze.

I hoist the strap of my bag higher on my shoulder, waiting. This is abnormal. I've had to exchange words with Elaine Young maybe twice this entire semester, and one was to apologize when I almost ran into her in the hallway. But that makes her the perfect person for this. She knows squat about me and is fully objective. Plus, from what I hear she's more level headed than my coach.

"Uhh, sure. But don't you have your own coach?"

I clear my throat. "I… I need a woman's perspective."

Now that causes the two women to exchange amused looks, and her assistant coach ducks her face—probably thinking that I can't see the smile on her face. But I can. Because I'm sky-scraper tall compared to her.

"Never mind." I sigh. Moments like this is when I wish I had a mother I could talk to.

"No, no. It's all right. Follow me to my office."

Coach Young motions with her hand and I walk behind her past the Bolts and Strikes locker rooms, the storage room, the gym, and down to the corridor that leads to the staff offices. There, for the first time, I veer right toward the Strikes' staff offices, instead of left to the Bolts'. Sections are divided by clear glass panels, and if anyone sees me walking into Coach Young's office they'll have questions.

But I need help, so I take the seat across her desk and wait until she settles in her chair. "What can I do for you, Mr. Tatum?"

"Please, just Brooklyn. I don't want to sound like my dad." I mumble as I fiddle with the zipper tab of my hoodie. "Well, Coach Green just told me I'm getting called to the pros."

Her dark eyebrows rise. "Wow, congratulations. But why don't you look anywhere near as excited as you should?"

"Because there's this girl."

"Ah." She leans back and her chair squeaks. "That's defi-nitely not something you could talk about with your coach."

"Right. He'd probably break a stick on my head if I tried."

"That would get him fired, but he'd probably blow your eardrums out until he loses his voice."

I wince. "Yeah, so. The issue is that this girl… she's everything. We've been friends since we were literally five years old. And I've been gearing up to ask her out at the benefit."

"Hmm." She presses her lips.

"And now I probably shouldn't. But I still want to. Except I can't say no to this offer, and like—I can't take her with me. She still has three semesters to go." I take a deep breath and slouch forward. "What do I do?"

"Talk to her?"

We stare at each other in silence. My eyes narrow until one starts to twitch. "Sorry, what?"

"Talk to her." She shrugs. "You can't pretend like nothing's happening. Your team will put out an announcement with the call-up and she may find out that way if you don't say anything. That'd be much worse."

I scratch my head. "But what if it goes wrong? What if I lose her?"

"Why would you lose someone who sounds like a lifelong friend of yours because you're moving away?"

"I—well…"

I almost say because I lost her once, except I didn't really. Liv and I found our way to each other, and eventually we picked right where we left off. Just like putting on a beloved pair of jeans you thought you'd lost.

The only thing that's different this time is that I want her. But it'd be selfish to use that as a talking point to change her life and mold it to mine. Even if I chose to stay, if I tossed away my hockey career, I'd be using her as an excuse to alter the course of my life and Liv wouldn't want that, either. Even if she doesn't feel the same way for me, she'd never want me to give up.

So no matter what I do, I'm going to lose her. But I should face it head on, like Coach Young advises. It's better to stay Liv's friend forever, than to try to mess with that.

"Okay," I say, my voice barely a thread. "I'll tell her everything."

I'll tell Liv that I'm going to the pros and that I love her, but that I don't expect anything from her other than what we are. I can be honest with her—I have to—even if it destroys me.

"Good luck, kid."

Nodding, I pick my bag up and after murmuring my thanks, I step out of her office. A few staff members watch me go, questions on their faces, but I'm glad that no one intercepts me until I get to my car.

I swallow hard, blinking fast in the dark even though there's no point in holding back tears. There's no one here to see them. There won't be anyone after I leave and I'm all alone on the other side of the country.

My phone starts buzzing in my pants and I try to ignore it. When it doesn't stop, I pull it out to check who has the worst timing in history.

"Dad," I say in a garbled voice when I pick up.

"Your Coach just called me with the news." Shit. I bang on the steering wheel. Of freaking course this is when Dad decides to show up. "Congratulations, son. I'll get to work on the paperwork on Mon—"

"I'm your son now?"

"Excuse me?"

"Now," I repeat in a flat voice. "When I'm moving to the opposite coast. That's when I'm your son."

"I—I'm not following."

Everything I've had bottled up for years and years finally spills out of my mouth. "You never called when I won a game. Or when I lost one. You forgot to call me on my birthday this year, by the way. But *now* I'm your *son*." I put some ugly emphasis on those two words.

"Brooklyn, what are you talking about?" He sounds flabbergasted.

"You've ignored me for years. Why the hell do you care what I do now? Or am I finally successful enough for you to notice me?" I don't give a shit that I'm weeping at this point. I'm so mad and hurt and sad. I don't care about anything anymore.

He repeats my name and adds, "Come home. Let's talk about this."

"No, I don't want to talk with anyone right now. I want to be alone, just like I'm going to be starting in January."

I hang up and turn the device off before he can even think of calling me again. Not that he would. I'm used to being without him, or my mother. But I never got used to being without my best friend.

What the hell am I going to do now?

CHAPTER 32
OLIVIA

"So, what kind of dress are we looking for?"

Brooklyn looks at me while he sips from what is potentially a kiddy-pool full of ice coffee. In the middle of a Wednesday afternoon. And in the winter.

Granted, he doesn't feel the cold and it's not just because he plays hockey, he just never has. It's probably because he's a human furnace. I can feel his heat radiating through his and my layers of clothes as we walk in the mall together, close enough to touch but not doing so. It would warm me better than the hot cup of tea I have my hands wrapped around.

"I guess something elegant." While he talks, the straw still sits between his lips and all my attention goes there. "But like, it doesn't have to be this huge, puffy, prom dress."

"A specific color?" I tear my eyes away from his mouth and glance at the store exhibits. Clothes, accessories, and home goods of all kinds wait patiently for people's wallets. I wasn't kidding when I said there's only dust and moths in mine, which is why we came here instead of a fancier store downtown.

"We both know it's going to be black."

I grin with my head still turned away from him. "Atta boy."

"Yep, you've taught me well." He clears his throat. "It'll also be easy for me to match."

"Oh." I whirl toward him. "Can you please wear a black shirt so we can both look badass and intimidating?"

Brooke blinks those emerald green eyes of his slowly. "We're already badass and intimidating, no matter what we wear."

"Pfff. They must not know you're actually a cinnamon roll, golden retriever, marshmallow guy."

"Excuse me!" He raises his voice in mock outrage that won't get him any attention, because this place is freaking empty and he can't fool his only audience. "I'm the best defenseman in Division I hockey right now. Opponents cower upon my sight—"

"Do they?"

"Hey." His frown now is for real.

I press my lips tight. "Sorry to break it to you, they're intimidated by your skills but not by your face."

He scrunches up said face. "Fine, I'm more the pest kind of D-man than the enforcer kind. But what's wrong with my face?"

My eyes flash to the faint scar right above the edge of his jaw, and I desperately wish I could kiss it. As if my lips could take away the hurt and finish healing it. But in the course of a few weeks, the blemish has become so familiar I almost don't notice it's there. It's just part of his face now—his beautiful, perfect face that will always haunt me every time I close my eyes.

"Nothing," I say, meaning it. But before he can say anything, I point at a store with my lips. "There's the place that will get me looking like a million bucks but actually set me back somewhere south of fifty."

"Wait, isn't this the place where you bought your actual senior prom dress?"

I squint up at him. "How do you remember that?"

Brooke presses his fist against his mouth and clears his throat. "Well, the tag was hanging from your dress like half the night."

That piece of news makes me gasp as we walk into the store. "And you didn't tell me?"

"I took it off when we finally managed to dance the one time."

Oh, I remember *that*.

His date, who was his girlfriend at the time, hogged him basically the whole night. I didn't have a date, which made me feel even crappier about myself the whole time. And when, at last, Brooke's girlfriend took a bio break and he found me for the dance we'd promised each other since like, middle school, I thought my moment had arrived. At one point he even leaned down and I thought he was going to kiss me, only to pull back quickly.

That moment was traumatizing at the time. I agonized the whole night about whether my expression showed how much I wanted him, and whether that had made him pull away. But I now guess it must've been when he tore the tag from my dress.

After inflating my chest with air, I expel it all out in a noisy sigh.

"Welcome," a sales associate says to us. Correction, to Brooklyn. She only has eyes for him, even though this store only sells apparel for women. "Can I help you with anything specific?"

His hand rests on my shoulder and he says, "We got it, but we'll call you if we need help."

Her smile falters a tad as she looks down at me. "You got it." I can't fault her for her disappointment.

As she leaves, my eyes fall on the rack she'd been blocking and I gasp. "Wow, that dress is so ugly it's almost offensive." It's this concoction of mesh and faux leather, all in a bright yellow highlighter hue.

Brooke squeezes between me and a busy rack, which means the front of his body brushes against my arm and fully paralyzes me. He plucks the dress by the hanger and offers it to me. "I dare you to try it on."

I unfreeze myself to roll my eyes and say, "We're not in middle school anymore, Toto."

"Speaking of dogs, I double dog dare you." There's a smugness in his face I don't appreciate, because if I refuse the dare he's probably going to come up with something worse.

"Didn't you say we have to kind of hurry up because you have practice soon?" That's one last ditch attempt.

Of course, he easily deflects it. "Aceituna, are you being chicken shit?"

"Fine." I snatch the awful thing from his hand until I see the size. "Wait, I need the right size."

"What are you?" he asks as he returns the original monstrosity to the rack.

I sigh. "M on a good day."

Deft fingers run through the hanger hooks, passing through the color tabs with the sizes until he finds an M. "Here you go. I'll wait for you outside the dressing rooms."

"Ugh."

I stomp through the store, equal parts annoyance and amusement swirling in my belly in the way only Brooklyn Tatum can create. At least the dressing rooms are spacious. There's a bench where I can set my tea down while I get undressed, and hangers to put my clothes so they don't drag all over the floor. I refuse to take off my boots, though, because the floor looks like it was cleaned last season if at all.

It's a bit too drafty for my liking and I shiver once I'm down to my underwear, removing the hanger from the dress. This looks like something that would work well at a nightclub in some tropical city, not the thirty degrees we're boasting this afternoon. But whatever, who am I to refuse a double dog dare.

But also, I'm curious.

See, this dress has a lot of see-through panels. After the way Brooke reacted the last time I wore something lacy, I wouldn't have expected him to be interested in seeing me in this. I'll happily pretend like this is some harmless little flirting, and not a prolonged goodbye where I have no idea how we stand.

I carefully step into the dress, making sure not to snag it with my boots because I don't want to pay for it. For a tense moment, it refuses to come up past my hips and for once, they may be a blessing in disguise. But then the dress slides right up and I have no choice but to slide my arms into the straps. As I pull it up, though, I can tell my bra will be in full display if I don't remove it. Unfortunately, it's one of those comfortable ones in the shade of my skin and it has seen better days, so I take it off. After I pretzel myself, I manage to zip the dress up and look in the mirror.

"Damn." My jaw hangs.

Brooke's voice comes from right outside the flimsy door. "Oh, I gotta see it now."

"Nope. You're not seeing this." I shake my head at myself. My assessment was right. This is a dress for a wild night out. Turns out the faux leather panels and trims hug places that have no right being highlighted—pun intended—during the day.

"I will tear the door off its hinges if I have to." He says this in such a deep, low voice, it makes me shake with a violent shudder.

I rub my hands up and down my arms to smoothen down the goosebumps. We both know I'll show him the dress. I know I'm dying to see his reaction. But I don't have to act like I'm so willing.

Grumbling, I unlock the door and pull it open.

Brooke's eyes bulge just like they did at O'Malley's the night I dressed a tad bold. But this time he doesn't throw a coat around my shoulders or something.

No, he slowly, very deliberately, takes in all the details. From the tight skirt that shows miles of leg through the mesh fabric, to the strategic cutouts around my torso, to the ultra tight top that enhances my otherwise modest chest. Finally, when his eyes lift to my face I know he can see the hot blush on my cheeks.

And it makes him smirk. The asshole.

He twirls a finger in the air. "Turn around."

"Wait." I run my hands down the back and what I feel is a lot of mesh, rather than faux leather. "I didn't check the back but it feels awful cool. Like there's not enough fabric."

His eyebrows pop. "Oh yeah? I can confirm that."

"No." Especially because I'm wearing granny panties. "I'm changing and then we're finding the actual dress we came here for."

"Actually, I selected a couple options while you were in there." He reaches to the side and brings up one. A chuckle comes out of him the second my eyes fall on it. "I double dog dare you."

"Brooklyn." His name comes out of my lips almost like a hiss.

This dress is the opposite. A pink ball of fluff with tiny hearts all over it. I feel like wearing this one even less than the yellow highlighter barf fest I'm currently in.

But I snag it anyway, and back into the dresser I go. He's still giggling like a five year old as I slide one dress off, and the second one on. But then I realize something. The cotton candy atrocity is also going to short-circuit him. I don't know if he grabbed it on purpose, but the dress is backless. And when I mean backless, I mean I have to hide my underwear because the back opening plunges that deep.

This time I open the door without warning. Brooke's eyes twinkle more than the Christmas lights adorning the entire mall. From the front, the dress is all puffy sleeves and a puffy miniskirt. Nothing terrible, although I've never seen him look at my thighs with such attention. I almost stay still for a while longer.

But nah, I turn. He chokes in his own saliva.

I look at him over my shoulder. "Did you pick this dress knowing that like half of it is missing?"

"I h-had no idea." He thumps his chest hard.

That time at O'Malley's, he reacted in a similar way. His coughing fit only abated after he'd buttoned up my jean jacket.

My eyes narrow. I think I got it all wrong back then. Brooklyn doesn't find me unattractive. It's just shocking to him that I am. The second I realize this, my pulse skyrockets through the ceiling and all the way to the moon.

Slowly, I turn back around and fold my arms. "Where's the other dress?"

"What?" He runs a hand through his blond hair once. Twice.

"You said you'd selected a couple of them while I was trying on the first one."

"Oh, right." He clears his throat as he reaches over again. He must've hung them from the door of the adjacent dresser. This time, the dress he presents to me is finally in line with what we're here for. At least on account of the color. "I think you'll actually like this one."

I feel the fabric between my fingers. It's silky but not as thin as the real deal. "Hmm. Okay." I take it from him and make a big show of heading back into my dresser at a snail's pace. Through the mirror, I can see his eyes glued to the expanse of bare skin at my back. I close the door and lock it, not because he'd ever try anything. But because I might. If he keeps looking at me like that I will.

Please, keep looking at me like that, I beg in my mind.

I hurry out of the pink dress to put on the black one. This fabric has zero give, so I slide it down from above. It's like it was custom made for my weird shape though. The drooping folds at my chest compared to how tight it fits everywhere else is actually very flattering.

This time, no matter how much I pretzel myself, I can't zip it up. It's fine, though. The dress fits like a glove, so I know one of my roommates can help me into it on the night of the event. But now I can't pull the tab down either, which means it got stuck on the fabric.

I contemplate whether to live in the dress forever, or to…

To… open the door, and ask Brooklyn for help.

I swallow so hard that I can hear it. My chest rises and falls with my rapid breathing. I'm going to do this, though. I have to test this new theory that he does think I'm hot. That the kiss we shared in the spring wasn't a fluke. That there could've been something between us if he wasn't leaving in a month.

"Brooke?" My voice breaks a little.

"What's up?"

"I need help. I'm stuck."

"'Kay. Open the door."

That sounds a lot more ominous than it should. But I open the door, even though I know this will change things.

Brooke's expression is serious as his eyes run down my frame. No laughter or coughing this time. Instead, he does something even more terrifying. He walks into the dressing room.

I take a step back, almost hitting the wall behind me. The door swings shut all by itself. As it clicks, my breath hitches.

Green eyes travel down the slope of my clavicle to my shoulder, down to my arm where the goosebumps are the worst. His lips curve in the corners. "You don't look stuck. This one fits you like a glove."

I shuffle awkwardly to present my back. "Not me, it's the zipper." I keep my face angled toward the mirror so I can catch every minutia. His eyelids lower, and I feel his gaze down my bare back like a caress. It skips past the zipper tab and settles on my butt.

For the first time in our lives, Brooklyn is openly staring at my ass. And his hand closes into a tight fist at his side like he's holding back from reaching out.

A weaker woman would collapse against the wall. I don't know how I manage to not be that weaker woman.

"Brooke?"

"Right." He jerks himself out of the trance, taking a step closer to get a proper look. I can't do anything to hide the shiver when his fingers brush against my back. "Sorry. I know you're ticklish."

I grit my teeth. That wasn't it. At all.

"Damn. This is really stuck." He grunts as he tugs on the fabric, which jerks me against him.

"Uhh." I lean my head back to look up at him. "You might want to be a bit more careful or you'll rip the whole thing open."

Brooke blinks down at me. Swallows hard. "I'm considering it."

The beat of my heart turns into pounding. His hands release the zipper and instead, cinch around my waist. His name falls out of my lips like a question, but all the answer I get his Brooklyn lowering his forehead to my shoulder. His skin feels like fire against mine.

"Liv…"

"Brooke?"

"I'm trying to behave here."

I grab his hands against my stomach. "What do you mean, behave?"

"I'm supposed to be your best friend. I *am* your best friend." His breath fans against my mostly bare back, making my muscles clench at the strength of the sensation. "But I don't have very friendly thoughts in my mind right now."

I bite my lip and ask, "What kind of thoughts do you have?"

A dark chuckle follows. "I really want to rip this freaking dress to shreds, throw you against the wall, and kiss you sense-less. And more. Definitely more."

Welp. This is when I collapse against the wall. It feels like ice against my forehead.

"Okay, let's be rational here," I say with a choked up voice. "If you rip out the dress, we'll have to pay for it and I still won't have something to wear for the gala."

Brooklyn snorts. But then he spins me around, and he doesn't have to throw me against the wall. The heat in his eyes alone is enough to melt me against it.

He leans an arm against the wall just over my head, and the posture brings his face almost level with mine. His eyes roam all over my face, as if searching for something. And for the first time since I've been crushing on him, I don't care if he can see how smitten I am. I run the tip of my tongue across my lips, savoring the coffee of his breath against them already.

Brooke sucks in air through his teeth, as if my gesture phys-ically hurt him. Faster than a lightning bolt, he holds the side of my neck and pulls me against him. His thumb runs down the length of my jaw until tucks under my chin to tip my head back. His eyes steal the breath from me.

"Liv. If we do this, we'll cross a line there's no coming back from." I'm sure he can feel the rapid pulse at the base of my throat against the heel of his hand, or how hard I swallow. His breathing is already fast, as if he'd been running to this moment. "If I kiss you right now, it won't be as a stranger. It sure as hell won't be as a friend either."

"I know," I whisper, my hands sneaking under his coat to fist around his sweatshirt.

"Is that what you want?" His jaw tightens as he swallows. "Say it."

"What?" I couldn't say my name right now if I had to.

"Say that you want me to kiss you right now."

"I… want…" I look into his eyes as I say, "You."

His mouth crashes against mine and I close my eyes, melting against him. I'd never describe our first kiss as sweet, but this one is downright bruising.

Brooklyn pushes his lips against mine, coercing my jaw open. I tilt my head back to give him full access, and we both moan when our tongues meet. His free hand slides down my back to the mound of my butt cheek, squeezing tight, bringing me flush against him and I gasp. But then, as his lips close around mine, that hand keeps going down until I feel a rush of air.

He tears his mouth away from mine and I open my eyes, about to protest. Except now Brooke drags both of his hands up my thighs, pulling the fabric of the dress up. I watch, confused but not upset at all. It only clicks when he wraps his hands around the back of my thighs and lifts me up.

Yelping, I close my arms around his neck so I don't slide right back down. Brooklyn looks up at me, eyes dark and hooded even as he smirks. "Don't worry, I'd never let you fall." He pushes me against the wall, hands sliding down my thighs until he wraps my legs around him.

I gasp. Joke's on him, I already fell a long time ago.

"Shut up and kiss me again."

"Yes, ma'am."

This time it's not as urgent. He kisses my bottom lip with all the care in the world, like maybe he knows it's already throbbing and swollen. But then he closes his teeth around it, so soft it doesn't hurt, but I feel the scrape of his teeth all the way down to my toes. The moan that tears out of my throat is so not safe for all audiences.

"Damn, you're so hot," he murmurs against my lips before kissing me hard once more. I grab a fistful of his hair, clench my legs tighter, and he's still not close enough. One of his hands holds my weight firmly under one thigh, but the other one travels higher. Not high enough. Not fast enough. And then his pants start buzzing.

Our mouths make a shocking sound as we separate. I keep my eyes squeezed shut, knowing that if I open them, there'll be stars dancing around his face.

We both breathe hard—him more so. Which is funny, seeing as he's the elite athlete here. His forehead rests on mine, our noses against each other. "I think that's my alarm to head to practice," he says in a low, husky voice that raises a shiver out of me.

By slow increments, I open my eyes to meet his. "Okay," I whisper. "Go."

He nods. "I'm going."

I bite my lip and gasp softly at how tender it is. He brings the roaming hand up to run his thumb against my lip. "I don't see you moving," I say against the pad of his thumb.

"I don't wanna move."

Puckering my lips, I place a little kiss on his finger. "Go."

Brooklyn groans, but he grabs me by the waist and lowers me until my boots touch the floor again. He keeps me there for a moment, tight against him. As he looks into my eyes, his hands travel across my back to the zipper. Two hard tugs, and it finally frees itself.

I suck in air as Brooklyn lowers the tab all the way down and says, "Promise me you'll wear this dress."

"Yeap. This is the one," I respond, the words jerky.

Brooke presses his smile against my lips and disappears out of the door just like that. Like we almost didn't just get frisky in here.

It takes me an extraordinarily long time to get changed. The sales associate glares at me the entire time she bags the dress, which, surprise, Brooke paid for on his way out. She probably heard the whole little episode. What she doesn't know is how hard I had to work to earn it, or how hard I'm going to have to work now to keep him.

CHAPTER 33
BROOKLYN

Olivia is avoiding me. Kind of. On Thursdays our schedules don't match, but on Friday night I have an away game and it gives her the perfect excuse to stay MIA the whole day. I invite her over to the library on Saturday, so we can finish our Spanish presentation and maybe also make out in the history section, and she claims to have A Thing Going On the Whole Weekend. She doesn't reveal what, though. But at least, she agrees to talk on Monday after our last Spanish class together.

Now, we sit together in class and she's definitely trying to pretend like I'm not here. I mean, I have my arm on the back of her seat, a leg propped up on my chair so I can sit facing her, and she still keeps her eyes set on the pair of students giving their final presentation downstairs.

It would be amusing if it wasn't so frustrating. She said, out of her very mouth that I thoroughly savored, that she wants *me*. I'm sure that hasn't changed in the span of five days. So why is she acting like this?

My phone buzzes against the table and I flip it around to find a text from my defensive partner.

GREAT DANE

Ready?

With one hand, I type up a response in return.

ME

I don't know

She's still being all weird

What if this makes it worse?

JAMES THE GOALIE

Well, if you don't tell her how you feel she's
going to stay even weirder amirite?

Since when did he get so wise? Or maybe he always was
and I'm only finding out now that I talk more openly with both
of them.

ME

K good point

Wish me luck, gentlemen

GREAT DANE

Godspeed soldier

JAMES THE GOALIE

Knock her dead

But like, figuratively

I slide the phone back on the table, face down. When I
glance up, Liv turns back to the front so fast it must make her
dizzy. My lips stretch into a smirk. I wonder if she was a bit
jealous that I finally paid attention to something else.

But it's okay, after today she'll know I don't truly pay attention to anyone else.

Her hair fell forward after she moved, and I want full access to her face again. I reach over, brushing my fingers against her skin as I tuck her hair back behind her ear. And since I learned her ears are sensitive, I linger there, playing with her piercings as if they were the point of my interest.

Sure enough, Liv shivers.

Her hand comes out like a whip against my ribs. She whispers, "What are you doing?"

I bite my lips hard so I don't laugh. "Nothing."

"Doesn't feel like nothing to me."

"Oh yeah?" I lean closer to her ear, her shoulder brushing against my chest. "What does it feel like?"

Her nostrils expand with a sharp intake of air. Like maybe she's only now realizing that she just admitted how my touch affects her. We're so close, if she fully turns her head we could kiss. But all she does is scoot far enough to gift me a fierce side-eye.

"Liv—"

"We said we'll talk after class." The finality of her voice makes me sigh.

I pull away and behave until it's our turn to present. As we walk down the steps together, it occurs to me that maybe she's being all weird because she feels physically attracted to me, but doesn't like-*like* me. That's possible. It's how I felt for the countless girls before her.

But her exact words in the dressing room were *I want you*, and not *I want to kiss you* like I originally asked her. So maybe my plan isn't as outrageous as it has felt in the past few minutes.

"Buenos días," she says in a perfect Spanish accent, only mismatching because she seems too polite. "Mi nombre es Olivia Rodriguez y éste es mi mejor amigo, Brooklyn Tatum."

What makes my eye twitch isn't how her name sounds so perfect in Spanish, while mine sounds so blah in English. But the fact she introduced me to the class as her best friend. I fold my arms, physically resisting the concept for the first time in my life.

I watch her as she continues with the introduction. Today she's in a grey button blouse and the same black pants that make every guy, including me, hang their tongues like cartoons. She's so freaking beautiful that she makes even standard business clothes become showstoppers.

I'm a beat too late to start my part, because I've been too busy ogling her like a fool. Clearing my throat, I say, "Les vamos a contar la historia sobre cómo nos hicimos amigos."

The lecturer said he wanted us to get more personal for this assignment, so Liv and I decided to make it about our friendship. How we became besties during a sad birthday party, to some other shenanigans like the time we cut class to go watch a Spider-Man movie at the cinema, to how she's the one person who has watched most of my games in person, to how I took a CPR class in high school for her.

The back and forth storytelling gets us some aww's and chuckles, which is already a much bigger reaction than most of the other presentations got. Among the audience, I spot our former group mates giggling up a storm. In contrast, the lecturer's expression tells me he's wondering what to make for dinner tonight.

I guess they're all going to get a shock pretty soon.

My ears roar as Liv recites the last words we have planned for the presentation. She points at me, because I'm supposed to be the one with the closer.

Except, I clear my throat and say, "Pero la historia continúa," in a gringo accent I can't quite shed no matter how much vocabulary I cram into my head.

Liv blinks hard. I reach for her hand and someone in the audience squeals.

"Brooke, what are you doing?" my best friend whispers.

"Shh, I'm trying to be brave here," I respond in a low voice, before raising it again. "Quiero escribir un nuevo capítulo contigo."

Her brown eyes widen. My whole face tingles and it's not doubt with one of those awful blushes that make me look like I have a rash. But I'll push through, because I want there to be no doubt in Liv's mind about what I mean. I want our story to continue, but not in the same way.

"No quiero seguir siendo solo tu mejor amigo." My voice lowers, because the next part of the speech is just for her. "Quiero ser tu novio."

Her lips part with a gasp.

A strident squeal echoes through the classroom. More noise explodes as all sorts of voices join in, or laugh, or coo—and I don't care. Because Liv's turned into a statue.

Her hand feels like ice in mine. I squeeze it a bit, to see if that snaps her out of the shock. But nothing. "Liv?"

Finally, she gives a sign of life by blinking so fast, her vision must be like the shutter of a camera. "You what?"

"I want to be your boyfriend," I say again, in English. Loud. "Not your best friend. Or just a friend. I want us to be together." I take a step closer to her, inhaling the scent of her skin. "I want you."

Tears spring to her eyes like it's a magic trick. But instead of jumping into my arms and kissing me senseless, she jerks her hand free and turns to dash out of the classroom.

There's more heckling than during an away game at the Bulldogs' arena, and the lecturer's straining his voice to keep the class quiet. I take off after Olivia. My stomach is so clenched, I fear I'm going to puke on my shirt.

She tries a door and I catch up to her as she's slipping through a second one. She tries to shut it in my face but I'm so much stronger. Still, I'm not going to wrestle her. "Liv, please. Can I come in?"

After a moment, she stops putting her weight against the door and I slip inside. The room is tiny and crammed with overflowing shelves of boxes, books, loose papers, and even dusty trophies. None of that matters. Liv stands in the middle and when she turns around, her face is rain and thunder.

"How dare you?" The question slips out of her throat like a growl and I freeze.

CHAPTER 34
OLIVIA

Brooklyn is pale. He swallows hard as he rests his weight against the door, shutting us inside the small storage room. I'm so pissed that he physically shrinks.

"How dare you ask me to be your girlfriend *now*." I throw my hands in the air so hard that when they fall, they slap my thighs. "Why now? After all these years?"

"I—" He opens and closes his mouth. "Because I'm a fool and I only realized I'm in love with you this year?"

I blink hard against the blurring of my vision, my feelings spilling out of my eyes in steady streams. His words knock the wind out of me, and I sound a lot fainter as I ask, "You what?"

The sleeves of his white shirt tighten almost to the point of tearing apart as he combs both hands through his blond hair, pulling hard as if he was the angry one now. "I love you, Olivia." Brooklyn drops his hands and just stays there, six feet away from me. "I've always loved you, I just didn't know it. But when you were gone, I missed you so damn hard I had to carve you on my skin."

He yanks the sleeve of his shirt so hard, the button goes flying. But he doesn't stop until the tattoo lines are showing.

"This? This was because of you. Because my heart has been so full of you, there was nothing left when you were gone. I tried to fill it with hockey or with other people and it wasn't enough. It was always empty. Until you came back."

With my hands pressed against my mouth, I say, "But now you're the one leaving."

The determination in his face cracks. "How… How do you know?"

Oh. So he *is* leaving. It's certain now.

"I—I overheard your coach and the scout talking two weeks ago."

"Two…" Brooke shakes his head hard. "Wait, is this why you've been acting so weird?"

"Yes." I bite my lip and shut my eyes. This will be a lot easier if I can't see him. "Brooke, do you want to know why I was so angry at you at that party, that I stopped talking with you for over a year?"

The only sounds from him are attempts at saying something and failing. The quiet extends uncomfortably, wrapping me in a cold vise I can only break free out of if I'm finally brave.

"That night…" I trail off, trying to use the sleeves of my blouse to blot out my tears. I keep sniffling as I talk. "That night, I had gathered my nerve to go confess my feelings for you."

He sucks in air so sharp, it makes me look at him. Never have I seen pain like this on his face. Not the time he skinned his knees after chasing me. Not after getting his cheek cut by a hockey stick. Not even when his mother left him.

"Liv." He shakes his head slowly, gulping so hard I can hear it. "You—You liked me back then?"

"Not just back then." My blouse can't absorb any more moisture and I give up. I just let the tears fall where they may. With a sad little voice, I say, "Since high school, or maybe before. I couldn't tell you exactly since when. Maybe since always. You've always been my one."

Brooke presses the heels of his hands against his eyes, like maybe he's trying not to cry. His jaw is so tight that a muscle jumps on his cheek. "I want to roundhouse kick myself right now. Or maybe I'll just stand very still and you can kick me instead."

"I'm not going to kick you." I sigh.

"Fine." The determination is back in his eyes after he drops his hands. "So what I'm getting is you like me, and I love you. We can make this work."

"You're wrong."

His eyebrows scrunch up in a mix of confusion and sadness. "You don't like me anymore?"

"No." I reach for his hand before he crumbles, and hastily add, "I mean, you got it wrong. It's not that I like you. I *love* you. I've always loved you."

"Oh." Air comes out of his lungs, so relieved that his entire frame sags against the door. His thumb runs against my hand. "Why do I sense a but?"

"*But* you're leaving."

Brooke nods slowly, his hair so messy that two strands arc over his eyebrow and almost into his eyes. "I am. But..." He leans down to grab my other hand. "That doesn't mean it has to be the end of our story."

"Brooklyn. You're going to be clear across the country."

"I know."

"And it's not like I can transfer to a nearby college so easily. I have a partial scholarship and in-state tuition here."

"I also know that."

"And I'm not going to let you pay for me, if that's what you're thinking."

His eyebrows squeeze. "Shit, I hadn't thought of that. Why not?"

"Because that'd be weird."

"But I love you," he says, as easy as talking about the weather. As if it didn't have the power to stop my heart from beating. He restarts it by lifting my hands, pressing his warm lips against one, then against the other. Green eyes set on me the entire time. "And I would do anything for you."

"Not that. It's not fair." My voice may shake, but my spine doesn't. "I won't strain your finances."

"Fine. Long distance it is."

"Brooke—"

"No, hear me out." He has his game face on, the one he uses for a faceoff. It's enough to make me clamp my mouth shut. "We just spent like a year and a half apart—fully apart, not talking to each other at all. And I came from the other side so besotted, I can objectively say I've never been in love before."

My heart soars—it's a balloon in the sky now.

I shake my head hard, trying to focus. "But—"

"No." He shakes his head hard. "You know I had girl-friends, but I never felt one percent of what I feel for you for any of them. I may have been slow and clueless, but I'm feral over you, Liv. We're talking raccoon in a trashcan at the back of a McDonald's type of feral."

I bark a sudden laugh, and it also brings a change in him. Brooke's face softens into a shy little smile.

"My point is," he continues saying, "Physical distance won't be enough to tear us apart. We're entwined where it matters." He brings one of my hands against his rock-solid chest, laying my palm flat against it so I can feel the fast drum of his heart. "Right here."

I rake my teeth across my lip. "This isn't so simple. We're talking at least a year and a half. You'll be so busy with training and games, you'll barely have time to come visit. You've seen what Max's and Aran's schedules look like. We barely managed to see them for Thanksgiving. And I'm going to be busy with school too. But even during breaks, I don't know if I'll have the money to buy plane tickets to see you. I'll have to get a job for that, which will make me even busier and—"

Brooke puts a finger against my lips. "We'll FaceTime every night. And text every day. I'll have games against teams nearby, and we can sneak out together in between. The team may send me back down, and I might just end up back the next semester—"

"That's not going to happen." I tilt my head to give him an annoyed look. "You're so damn good, they'll never send you back down."

Brooklyn ignores that. "We can do this. I want to do this." His arms come around me, bringing me against his body. "I'm asking you to want to do this. Please?"

I let out something that sounds like a whine and a moan, dropping my face against his delicious chest—hard, warm, his own natural scent more potent than his fancy cologne. If only we could stay like this forever, wrapped in each other at last.

"There's nothing I want more," I admit in a mumble. "Brooklyn Tatum, I've wanted you for so long, it hurts like a literal thorn on the side."

"I'm sorry." He drops a kiss on my head.

I sniff against his chest. "And I can't believe you finally want me back when you're freaking leaving."

He buries his face in my hair, inhaling deep. His hands run up and down my back, warming me. "I'm leaving but I'm not leaving *you*. Ever."

"What if you meet someone else?"

"What if *you* meet someone else?" he counters.

"I mean, of course I will. Life is a constant parade of people."

He yanks my blouse out of my pants and sneaks his hands underneath so fast that I can't even react.

And then he tickles me.

I squirm and try to elbow him, but the attack only stops when he hugs me tight once more.

His hands are still under my blouse, and I pant against his chest. "My point is, you might meet a stunning woman in your new town who makes you realize that your childhood best friend is a cleaning mop in comparison."

"Olivia Rodriguez, how dare you speak that way about the woman who makes me wake up sweaty and gasping in the middle of the night?"

The one who gasps here is me, because he says all that wild stuff while at the same time, fisting his hand around my hair and pulling my head back to look up at him. His touch his gentle but unyielding.

"You make me take cold showers in the winter, Liv." He dips his head, saying the words against my lips. "I didn't lie when I said you make me feral. If you've seen me skate funny, it's because I started thinking about you in the middle of a game."

"Brooke!"

He grins. "No one else can, or will ever do that to me."

I'm ashamed to report that my knees buck and I only keep standing because of his arms around me. "I had no idea," I whisper.

He casually lowers a hand to my butt to press me flush against him. A little sound escapes from my throat that makes him grin even more. "What I want to know is… do I make you feral too?"

"I—ugh. Are you seducing me in a dirty storage closet?"

"Is it working?" His lips feather against the corner of mine. Brooke tilts his head to the other side, our noses brushing for a second, but instead of peppering a soft kiss against the opposite corner of my lips, he runs his tongue against them.

I push him against the door, hard enough that it stuns him

for a moment. Then I grab two big fistfuls of his crisp white shirt, and in perfect imitation of a hockey enforcer trying to throw their opponent down on the ice, I yank it up so hard it comes clear over his torso, his head, and off his body.

"U—Um, Liv?"

I toss his shirt over my shoulder and say, "The answer is yes."

Brooke's eyes are as wide as saucers, intent on my hands as I place them against his bare chest. Just that contact is enough for his skin to break into goosebumps all over, for an unmistakable flush to settle on his chest and neck. He swallows hard as I trail my hands down, tracing every ridge of muscle, my nails softly raking against his velvet-soft skin until they hook around his belt.

His hands close around mine. "I want to continue this some place else where no one will hear us."

"You're right," I say, but neither of us moves. "Can I kiss you, though?"

"Oh yeah, please."

I grab the sides of his face until our lips smash together. His hands find the bare skin of my sides, and not even a second later he's yanking off my blouse too. I don't even have time to gasp before he's kissing me again.

His body pushes against mine, walking me back until I'm against a rack. Hooking an arm around his neck to keep him close, I run my other hand up his arm, mapping the shape of his muscles, his shoulder, his clavicle, feeling the strain of his neck muscles as he devours my mouth. We breathe hard, our lips smack and suck, hungry for each other. But the best part is where our fevered skins touch. We've kissed before, but this part is new.

I guess all of it is.

Brooke tears apart, his chest expanding and collapsing fast

as he gulps for air. And I'm not faring any better, except my vision is a blur of his face and exploding lights.

"Does this mean we're doing it?" he asks, panting against my mouth.

I'm so dizzy, all I manage is to ask, "It?"

"Perv." He chuckles, even though he's the one who started it. "I mean us."

I bury my face in the crook of his neck, breathing through my mouth in my haste to get oxygen to my brain. Fast. But even if my mind was in its normal frame, I'd still answer the same.

"Yes." I mouth the words against his neck. "We're doing this. Us."

CHAPTER 35
BROOKLYN

Liv shivers as we walk up to the hotel where the benefit gala is held this year. I paid for valet parking so the exposure to the winter weather was minimal, and I bring her closer against my side as I run my hand up and down her arm. "Cold?" I ask.

"What?" She looks up at me, almost as if she'd forgotten where she was. "No. I just have regrets."

"About me?" I put my free hand on my chest.

"No. About this dress." That's when I notice she wasn't shivering but trying to stretch the material of her dress. "It makes my huge hips look huger. And this little jacket is way too short."

She's talking about the same black dress that made me lose my mind in a store's dressing room. She paired it with some fluffy black jacket that looks equal parts cozy and elegant, but stops right at her waist and highlights precisely the curves that made me think with my pants when I saw her in this dress.

I slide my hand past her arm, sneaking it below the jacket until I find her waist. Liv's breath hitches and she turns to look at me. If she hadn't put so much effort into her makeup I'd be ruining it right now, never mind the fact we're standing in the middle of the hotel lobby. My hand continues its journey lower over the swell of her hip, and it parks right on a spot I now know quickens her pulse.

Dipping my head lower, I run my nose across her warming cheek until I find her ear. I whisper very softly, "Your hips are so perfect I want to bite them. I won't accept any slander." And for emphasis, I give her a little squeeze.

Gasping, she steps all the way out of my embrace and fixes up her pristine clothes. "Brooke, we're in public. You need to behave."

"How can you expect me to behave when I've been resisting you for ages?" I finish the question with a whine and an attempt to grab her. All I get is her hand in mine and I guess I can settle for that.

"*Ages*, you say when it's only been like nine months since we kissed for the first time." She snorts as she pulls me to follow the signs leading to the event hall. "What about me? Should I be acting like a feral raccoon because I've been resisting you for longer?"

I tug her hand hard and she yelps as her body follows the momentum. The twirl lands her right against my chest and I close my arms around her before she can react. "Yes please," I say, brushing my nose against hers. "I'm finally all yours. Unwrap me like candy."

Her eyes dart around but there's no need, I said those words low and slow, only for her.

"Well, I'm not the one who's busy making hasty arrangements to move across the continent."

I sigh, dropping my forehead against hers. "I'm sorry. But I promise I'm all yours between Christmas and New Years. Should we go somewhere that week? Or… book a hotel room?" I wiggle my eyebrows.

Liv's eyes narrow. "Actually, not a bad idea."

As I freeze, she easily frees herself from me once again. Only when I realize that she's walking away—because my eyes are absolutely glued to her swaying hips—does my brain kick-start again. I run after her and when I catch up, I ask, "Wait, for real?"

"Mina, hi!" Liv says, completely ignoring my very legit question.

Her friend appears in my field of vision, wearing some red dress that matches the tie Dane's wearing. "Liv, you look absolutely stunning, oh my goodness."

The two girls hug it out and Liv says, "Have you looked at yourself in the mirror? Because you could stop traffic."

"Is it because her dress is red?" I ask, which gets me two glares. I turn to Dane. "What?"

He's laughing at me. "Dude, you're such a dipshit. I'm going to miss you."

I put a hand on my chest. "Aww, don't make me cry. You'll ruin my makeup."

"Liv," the other girl says. "Your new boyfriend's hot but he's kind of…"

"Yep." My girlfriend—oh my shishkebab, I'm still not used to the novelty—sidles up against me, her eyes sparkling with affection as they turn to me. "He's something else." Okay, not affection. Amusement.

I drop a kiss on the tip of her nose. "I'll have you know, I'm leaving college with an excellent GPA."

"Sure…"

"For a busy Division I athlete."

"Right." Her teasing stops the second I squeeze her hip again. Clearing her throat, she turns back to her friend. "Anyway, congratulations you two! I heard you became an official couple already."

"What?" I whirl around. Sure enough, Dane's arm is also

around Mina's shoulder in a way that is too affectionate for a casual date. "When did this happen and why did I miss it?"

"You were busy being a Division I athlete, trying to come up with ways to get your girl bestie's interest, and eventually also getting called up to the pros." Dane checks a finger for every one of the points. "Anything else?"

My girl bestie shifts in my arms and I feel her eyes boring into my face. "What's this about trying things to get my attention?"

"Traitor." I growl at Dane.

"Oh, look. Let me go say hi to Jamie who I've already said hi to earlier. Let's go, Mina."

The two of them leave while absolutely in stitches. I'm torn between being glad that I won't have to put up with that duo after I'm gone, and also being absolutely bummed about it.

"So?"

I take a deep breath. "Fine, I'll confess everything. I might've asked Dane and Jamie for advice to see if I could get out of the friendzone. But despite how he made it sound, it was only one time."

"Ugh, you're so damn cute." Liv lays her head against my chest, both of her arms coming around my waist.

"Cute? Me?" I scoff against her hair. "Sexy, yes. Irresistible for sure. I've even been told to drop hockey and pursue modeling. Maybe Hollywood."

She lifts her head to place her chin against the lapel of my tuxedo jacket. "All that plus cute. Sweet. Adorable. Like a cuddly teddy bear."

I hum from deep in my throat, recognizing those as the fighting words they are. I'm happy to let her think they're flying over my head, and I'm making a little retaliation plan when I get interrupted.

"Didn't think I'd see you at this place." It turns out to be none other than Kyle Warren and two of his senior goons.

I probably look like I'm sucking a lemon but it's just confusion. "What?"

"Yeah, thought you were too important for these things now," one of the other says.

"Besides," adds the third guy. "It's not like it matters to you anymore if we get more funds from boosters or whatever."

Liv tenses and before she gives them the spectacular verbal lashing I can feel gathering in her chest, I just say, "Of course I care. I'm still the captain until Dane takes over, and if you have any issues about that you should take it up with Coach Green."

Kyle raises his hands toward his buddies. "Dude, we're not being sarcastic. We really thought it was how you were gonna be."

"Oh." I lean back, blinking down at them because they're shorter. "So… Basically, you thought I was gonna act like Liam?"

"Yeah, I guess."

Liv looks up sharply. "Is that the guy who…"

The guy who caused our rift only to screw with my head? "Yep." I cringe.

One of the other seniors says, "I heard Liam got kicked off his pro team for slacking off."

"But you're not like that, huh?" Kyle does something unexpected: he bumps his fist on my shoulder all buddy-buddy like. "You made us play hard during your captaincy and now here you are, still giving a damn even though you have a foot and three quarters out the door."

"That's my boyfriend, all right," Liv says in a proud voice.

My chest swells with something bubbly. I nuzzle her hair to whisper in her ear. "I like it when you're proud of me."

She digs her elbow against my ribs.

"Anyway. Congratulations and… thanks?" Kyle cringes, red tinging his cheeks and I don't know if it's because it was hard to say that, or because of how obvious it is that Liv and I are this close to tearing each others' clothes off.

I drop my arm from around Liv to offer my hand. "Thanks, man. I'll still be rooting for the Bolts to the end." I end up shaking hands with all of them before they move on to attack the buffet table.

I pull at my shirt collar. "Well, that was something."

"Why do you look so surprised?" Liv tilts her head, her eyes seeing right through my soul. "Did you really think you weren't leaving a mark?"

"I—uh. Yeah. Maybe." I shrug. "It's bittersweet as hell. I'm not leaving any records or big legacy like your brother or Max."

"The news article announcing your departure from the Bolts said you're the shortest tenured captain in the organization so far. That's a record." She chuckles as I turn even more sour, but everything's okay again when she takes me by the hand. "But seriously, as you can see, more people like you and want you to succeed than you think."

"I'm just not used to it, I guess," I say, trailing behind her on the way to the food table. There's a line, of course. "My own dad hasn't even called me after the whole…" I told her everything about that conversation a few days ago, so I don't need to go into detail for her to know what I mean.

She shifts her hand to slide her fingers between mine, squeezing tight. "Maybe this time it's because he doesn't know how. Haven't you thought about reaching out yourself?"

I have. A lot. But maybe I'm the one who doesn't know how. This isn't even like when I was trying to reach out to Olivia again after a year and a half friendship hiatus. This is worse. The last time I had an actual conversation with my dad was… I don't know, sometime before he met his current wife?

Before I can find a way to voice this, someone cuts in line

for the buffet right before us. But it's not anyone trying to get to the food first. Instead, a blur tackles my girlfriend.

"You look so gorgeous!" it screams. "And I told you he was putty for you!"

Liv's face is smushed into the hug. "Uhh…"

"Liv's the gorgeous one and I'm the putty? Sounds about right," I jest.

Finally, the two girls tear themselves apart and the newcomer gives me the time of day. It turns out to be Dee Meyer from the Thunder Strikes.

"You guys make such a cute couple. And about damn time." Dee shakes her head as if she couldn't believe how long it took us to get our heads out of our asses. Meanwhile, I snap my fingers because she's preaching to the choir. She offers a sharky smile. "But anyway, Tatum. Don't get complacent now that you think Liv is all yours. We may go to parties and other places where tons of hot guys will drool over us."

Liv presses her lips for a moment. "What are you doing?"

"She's trying to see if I get uncomfortable or jealous." I fold my arms. "And I sure am. You think I don't know Liv's hotter than the sun and that there are better guys out there?"

She glances at Liv. "He's sharper than he looks."

"Not really, I'm just honest." I pluck Liv from her hold and bring her back toward me. "I know I have to work hard to make this a success."

"As long as you know… We'll be rooting for Liv, and since she seems to want you, I guess that means we'll be rooting for you too." Dee sticks her tongue out at me before waving her fingers and heading back to wherever she came from.

"My friends don't hate you, if that's what you're wondering," Liv says once they're gone.

"I know. I'm glad they'll look out for you when I'm gone."

She sucks her lower lip in to bite it and keeps her attention on the buffet. Aside from pressing logistics about my impending move, we haven't talked very much about what life is going to be like afterward. This is one of those cases where it's easier to go with the flow than to think too hard about things, which is more my area of expertise than Liv's. I raise her hand and press my lips on the palm, before it's our turn to grab plates.

It takes us longer than everyone else to peruse the offerings on the table. Each dish only has a little card listing the main ingredients but not all the details. We end up having to find someone from the catering staff to get enough information for Liv to select a few tiny tarts, a handful of fries, and a salad.

"Hold." I demand once she serves herself. I swap out plates so I can comb through her salad with my fork. Then I swap again. "Coast clear."

"Roger that, captain." She spears a forkful of fries. "But I brought an EpiPen just in case."

"Where?" I roam my eyes up and down her frame. Her clingy dress has no pockets, and I don't expect any in her little jacket.

"Oh." She facepalms with the hand carrying the fork. "In my clutch. But I left it in your car."

I squeeze my jaw. "Liv, that's no bueno. Take my plate, I'll go get your purse."

"It's okay. The caterer just said—"

"But just in case. Let's—"

"Tatum!" We both suck in air as Coach Green heads over, two men in tow. I don't know who they are but I recognize the expensive cut in their suits. These are either boosters—St. Cloud alumni with pockets deep enough that they get buildings named after them—or sponsors from some wealthy organization.

I almost forgot this is actually what we came here for.

Shifting my plate to my left hand, I offer my right to Coach for a handshake. "Coach, great to see you."

"Right back at you, son. Thank you for dropping by when we know you must be busy with the move." He frees his hand to point at the other two. "These are my friends Lenny Farrow and Maurice Beaumont."

I squint. The names ring a bell, even if the faces don't.

"They're my good friends from when we played in the NHL a decade ago," Coach finishes saying, giving me a look that clearly says *play nice or else*.

Oh. This is a third category I hadn't considered.

"And you're Bryce Tatum's kid, right?" One of them shakes his head. "We played against him back when. Real pain in the ass."

Yeah, I guess that's where I got it from. It's also why their names were familiar. Either Dad must've mentioned them, or I simply heard them when I used to watch his games growing up. But like most of my childhood, I put any knowledge of them in a vault in my mind.

I wonder if Coach's a bit tipsy because he says, "Brooklyn here isn't just *the* Bryce Tatum's kid. He's the Bolts player who has been called up to the pros the earliest, that's how good he is."

Mr. Beaumont whistles. "Now, that's a feat not even your father achieved."

I hope they can't see the heat creeping up my face. "I, well —" A tug behind me makes me turn. Liv's looking at me funny. "Oh, where are my manners. This is Olivia Rodriguez, my girlfriend." I push her gently by the small of her back.

"Lovely to meet an even lovelier young lady," Mr. Farrow says.

Liv shakes his hand but her attention stays on me as she clears her throat. And again.

Every fiber of my being focuses on her.

She's working her mouth, running her tongue against her palate. Like it's itchy. And she's not saying a single damn thing.

Sucking air, I push my plate onto Beaumont's hands because he's closest, before taking Liv's plate and dumping it on top of mine. "Sorry, sorry. I think my girlfriend's having an allergic reaction." I hold her face. There's no swelling yet but she's paler than before. Not even the makeup can hide that. "How bad is it from one to ten?"

"Two," she wheezes out. "But changing fast."

"Shit."

I don't care if we're making a scene. I bend down to pick her up in my arms. She grabs tight onto my neck. I don't even have time to apologize again before I'm bolting out of the event hall.

CHAPTER 36
OLIVIA

I'm sorry," I rasp weakly.

"Shut up." Brooklyn grits out the words not unkindly. His eyes are wide and forehead wrinkled, the same sheer panic that has taken over him every time I've had an allergic reaction. "I should've been more careful. I should've—Key?" He all but shouts at the valet outside.

The poor guy takes one look at me and immediately guesses that something's wrong. Maybe my face is swelling up already.

Only one thing can make me sick so quickly. Peanuts.

But the caterer didn't mention peanuts anywhere.

"Black Jeep Gladiator," Brooke says, panting. That's probably more from the stress of the situation than from the physical effort of carrying me.

My own heart races faster than a rabbit being chased by a wolf. This is bad. Like really, really bad. I try squeezing Brooke harder to comfort him but instead I sag against his arms. Brooke has to hoist me up again.

"Uh—Uh… Here."

Brooklyn swings me a bit as he snatches the keys. "Where are we parked?"

The valet points to my left. "That way. Second row, I think."

Brooke takes off again. The night is cold but above freezing, and the snow's melted into puddles that squelch under his dress shoes. "It's going to be fine," he says harshly. "We'll make it in time."

I can't speak anymore but I try to nod, and that makes me dizzy. I start praying because this is going south at breakneck speed.

Some beeping makes him change tack, and I realize a second later that it's because he's found the car. With me in his arms, he maneuvers to open a door. Grunting, Brooke strains forward to sit me down. My arms automatically grab at whatever they find. I squeeze my eyes shut against the noises. The car's swaying worse than the earlier bounce in Brooke's arms.

I try to say his name but it's a gurgle.

"I'm here." Brooke appears before me again and dumps something on my lap.

It's my clutch and he's fiddling with the tab. He rips it open on pure strength alone and everything goes flying. The EpiPen lands between me and the seat and he fishes it quickly. He's done this enough times that he's as efficient as a doctor when popping it open. But I'm sprawled weird on what I now recognize as the backseat. He bites the device to drag me closer to the edge of the seat by my hips, and lifts my dress so fast a tearing sound echoes through the cabin. Without needing a warning, he stabs my thigh with the EpiPen with clinical precision and we hear the click that tells us he did it right.

We're both breathing hard as we wait for the adrenaline to be injected into my system. A strand of blond hair escaped his pomade, and it flies up and down with his breaths. After three seconds, he chucks the injector away.

"You doing all right?" he asks, his hand massaging my smarting skin. The only response I can give him is to cringe. "Okay, lift up your legs. We're going to the ER."

A pained little moan escapes from my chest but I manage the task. Once my legs are up, propped against the passenger's and backseat—and who knows what I'm flashing him with— he shuts the door.

I drop my head back and curse myself. Why is this happening tonight? Or at all? It's not like I was super careless.

The driver's door opens and the entire cabin rocks as he hauls himself in. A series of noises follow. His door shutting. The click of his seatbelt. The engine roaring to life and the electronic noises of the dashboard lighting up. His A/C swooshes with ferocity, and I feel the heat hit me right away. My muscles relax a tad. Sweat trickles down my skin but it's the cold kind.

He peels out of the parking lot so fast that the tires squeal. After working my throat a couple of times, I manage to say most words of a sentence. "Sorry. Will be fine. Slow."

"No, I'm not going to slow down." I can tell he's speaking between his teeth. "I'll get you to the damn ER and deal with the speeding ticket later."

"No! Your… career—"

"Screw that. You're in danger!"

"Just… careful."

"I am. I will be." He gathers a deep breath. "I'm just going to drive ten miles per hour over. Maybe twelve, okay? Fifteen at most."

"Brooke…"

"Hey, you're talking more. The adrenaline's working, right? Did you keep your legs raised?"

"Ye…" I can't manage the *s* sound, but a wheeze fills in the blank.

"Okay. Hang on, Liv. We're almost there." The car jerks a

bit at a sharp turn and we must really be almost there. The hotel was downtown and the main hospital in town is probably ten minutes away at most. "What do you think caused it?"

I cough out the word. "Peanuts."

"Shit." After a pause he says. "I have to come clean. I'm going faster now." I clear my throat aggressively. "Okay, I've slowed down a notch."

I'd laugh if I wasn't technically dying right this second.

"I'm going to sue the shit out of that caterer."

"No!"

"Fine, I'll give them a really shitty Yelp review."

"Ye… Good."

He barks something that sounds like a cross between a cough and a laugh.

"My… fault."

"Liv, no. It's not your fault. They're the ones who hid the murder nut in the food."

"But… pen?"

It takes him a moment to deduce what I mean. "Ah." For a long moment he doesn't add anything further. But then the car's jerking to a stop and he's rushing out. This time, he opens the door at my head and pulls me out by my pits. Pivoting me, he lifts me back in his arms. My head lolls on his shoulder and I'm not sure he's even shut the car door before he's running away.

I'd recognize the swishing sound of the ER doors in my sleep. Harsh lighting assaults my retinas. Above me, Brooke hollers. "Excuse me! My girlfriend's having an anaphylactic reaction to peanuts."

Atta, boy. Loud, clear, to the point.

Sure enough, not even a second later, he's placing me on a hospital bed. After Brooke gives me a sloppy kiss on my forehead, I'm wheeled away.

*

An oxygen mask, an IV latched onto my arm, a tiny hospital bed shoved in a corner, and an even tinier chair beside it, aren't quite the nicest setup for a date. But after the ER staff are done assessing me and settle me to wait out the rest, Brooke joins me on that little chair dutifully. Even though I'm pretty sure his ass is spilling on all sides from it.

He hasn't let go of my other hand ever since we've been abandoned out here, while the doctor and nurses take care of the sparse other patients. This is also not his first rodeo in this position, and as much as I love him for being here during every scary moment, I also hate that I've put him through it.

"Sorry," I repeat through the mask.

His eyes follow the motion of his thumb sliding across my skin. "Stop apologizing, woman."

"But I ruined the night."

"The freaking peanuts did." His brow tightens. "I can't even figure out where they were."

"I think it was the fries." I close my eyes. "They had the same color as the ones from O'Malley's. I should've made the connection before all this happened."

The chair squeaks and then he's resting his head against my hip. "Again, not your fault." Slowly, I free my hand from his and bring it up to his hair. He sighs audibly as my fingers work against his scalp. "I got so scared, Liv."

My chin trembles. I let tears roll down my temples. "I'm sorry for scaring you."

He shakes his head against me. Funny how despite everything, that can shoot fire up and down my body. I glide my hand through his hair to the back of his head, until I find his neck and stop there. I just need to feel his heat to know everything's going to be okay.

Of course, that's when my family shows up.

"Olivia!" The scream belongs to my mother.

"I will kill you." That one, to my brother.

Both Brooke and I spring. He swivels around on the chair. I push up myself to sit on the mattress. Pulling up the oxygen mask for a moment, I ask, "What the heck are *you* doing here?"

Maddie responds instead, "He's still out with a groin injury so we came home early for the holidays. Sweetie, are you okay?"

I try a different tactic. "This is an emergency room. I'm pretty sure you're not all allowed in at the same time."

"Thankfully it's a quiet night," Dad says, slide around the other side of the bed to check my IV as if he knew what to look for. Or maybe he does, because this sure as hell is also not his first rodeo. "Are you doing okay, mija?"

"Yes, thanks to Brooke—"

"What did you do?" Aran all but growls at him.

Brooke opens and closes his mouth. "I—"

"He saved my—"

A gentle hand combs my hair. "Ay, mija. Qué susto me llevé."

"Mom, it's o—"

"*You*." Aran points at Brooklyn. "Out. We're going to have a talk."

Brooklyn leans forward to start getting up, and I squeeze his shoulder tight. "You're not going anywhere."

"But—"

"And *you*." I turn the full power of my laser beams on my brother. "Why do you think this is Brooklyn's fault every time?"

"Because he's always at the crime scene!"

"Ever stop to think that actually, Brooke is the one saving my ass each time?" I grunt in frustration.

Meanwhile, my silly boyfriend runs a hand through his messy hair and says, "Your brother's right. I should've been more careful every time. I should—"

"Stop." I raise my palms. "Everybody stop. I get how crappy this is every time it happens, and how it must make you all feel. But this is my responsibility. *Mine*. I don't need you—" I point at my brother and then at my boyfriend. "Or you to think this is on you to solve, okay?"

"But Liv…" Brooke reaches for my hand again. "What happens after I leave?"

My brother's eyes zero in on our joined hands. It occurs to me that I haven't told my family yet that Brooke and I are a couple now. Maddie understands her Neanderthal husband very well, though. She puts the palm of her hand on his chest, effectively blocking him from throttling Brookie.

Sighing, I return my attention to my blondie. "The same thing that happened the past year and change. And that will happen the rest of my life, even when we're together again… I carry on as usual."

That answer almost seems to hurt him more. "Do your other friends know the steps? CPR? Do they have the routes to the hospital memorized?" Everyone's looking at the back of his head, and I don't know if he realizes what he's admitting in front of most of my family.

I blink hard, holding back tears.

"Like you?" I shake my head. "No, but they can learn."

Aran's frowning. "You have all the routes memorized?"

"I—Yes." Brooke scratches the back of his head as he glances back at my brother. "Don't you?"

"No."

"What he means is that he's impressed you care about his little sister to that degree, and that he gives you permission to date." Maddie grins.

If anything, Aran's expression darkens even more. "That's not what I said at all."

"You guys are finally together?" Mom's smile blooms as if we were giving her an early Christmas present.

"Um, yeah."

"I gotta text your sister." Dad paws at his coat until he finds his phone. "She's going to blow a… what's the word?"

"A fuse?" I cringe.

Maddie's laughing now. "Yeah, especially because she just won the bet."

Brooklyn scrunches up his face. "What bet?"

"Nothing." I wave the words away. "I can see a nurse glaring our way, so can you all please go home?"

"Come." Maddie herds her husband and my mother, since they're closer. "Let's wait at the lobby."

My mom motions at Dad. "We have to go settle the bill, Arturo."

"Ah, verdad." Dad cringes and I wish a black hole would swallow me. Luz and I have eaten into any hope of our parents ever retiring. I guess now only me, since she's officially on Max's insurance.

Brooke collapses on the tiny, squeaky chair after they're out of sight. "Wow, for a second I thought I was gonna land on the bed right beside yours."

I slide the oxygen mask back down and lean back on the bed. "Did you forget you're bigger than my brother again?"

"Yep. He's scary as hell." Why is there a sheepish expression on his face? "He and I used to scare off any creeps around you pretty good in middle school and even in high school."

"You did *what*?" I gape. "Are you two the reason why I could never get a boyfriend?"

"Maybe?" he squeaks.

Sarcasm drips all over my words. "So it wasn't because of my food allergies? Or my taste in music? Or even my hips?"

"Nope, no, and hell no." He hunches over to rest his elbows on the mattress. "Liv, I'm serious. Are you going to be okay when I'm not around? I can still stay. They haven't—"

I squeeze his lips between my fingers until they look like a duck's bill. "I'm not going to be the reason you can't live your life. And my allergies won't stop me from living mine, so zip it."

"Fine." He breathes the word out from the side of his lips. Shaking his head, he frees himself from my grip. "But you'll let me know if something ever happens."

"Of course." I run my hand down the lapel of his tux, trying to fix it up. "Just like you'll also let me know if something happens to you, right?"

"Yes." He tilts his head. "But you'll watch my games too, right? I can only play my best when I know you're watching."

"I'll watch every damn game even if it kills me."

Brooke presses his lips to hold back a smile. "So basically, we're going to be worried to death about each other the whole time."

"Exactly."

My fingers stretch apart as he slides his in between. "All right. We're doing this."

CHAPTER 37
BROOKLYN

"We're doing this?" I ask and I'm afraid to admit my voice shakes.

"Not if you don't want to." Liv makes our arms swing, joined by our hands as they are.

Taking a deep breath that fills up my lungs with icy air, I make a conscious decision to shut my fears out and just go for it. I ring the doorbell to my dad's house.

"I'll be here every step of the way," she says beside me.

My chest explodes with a burst of something, and the only way to release it is by capturing her face between my hands and pressing my lips to hers. Liv makes a humming sound from her throat that makes my heartstrings thrum. I savor her lips slowly, mine working in tandem with my tongue to map her silky softness.

Of course, that's when the front door opens.

"Eww." No doubt that's Lee.

Olivia's and my lips make a loud smacking sound as we separate. As greeting to my half-brother, I say, "Hey, twerp. Is your father around?"

"First of all, you're the twerp." I give him a shit-eating grin that seems to annoy him further. "Second of all, he's your father too. And third of all—or just third? Whatever—and third, it's Christmas, *you twerp*. Where else do you think Dad would be if not home?"

"Wow, that's cute. You already know how to chirp back." I pull him into a headlock faster than he can react and rub his hair. "Who taught you that, huh?"

Behind me, Liv sighs. "Brooklyn, unhand him. Absolutely no one enjoys your headlocks."

"Wrong. I do." But I do release him. I try my best not to laugh as he fixes up his hair and glares the shit out of me.

But his expression softens when he looks at Liv. "Erm, thank you."

"Hey, she's taken." At the look on Liv's face, I say, "What? I recognize those eyes. They're those of a tween developing a crush on a hot, older girl."

She cocks an eyebrow. "You'd know, huh?"

Oops. I've walked into a mine field.

"Well, we better go in before we freeze out here," I say amiably and guide her inside.

"Do you still think Luz is hot?"

"Hmm, I wonder where Dad is." I busy myself hanging my beanie on the coat rack and unraveling my scarf.

"Oh, so you do?"

I snort. "Please, you'd punch me if I said she isn't."

"True, no one can say any crap about my sister other than me." After a pause, she asks, "But I'm hotter, right?"

Relieved that this question's easy, I say, "Of freaking course. You're the hottest girl in the entire planet."

"You guys are gross," Lee says before shouting, "Dad! Your other son is here!" His feet patter away from us after that, no doubt back to playing with whatever his parents bought him.

The one who finds us first is Lauren, though. "Merry Christmas, kids." We return the greeting and she ushers us to the kitchen. "Eggnog? I made it with coconut milk, in case you visited us, Liv."

"Sure," I say as I hold the barstool for Liv to sit comfortably. She says she doesn't like it when I do things that she can do herself, but I do like it. And that's just one of the little things we've had to adapt to now that we're out of the friendzone and into coupleville. Another one is when she dresses super sexy for a night out. That one I don't like because there are too many creeps out there, but she does. Compromise and all that.

Lauren pours two hefty cups of eggnog for us and one for herself. After a little toast, I take a sip and—

Start coughing.

Liv clears her throat. "Erm, Mrs. Tatum. I think you gave us the one for adults."

For alcoholic adults. Not even a shot at a Bolt House party has ever given me a kick like this.

"Don't tell your father, but I think you're old enough," Lauren says with another sip of hers. "Is it too strong, though?"

"A bit?" Liv's eyes are watery. So… not just *a bit*.

But my step-mother shrugs. "Oh well."

Liv and I exchange a glance. Her face reads the exact same thing I'm thinking. Which is that we *cannot* laugh, no matter what.

Heavier steps than Lee's descend down the stairs and I tense. Immediately, my girlfriend slides her hand to my knee and gives it a healthy squeeze. Healthy, I say, because it elicits a totally healthy reaction out of me that travels all the way to my blushing cheeks.

I clear my throat to center myself as Dad appears before me. He kisses his wife's forehead before facing us, his expression even more drawn than usual.

"Son."

"Dad."

"Mr. Tatum." When he turns to Liv, she adds, "Merry Christmas."

"Of course. Yes. To you as well."

Silence.

I take another sip of the eggnog. Now that I know what to expect, it doesn't hit me quite as hard. Though it's still funny how a chilled beverage is warming me up so fast.

Liv smacks my thigh with the back of her hand and I jolt.

"Right." I place my glass back on the counter. Why is this harder than the prospect of playing professional hockey players in a couple of weeks? I tap my fingers on the cool granite counter surface, and talk to them rather than to my dad. "So, um. I wanted to apologize. For last time."

Even more silence.

I dare a peek at my girlfriend. She's nodding at me, short hair brushing her jaw with the motion. I've already said my due, so it's probably fine if I whisk her upstairs for some of the teddy bear cuddling she claims to want, right?

But Dad makes a raspy sound from his throat. "I should be the one apologizing."

"Huh?" My head whips up.

"Your father has been doing a lot of thinking after your phone call." Lauren draws circles on Dad's chest with the palm of her hand. It occurs to me then that she's doing the same thing Liv's doing with my knee. Soothing me. As if Dad was nervous too.

Huh? I repeat in my mind. What the hell does he have to be nervous about?

"I… I had no idea you felt that way." Dad leans his hands on the counter, and I notice he's tapping his fingers too. "You've always been so independent. I thought—I thought you didn't need me. Which in hindsight makes me even more of an asshole."

"You're not an asshole, honey," his wife counters.

"I am. My therapist said I used that as an excuse to pull away from Brooklyn because he reminds me too much of Natalie."

Lauren's appalled. "Did your therapist call you an asshole?"

"No—"

"You go to therapy?" Liv squints at him, trying to picture it.

I latch onto something else entirely. "How in the freaking hell do I remind you of my mother? I couldn't be more different from her."

"I know, Brooklyn. I know." He runs a shaky hand through his hair, darker than mine. "It's just your face. You look so much like her."

That lands like a kick from Manny Pacquiao to the solar plexus. I open and close my mouth, but only air comes out.

"That's entirely a me-problem," Dad says, raising the palm of his hand. "And I took it out on you without even realizing it until you yelled at me. I'm…" His voice softens. "I'm so sorry, son."

Ah, shit.

I hang my head, squeezing my eyes tight. I freaking refuse to cry over this.

But then Liv's closing her arms around me. I bury my face in her chest and she hides me from the world.

Apparently Dad's not done yet, though. "And you were so right. I've been a t-terrible father." He pauses and I hear a sniff. Two. He clears his throat and his voice comes out stronger now. "I know it's too little, too late, but I'm working on this with my therapist. I hope you can give me a chance to make amends when you're ready."

"Good job, Bryce." Lauren whispers to him, though not low enough that I miss it. "Aren't you glad we rehearsed?"

Liv's chest rumbles with her voice. "But you didn't know we were coming."

"No." Lauren's laughter twinkles. "But Bryce was planning to deliver this speech while seeing Brooklyn off at the airport next week."

Liv and I snort at the same time.

That sign of amusement makes her pull away. She smooshes my cheeks between her hands and runs her thumbs across them, wiping away the moisture her clothes didn't catch. Her sweet little smile makes my chest do something funny.

"Aren't you glad we decided to come?"

"Yes." I sound like a little kid with my face all smooshed between her hands. Meanwhile, I run mine up the back of her thighs to remind her I'm not a little kid. Just in case she forgot.

I don't know if Dad can guess at what's happening behind the counter, but he clears his throat. "Anyway, are you staying with us for the last days? Your bedroom *and* a guest room are ready for you two, if you want."

"Sorry, Dad." I lean way from my girlfriend's manhandling hands to look at him and his wife. "Liv and I already have plans." Plans that I can't tell him about, if I go by the gentle warning behind the words *guest room*.

"We're going to my parents' next," Liv says, and clever girl that she is, she drops that half truth without adding the other one. We rented a literal cabin in the woods where I'm going to show her how spectacularly, unbearably hot I find her.

We spend a couple more hours at my dad's, which includes some street hockey with Lee and some of his friends from school, and head over to Liv's to have lunch with the entire clan, including both of her siblings and their spouses. It's pretty wild that soon I'm going to be playing against Max and Aran.

But the real dream coming true is finally getting actual alone time with my girlfriend, my best friend, the love of my

"*Girl!*" I shout back.

"Giiirl." Dee hauls us in a massive group hug. We all compete to hug each other harder, but in truth, Dee's got us beat. She's the one who just got invited to the women's Olympic hockey team, along with luminaries like Ryan Avery—friend of Aran and Maddie—and JT Brewer—my sister Luz's bestie from her Thunder Strikes days.

"Okay, I need to breathe." I tap Dee's shoulder and she releases us.

"Can you believe this? We're done with education *forever*." Mina drags the last word for emphasis.

"Speak for yourself. The master's in public health and nutrition of my dreams awaits me." I bend my hand in a delicate way.

"Nerd."

"Yes."

"I hate that we won't be living together anymore." Mina lips form a downward arch.

Dee nudges her with her elbow. "But hey, you're moving in with your new boyfriend so that's a major upgrade."

"I mean, yes." Mina doesn't sugarcoat it and I start laughing.

"I'll miss you guys so much." I put my arms around their shoulders and hug them again.

"But *you*. You're the one who must be the happiest." Mina tips her chin down and gives me the evil smirk that is capable of making an entire Division I hockey team do her bidding. And that's definitely not because she's the girlfriend of said team's graduating captain.

I lift a shoulder. "Well, it's not a competition."

"You don't need to lie in front of us."

"Yeah, okay. I'm excited enough to power an entire continent." I press my hands against my warm cheeks. "I can't believe I'm moving in with Brooklyn."

"I can't believe you guys did long distance for a year and a half." Mina shakes her head. "I could never."

Dee scoffs. "Yeah, you could. You'd follow Bloom to the ends of the earth."

"Heck yeah. I have to be there to keep those puck bunnies away." She winks, knowing full well she was one such puck bunny once upon a time.

I recognize some approaching figures over her shoulder. "Oh, time's up, guys. The whole Rodriguez clan makes landfall in T-minus one minute. See you at the party later?"

"Of course."

"For sure."

The fact they say this at the same time, and that Dee's wearing the same sinister-Mina expression, gives me pause.

But then a set of pincers wrap around me. "¡Mi hermanita se graduó!" Luz's obnoxious voice pierces my eardrum.

"Ugh! Get off me, you oaf. You're gonna squish the baby."

Luz places a loud kiss on my cheek and pulls away. I turn to find her massaging her pregnant belly. "Baby CR wanted to hug you too." My dork of a sister and her dork of a husband are calling their upcoming firstborn by the initials of their last names, because they refuse to give us any hint on whether it's a boy or a girl.

Max gives me a one arm hug. "Congrats, Oliva." Of course, he's joined the family tradition of calling me by some variant of olive, but in Italian. I hate them all.

Mom's all sniffly as she hugs Dad. And his eyes are misty eyed too. "Our last baby is all grown up now, Arturo. ¿Qué vamos a hacer?"

"Jugar golf?" He suggests, dabbing at his face with a handkerchief.

"Auntie!" This is the only word, aside from Mommy and Dadda, that my niece can say so far. Which is helpful, since aside from Luz and I, she has Maddie's sister.

I pluck her from her mother's arms and smush my face in her belly, which always makes her laugh. She clings to my neck as I look at her parents. Aran grunts, and his wife translates, "We're so proud of you."

I love Maddie, and only Maddie.

"Thank you, guys."

I can't help trailing my eyes past them to the expanse of the plaza that leads to the public entrance of the arena. There are clusters of people everywhere, families and friends of the grads taking pictures, hugging it out. It's a moment of relief, joy, and pressing nostalgia.

Right now, I'm trying my hardest to not let sadness overpower me. This should've been another one of those important milestones that Brooke and I shared together. It was why we busted our behinds to get in the same college. But life had its own plans, anyway. And I guess it's not right for me to expect him to come today, when I'm literally flying tomorrow to officially move in with him.

He'll keep playing professional hockey for the team of the city I'll be doing my master's at. I can't believe how perfect that is—it almost feels like a reward after all this time apart.

Aran reaches his hands toward me to retrieve his daughter, and I comply with a mild protest. Then *I* get lifted off the ground.

Squeals explode from my chest at the vertigo. My diploma and bedazzled hat go flying off. A second later, I land on powerful arms and I recognize the scent of expensive cologne and warm boy. When I open my eyes, Brooke's grinning face peers down at me.

My brain catches up to what my nose knew first, and my jaw drops.

"Hey, Liv."

"Surprise!" the voices of my former roommates shout in unison from nearby.

It finally clicks. This is why they looked so devious. They were planning this behind my back.

I stretch until I free my arm squished against his chest and bring it around his neck. With my free hand I touch his face, just to make sure this is real. The faint scar from a year and a half ago is still there on his jaw, and that's how I know I'm not dreaming.

"It's you," I sigh the words.

"It's me." Brooke presses a quick kiss on my lips that makes someone coo. My sister, I'm sure. When he pulls away, he asks, "Did you really think I'd miss this moment?"

"Well. Your team's in the playoffs, unlike the losers over there."

"Hey!" Max laughs.

My brother grouches. "We'll see about that next year."

Slowly, Brooke tips me to one side until my feet touch the floor. He doesn't let go, though, and I'm in no hurry to go anywhere else. "I mean, we still have to travel tomorrow but I definitely couldn't miss this day. Especially when I may have already tattooed it on my side."

"What?" My eyes bulge. "That's only supposed to be for important dates." That, I learned at a certain cabin in the woods. The numbers I'd seen tattooed on his ribs were the date he was drafted. Since, he's added the day we officially became a couple and the day he scored his first goal in the NHL. That day he broke a franchise record of youngest offensive defenseman to do so, too.

"Today's an important date." He pushes my short hair behind my ears, and slides his hands down my arms until he joins our hands. "It's not just your graduation or what would've been mine."

I rack my brain, trying to think what else could be a big deal. "Are you getting a raise? Surely not getting traded so soon. Or did you land that massive sponsorship deal your agent's been negotiating?"

"Nope." He pops the *p* with gusto. "Today, I'm going to win by shutout. And so will you."

"Huh?" I glance around, but clearly no one's going to help. My family and friends watch this bizarre conversation with entirely too blank expressions. When I turn back to my boyfriend, he's in one knee.

I freeze.

Brooklyn's eyes glint like pure emeralds under the sun. There's a soft smile on his face, like he's not nervous at all. Like he's not doing something completely shocking.

"Aceituna."

"Brooklyn." I growl. "What are you doing?"

"You know what my job is, right?" His voice is gentle but unwavering, his hands warm around my cold ones. "I have to do whatever I can to prevent goals, and see if I score some as well."

"Right." I blink hard.

"But there's only one game in my life where it's not about scoring goals. It's about both sides winning, together." His eyebrows rise. "I'm talking about us, in case it wasn't clear."

"Yeah, I'm following."

Someone snickers behind me.

"'Kay, good. Just checking." Brooke pauses to grin. "That's why it's the only game where both of us can win by shutout, you see, where it's not about scoring points against each other at all. We protect each other. We push each other to succeed. We catch each other when we're down…"

I swallow hard. "You don't need to stop, I'm still following."

Brooke rakes his teeth on his bottom lip and releases it to a little smile. Maybe he's more nervous than I thought.

He shifts his hold to take both of my hands in one of his.

The free one rummages in his pocket. My heart kicks and roars to a full throttle. Everything around us disappears from my vision. My mind records this moment for replay the rest of my life. There's only sweetness in his eyes as he brings forward a ring. The gasp that comes out isn't mine. I've become a statue.

Only when his eyes lower to the offering do I tear mine from his. The ring is a white band, simple but sleek. And atop sits a shiny black rock. I have no idea what it is, but immediately a thought pops into my head.

Wow, that is so me.

Next thing I know, everything's blurring because my eyes are raining.

"That year and a half when you shut me out was the worst of my life," Brooke continues saying in a soft, low voice. "And the past year and a half away from you has been the hardest. Now, I don't want to waste a single second more."

"B-Brookie…"

"So, Liv. Aceituna. Oliva. Olive. Bestie." I hiccup a laugh and he places a kiss on my hand. "Olivia, will you marry me?"

I drop to my knees, burying my face in the crook of his neck and hugging him tight. And in front of my entire family and friends, I say in my best Spanglish, "Sí. A thousand times sí!"

EPILOGUE

BROOKLYN

"I can't find the rings."

For someone who spends so much of his time on the ice, never have I turned into precisely that until this very moment.

Glad to see I'm not the only one, though. All movement in the room stops, every single man transforms into an ice sculpture like the kind my step-mother commissioned for the reception later tonight—two swans or something.

I stop breathing in the middle of putting in my favorite cufflinks, a miniature of the Stanley Cup my team and I won last year. Through the mirror, my eyes find the face of my brother and at least he does look like he regrets uttering those words very much.

However, I still sound angry enough when I ask, "You *what*?"

From the corner of my eye, I catch Dane cringe. "Oh, boy."

"I didn't lose them." My fifteen-year-old brother stuffs his hands in the pockets of his dress pants, brow furrowing with a mighty fierce look that cowers his hockey opponents but not his big brother. "I just left them on a table when I went to the restroom, and they were gone once I returned."

"Usually," Aran mutters in a sinister voice, "I make threats on the older Tatum, but now I may consider changing the subject. If you ruin my sister's wedding—"

"And mine," I add sardonically. "But anyway, no need to threaten anyone because this won't ruin the wedding. We'll fix it."

"Right." Max abandons his glass of brandy—the same fancy little beverage we've all been hydrating ourselves with while getting ready for my wedding—and gets up from his leather chair. "All we need to do is look for them."

Jamie raises his hand like we're in a classroom. "But wait, what if someone stole them?"

I narrow my eyes. "We're the only guests in this hotel. If someone dared to steal my wedding rings, I will sic the Aran Rodriguez on their sorry ass."

To illustrate, said goalie cracks his knuckles.

"Maybe let's try to not have any murder in my sister-in-law's wedding, okay?" Max chuckles.

"Right." I look up at the ceiling as if I could find my patience hanging from it. With a deep breath, I turn back to my brother. "Let's start at the crime scene."

"But I already looked at every nook and cranny," he whines.

"You're just a defenseman like your brother. Don't act like you have the best eyes in this room," Aran retorts dryly. "Let's go."

"Fine." Lee didn't grow up under the shadow of Aran's threats to his life, so he has the nerve to roll said eyes at the massive goalie who could still snap me in half.

For the first time Aran narrows his eyes at someone other

than me. When his attention falls on me, it's only to motion with his head that we should get going.

It took him a while—almost the entire time Liv and I have been dating—for him to get used to the idea that I'll always been in his life. But I think this is the first time Aran and I are on the exact same page. We both don't want this wedding to be anything but perfection, which is what my fiancée deserves. He's the first one to vacate the gentleman's dressing room, since he's closest to the door.

I'm the only one who isn't fully decked with tie and jacket because the photographer is supposed to drop by any second, but I don't care about that. Not when we have a major emergency. I leave the room sans tie, vest, or jacket, with one cufflink secured in the sleeve of my shirt and the other one in my pocket.

Our heavy steps echo around the hallway as we follow Lee to the hallway. A little sideboard loaded with a gigantic flower arrangement sits in between the doors to the women's and men's restrooms.

"Dude," Jamie says with laughter in his voice. "Why did you even come here when we have a private bathroom in our suite?"

"Whoever was there before me left it stinking up so bad I almost barfed." Lee stretches his mouth in the universal gesture of *yikes*. "It was honestly unlike any stank I've ever come across in my life. Worse than a public trash can."

"Oh that was me, sorry." Dane grins. "That happens sometimes after breakfast burritos."

"Wow, I feel so bad for Mina." They're still going strong and probably the next couple in line to tie the knot, but maybe I should advise Mina to save her lungs. And stomach. Horrified, I add, "Do whatever it takes not to fart during the wedding or else."

"It's all good. I think I got it out of my system."

"You think?" I scrunch up my face.

"Let's divide and conquer," Max chimes in with the voice of reason, probably because he's the eldest of this weird bunch. "Aran and I can check the men's restroom in detail. The rest of you should comb through this entire hallway."

"Aye captain." Dane salutes because, funny enough, Dane's now a teammate of Max's, and the latter is the captain.

"I'll take the flowers and drawers." Jamie does a finger gun at the arrangement.

My brother protests. "I didn't leave the box in any of the drawers."

"But you never know." Dane shrugs. "Didn't I see you sneak a drink from your father earlier?"

Lee's face heats up. "Trust me, if I was drunk I'd really have puked all over the bathroom after your biological bomb."

I expel all the air in my lungs and push my cuffed sleeve to check the watch. "Gentlemen, we have just shy of an hour to find my wedding rings. Let's focus."

With that, there's no more fooling around. Max and Aran slide into the men's restroom to start the search. Dane and Jamie inspect every nook and cranny of the table, and even go as far as dismantling the flower arrangement. Lee paces up and down the hallway, scanning the carpet and any piece of furniture in the way.

Meanwhile, I force myself to do something that doesn't come natural to me—and that is to think.

Would not having rings available be grounds for stopping the wedding? Because no way I'm letting that happen. I'm walking out of church today with Olivia Rodriguez as my wife, and not even a lightning storm will prevent that. But she'd also be upset to find out we're starting our marriage with a blunder already, and all I want is for her to be happy.

The thing is that even if my brother acted like a stooge and lost them, all because of Dane's nasty farts, he would never lose them on purpose. The box is kinda big, hard to put in one's pocket, with a velvet casing that can't get wet. I get why he wouldn't want to bring it in the restroom with him.

All this leads me to think that someone took it.

And I don't mean that they took it with ill intentions. The only guests at the hotel are family and friends—Dad and I made sure of that. And the hotel is a small boutique one with a limited amount of staff, no pedestrian traffic, tucked in a wooded piece of land removed from the main town. If this was a mystery, it would be the simplest one.

I'm sure someone saw the box, recognized it, and took it to keep it safe. But if so, who did it?

I pluck my phone from my pocket and start blasting texts to a bunch of people.

This is when the photographer arrives, no doubt coming from the bride's suite on the floor above. He takes one look at Dane crawling on the floor to check under the table, at Jamie rearranging the flowers, my brother with handfuls of seating chair pillows, and at Max and Aran stepping out of the men's restroom with faces red from some kind of effort.

"Um, is this a bad time?" the poor guy asks.

"Have you seen a white velvet box yay high?" I make the rough size of it with my hands.

"I'm afraid not."

While I sigh, Aran turns to my brother. "Are you sure you went into the men's restroom?"

Lee splutters. "Of course I did! What do you think I—"

"Just checking," Aran grouches.

"I'm pretty sure someone took it," I say, following it up with my deductions. I don't appreciate how every single one of them looks impressed by the fact that I do, indeed, have some neurons inside my extremely good looking blond head. Annoyed, I finish with, "And anyway, I think we should split and talk with all the guests until we find whoever has them. There's only one problem."

"Time?" Max raises his eyebrows.

Somberly, I shake my head. "No. My future wife can't ever find out."

There's unanimous agreement from the men and the teen, and together with the photographer at my heels, we split in all directions.

OLIVIA

"The men are acting weird," Mina declares as she walks into the bride's suite.

"When don't they?" I take a careful sip of the most delicate champagne flute I've ever seen. I'm afraid if I hold it too tight, it may crack and pour champagne down my wedding dress.

"Fair, but this is weirder than usual."

"What are they up to?" my sister asks from the windowsill. She's in the same soft periwinkle dress as the rest of my bridesmaids, which includes Dee, Mina, and Maddie. My mom is the only one in a deeper blue, but still in the color scheme reminiscent of the college all her kids attended.

"They seem to be like, interviewing guests." Mina folds her arms, lips twisted in a grumpy way. "Except they wouldn't tell me what the deal is."

Dee pauses from pouring herself another mimosa. "Suspicious."

"Very."

"What are we gonna do about it?" Maddie asks.

My shoulders slump. "Well, I can't go out there in this to find out." I motion at my incredible wedding dress, a mermaid cut cream number with delicate beading that makes it shimmer when I move, giving me the look of a real mermaid just emerged from the ocean. It's gorgeous. I feel absolutely beautiful in it. I can't wait to see Brooke's reaction to it. It's not that I'm superstitious, but I don't want to ruin that moment for myself.

"Leave it to your big sister." Luz lifts her long skirt to not step on it as she gets up. "Because it turns out that I have a big weapon."

I cock an eyebrow. "What's that?"

"A husband who does whatever I want."

"Oh." Maddie snaps her fingers. "I too have one of those. I'm coming with."

"Yo también," Mom says, and joins the other two women as they walk out.

"Show offs." Dee sighs.

Mina joins her at the bar. "Right?"

"Pff." I shake my head. "As if you two also didn't have guys who are wild over you in the wedding party."

Dee grins, her cheeks deepening in color. "Well, Jamie and Dane aren't our husbands yet."

"Yet." Mina narrows her eyes. "That's the key word."

We ended up dating the same group of hockey bros we went to college with, but wilder things have happened in my life. Such as me legitimately getting a job as a nutritionist for Brooke's team, and also releasing my first book of allergy friendly recipes.

"I still can't believe that we'll never be able to breathe non-stinky air," I joke about the unfortunate side effect of living with men who sweat for a living.

"Don't get me started on that. The smells that come out of the digestive tract of my boyfriend are criminal." Mina pretends to gag.

"I honestly stink worse than mine, but I'm starting to think that his nose doesn't work." Dee elegantly drapes herself on a settee, champagne flute in her hand.

Mina closes her eyes. "I wish my nose didn't work."

While I'm chuckling, the door opens again and the three women in my family walk back in. Maddie's the one who breaks the news.

"Turns out that your future brother-in-law lost the rings."

You could hear a pin drop.

My eye twitches. Slowly, I set my champagne on a nearby table by the floor length window. I remind my reflection that a blood stain would look much worse on my dress than a splotch of champagne, and that's a good enough reason to not commit murder.

"Someone bring me Brooklyn."

They all look at each other.

"Isn't that bad luck?" Mom asks.

"Rather, I'm suddenly concerned about Brooklyn's physical integrity." My sister bites her lips.

"That's not it." With a few steps, I plop myself on the window sill with no elegance. "I just want to make sure he's not freaking out about this."

"Awww."

"That is so sweet."

"You guys are so in love."

"I'm gonna cry."

"No, don't ruin your makeup. The makeup artist already left."

I stare at them in a deadpan, but the only one who gets the hint is my mom. In a complete mother hen move, she starts herding the unruly women toward the door, saying, "Let's go find the broom. I'm sure we can find a way for him to not see the bride, so we can keep the good luck."

They're all flutter and chatter as they leave the room, and in the ensuing quiet I strongly regret Brooke's and my policy of no cellphones during the preparations. The whole idea was to heighten the excitement, but now I wish I could just call him.

Maybe ten minutes pass before the door opens softly and Brooke pokes a hand in to wave at me.

"Um, Liv?"

"I'm here." My dress rustles as I head over to him and clasp his hand in mine. "Hey, blondie. Are you coming in or not?"

He sighs heavily. "As much as I want to see you, I don't want to add more bad luck to today. I was told you heard."

"Yep." I make the *p* sounds pop, and his hand squeezes mine harder. "You shouldn't have tried to keep that from me."

"I just didn't want to worry you."

"But it's okay for you to stress by yourself?" I lift his hand to press my lips on the warm palm. "That's not what marriage is about, you goof. We're supposed to share the good and the bad, in sickness and in health and all that."

"You're right," he mumbles beyond the door. "Well, I feel like a definite goof now."

"And you should be. I'll marry you with hair ties if I must."

"I don't think I have any of those, but I'm sure the reception desk will have some rubber bands."

My face splits into a grin. "Those would work too."

Brooke tugs at my hand and I go with the motion until my arm pokes outside. I stiffen as his breath fans over the back of my hand. And then, ever so softly, he presses his lips to my knuckles like something out of a regency romance.

Except Brooke being Brooke doesn't leave it all sweet and chaste. Nah… His lips work a little on my big knuckle, the moist warmth promising a lovely, delicious wedding night. My knees weaken and I have to hold myself by the door frame so I don't swoon.

"Thank you," he mutters all of a sudden.

My voice is throaty as I ask, "For what?"

"For marrying me even though I'm a ditzy blond who managed to lose the wedding rings on his wedding day."

That tears a little laugh out of me. "I love you not despite that but including it, you know?"

"And I love all that you are," he volleys back easily, not like he's just said the most beautiful words a bride can ever hear. "So we're still on?"

"Oh heck yeah. We're still in the game. Just promise me you won't try to shut me out every time something happens in the future."

"You have my word."

With that, the wedding proceeds. Even though rain pours while we drive to the church, and one of the groomsmen expels some noxious gas right before the ceremony starts, and the ceremony gets interrupted when the rings box appears in my niece's flower basket, we make our vows and are pronounced husband and wife.

It only hits me as we walk up the aisle together, our eyes trained on each other's and not on the way, or on the happy congregation around us, and Brooklyn enunciates the words…

"My wife."

Heat climbs up from my chest, my throat, to my face, and I have to blink back tears. Because at last it clicks on me that I made it, I married my best friend—the man I've loved my whole life, and who will love me back the rest of it.

I return, "Mi esposo." And we stop at the entrance for one more kiss to start the rest of our lives.

THE END

*

*Thank you for reading **Shutout**! I hope you can take a brief moment to leave a review on Amazon.*

Here are my other works if you're craving more closed door sports romance:

Book one in the St. Cloud Hockey Series, **Faceoff***, is a rivals to lovers romance.*

Book two in the St. Cloud Hockey Series, **Overtime***, is a grumpy x sunshine romance.*

Mistlefoe *is an office rivals to lovers Christmas romance, loosely linked to Faceoff.*

Preorder **Wild Pitch***, book one in my upcoming Wild Baseball Romance series where the team's hot pitcher becomes our heroine's dating coach.*

Sign up for my newsletter at MARILOYAL.COM to download **Set Me Up***, a free volleyball romance novella.*

Happy reading!

GLOSSARY OF SPANISH VOCABS

Chapter 4

- Cojones: men's dangly bits (see also in Chapter 6).
- La madre que lo parió: the mother who birthed him.

Chapter 7

- Aceituna: olive (see also in Chapter 8, 11, 15, 18, 23, 24, 32, 38).

Chapter 8

- Oliva: another word for olive.

Chapter 14

- Obvio microbio: this is a semi rhyme in Spanish that literally translated makes no sense (obvious, microbe).

Chapter 18

- No me digas: don't tell me.

Chapter 21

- Buenas noches: good night.
- Gringo: word used for non Latin Americans, more often for White people (see also in Chapter 33).

Chapter 22

- Tú: informal *you*.
- Usted: formal *you*.

Chapter 23

- Espero comenzar mi carrera en la NHL dentro de dos años: I hope to start my NHL career in two years.
- Suena muy interesante. ¿Cuál es la parte que más te emociona de convertirte en un jugador profesional?: It sounds very interesting. What makes you the most excited about becoming a professional player?
- Lo que más me emociona es formar parte del mismo equipo con mi amiga, Olivia: What makes me the most excited is being part of the same team along with my friend, Olivia.
- ¿Cómo es eso posible?: How is that possible?
- Es que mi sueño es ser la nutricionista de su equipo: It's because my dream is to become his team's nutritionist.

Chapter 24

- Pabellón criollo: translated would be "creole pavilion," which means absolutely nothing to us, except that this is the name of the national dish in Venezuela (white rice, black beans, marinated pulled beef, side of arepa and fried sweet plantain).
- Carne mechada: marinated pulled beef.
- Mierda: shit/crap.
- No bueno: *not good* in improper grammar (see also in Chapter 35).

Chapter 29

- Correcto: correct.

Chapter 30

- ¿Quieres unas arepitas, mija?: Would you like some arepas, my daughter?
- ¿Qué? ¿Tienes que hacer un laundry?: What? You have to do laundry?
- Aceitunita: little olive.
- ¿Qué pasa, Olivia?: literally translated would be *what's happening, Olivia?* But the meaning is more akin to *what's wrong, Olivia?*

Chapter 33

- Buenos días: good morning.
- Mi nombre es Olivia Rodriguez, y éste es mi mejor amigo, Brooklyn Tatum: My name is Olivia Rodriguez, and this is my best friend, Brooklyn Tatum.
- Les vamos a contar la historia sobre cómo nos

hicimos amigos: We're going to tell you the story of how we became friends.

- Pero la historia continúa: But the story continues.
- Quiero escribir un nuevo capítulo contigo: I want to write a new chapter with you.
- No quiero seguir siendo solo tu mejor amigo: I don't want to keep being your best friend.
- Quiero ser tu novio: I want to be your boyfriend.

Chapter 36

- Mija: mija is a colloquialism of "mi hija" or my daughter but used widely beyond mother/daughter relationships.
- Ay, mija. Qué susto me llevé: Oh, my daughter. That was so scary.
- Ah, verdad: Oh, true.

Chapter 38

- ¡Mi hermanita se graduó!: My little sister graduated!
- ¿Qué vamos a hacer?: What are we going to do?
- Jugar golf: play golf.
- Sí: Yes.

Epilogue
Yo también: me too.
Mi esposo: my husband.

ACKNOWLEDGMENTS

I can't believe that the series is over. This is probably what parents feel when they send their last child to college, wanting them to succeed and trace their own path but also being afraid for their kids, and sad for their new loneliness. Now the St. Cloud Hockey Series isn't just three little stories in my head, they're also yours. That's both terrifying and exciting, and it couldn't have happened if it wasn't for the people in my life.

And well first, *always*, thank you Lord. Contigo todo, sin ti nada. Now for the actual people:

To Avery Keelan and Tamara Lush, a special thanks for keeping me afloat while my mental health struggled in the course of these releases, for advising me when I got too in my head, and for the funny memes.

To Aimee who kindly and patiently puts up with my weird questions about when to use *in* or *on*, even though it's been like 15 years of the same. Sorry/thanks!

To Enni at Yummy Book Covers who not only is the best cover artist in my modest opinion, but also a stellar human being.

To all my readers, whether you came onboard from the humble Faceoff beginnings, joined during the Overtime era, or are reading Shutout first. Thank you for allowing me to compete against TikTok, Netflix, kdramas (oof, this is an honor), and all the other cool things you could be doing but instead chose to read my book.

Special thanks to my ARC readers and hype team for spreading the word about this newcomer called Mari Loyal and her books full of feels and giggles. Without you I'd be screaming into the void by myself.

Last but not least, I want to thank my mom and my sister, and my dad up in heaven. Thank you for encouraging me to keep going, and for helping me when I struggle. Los amo con todo.

ABOUT THE AUTHOR

Mari Loyal was born and raised in Venezuela, a baseball country that only cared about another sport, football soccer, every four years. As such, she decided to make hockey her whole personality because she had to make a point of being different. These days she no longer suffers from Not Like Other Girls syndrome and is very happy to be in the sports romance fandom. She writes closed door romance with a Latin American flair and an abundance of cinnamon rolls heroes. She also enjoys eating cinnamon rolls (the confections), in her spare time.

Sign up for my newsletter at MARILOYAL.COM